THE CONGRESSMAN'S DAUGHTER

Novels by Craig Nova

TURKEY HASH
THE GEEK
INCANDESCENCE
THE GOOD SON
THE CONGRESSMAN'S DAUGHTER
TORNADO ALLEY

THE CONGRESSMAN'S DAUGHTER

CRAIG NOVA

DELTA
FICTION

Delta/Seymour Lawrence

A Delta/Seymour Lawrence Book
Published by
Dell Publishing
a division of
Bantam Doubleday Dell Publishing Group, Inc.
666 Fifth Avenue
New York, New York 10103

This book was written with assistance from the National Endowment for the Arts and I want to express my gratitude for it.—C.N.

This book is a work of imagination, and no character in it is drawn from any person, now living or dead.—C.N.

ISBN: 0-385-29716-5

Reprinted by arrangement with Delacorte Press/Seymour Lawrence

Printed in the United States of America

Published simultaneously in Canada

May 1989

10 9 8 7 6 5 4 3 2 1

BG

For Tate

BOOK I

What Love Costs Daughters

I know more secrets than any man I have ever met. Perhaps this is because I am reticent and a good listener, and, my God, the things people have told me right here, in this old house with the shutters banging in winter. What things! Maybe when it all comes out, people are too tired to be ashamed: they speak in a flat, clear voice that is easily understood. No details withheld. I'd like to point out that I am not so much dull as discreet. I've had some experience with the world. Anyway, I have a story to tell you.

When Alexandra came home to bet on the fish, she was nineteen years old, six weeks pregnant, and unmarried. She didn't want to be married, not then. The fish was an old trout, speckled, enormous, a cannibal . . . it lived in a pool in a stream off the river. I'd see it from time to time, waiting in the slime green shadows of the pool, gently finning among the dark rocks, waiting for some small, living thing to make a mistake.

Of course I am infuriated with the people I want to tell you about. They couldn't talk to one another, couldn't settle their differences, couldn't make amends behind closed doors, and be done with it. There was no understanding, and they were, in some ways, so silly. But that's the least of it. I had to sit here and watch, and when I knew what was going on, I was trapped by them, and unable to walk down the road and stand in front of that house and call the liar into the road . . . I would have done too much harm.

I live in New England. My father left me well fixed for money, but I haven't been idle. Gossips are idle. I studied engineering at Berkeley and have spent my time in soil conservation, water management, and over the last thirty years I have repaired trout habitat. I haven't made much money at it, but, then, I haven't had to. Brown trout are a dirty, German fish, but brook trout need clean, clear water. Anyway, I am older now, with a hump on my back, waiting for spring when I can go dig in the garden with my smelly dog. I like milk snakes in the garden. My dog doesn't. He kills every other one. I live alone, eating my own harsh cooking, giving the leftovers to the dog. He's getting fat. I am a widower.

I was never frail physically. I did a lot of the work myself, building wooden barriers to stop the silt from filling the streams, and I dug the trenches to bury good long deadmen, those posts that anchored the barriers. I walked through Patagonia, and climbed the Andes. When that liar came to live down the road, I was tempted to drag him out of the house and there, for all the world to see, I should have . . . but I did nothing. In those days all I had were suspicions.

I can see order is needed, and that I'll have to attack the problem as though it were one of engineering, to think of so many gallons of water moving through a space so shaped, the water hitting a far bank of rocks and pebbles in so much hardpan of a certain thickness. . . . I have not always been this angry. Perhaps it's the age.

As I have said, I live in New England. My house is old, two stories, has white siding and black shutters, two large maples in front. They are getting ready to die: the leaves have small bumps. I noticed it this spring, as though each one had a pin stuck through it again and again. I have a hundred and fifty acres, mostly in woods, but thirty acres in fields. I keep them mowed and they are poorer each year. No nutrients are added. I have no cows, no manure spreader. There's an old barn, in good repair although it's drafty. There's the vegetable garden and a large lilac. There are the flower beds, in which I've planted

white Everest phlox, and White Admirals, columbine and begonias (Judy Langdons are a favorite), delphinium, and some lilies,
mostly Prairie Sunsets. There's a new bird feeder that looks like
a spaceship, a cemetery across the way. I can see the Sugar Wolf
River from my living room.

My neighbors were Harlow Pearson, his wife, Anne, Xan
Thu, their houseboy, and their daughter, Alexandra. The story
is about Alexandra, more than anyone else, and she is still my
neighbor, sitting in what was Harlow's house. . . . Harlow is
dead, and so is Anne. I remember Harlow in his middle fifties,
tall and slender, broad in the shoulders. His hair was white,
although not pale, not like dandelions, but harder, still having a
metallic color. He walked with a straight posture, and wore, in
summertime, white pants and a pullover sweater. He was a
gambler, or had been when he was younger. He once said,
"Life's a gamble," and the horror was he believed it, and I'll bet
he would have said, "Love's a gamble." What can you say about
a man like that? That he was too dumb to walk the face of the
earth? There were times when I detested him, and then he'd
show up with three dozen fresh oysters, which smelled and
tasted of the ocean, and we'd sit in my kitchen, shucking them,
eating them with horseradish and that Australian beer he always used to have. Swan. Or, he'd take me to the county fair,
where there was an enormous rat on display, the size of a small
pig. "A killer rat" it was called. I have always had an interest in
oddities. At these times he looked at you, and his eyes suggested
he understood exactly what you wanted, although he wasn't
sure he'd give it to you. It had its effect on his beautiful daughter.

He was a good fly fisherman, better than I was. When Alexandra was growing up, he was in Congress. He won his first election in 1958. It was a dull, sleepy time for the country. There
was nothing exciting, not really, and Harlow went to Washington more for being presentable than anything else. Well, he
went there in the midst of that dull, sleepy time, when we
seemed destined to go on forever in a hazy lie about ourselves.
He served until 1966, when he lost an election. I don't think he
was even surprised about the loss: the country had changed, or
was beginning to, and he knew he didn't fit so well as before.

On that November night, when it was clear he had lost, he came to see me and said, "The hell with them. I did my best. . . ." And then he cleared out of Washington and came back to New England. An aide did the packing and the moving. I was puzzled by the speed, by the abrupt change of it all, but later I had my curiosity satisfied. I remember, in the weeks after the loss, that the two of us sat in my house staring at the television, on which there were shown young men and women, their hair long and golden as they funneled into a run-down part of San Francisco. Harlow stared at them, blinking now and then and drinking bourbon. Anyway, Alexandra was nineteen when Harlow lost the election.

I watched Alexandra grow up. I am at the end of the road: beyond my house there is a farm road that goes between stone walls. After a while it turns into not much more than a trail and even the stone walls disappear. Then there are beaver ponds, hillsides covered with birch, maple, and pine. There are mountains beyond, and the wind from them blows against my house in winter. It is a mile from my house to Harlow's, and five miles beyond that to the closest paved road or house. Alexandra was forced to come my way, since there wasn't anyone else around. The woods beyond my house were beautiful, and when she was a child, I was always good for a tuna sandwich, a bag of chips, or some other forbidden thing. I still remember the look in her eyes when she was ten and having a bag of chips. When it was almost empty, she sat with her head thrown back, the bag held up, her tongue just touching the last golden bits. Then she blew the bag up and popped it. Both of us laughed.

It seems when she was growing up, she was always passing my house. I'd look out the window, in the summertime, and see her walking, at the age of six or seven, wearing overalls and tennis shoes, her hair blond and almost white from the sun. She went along, poking mushrooms with a stick. Sometimes she waited in front of the house, until I came out and asked her in. She was a polite little girl, and she wanted to entertain: she told me the jokes she heard as though I had never lived. Then she passed on a bike with learner wheels, then without them. I'd see her in winter, when she was long, gangly, and twelve, the features of her face seeming too large, lips almost swollen, eyes large, nose straight and fine, but still childish, and I never looked more than twice: it was just Alexandra, on skis, or foot, snowshoes, on a bike, or on the horse that Harlow had for her one summer. We still had our lunches, snacks, snowball fights, and walks. She thought of me as something of a scientist and she asked questions that were embarrassing, her grayish large eyes set on my face, her large lips swollen, her skin smooth and pale while I looked for the right words. When I was a little clinical, she supplied, to my horror, the slang. She told me, too, in a frank, unaffected way, which boys at school she had a crush on, and why. She thought one would be beautiful, and she wanted to see him walk around her with no clothes on. It would give her pleasure. She had a healthy interest, and I listened.

And, of course, one early summer day, I looked out the window and saw a young woman coming along the road and strolling into the woods beyond my house. Her hair was shortish, blond, and fell over the straight features of her face. She walked with her shoulders square, her head up, her stride a little slow, her hips making a slight dip. When I went outside, she turned, looking over her shoulder, and smiled. I hesitated for a moment and then went out, smiling myself as I came from the shade of the house. She blushed. Of course, I was a little in love with her, even then, at that age, but it changed absolutely nothing. Nothing at all. We became friends. I was in my late forties.

We became good friends, too. Maybe I cooked something a little more elaborate when she came for a snack, something light and tasty. We ate fruit in the summer, grapes that were pale green, dusty, beaded with moisture, and peaches and dark plums. There were things I had grown. She ate with a healthy appetite, showing her teeth, asking questions, confessing things. She trusted me, and I was a decent man.

It cost me something. I wouldn't deny it for a minute. But, I was a good friend and I listened. She came to my house, sometimes calling first, but at other times she'd walk up the road when she knew I was at home and then, when I saw her, I asked her in, almost as though she were seven or eight again. There was a lot of chitchat, but later, there were those rare occasions when she stood on my step and looked into the house, her face white and her hands damp, cool, and asked if she could come in,

and then she sat before the fire, not looking at me, and speaking
in that soft, almost breathy, beguiling voice. I didn't know what
to say, so, of course, I kept my mouth shut. I think she appreci-
ated that.

I never liked Alexandra's mother. She was tall and slender,
with light-brownish hair. Her name was Anne. What she really
wanted out of life was a good time. I have never seen a woman
more miserable than she on the night Harlow first won an election. She wanted to live in Paris or London and New York, and
she thought, when she married Harlow, that she was going to
get it. She could never understand why Harlow hung on to the
house in New England, but after all it became clear. He needed
an easy congressional district.

In fact, the district turned out to be anything but easy. The
first election was a hard, angrily fought one. Of course it was
dirty, and Anne was surprised by the things people said about
Harlow. The ugliness of it, the plain cynicism, shocked her.
. . . The election was decided by ten votes. There were re-
counts, lawsuits, but that's what it finally came down to. Ten
votes. I saw Anne after that counting the number of people in a
room at a dinner party, and if there were ten or more, I saw her
obviously thinking that these people, the ten guests in her dining room, were responsible for her disappointments. They
could have voted against Harlow. There were times when she
looked at her dinner guests with a barely noticeable but still
definite hatred.

She wasn't a shrew . . . that's the best I can say for her. She
was miserable, and then sick during the time after Alexandra
was fifteen. Anne had had a mastectomy and was obviously dying, and she hated to see the figure of her daughter. She wasn't
much comfort to Alexandra, and certainly wasn't good company. She wouldn't answer questions, either. Maybe that explains why Alexandra spent so much time in my house and
continued to come over the years. When Anne was sick, she
demanded to be taken to shop in New York, Paris, or the Caribbean, but when she packed her bag, she said, "No, no. I don't
want to go anywhere. I'm too tired and I want to be left alone."

Alexandra was fifteen when Harlow taught her to fish. I was
always surprised he hadn't done it sooner, since by the time

Alexandra was eight, she was going with Harlow and sitting on the bank and watching while he covered the water of the Sugar Wolf, White, or Tweed rivers, his casting being delicate, the line cutting through the air and floating over the water. I don't know why he didn't see how much she wanted to learn, if only because of the beauty of it, the lacquered bamboo, the silk wrappings as bright as Christmas balls, the chrome guides, the polished Hardy reels, the wood of the landing nets, the heavy, solid sense of waders, the delicacy and color of the flies themselves, and the sense, for a moment, of participating in the rise of mayflies . . . well, perhaps I'm overstating it, but after all I've spent thirty years of my life trying to keep the fish alive. Alexandra wanted to learn. It was the kind of beauty she enjoyed.

There were those winter evenings when she came to visit, bringing the cold air with her, and asked me what flowers I'd plant in the spring, and I'd tell her phlox, and Pure Whites, and thyme around the flagstones. She came in the spring when the frost was out of the ground and we'd plant them together, and when they bloomed, I'd see her in the morning, already out there, bent next to the things we'd planted, her voice coming up to me, when I went outside, in a small bark of laughter and a hum of pleasure as she put her nose to the petals. Of course she wanted to learn to fish.

If nothing else, Harlow had taught her not to ask for things. He was a difficult man and resisted direct requests. If asked right out, he'd refuse and become stubborn (precisely as stubborn as a gambler who thinks that a number on the wheel should come up since it hasn't for a thousand times and continues to play it, even though the number doesn't come up a thousand and ten, and twenty, and thirty times). The way to approach him was to be indirect, to make a proposition he could add things to . . . this meant compromise, especially if your needs were clear and sharp. Other people learned this, too, and it probably helped Harlow in Congress, since he had the reputation of being able to deal if he weren't approached too directly. It helped him up to a point. Anyway, Alexandra learned not to ask directly, and so she sat on the bank, probably already knowing how to fish, but waiting to be offered the chance to learn some of the finer things at the hand of her father.

In the late spring after I had seen Alexandra walking as a young woman past my house, Harlow came to visit. He brought oysters and beer and we ate them and then went on drinking bourbon until two or three in the morning, and I remember him bumping into the door frame on his way out, where he stood before my house, his hands in his pants, the lower panels of his jacket held at his sides by his arms, his handsome, drunken face set on mine. "Maybe you should marry Alexandra," he said. "Right now . . . as a kind of conservator." Both of us laughed. How hard I laughed, although even then I was thinking, the silly ass, how can he talk that way . . . it's just a little too close to the truth, not in fact, but in feelings. He was that way. He stood there, swaying under the stars, and then sighed and said, "I don't know what to do about her."

I wanted to step out into the cool air, close to him, and even look down at him, since I was a little taller, and grab the expensive lapels of his expensive jacket and say, "Don't be a fool. You have to do nothing aside from leaving her alone. She's just fine." But I didn't. I stayed in the doorway, leaning against the frame and said, "Teach her to fish."

There was something else, too. Alexandra had alarmed him by asking about his life in Washington, and he had become stubborn and angry. There were always rumors about him, and, of course, they were true. Harlow had told me himself when we drank until the early morning. He didn't brag, but confessed, in that same flat and and tired voice. Alexandra had heard about one of the women he saw there, the tall African, with an elegant carriage, greenish eyes, and who spoke perfect French, and whose only concern was raising money for her country. She had no scruples about her methods. Absolutely none, and by God she shouldn't have! Who would criticize her? There were other women, too. Not as interesting or as smart, probably. With ordinary ambitions.

I know Alexandra had asked him about what he did in Washington. He had stood in my kitchen, his face already set in the stubborn expression of a man who hates directness, and said, "But what could I tell her? How could I explain?" He was probably right about that. Although Alexandra would have listened, and if she didn't understand, she was smart enough to store the information, if only to be digested over the years and understood when she was her father's age. But she did want to know, and not only because she was confused about what was happening to her mother and father, but because of herself as well: was she condemned to the same life as her father, was it going to be passed down to her, and was it so horrible after all? I was amazed that she was thinking about it in such a fashion.

More than anything else I had misunderstood how angry Harlow was. I had dismissed his talk of a "conservator" as drunken babble. There was no reason to take him seriously. After all, I knew he loved her and that he was proud of her. But really proud. It was at this time that Alexandra began to go to Washington with him, to the dances and parties there. I've seen pictures of Alexandra in those dresses Harlow had made for her. They were seamed along the rib cage, made of silk, and left her shoulders bare, and in one of the pictures the two of them are dancing, Harlow looking down at her, gently touching her back and the tips of her fingers, his hair lighted by the chandeliers. He wore evening clothes, black tie, and they fit him perfectly. It was at one of these dances that Harlow said, "Would you like to learn to fish?"

Harlow started to teach her in the field next to his house. They took a walk before the lessons began, and went through Harlow's fields and woods, along the river and finally up the banks of a tributary. In the middle of it there was a pool, shallow at the tail, but deep everywhere else. They kept their eyes on the water, being soothed and drawn by its depth, and as they stood there, in the cool spring afternoon, they saw something move. The water was clear and made the bottom appear close, although the stones there were distorted and flat. The fish rose from the bottom and took a nymph that was struggling on the surface. It was a slow, quiet rise, coming out of water so deep and clear as to make the trout seem to be rising through the wrong end of a field glass. It seemed to come from someplace beneath even the bottom of the pool, from those green shadows among the moss- and slime-covered stones that were barely visible themselves. It took the nymph and left a dimple, a hole in the surface that was a little smaller than a thimble. The fish then sank again, disappearing or falling back into that place from which it came, showing, before it left the surface, its sides, the spots on them, each one surrounded by silver. It was that brown trout, thick in the belly, infinitely patient, heavy. I was always amazed that the pool could support so enormous a creature and even did some work there to find out why. The stream above was the perfect mixture of gravel and light and the insect life was amazing. The hatches of caddis flies were thick, as numerous, it seemed on some nights, as moths around a light in summer. And, of course, after a certain point, these old fish become cannibals.

Alexandra told me that she was amazed by the place, the wet silkiness of the water, the silence there after the fish had sucked a morsel off the surface, the quietly living and brooding aspect of the pool. She and Harlow stood there, looking into the green water, feeling it on their hands and faces. Maybe that's when Alexandra asked again about the African woman, the one with the tall, perfect carriage, the lips that moved slowly as she spoke French, her expression cool and maybe even a little haughty as her eyes lingered over Harlow's face, the expression in them saying, Well, when are we going to get around to it?

Harlow took Alexandra into the field on the other side of the stone wall and gave her a fly rod and reel. He worked out some line, and taught her to cast, to make a tight loop as the line sailed out in front of her and to hold the fly rod so that the line rolled out gently on the grass, in which it made a thin, straight crease. After a while he tied a leader to the line and put on a white fly, too, after breaking the hook off it. Then Alexandra began to cast the fly where she aimed, and over greater distances, too, double-hauling the line and shooting it, already beginning to make small bets with Harlow about how close she could come to the handkerchief Harlow spread on the ground for a target. After the lessons Harlow sent away through the mail for a pair of ladies-cut waders.

The Sugar Wolf River in springtime is fast, the color of coffee with milk in it. It's fairly deep. The bottom is pebbly in most places, although the pebbles are large, as big as a fist, and in the chutes and runs between the pools, the brownish water is topped with a foamy, whitish fluff.

The lessons continued after the ladies-cut waders arrived,

brought up the road by the UPS truck. Alexandra got into them, smelling the new rubber and glue, and she and Harlow went down to the river. Harlow wore his waders, too, and they went out into the current, always watching where they stepped, feeling the water pull at them. When they went far out the first time, Harlow took her by the hand, and they waded until Alexandra could feel herself becoming buoyant and about to be washed downstream. But soon she was making bets with him about the wading, too.

In the first season they went down to the river after a rain, when the water was high. Alexandra then began to work upstream, feeling the weight of the water against her, her eyes on the bottom as she worked to a large rock she bet Harlow she could get to. They did this in the late afternoon sometimes, and Alexandra saw the clear water of early summer turn dark green and then the color of oil. But even when the water was dark and so deep she couldn't see the bottom, she went ahead, to the rock, or through the pool, and then she came back to the shore and stood next to Harlow, her face wet, water dripping from the waders. Harlow took the wallet from his jacket and counted out the bills. Alexandra delighted in watching him then, since, for the moment, everything was clear.

There was one other bet about wading. In the first spring that Harlow had given her lessons, they had been standing at the edge of the river. The water was high, the color of hot chocolate, and there was a rock about twenty yards from shore. It stood out of the water and had a large brownish and white wave in front of it, as though it were the prow of a ship. Alexandra bet Harlow she could wade to the rock, and Harlow had taken the bet and watched as she went out. When she had been almost to the rock, she had fallen. The water slapped her face and then she had begun to swim, finally getting her footing. She came back, wet, smiling at her father, already having her hand out, but found, when she stepped from the stream, that he wasn't going to take the wallet from his pocket.

"The bet was for wading, not swimming," he said.

"I made it," she said, "and back."

"No," said Harlow. "That wasn't the bet."

Alexandra had stood, shivering, staring at her father with her hair dripping and feeling her clothes that were soaked and the waders that were filled with water.

"I want the twenty dollars," said Alexandra. "I won it."

"No," said Harlow, and he began to walk toward the woods.

Harlow walked for a little way, went into the woods and then stopped and turned. He came back down to the bank and stood on the round stones there. He took his wallet from his back pocket.

"Here's ten dollars," he said, "we'll split the difference."

Alexandra had taken the money before she realized it was only half. Harlow turned and walked back into the woods and Alexandra was left with the ten dollars, which she held in her wet fingers, already knowing that the ten dollars didn't separate them into a winner and a loser, but the opposite: It bound them together. He wouldn't take the ten dollars back either, when she tried to give it, wouldn't even let her accept a clear defeat.

After collecting the ten dollars, she came down the road to my house. Her hair was wet, and the bright blue-and-red plaid shirt she wore clung to her sides. Her blue jeans were as dark as when they had been new. Only her shoes were dry, since she had taken them off to get into the waders. They were white and covered on the sides with the mud from the road. She looked cold when she came right up to the door. Her lips were dark, like the color of very ripe raspberries, and her skin was pale. She was shivering a little in the breeze, and when I came to the door, holding the book I had been reading (a history of the Nile), she held out the ten-dollar bill. "Here," she said, "I want you to buy me a bottle of champagne."

She came with me to the store, and then we drank the champagne at my house. Alexandra's clothes were almost dry, at least her shirt and her hair were. We drank the champagne fairly quickly. I remember, when she got up to leave, the wet print the seat of her jeans left on the chair in the sun room and the sound of the mosquitoes striking the screen there.

Maybe that was the first time I was really angry at the man. What was she? Sixteen? Seventeen? And at that age she was sitting in that lovely room, in the light, getting half smashed. How could Harlow have been so asinine? He wasn't a gentleman. The fishing had come out all wrong for him, since it had turned into a kind of definition, a kind of directness, and there were times when he hated that. Well, all right. I was infuriated, but what could I say, "The man's a fool?" I tried to criticize, or to at least begin to say a tenth of what I thought, and she bristled, probably all the more so because she knew I was right and loved him anyway. I stopped, and it was the last time I said a thing against him: I saw it just made her panicky.

Alexandra hated vagueness. She admitted as much that afternoon. As the years passed, Alexandra felt the lack of understanding between her father and herself, and there were times when it seemed to be a physical sensation, as though she had walked through a spiderweb and felt it stream behind her, leaving its airy, maddening tug.

There were times, though, when the fishing worked better. At the best it was a compromise. They'd get up in the morning, sometimes very early, when the air was damp and cool. They put their things into the back of Harlow's Jeep, their waders, vests, fly rods, and a lunch, too, in a basket. Chicken sandwiches wrapped in waxed paper, little pickles, cold potato salad, two bottles of Swan beer, a slice of chocolate cake. Then they'd drive to Otter Creek and fish. I used to see them, coming home in Harlow's Jeep, with the windshield down, combat style, Harlow tall and thin and tanned at the wheel, and Alexandra next to him, feeling the wind on her face and hanging on, her eyes set directly on the road ahead.

Alexandra came to me after one of these days, and she leaned against the stone wall that runs along one side of a flower bed. Whenever I break a plate, or something made of glass, I put it on the wall to keep the snakes from sunning themselves there. They don't like the sharp edges. Alexandra was sunburned. She ran a finger along the shard of a crystal vase I had left there, and she said, carefully moving her finger over the knifelike piece of crystal, "I caught a big rainbow today. Its back was green and covered with black spots. Its sides were bright. I guess they were its spawning colors. . . ."

Her finger touched the end of the crystal.

"We're not so selfish, are we, to leave my mother alone?" said Alexandra. "My mother wants to be alone. You know she's dying, don't you?"

I said I did and that I was sorry.

"I'm a comfort to Harlow," she said, "so long as I'm quiet. But that's something. He thought the fish was beautiful, too."

Alexandra was sent to an all-girls college in upstate New York. I think she enjoyed the place, the cold, isolated winters, the regularity, maybe even the discipline. Things were clear there. Perhaps it was part of Harlow's desire for a "conservator" that made him pick the place out. At the time, it didn't matter to her. She was learning things and was happy at it. She did well, and seemed to have a gift for mathematics. She thought about men, too, probably because there were none around, aside from the dry leaves who were her teachers. She wrote me letters. She wanted to know what men were like. Not the smooth, pretty boys she had known. Those she understood. But grown men. Well, what could I say, that we're not all the same in the dark, and that we're certainly not all the same in bright light, either. It seems we spend most of our lives in bright light. The liars are the worst, of course, I could have told her that.

In the fall of her second year, Alexandra's mother died. Harlow called Alexandra and she came home, taking a bus and then getting a taxi from town. Harlow was alone in the house, aside from Xannie, the houseboy. Alexandra came up to the door and Harlow let her in. They discovered that they had been mourning for years, and they sat quietly in the living room, not saying much. I think that both of them had cared for Anne, but the disease had been hard on them all, and Anne had been reduced by it. And, of course, Anne had never been comfortable or warm, especially after Harlow had won the first election. Alexandra and Harlow sat silently in the front room, and while they sat there Alexandra looked up at the clock that sat on the mantel.

It was a big clock, with a round face, through the holes of which there was a hint of gears, rods, old springs. The face itself was covered with painted animals, deer with their heads at the ground, hawks in the air overhead, wings spread, talons drawn. There was a bear in a tree. Below the face there was a painted door, a glass one on which there were green fields, mountains, and a farmhouse. It had almost no perspective and looked as though it had been done by a talented child.

Alexandra stood up and moved around the room, already feeling the coldness there, the emptiness her mother had left in the house. She stood in front of the clock and reached for the small handle of the door. She opened it, as she had done years ago to see the gears, but now they were blocked by some letters in envelopes that had already been opened. Alexandra had looked there many times as a child. The place wasn't used to hide things, not regularly anyway, and Alexandra took the letters down, seeing her mother's name there, written in a man's squarish hand. Without even thinking, really, Alexandra began to read. Perhaps it was her mother's death that allowed her to do it, since at the end there doesn't seem to be much need for secrecy or for privacy, either, although this is sheer illusion. Harlow let her read them.

He had every reason to be angry. After all, his wife had died and she hadn't really had much use for Harlow or for his life, either. She hadn't enjoyed her child, and had been denied, or so Anne thought, the important things in life, dinner in Provence, or Italy, good European hotels, the quiet hush of civilized life. I can't tell you where she got such grand ideas. Harlow had put up with her, had even been charming about it, up to a point.

The letters were dated a few years before, from the time when Alexandra had been twelve and thirteen and her mother hadn't been sick. Anne had been a pretty woman in those days. The letters were from a man, and Alexandra stood before the fire, reading each sheet, with Harlow sitting behind her. She told me she had wanted to stop, to fold them up and to put them away and sit down in the silence of the room again, but even as she turned each sheet, she knew it was too late for that. And when she was done with them, still seeing or hearing the phrases of them—"the look in your eyes at that moment . . . the unbelievable heat . . . at the time"—she turned to Harlow.

"You can burn them," he said, "I've already read them."

Of course, *he* should have burned them. Perhaps he was so angry as to be confused for a moment, and wanted the letters exactly where they had been, as though to confirm what he knew. They hadn't been hidden. They had been left for him. I

suppose he was trying to recall those days when Anne had sat
before the fireplace, sick and uncomfortable. She might have
been reading the letters over and had been surprised by him
and had stuck them into the clock, but even Harlow couldn't
convince himself of this.

The letters were filled with details, with all kinds of things
. . . Anne's fears of being caught by Harlow, the places where
she had spent time with the man, that Anne had left some
clothes in his house, the scent of her in the morning, under the
sheets. Men are such fools about these things. They can stand
infidelity if they don't think about the moment it takes place.
It's easier, I can tell you, if it just seems like an absence, a
strangely long time at the supermarket.

It was neatly done. I have already said I didn't like the
woman. Harlow was left, sitting there, not able to tell whether
the letters had been left accidentally or not, although being sus-
picious they had been put in the clock with a purpose. I guess
he hadn't burned them because he wanted to go through them
again and again, looking for some clue, something that would
tell him his wife hadn't hated him as much as the letters made it
appear. He would have forgiven her a passion, a long, intense
. . . I don't know what to call these things. An affair! That's the
word I'm trying to avoid, since it seems so cheap. Anyway, he
would have forgiven her that. But vindictiveness was another
matter.

Alexandra burned the letters.

"Why did she do it?" she said.

"Do what?" said Harlow, looking up. "Take up with him? Or
leave the letters to be found?"

"Both," said Alexandra. "Do you think she left them?"

Harlow shook his head, and Alexandra knew it was a refusal
to talk and nothing more.

"Why was she so lonely?" said Alexandra. "Couldn't she talk
to you? Had things become that complicated?"

Harlow said nothing. Alexandra looked at the letters, the
pages of them slowly coming apart in the coals, the thin and
now delicate sheets opening and closing like some large black
butterfly. Alexandra told me later that everything she did was
wrong: she could feel him becoming harder and more distant

with each question. And she needed to know. She was nineteen years old and the years before her seemed frightening. Was she condemned to these things herself, and what pleasures were there? Harlow wouldn't talk.

Alexandra didn't stay at home as long as she would have liked. She said the pressure was too much. They were perfectly polite, and there was a lot to do. Everyone was prepared for the occasion and that meant it was a large one. After a week, though, Alexandra went back to school.

Harlow knew there was something wrong, and I think even he was ashamed. God knows he tried to do something about it, and, of course, that made it worse. That's where he was a fool: he wasn't equal to his own good intentions, and, of course, he was arrogant enough to announce them when he couldn't live up to them. He didn't like the feeling in the house, and everything in it seemed to have a sharp, uncomfortable edge. I don't think he could remember who came to pay their respects to Anne, and when I came, I wondered why he stood in the living room, staring at the clock. I thought he was worried about time, about how it slips through your fingers. And, to be honest, that's what he should have been thinking about.

Harlow's study was upstairs, down the hall from Alexandra's room. He was sitting in it when Alexandra was packing the small bag she had brought from school, and when she came down the hall with it, walking through the pressure in the house, Harlow called her into his room, and said, "Will you come fishing next spring? Maybe we'll talk then. Okay?"

Alexandra stood in the hall, holding the suitcase in front of her knees.

"Okay," she said.

Then she came into the room and put her arms around his shoulders, really holding him. She was probably crying. For a moment the pressure in the house was gone, so much so that she could sense the two of them together, and how long the dying had really been. Harlow had looked up at her, and his eyes, his glance, again suggesting that he knew exactly what she needed. And he had even given her some of what she needed then, since, she later told me, she had been terrified of leaving the house when it had been filled with coldness and pressure. The house felt better now, and she was free to go.

Yes, well. He should have promised nothing. Not a thing he couldn't live up to. I don't think he had any idea how serious she was, although he certainly found out. And look what it cost him, too! Alexandra was smart, reasonable, and for the moment relieved, because at least he had given her that. Of course, it made things worse later, because she had gotten used to the idea, and the anticipation of more.

She picked up her bag and left. Nothing seemed more reasonable to her than waiting. After all, the man's wife had died, had infuriated him. It seemed reasonable that he might be reticent, that he was confused and angry and wanted to be left alone. Things seemed clear and understandable, and for a moment those phantoms, those fears about the time ahead of her, disappeared, just vanished the way they do on a fine, clear morning. She wrote letters to me, sharing her secrets, and asking, too, about what I was going to plant in the spring. There were some terrible jokes going around and she sent them to me, saying they were awful. They were, but I was strangely glad to have them. She and Harlow even set a date to fish together, she told me in a letter, so she had that specific, clear time to look forward to.

In the springtime, Alexandra packed a bag to come home to keep the date, and when she was putting her things into it the mail arrived at school. There was a letter from Harlow, saying that this year he had decided to fish in Yugoslavia. He was going alone.

Alexandra sat for a minute on her bed with her letter in her hand, but only for a minute. Then she finished packing her bag and another, too. There were things that she had bought at school, and they didn't fit in the bags she had, so she went to town, hitchhiking along the road, and bought a large, cheap trunk, and filled it, too. She wrote a note to Harlow, and put it in the mail. It said, "Good luck in Yugoslavia. I've gone to California."

He showed it to me when he returned. Alexandra had gone, and had disappeared. Her mother had left her four hundred a month. Not a fortune, but enough to live like a student. And she was clever, too, about not being found. She borrowed the entire year's income from her mother's lawyers, and went to San Francisco. This was in 1966, and if there was ever a year to disappear in California, that was it. She had no use for fads, but was glad there was one to use as a disguise. Harlow thought she was in some communal apartment in Haight-Ashbury, eating with the Diggers, and the rest, but it shows how little he knew her even then. She got a job, for an accountant, rented a small apartment, took some courses, and thought about things. She bought some clothes, some short skirts, which she loved. She made a picture into a postcard by putting a stamp on the back and sent it to me with a note saying, "Everything's OK, what do you think?" In the picture she stood in front of a bar by the bay, her hair longish, her skirt as short as in the pages of French *Vogue*, her smile so real that I found it hard to believe she wasn't in my house in the middle of that hard eastern winter.

Harlow had the gall to feel injured, and to ask me what he had done that was so bad. What can you say to a man like that? But, after a while, it even dawned on Harlow that he was in the wrong. He didn't admit these things very well, but he tried. He called the police in San Francisco repeatedly, got in touch with a service that specialized in finding young people who had disappeared, tried to trace her through the one check that had cleared Anne's lawyer's bank. The police didn't find her. She wasn't on the streets with the others. It served him right to think about her that way.

I gave him the card, though, as soon as I had got it. I walked down the road in the middle of winter, seeing the mixture of sand and ice there that seemed dirty and harsh. I knocked on his door and offered the card and Harlow stood in his shirt sleeves in the cold and said, "My God. My God. She's all right. My God."

I turned and walked back down the road. Of course, I was ashamed of myself, that I had even considered keeping the card, or not showing it to him. He didn't give it back. And he didn't take warning from it, either, since he couldn't see the danger in front of his eyes. Alexandra had grown up, and it wasn't so much what the world could do to her as what she could do to Harlow and his smug stubbornness.

When she came home in the spring, she was, as I've said, six weeks pregnant. She wasn't married and had no desire to be married to the father of the child. So there it is. There are times when I am infuriated by the monstrosity in this, as though life were waiting for her, or for all of us, to make that small mistake, to relax and to be at ease or soothed and to think, for a fatal moment, that life doesn't have some brutal use for us. Any fool could have seen it coming, but not me, and certainly not her father. She called Harlow to let him know she was on her way (although she hadn't yet told him about the child), and he came down the road to see me. He stood in front of the sunroom, where I was putting up the screens, and said, "You see. Everything's going to be all right. Sometimes it's best just to hold out."

I am surprised how angry I am, even to this day, when it's all finished, when we've come to the end, or the end as I know it. I've had long winters with heavy snow, when the temperature was below zero for days on end, to think about what happened and the details of it. Perhaps I am so angry because I have added a thing or two, a detail that never took place, but one that seemed to be appropriate, however difficult it might have been to imagine. You can trust me. I am not a liar, but I have spent those winters and some pleasant summer days, too, going over the secrets here. Some of them, I suppose, are mine.

Getting on the Boat

 Once Harlow told me that when he was gambling, the world seemed bright and clear, the edges of everything lined and clean, purely cut. He liked European casinos, especially those with chandeliers and chamber music played by musicians in evening clothes. In the old days, he had taken Anne to them, and she was calmed and happy there, even when Harlow was losing money. I think it made him feel as though he were somehow participating in the world, and he liked that. He hated to be a bystander. Once, he tried to explain gambling by saying it was the difference between walking through an abandoned orchard with a gun and a dog, looking for grouse, and just walking.

I know he never lost that much money. In some things he was just lucky, and there were times that even when he lost, something came of it. Harlow's houseboy's name was Xan Thu, and in America he was called Xannie. His parents had been members of a remote Asian tribe, and Harlow hired him because of a bet, or two bets, one made by Xannie, and one made by Harlow, both of which they lost.

In 1950 Xannie was working as a groom at the racetrack at Ipoh, in Malaysia. He spent his nights there, too, sleeping at the back of a barn, his bed made on bales of hay, on which he stretched out, hearing the rustle of it and feeling the itch through a thin blanket he spread there and smelling the dusty, grassy odor. He was tallish, thin. He took his meals alone, eating while he squatted and leaned against a stall door, or in the room where he slept. There were other grooms, too, and they found their places to sleep in the barn, each one having a small bag in which there were kept a few personal things, a book, a photograph, a comb, an extra white shirt, a dark pair of pants.

The man Xannie worked for most often was half French and half Burmese: he was heavy, bald, and had greenish eyes. His skin was smooth and a brown and olive color. His suits were made in London, and he wore a large gold watch that gave the time for any place on the earth. The man's name was Pierre Boutielle. There were times when he couldn't sleep and came to wake Xannie up.

"Are you sleeping?" said Pierre.

"No," said Xannie.

"Have you seen any thieves?" said Pierre.

"No," said Xannie.

Then Pierre said, "Come outside." Xannie went with him, and Pierre gave him an American cigarette, a Camel, and they both smoked, feeling the wet Malaysian sky, and seeing the clouds floating along, made visible by the sickly light of the city.

Pierre told Xannie about the places he'd been. He said Parisian women and Dutch women, too, would do anything for money, that New York was filled with madmen, that there was a desert in Yugoslavia. America had more food than anyone thought imaginable. There were Malaysians and Burmese who had made money gambling and in restaurants in America, and some had become doctors and university professors. There was a Burmese pediatrician in Chicago. . . . Xannie smoked a cigarette and thought about piles of food: he saw a cone, high as a volcano, that was made of rice. He smoked the cigarette down to the butt, burning his fingers.

Pierre had a horse he'd bought in the Philippines. It was a good horse with fine breeding and had originally come from Lexington, Kentucky. Pierre was concerned about the horse, afraid that it would be stolen, and he spent nights looking into its stall, saying that there were dishonest people around, and that you had to be on guard against them. Pierre had once gotten drunk in town and fallen asleep in an alley, and when he had woken up, he saw that someone had stolen his shoes. They had been white shoes. When Pierre stood and stared into the stall, Xannie was with him, wanting to hear about the Parisian and Dutch women and the food in America, but he only stared into the dark stall, hearing the restless movement of the horse. When Pierre felt reassured he said, "Let's go for a cigarette."

The horse was worked regularly. One night after the horse had been pushed a little harder than usual by a trainer, Pierre came into the room where Xannie slept and woke him by shaking his leg, and then told Xannie to go into town (in a taxi) and to bring a veterinarian. It was after one o'clock in the morning and Xannie was to tell the vet that he had a sick dog. Pierre gave Xannie a package of Camels, and Xannie rode in the taxi, with the windows rolled up, smoking a cigarette. He brought the veterinarian back, a Frenchman who looked carefully into the taxi and who waited for it to air out before he got inside. When they got back to the track, Xannie was left alone in front of the barn to watch while the veterinarian went into the barn to take a look.

In the morning the horse was gone, but the next night, about one o'clock in the morning, it was brought back. The veterinarian had taken the animal to his clinic, where he had an X-ray machine and a table for the horse, and soon the doctor was back again to talk to Pierre and to show him the strange black and white photographs of a bone in one of the horse's feet. There was a long, definite crack in it, and the veterinarian told Pierre that one good hard run, and the bone would break. The veterinarian said the foot would "explode." It was best to sell the animal right away, he said, and then he left.

For a few days Xannie heard nothing, but in the middle of the night Pierre came into his room and asked if he was sleeping and if Xannie had seen any thieves. Xannie noticed that Pierre didn't say thieves with the same horror as usual: there was a softness in his tone that verged on the affectionate. Xannie said he hadn't seen any thieves, and then he and Pierre went outside to smoke. Pierre had been drinking, and he weaved from side to side as he said, "You know that goddamned vet blabbed. Everyone knows about the horse. How the hell can I sell him now?"

Pierre hadn't offered a cigarette and Xannie looked at the lights of the city. When Pierre spoke he gestured with the hand that held the cigarette, and the orange tip of it streaked through the night, making lines that looked like neon tubing, and Xannie watched the bright curved shapes and listened to Pierre's deep breathing.

"Is the horse insured?" said Xannie.

"Yes," said Pierre.

They both looked at the lights of the city and the gray and yellow clouds above it.

"Is it insured for theft?" said Xannie.

"Yes," said Pierre.

"It would take a stupid thief to steal a lame horse," said Xannie.

"Not everyone knows," said Pierre, "and is it my business to worry about the brains of thieves? They've been known to make a mistake or two. Look."

He pointed to the horizon, at a light there, which was in the direction of the jail in Ipoh. Behind them there was the large wooden barn, the sense of the animals in it, uneasy in the stalls filled with sawdust.

"It can be arranged," said Xannie.

"I want to know nothing about it," said Pierre.

They stood side by side. After a while Xannie said, "Six hundred dollars. Tens and twenties."

"Three hundred," said Pierre. "I am not a rich man."

"All right," said Xannie, "three hundred and fifty and a set of papers for a horse with different breeding. Bad breeding, a different color, but the same age and sex."

Pierre sighed and said, "All right. Would you like a cigarette? A Camel?"

Xannie took one and lighted it, pulling the smoke into his mouth and standing there, watching the lights of the city, the large, lumpy clouds, and thinking, while he heard the horses moving in the stalls behind him, of the Parisian and Dutch women and of the piles of rice as big as mountains.

The next day the horse and Xannie were gone.

In 1950 Harlow was in the navy, and he spent some time in Malaysia, at Ipoh. Ipoh is a crowded city, and during the monsoon it rained so hard it made you feel as though you were standing in a shower with your clothes on. The sky turned purple during the monsoon, dark as an ugly bruise. Anyway, one day Harlow was walking down a street that was lined with closed-up shops and warehouses. The shops were shut up with metal doors that rolled down from above the windows, and the warehouses had large padlocks, some of which were old and as large as a book. At the back and front of each building's roof there were rolls of barbed wire. The warehouses were used on a short-term basis, and could be had for as little as twenty-four hours at a time. Harlow walked down the street and stopped in front of one that held bicycles. The city was filled with pedestrians, cars, motorcycles, and bicycles, but Harlow had never seen a horse in it. There wasn't enough room in the city for horses. He stopped in front of the bicycle warehouse because he had almost stepped in a pile of horse manure.

The door to the warehouse wasn't locked, and when Harlow pushed it open he saw by the dusky light in the street that bicycles were stacked on the floor and hung from the walls and rafters. When the light from the street hit the wheels of the bicycles, they looked delicate, almost fragile, like the spokes of an umbrella without the cloth. After a while, Harlow heard someone say, "Close the door."

Harlow pushed the door shut, and the hinges made a slow, insect-like screech. He didn't close the door completely. When he turned around, an electric light came on, and the bicycles were clearly visible, hanging in the air overhead. At the back of the room, which was narrow and not very long, there was an Asian man, dressed in a pair of dark pants and a white shirt, who was holding the halter of a horse. The horse, even in the dim, yellowish light, was clearly a Thoroughbred.

Harlow came a little closer, stepping over the bicycles and looking around the warehouse, but he saw no one else. There was only the uncomfortable, confined horse, the Oriental man, the gray walls of the place, the shiny spokes of the bicycles, and the piles of black rubber tires and inner tubes, many of which had been patched so many times as to look exotic, like the coils of some enormous pink-and-black snake. Harlow and the Oriental man didn't stand close together, but they each took a long, frank look into the other's face, and while they stood there it became clear that what had begun as an intrusion or perhaps even a burglary had ended, for a while anyway, as a limited partnership.

Harlow introduced himself. The man said his name was Xan Thu. Harlow ran his hand over the horse's cheek, along the muscled, arched neck, and down its chest.

"Where did you get the horse?" said Harlow.

Xannie blinked at him.

"Is it stolen?" said Harlow.

"No," said Xannie, "it's not hot. But, in all honesty, I'd have to say that it's a little warm."

"Hmm," said Harlow, "how warm?"

Xannie blinked again.

"Let's put it this way," said Harlow, "do you think anyone at the track here would recognize it?"

"Anything is possible," said Xannie.

Harlow looked over the horse a little more. When he faced Xannie again, he found on a crate next to Xannie's elbow a piece of newsprint. It hadn't been there before, and when Harlow picked it up he saw it was a past-performance sheet, two months old, that had come from a track in Manila. It had been neatly folded, but was still watermarked and yellowed. In the center, circled with a lead pencil, there was a chart for a three-year-old horse that in fifteen starts had showed in three, placed in three, and won nine. Harlow recognized the breeding.

"What do you say," said Harlow. "Why don't we run him at the track here?"

"There's the problem of being recognized," said Xannie.

"We can fix that," said Harlow. "Let's change the color."

"Yes," said Xannie, looking at the horse and making a low gurgle of pleasure. "Let's change the color."

"What's the penalty for stealing a horse here?" said Harlow.

Xannie said it depended on the owner. Some had been known to take the law into their own hands. Both Harlow and Xannie had seen the tattooed gangsters in the city, some of whom had a stump instead of a finger, the digit given to a hoodlum as a gesture of loyalty. Harlow looked over the horse again, read the performance chart, took another frank look at Xannie's face.

"I wouldn't want to have any trouble," said Harlow.

"No," said Xannie, "isn't that why dyeing the horse is a good idea?"

Harlow sighed and said he guessed it was. Then he went out of the warehouse and down the street to the avenue, where he took a taxi to a grocery. The taxi waited while Harlow bought ten packages of black RIT dye, two natural sponges, and a stack of towels. Then he got back into the taxi. When they were close to the warehouse, Harlow told the driver to let him off on the corner, and as he walked along the street, he looked over his shoulder.

Xannie and Harlow found a galvanized tub and they filled it with water. They mixed in the dye, a little at a time, and while they stirred it around each looked into the other's face, obviously thinking about the odds on the day they'd race the horse. Then they went to work, neither one of them saying a word about the color, since both of them had already decided on gray.

Harlow dipped a sponge into the tub and tried it against the horse's withers, and Xannie used one of the towels to rub the place dry. They stood back and admired the sickly gray-black color. Then Xannie took the other sponge and they went to work, rubbing the dye into the horse's coat, drying it, and standing back to judge the change. When they were done, the horse was covered with the doubt-inspiring color, which was suggestive of bad breeding and lousy nerves. More than anything else, it was the color of a weathered headstone in a New England cemetery.

Harlow went to the back of the warehouse, where there was a cold-water tap, and washed his hands, feeling the cold lather and seeing the stains of the dye under his fingernails. When he came back, he found another piece of paper on the same upturned box on which he had first seen part of a past-performance chart. This one was heavier, and the printing was better, and there was a fine scroll around the edges of it. It looked a little like a certificate of stock, and at the top there was a description of a gray three-year-old Thoroughbred. The breeding was given, too, and it didn't look very distinguished.

They put the empty packages of dye into the sack Harlow had used to bring them from the store. Xannie said he'd burn them in the alley. It was still early in the day, and Harlow said he'd get to the track and look around for a jockey. Then he went back to the corner and found a taxi.

In the evening, two hours after the last race, Harlow returned with Harry Laue. He was dark, overweight for a jockey, and a little drunk. Harlow opened the door of the warehouse, and Laue stepped in. Xannie was feeding the horse from a bucket. There were some carrots, too, and Xannie held them up, one at a time, and pushed them between the opened lips, and the regular, moving, and faintly curved teeth. Laue stepped up to the animal, went over it, and said to himself as he touched the muscles, the neck, the legs of the thing, "Well, well, well . . ."

"What do you think?" said Harlow.

"I got two thousand in the bank," said Laue. "I'm getting it out." Then Laue went back to the horse, his small, callused hands going over it again, and from the dim place where he bent down, Harlow and Xannie heard his half-sober chuckling. "That two thousand was for leaving town. Can you imagine what it would be like to be trapped here?" He went back to chuckling again, his fingers now carefully going over the horse's legs.

Two days later the horse was entered in the eighth race at Ipoh. Harlow and Xannie walked around the track, feeling the excitement in the air, which was definite enough to be almost smoky. They drank Scotch and soda in tall glasses. Xannie had a pair of dark glasses, and he took them from his pocket and put them on and looked around, and then took them off, fiddling with them while he drank long swallows. Xannie had three hundred dollars and Harlow had nine hundred. They found two chairs and sat in front of the tote board, their faces blank and bored. When the first prices went up, the horse was listed at fifty to one, and when, before the race, the price went to ninety to one, Harlow and Xannie bought two more drinks and went to the windows, before which there were long lines of people, Malaysian, Chinese, even English and Americans, not to mention a lot of French, all figuring on forms with a bit of pencil and looking over their shoulders through the smoky air, seemingly expecting that someone or at least some news was coming up behind them. Xannie asked if the clerk would take his watch, too, for fifty, or thirty, or ten and even five dollars, but the clerk looked at the watch, bit it, and then gave it back without a word, only pushing Xannie's tickets across the stainless-steel counter.

Before the race, when the horses were being led to the gate, the gray being put into the first position, Xannie said, "What if we win? How the hell are we going to get the money out of here?"

Harlow opened the jacket of his dress whites and inside there was a service .45 automatic in a holster, which was worn high and to one side. Harlow left his jacket unbuttoned, not because he cared about the pistol showing so much as wanting to be able to get to it easily.

It seemed as though the gray horse came out of the gate a length ahead. And at a distance, as the horses ran from the gate along the long backstretch of the six-furlong race, Harlow and Xannie saw the odd sealike and gentle movement of the horse as it seemed to stretch out and lift off the track a little, moving faster than even they had hoped. Before the first turn it was five lengths ahead and still gaining, its tail out and flying, its mane out like a flag, too, as Laue tried to rein the gray horse back a little, since even at Ipoh there were some standards to worry about.

In the turn it looked as though the horse was going too fast to make it. More than anything else, there seemed to be a momentary straightness in its path, a tangent that, if followed, would take it to the fence. The people in the stands were already standing and screaming, but in the moment the horse seemed to step out from the path it should take, the screams changed to a long, deep groan. The horse continued to go straight, although not for long. It dipped a shoulder and then turned a quick, high cartwheel, in which Laue and his tack and the horse's mane and tail blended together. The circular motion of the animal and the color of it appeared for the briefest instant like a puff of smoke from an explosion, a light, streaming collection of gray on gray, with a boot, a stirrup, a hand, or a bit of silk, a sharp hoof flashing into the clear air and then disappearing again into the confusion. The horse hit the ground, rolled over, and tried to get up, but didn't.

Harlow walked through the crowd, and Xannie hung on to his jacket, which pulled him along until they came to the rail. Harlow jumped over and began running across the soft, loamy soil of the track, which was deep and made the long run seem dreamlike and difficult. Harlow crossed the infield grass, and as he went the people from the stands came behind him, the crowd of them spreading into a large V.

Laue was standing and looking at the horse when Harlow arrived, and for a moment, while the horse pawed the ground and tried to get up, falling each time it put weight on the broken leg, its head rising and sinking with the effort and the pain, Harlow and Laue looked at each other until Laue said, "It'll have to be killed." And as Xannie came running ahead of the crowd that streamed across the infield, as the stewards drove in a Chevrolet pickup truck from the side of the track where the grandstand was, Harlow took the .45 pistol from under his coat and stood before the horse and shot it between the eyes, once, and then again, and the horse gently and slowly put its nose onto the soft loam of the track. As the horse lay still the crowd arrived, Xannie at its head.

Xannie stood on the side of the horse opposite Harlow and wailed, throwing his arms into the air, crying openly. Harlow stood with blood on his dress whites, still holding the gun. People crowded around him, looked at the horse, and then were pushed aside by others, who were talking quickly and screeching, gesticulating, showing with their hands how the horse had gone straight and then turned end over end. Xannie screamed at Harlow, now speaking not English but a Chinese or Malaysian dialect Harlow understood not at all. A young man in a blue work shirt with a tie said to Harlow, "He wants the gun."

"Why?" said Harlow.

The young man spoke so quickly that his cheeks seemed to flutter.

"He wants to shoot himself," said the man in the work shirt.

Xannie stood on the other side of the horse, one hand out, the other making gestures toward his open palm. The crowd around the horse made a muttering, a slight, endless babble.

Harlow put the pistol into the holster and said, "No. Tell him to come along."

Xannie stood on the other side of the horse, palm still out, his cheeks marked with tears.

"All right," said Harlow, "tell him I'll take him to America."

The man in the work shirt shouted, opening his mouth so wide as to make a web of his cheek when he spoke. Xannie stared at Harlow. Then he spoke in the language Harlow didn't understand.

"What's that?" said Harlow.

"He wants to know if it will be by boat or airplane," said the man in the work shirt.

Xannie and Harlow stared at one another, and as they did so, with the crowd around them, it began to rain. The sky was purplish, dark, looking bruised. The clouds had no texture. Instead they came in one piece, only marked by the perfect silver lines of rain. Harlow and Xannie both stared at the horse, and in the heavy rain they saw that the water running from it was getting a little dark, and that when it streamed into the red soil of the track, it left black marks that reminded Harlow of a woman's cheeks when her mascara began to run. The stewards began to look at it, too. Then Xannie climbed over the horse and said, in his crisp, accented English, "It's all right. I'll take the boat."

They turned and pushed through the crowd and walked through the heavy mud of the track, their feet becoming large and misshapen with it, their fingers and knees still trembling as they went toward the grayish grandstand with its weblike and smoky supports, and as they went by the rail there was a man standing against it. He was bald, heavy, wore a dark suit made in England, and his skin was an olive-brown. His eyes were green. He was a little drunk and he had been been crying, but now he said, his voice watery and sibilant, while looking at Xannie, "Carrés d'agneau, truites de rivière grillées, homard à la creme. L'argent pour les femmes."

Roast young lamb, grilled trout, lobsters in cream. Money for the women.

They continued walking, and the crowd closed in around them, obscuring the track, the grass of it, the white rail, and making a sound like running water, but as they went, there still came over the noise of the crowd the steady, half-drunk voice of Pierre, as he shouted, "Saumon glacé à la parisienne!"

Glazed salmon!

I first heard this story years ago, when I was having dinner at Harlow's house. Xannie hadn't been in the country long, and Harlow had moved into his father's house and brought Anne, Alexandra, and Xannie to live there. Harlow was already inviting to dinner some local . . . allies, and one of them asked Xannie what he would have done if Harlow had passed over the pistol, but Xannie only stared at the man and said, "It's nice to be in America, don't you think?"

I liked Xannie, and we shared the secret. Or more than just one secret. I waited for a time when we were alone and then asked him in a mild, friendly, and sympathetic tone how long he had waited in the warehouse for Harlow to come along.

Xannie stared at me full in the face and said, "Have you ever been to Malaysia?"

It came out slowly. Every now and then, when Xannie came to ask for help with his income tax or with a mail order form, he'd mention Pierre Bouteille, the stables, the X rays of the horse, the papers. He knew that once he had the horse, all he had to do was to sit tight: the right American would come along. There were a lot of us in Ipoh at the time. I don't know why. And, of course, no American can resist fixing a horserace. We're fascinated by these things, since it's an American version of sophistication. In the Orient, Xannie said, things are more ordinary. He once had a ticket for a horse winning a race in Malaysia, and when he went to cash it, the clerk slammed the window shut, saying that although Xannie had the winning ticket, the horse wasn't supposed to win. Xannie had almost formed a partnership with an enlisted man from Mt. Sterling, Kentucky, but at the last moment he backed out, since the enlisted man didn't look like he had the money for a trip to America. Xannie waited for Harlow to put his head in the door.

Xannie had been certain, too, that no American in the world would let him use the pistol on himself. He had been waiting for the moment when an American would stop him. Xannie had banked on it. If you figured this out, he became your friend.

And after we had stood in the kitchen, where I had asked Xannie about it, and where we stood, bobbing our heads to each other in a display of ceremonial politeness, he began to walk down the road to my house on his days off, in summer wearing his pleated cotton pants, a white shirt, and carrying a black umbrella. He hated the sun. Rain too. In winter he came along the road in insulated boots, down pants, and a parka. Whenever there was an assassination, Xannie was at my door, explaining it as he came into the house. Assassination was his specialty.

Down by the Riverside

When Alexandra came home from California, she drove a 1955 Ford station wagon. She wanted to drive across the country, and had bought the car to do so. It didn't leave her with much money, a couple of hundred, I'd say, and by the time she got to town, I don't think she had more than twenty dollars. She hadn't made much money, and the four hundred a month was gone for the year. She wanted to drive, she said, because she didn't think she'd be getting out for a while.

She'd never seen the country. The Ford was blue, a color that was weathered so it looked like the sky on the first pale spring day of the year. She wore, for most of the trip, a pair of jeans, a T-shirt, and a pair of tennis shoes, which had been white but were now gray and had knots tied in the laces. She went over the Bay Bridge, seeing the water there dark blue, windblown and flickering with sunlight. In the San Joaquin Valley the fields had already been planted and were green with fuzz, but the size of the fields and the absence of buildings aside from silos made the new things coming up look false, like Astroturf. She was glad to get into the Sierras and to have the smell of pine and humus made of bark and needles. She watched the temperature gauge on the Ford. The gauge began to move upward as the

Ford climbed, and when she came to the top of the pass, seeing the white mist from the Ford's radiator twisting and disappearing above the hood, she thought of New England and of the stream near her father's house, the pool where the fish rose from the dark green slime and shadows of the bottom.

Alexandra crossed the Mississippi early in the morning. She stopped just before the bridge and went down to the river, seeing the wide water, and being able to feel the tug of it, the pull toward the ocean. For a moment she wanted to take off her clothes and bathe there and to towel her skin, feeling the silt of the river, but the water was cold and she was afraid of the shock. She put cold water on her face, hoping it would make her feel a little less nauseated. It would be easier to drive that way. She went through Ohio and Ashtabula County, where she spent the night and saw, in the morning, ducks and geese on the Pymatuning Reservoir. And finally, when she came to New England, she had that twenty dollars left. She looked at the gas gauge and tapped it with her finger, hoping the needle would rise a little, but it didn't.

Alexandra stopped at Billy Watson's Mobil station just outside of town. Billy's son was sitting in a chair with a broken seat next to the Coke machine. The station has two gasoline pumps, a rack of oil, and a light standard. In those days Billy or his son pumped the gas, but now Billy's son sits behind a glass booth and you talk to him through a microphone when he takes your money. You fill your own tank. But then Billy's son was enjoying the spring weather after a long winter of snow plowing and pumping gasoline in the cold.

"Is it all right if I use the bathroom?" Alexandra said. "It might be a minute or two."

"Sure," said Billy's son, "it's okay. Take all day if you want."

"Thanks," said Alexandra.

In the bathroom she put the suitcase on the toilet seat and opened it there. Inside, on the top of her clothes, there were some towels, a washcloth, and a bar of soap. Alexandra put one of the towels on the stained concrete floor, stood on it, and undressed. She washed the sink with the soap, which was pink and had come from a motel in Nebraska, then filled the sink with water and put one of her long, slender legs into it. She soaped the shin and calf, picked a razor from the suitcase and began to shave. When she was done, she rinsed, switched legs, and began again. She shaved under her arms, and then put the razor back into the suitcase. She gave herself a sponge bath and felt the rough texture of the terrycloth. Every now and then she heard the sound of the bell as a car ran over the pneumatic tube stretched over the cement next to the gasoline pumps. Alexandra filled the sink and wetted her hair and took some shampoo from the suitcase. She worked it into a lather, and scrubbed, looking at herself once in the mirror and seeing there the reflection through the spotted glass of a young woman with smooth fine features and grayish eyes. The lather was thick and made her seem as though her hair was white and curled tightly. She rinsed her hair and dried it, hearing the sound of the dryer loud in the small bathroom. She put on a brassiere and stockings and then opened the door a little and asked Billy's son if he'd bring her the dry cleaning from the car. He handed it through the door and blushed and Alexandra thanked him. He stood outside the closed door and said, "You're Harlow Pearson's daughter, aren't you?"

"Alexandra," she said, "that's right."

"I heard you were out west someplace," he said.

He waited for a while, and then went out and sat in the chair by the Coke machine. Alexandra put a little makeup on, just a little to make her skin whiter and her eyes seem more gray, and then she dressed and put everything back in the suitcase. She wore a white cotton skirt, a silk blouse, and she put a scarf around her neck. She wore shoes with a longish heel and walked out of the bathroom, carrying the suitcase, and waving to Billy's son, who sat, chair tipped back, staring at her.

Of course, Alexandra didn't want to appear before Harlow looking as though she were desperate. And there was something else, too, in that she had never felt more . . . pretty. And, of course, it wasn't just appearance . . . she had become a young woman and was privately fascinated by it. The pregnancy seemed to her to be part of her worthiness. She wanted to let him see the beauty of it and perhaps even to flirt with him a little, as a kind of celebration. Rules didn't mean much to her and she accepted the pregnancy almost as a kind of reward. She was a child, you understand! She was as glad of it as she was of a sunrise, pleased by it, and certain, in a more profound way, that she wanted to have the child. Perhaps it was the closeness of her mother's death. I know, after my father died, I had a wild longing to have a child. Then my wife was alive and we did have a son. I'll never forget the joy and the piercing regret at the time when I knew my father would never see the child. Maybe it was like that.

Alexandra left the Mobil station and drove north, out of town. She went along the Sugar Wolf River. The river was high and brownish, the white arms of foam behind the rocks turning back on themselves. When she passed the covered bridge, she pulled to the side of the road, where there was a bench and some green trash cans. She took a bag from the car, in which there were crackers, cheese, and a knife and that folded twenty-dollar bill. She left the money in the bag, but she took out the knife and the cheese and the crackers and sat there, slicing and eating the cheese and being buffeted by the wind as the trucks sailed by. On one of them there was written in dust, in large block letters, a sign that said SHOW ME LEG.

Alexandra stared at it as the truck went along. She finished the last of the crackers and cheese and got back into the car, still feeling fresh and clean and not quite so hungry, either. After a while, when she was going uphill, she passed the truck, and when she went by she pulled up the white cotton skirt, showing the skin at the top of the stockings, her knee and long leg, and as she went by the truck driver sounded the air horn again and again, the long blasts following her as she went along the river. And, as she went by, she put her head back and laughed, showing her white teeth and the shape of her mouth and filling the Ford with her sharp, barking laughter. I was shocked by this, but she looked at me, her eyes steady now and said, "It was just a little fun." Then she looked away and said, she had a few desires of her own and they weren't so easily satisfied. I can still see her, though, coming along the river in the Ford that was almost out of gas and the air horn sounding, echoing over the water and through the valley.

She turned up the road to Harlow's house.

Harlow's house was ten miles from town, along the river. At

one time it had been a farmhouse and it was covered with
clapboards and had green shutters and it sat on top of a slight
grade. There were fields below it that ran all the way to the
river. The fields were edged with trees, mostly greenish aspen,
and sometimes in the early spring after the leaves had come out
and there was a breeze, the undersides of the leaves flashed and
sparkled and had the same texture as the light that came off the
river. The house had two stories and a slate roof and two chimneys, one at each end, and in front and at one side there was a
small orchard. It had thirty trees. At the road, which separated
the orchard and the house from the fields that ran down to the
river, there was a white fence and an arbor, which was covered
with roses. Harlow probably owned five hundred acres, most of
it in timber. There were only fifty or so acres in fields.

The vision of the house was always startling. You went along
a road for a long time. It was a dirt road and it went through
flat, wooded land, and then you came to open fields with the
river in the distance and Harlow's white house above the road.
It seemed to command the place and made the landscape there
seem separate from the outside world, clean and preserved, not
decayed in any way, not weak. It was always striking to see,
especially in summer, when the shutters seemed so green and
cool and reserved, and the white clapboards looked frosty and
correct.

Alexandra had called Harlow the night before from a phone
booth in New York State. I think he had been up all night after
that, and in the morning, when the grass was wet and glassy, he
came down to see me and walked around in my garden, poking
at the mounds of black soil I had tilled. After a while he turned
and said, "I just want to start over. That's all. If she'll just . . ."
He didn't finish, and I was left thinking *just!* Just what? Just not
have needs, I suppose. Of course, he felt wronged, because he'd
been miserable since she'd left. Of that I'm certain. He didn't
want to explain himself, not to Alexandra or to anyone. I think
it embarrassed him, but, my God, he wasn't living on an island
in the middle of the ocean. I've always thought the greatest gift
a father could give was to let a child know exactly who he was.
What was the point of lies? He stiffened in the yard, before he
left, and said he wasn't going to be pushed around. And, when

he thought I'd gone back into the house, he took from his back pocket the card I had given him, the one with the photograph of his daughter standing on a street in San Francisco.

Alexandra had brought presents, too. A heavy, armored pair of Zeiss field glasses for Xannie and a pigskin coat for Harlow. She had bought them before she put the rest of the money into the car. Alexandra had always liked Xannie, or more than liked, since he had brought her up as much as her mother had. Xannie had told her, time and again, that what she wanted to be in life was a "tough mutt."

Alexandra drove the Ford up the road, seeing the house and the top of the gentle rise. She stopped the car and got out into the warm morning. It was the middle of spring. She picked the heavy field glasses off the front seat and then walked through the arbor in the stone wall and through the orchard. The field glasses were slung by a strap over her shoulder.

Harlow was waiting just behind the door, and he saw her coming between the trees, which were in bloom, the white petals showing their reddish, almost painted-looking centers. He stepped out and down the brick steps of the house and then Alexandra stood next to him, her eyes set on his. Neither one of them smiled. She looked very pretty in the sunlight.

After he'd greeted her, but not touched her, not shown in any way what those winter nights of her absence had been like, he said, "I know what's been eating at you. So we might as well get it over with now. I've got your things inside."

"What things?" said Alexandra.

"Your waders and fly rod," he said. "Aren't you upset about a missed date to fish? Isn't that what you came home for?"

Alexandra looked at the whitish, ice-colored hair of her father and stepped a little closer to him.

"Yes," she said, her voice seeming soft and careful, "I guess that's right."

"Good," said Harlow.

He reached back into the house and brought out her waders. They had been patched in a few places with red rubber. Harlow had taken them out the spring before and this one, too, and filled the legs with water to see where there were leaks. Alexandra reached out for them and the fly rod and vest, too.

"Wait a minute," said Alexandra.

"What for?" said Harlow, stiffening a little in the doorway.

"I'll need some other shoes," she said.

"I'll get them," said Harlow. He went upstairs.

Xannie stood behind the door. In his hand he had a catalogue, since all of his clothes came through the mail, from Brooks Brothers, L.L. Bean, and Dunn's. The catalogue was from Nudies of Hollywood, and Xannie had it turned open to a page that showed rows of western boots.

Alexandra slipped the field glasses from her shoulder.

"Xannie," she said. "Xannie."

He stepped out, into the light, blinking at her and holding the magazine from Nudies.

"I brought you something for the races," she said.

She held out the glasses and Xannie took them. He bobbed his head a little and took Alexandra's hand and gave it a quick squeeze. "Thanks," he said. He stood there, still blinking, feeling the weight of the field glasses. After a while he said, "What's wrong?"

"What makes you think something's wrong?" said Alexandra.

"I don't know," said Xannie, "sometimes I think I've got a nose for trouble."

They both turned and looked at the car as it sat in front of the house. It was dusty and there was rust along the bottom of the doors. The dust was fine, white, and made the windows have a pale milky quality. The license plate seemed alien, peculiar in the cool air of New England.

"Listen," said Xannie. "Be careful how you tell Harlow. Okay?"

Then Harlow came down with the shoes and Alexandra went into the living room and sat down and took off the ones she was wearing. As she bent over her foot, tying the laces of the short boots, she heard, from the mantel, the sound of the clock there, the steady ticking of the gears at the top of the pendulum. She thought of how it sounded in winter, when there were two feet of snow on the ground and it was ten below zero.

Harlow waited until she was done, and then he bent next to her and opened the aluminum fly box he carried and showed her the small dandelion puffs of flies there. Most of them were gray or bluish. "I tied these last night," he said. "I'll put some on your drying patch." Then he bent over her, still not touching her, as he put them on the patch of lambskin on her vest. She held the vest in her hands and felt the gentle tug as each fly was hooked through the fleece. They took their things and went into the sunshine. Harlow carried a basket, too, that he had packed in the morning.

Xannie stopped them in the orchard. There were four or five morels growing there, and Xannie picked them and dropped the small mushrooms, each one with a textured cap, into Harlow's basket. Then they went through the field beyond the orchard and into the woods. The maples weren't filled out yet, although the leaves at the ends of the twigs and branches were pinkish and emerging: they had the shape of the open beaks of young birds. Below there was the flash and blue glint of the river. Harlow went down to it, leaving Alexandra alone. She took off her skirt and stockings and stepped into the waders, feeling the coolness of the material against her bare skin.

Harlow gave her a fly rod, already strung up, and she waded out. Soon the mayflies began to come off the water: they were delicate and gray and they reminded her of the flowers on the apple trees in the orchard. She had unbuttoned her blouse to feel the sun on her neck and shoulders, and some of the mayflies landed on her skin. Soon they rose from her, and they seemed to be emerging from the white material, lace, and the pale skin of her shoulders and neck.

Alexandra hooked and killed two fish, and they made a banana-shaped weight in the pouch of her waders, and she stood there, feeling the mayflies' light touch against her skin. She was scared, and the light touch of them set off a shudder, a cold run of panic that slipped down her legs, and into her boots, where there was the cool pressure of the river. Then she waded ashore and changed into her skirt.

Harlow didn't catch anything, but he cleaned and cooked the fish. When they were brown and crisp, Harlow put them on a plate, along with the morels, and then Alexandra and Harlow sat opposite one another. The mushrooms were smoky and the fish had a strong taste of the river, and soon Alexandra was left with a comb of bones on her plate.

Alexandra told me she didn't think they'd ever get there, but they finally walked up the tributary to the large, deep pool. At this time of the day its surface was blue as the sky, but when Alexandra stood in the shadows she could see the stones, the brownish green moss, the sluggish, haunting shadows there. The pool was cool, and as she watched, something stirred. Or maybe it was just her imagination. She had been thinking about the fish, the enormous old cannibal of a trout, since the moment she had stood in the used-car lot in California, kicking the tires of the Ford and drawing a bead on her father.

It was important that the two of them seem ordinary. Alexandra's hands were sweating, and she was having trouble breathing easily. Her knees were weak with the effort of standing there and looking into the dark green water. There was a little breeze. Alexandra said there was the slight, insane creaking of the pines nearby. She stood there, her face seeming bored or tired, pale with lack of interest. But she was thinking, as she stared at the water, Well, what if he doesn't go for it? What then?

I don't think there was ever any doubt about what she intended. She came to trap Harlow. She probably started to think about it when she went to the used-car lot in San Francisco and bought the station wagon to drive across the country. I'm sure, as she stood under the winglike flapping of the small flags in the lot, she was already thinking about the fish that lurked in the mossy and green shadows of the pool.

All Harlow wanted was for things to be as before, when they had gone to fish and had driven in the Jeep with the windshield down flat, combat style. And even though he didn't take any warning from her leaving, he certainly knew what it was like to live without her. He had sat in that old house of his, hearing the snow washing against the windows, wondering where she was or what she was doing. He said he was so glad, when he saw her walking up the flagstone path to the house, that he thought he was going to die. He believed it was possible to die from happiness. He said his heart couldn't tell the difference between grief and joy. Perhaps that's why he tried to avoid them both. I'll never forget the times he came to see me, in the middle of winter, his face marked with the certain knowledge of what it was like to sit in his house, feeling the aching tug that came from having his daughter gone and not knowing where she was. Well, he was glad to see her, although he was too arrogant to see she was desperate.

California hadn't been easy for her. She'd been tricked there. Or worse than tricked: changed. She had found a job, rented an apartment, and then run across the man who was the father of her child. He was an older, dignified man who seemed to know everything about her, so much so that Alexandra hadn't even considered getting pregnant, since what they did seemed more an exercise in comfort and understanding than anything else. The man was soothing. Alexandra had been pleased by him, forgetful of her mother's death and Harlow's aloofness. And no one was more surprised than Alexandra when she discovered that the ordinary world had been there all along, just waiting, and finally revealing itself in her pregnancy. The shock that the man was already married wasn't anywhere near as hard to take as the fact that she had been lulled. The older man was a sentimentalist. What else can explain the fact that he was cavalier when he was smart enough to know better? At least Alexandra didn't go to the old fool for help. What could he have done, invited her to live with his children, one of whom was just a little younger than Alexandra?

She told me she was all right until she saw Harlow's house: the first glance at the white clapboards and green shutters, the yard and the orchard she had known all her life, brought her to a panic she could almost feel on her skin, as though it were itching. After all, her father wasn't easy to trap. There wasn't, I don't think, anything cynical in her. Trapping him was the only thing left for her.

So, Alexandra and Harlow stood by the pool, looking at the dark shadows, the deep stones covered with moss, and the bottom itself, which, in places, was so dark as to be invisible. They had some chitchat. Or Alexandra made it seem as though they were just talking to no real purpose. I imagine Alexandra yawned and turned to Harlow, showing him the tears along the lower lids of her eyes. Down below, in the water, something turned over and showed a flash of light on its long, silver sides. Alexandra noticed it but didn't say anything. Of course,

Harlow started talking about the fish. Alexandra looked uninterested. Harlow talked about what a creature the thing was and how hard to catch. Alexandra probably shrugged and began to turn away, saying, in a sleepy, half-interested voice, "Oh, he wouldn't be hard to catch."

"Do you want to bet?" said Harlow.

"Yes," said Alexandra, now standing next to him, looking into his face, although she spoke, from inertia I guess, with that same half-bored, breathy voice.

"All right," said Harlow, "I'll take that bet."

He turned and looked at her. The poor son of a bitch. I think in that moment he was happy. Everything was exactly the same as it had been. Alexandra was home, safe. They'd gone fishing and they were going to have one of their bets. Like the one they'd had for wading. It was just like old times.

Soon they were arguing, almost screaming. I don't know what set it off exactly. Maybe it was Harlow's anger from winter when she was gone. How dare she leave him like that, without a word? Well, she stood there, blinking at him with disbelief. Hadn't he gone to Yugoslavia, hadn't he abandoned her? Well, said Harlow, there were reasons. He needed privacy. Alexandra said she wasn't so concerned with the reasons anymore. She only wanted one thing and that was that she'd be able to depend upon him for the bet. She didn't want him to run away.

It went on that way. They stood opposite one another, their faces coming closer together, their voices rising off the hard, flat surface of the water. The thing there in the dark, the fish, turned on its side again and showed a tantalizing flash of its silvery flank. It looked like a piece of aircraft aluminum that had been turned, in the water, for one moment toward the sun.

Harlow said he wasn't going to run away. What did she want to bet? Was it money? Alexandra wouldn't answer him directly. Time and again she came back to asking him if she could count on him. Would he betray her? Would he leave before things were resolved? Could she be certain of him, no matter what? He said she could count on him. He wouldn't leave.

"All right," he said, "what will we bet?"

"I want some help," she said. "If I catch the fish, you'll give me some help."

"What help?" he said.

"Just some help," she said.

"What help?" he said. "What do you want?"

But she went back again to insisting that he'd give her a chance to resolve things. Could she count on him? Absolutely count on him? No matter what? He wanted to know what she took him for, some dismal liar? Their voices rose again, trapped between the two low ridges on either side of the pool, which made what they said have a strange hellish and echoey quality. Harlow agreed. Yes, he said, no matter what. Then Alexandra told him she was going to have a child.

Of course, he thought it was time to have a frank talk. He gave her every argument you could think of. He was good in an argument. Most of the ones he gave her made her stare at him, her eyes wide with rage. She told me that she wasn't absolutely sure why she wanted the child, aside from being able to say it was a large, definite thing that would come into her life. Perhaps she thought it was a matter of turning every insult and lie, every bit of evasion of the last few years into something that was worthwhile and good. The more Harlow argued, the more she was certain. Well, he'd spent a lifetime avoiding her, and now he expected her to believe him. Near the end, he was reduced to repeating himself and then they both stood silently, watching something flash and move in the depths of the water.

He thought Alexandra was having the child to hurt him, in the same way that her mother had left the letters in the clock for him to find. So, his voice rough with anger, he said to her that he'd keep the bet. And if she hadn't caught the fish in two weeks, then she'd come with him to Sweden, where they'd "get rid of it." That's the way he put it. Alexandra agreed.

Then they turned and went down to the river, where they picked up their things and went home, the two of them walking along, appearing to be as ordinary as possible. Both of them wanted to pretend, for the moment, that nothing had changed. They went through the fields, their legs swinging out, in the same cadence as the ticking of the clock that sat on the mantel in the house.

Alexandra came to see me that afternoon, and she sat in the sun room, her hair bright with the rose and golden light behind

her. There were insects outside, rising and falling on a fountain
of air, each one a small, bright fleck that had the same color as
the sun. I gave her a glass of lemonade, which she drank slowly,
her eyes set on nothing at all. After a while she thanked me, and
then went back to Harlow's house.

Harlow came, too, and he said there was nothing else to do
but to go along. At least he understood he was trapped, although he was horrified that the two of them had been working
on it for years, so that one afternoon they'd find themselves
standing by a pool of water, feeling the thing close around
them. I offered him some lemonade, but he waved me away, his
face showing exasperation, and when I brought two long cool
drinks with bourbon in them, we poured them down so quickly
as to make our noses ache.

I asked him what he was going to do, and he sat there, rattling
the ice in his glass, and then he said, looking up at me with an
unpleasant expression, "Why, I guess I'll go down there and
catch the thing myself. That way she won't have a chance, will
she?"

His face had that hard, gambler's stubbornness. If he caught
the thing, he'd have it mounted to hang on the wall. Then he
got up, thanked me for the drink, and went down the road, his
figure receding through the reddish bits of insects that rose and
fell in the last light of the afternoon. The poor fool. He hadn't
learned a thing.

Perhaps I have given an incorrect impression of Harlow. I've
made him out to be equal to his daughter, or at least energetic
enough to struggle or gamble, or whatever they called it. But
that's not the case at all. He was anything but that. He was, if
anything, unsure and angry. His wife had died and he had lost
an election, so he had no work, nothing he could count on. His
daughter had been gone close to a year. It was a dangerous time.
And maybe the danger of his position made him all the angrier.
It's not an easy moment when you realize you haven't escaped
life at all, or those horrible things that happen to others, or
when you realize life is only rearranging itself in that phantom-
like way and that soon it will kill you. Whenever I think of this,
I feel a cold tingle, but then I slap my smelly dog and go about
my business.

Mad Katherine

 Alexandra told me, too, that at this time she began to dream of Mad Katherine, the hunter. When Alexandra was nine and ten and eleven years old, I told her Mad Katherine stories. Alexandra delighted in them, but they came back, at night, and weren't delightful then. Mad Katherine lived in the woods along the Sugar Wolf River a hundred years ago. She had a tent of skins and ate what she could trap or shoot. She killed hundreds of deer and eight bears. Mad Katherine walked to the towns along the river when she needed to buy thread or some salt. She was dressed in skins and showed her scarred face. There were lines on it, around the eyes and across the nose, long, whitish marks that looked like pieces of knotted string. They came from her fights with bears and men. Mad Katherine had a daughter, too, and when she went to the woods to live on berries, venison, and fish, she left the girl behind, in town.

In the town library there are handwritten accounts of her, left by people who had seen her, and I had gone through them, turning over the paper that was ginger-colored and covered with ink that had faded to a light purple. I told Alexandra a story when she sat opposite me on a summer afternoon, eating a cucumber sandwich and a bag of chips. She wanted to know where the daughter stayed and I couldn't tell her.

Now, in her dreams, Alexandra saw Mad Katherine walk toward a deer, which was on the ground and bleeding from the shoulder and nose. Mad Katherine took a knife from her hip and the blade of it was sharp and polished. The blade became the center of the dream, looking like a sliver of frozen water in the landscape. The knife reflected the sunlight and brightened the dream's thin fog. Or sometimes she saw the deer on the ground and Mad Katherine approaching it with only a piece of bone, a deer's leg from another time, having even given up the knife that came from town. Mad Katherine stood next to the deer and took a stone and began to crack the leg she carried so she could make a knife of her own. Alexandra woke to the dream's muted hammering, and as she heard the sound of it recede into the darkness, she thought, There must have been other solutions. Why didn't you go to New York or Chicago? What about an escape? And what about your daughter? Didn't you ever sit on those ridges above the river and stare into town at the lighted window in the house where your daughter stayed? Did you begin to hunt and fish and live in skins along the river because you wanted things to be clear? So you'd have no complications? And what did you do with your evenings or with soft, warm afternoons?

Hammer and Tongs

 Even though we live in what is called the "country," we still have a town, too. It is the place where we go to buy a washing machine, a dryer, to shop for food, have our glasses adjusted, our teeth fixed, hair cut. The town, I'm afraid, needs a little explaining.

The town is not pretty. At times it reminds me of industrial England, in the Midlands, say. Or of the mill town it once was. There's an old section, a street lined with brick buildings from the nineteenth century. They have flat, soapstone sills and curved arches at the top of the windows. The roofs are flat, mostly, tarred now, and around the windows there are long black stains. The buildings are built side by side, one against another on a street that goes down to the river, and the aura of New England rigidity around them is so prominent as to make the buildings seem cold with it. I have even touched the gray weathered bricks of one of them on a July afternoon when the temperature was a hundred, just to see. And even in the heat I could feel the terror of the women who walked by the brick buildings a hundred years before.

The town isn't old-fashioned, or not without improvements or changes since the nineteenth century. On both sides there are gas stations, muffler shops, shopping malls, hardware stores, nurseries, hamburger stands and pizza places for people who are afraid to get far away from the highway. In the old part of town, the dark buildings have been made into apartments, and there are stores now in which you can see records, health food, books, or dress shops with windows where bikini briefs and transparent brassieres are displayed. There is a dating service and a video arcade. A gourmet food shop and a stockbroker.

We have the Critchfields, the Keiths, and the Thachers. My mother was a Critchfield. They have been here for generations. It is amazing how many of them still have money, and they stretch it out in the old houses they own. Their children go away to school, but they almost all return, since it's a shock to them that the rest of the world has no awe of a Critchfield from southern New England. Harlow's family had been here for a while, but not nearly long enough to be thought of as anything more than marginal. We have storekeepers too, and there is a rich political life. There are poor people, who originally built small houses around town, but recently they have begun to live in trailers. There are hard-working, honest people whose parents lost farms and came to town to work hard there, too. There are doctors, lawyers, accountants, dentists, real estate brokers, bookkeepers, store owners. And, as I've said, Critchfields, Thachers, Keiths. You'd think everyone would mind his own business. They don't, of course. Maybe it's the long winters that make them the way they are.

And that's what I want to come to. Some years ago there was a young woman in town. Her name was Sally. She wasn't from around here, not originally, and I imagine she came from across the river. But for a while she was here, working in a factory outside of town called Flash-a-Matic, where they made spark plugs. It's gone now, but when Sally worked there she found a young man and got pregnant. Or maybe there was more than one young man and she didn't know who the father really was, or didn't care. She had the child, a little girl, and lived alone with her in an apartment in a building by the river. Or tried to. I'm amazed she held out as long as she did, since the women of the town, those who organized the garden parties to benefit the museum and library, the women of advanced ideas, those who

canvassed for the right candidates and who gave money to the
right causes, those same women hounded her.

They began by offering help. Or what appeared to be help,
but which was just getting a foot in the door. They immediately
presumed Sally was their responsibility. Of course, they didn't
see the condescension in this. They sent food and clothes and
the smallest amount of money, and soon they were talking
about the welfare of the child. They arranged for the social
worker to offer counseling and to have the child "tested" to see
if she needed "assistance." The results were private, of course.
The women would tell Sally only that the "case" had been "sent
up" to the state capital. There were times when I'd see Sally
with her daughter, the two of them walking along a sun-filled
street in July, looking in the windows, or just walking, Sally
holding the girl by the hand. Of course, the women in town
kept her from having a job.

As a matter of fact, I gave her a job. Not much of one, to be
sure, but at least I found out how the rigamarole worked. My
wife needed help with our son, who was a few years old, and I
hired the woman. She walked up the road from town when I
couldn't pick her up or when I was away, and I can still see her
coming along that long road, leading her daughter by the hand,
coming through the dust and the golden insects of the afternoon. She did good work, but soon I got a call from the accountant's wife, who said, in passing (only in passing), that it was too
bad that Sally was working in the house, since her little girl had
been known to hurt the other children Sally looked after. It was
probably jealousy, she supposed.

Sally was smart enough to see what was going on, and she did
her best. In all her innocence, she thought it would be possible
to make friends with the women. Maybe if she could talk to
them, they'd leave her alone. She thought about it for a while.
The truth of the matter is that she was hungry a lot of the time:
it was hard to find almost any work at all. They wouldn't take
her back at Flash-a-Matic, and she wouldn't take from me anything beyond what was fair. I increased her hours, but she
could see what I was up to, and while she worked more than she
thought was right, not as much as I offered. Well, she decided to
have the women in town to lunch. She picked out some invita-

tions and mailed them. They were tasteful, severe cards and she had carefully written the time, date, and address. She bought some things to give the women for lunch. She did some cooking, cleaned the apartment, ironed cotton place mats and napkins. The first call came, I guess, in the morning. The accountant's wife said her child was ill and she couldn't make it. She was sorry. Sally hung up the phone and began cleaning the windows. The next call came when the quiche was in the oven. And it went on that way, every ten or fifteen minutes, until all of them had called. What she made was typical of her: she'd read in some magazine about quiche. Her daughter told me, a few days later, that she was tired of eating cheese pie. Did I ever eat cheese pie?

Anyway, they hounded Sally out of town, forced her to one of those new cities in California. I often wonder what became of her there. It all happened so smoothly, without effort, and it was impossible to single any one out and say, You. You're the one who's responsible. They were too clever for that. One day Sally was gone and no one said a word.

Alexandra knew this story. As a matter of fact, when she came to see me after making the bet with her father, she was insistent on going over it with me again . . . she wanted more details, more names. . . . But, as I've said, the people involved were vague and clever. And Alexandra knew she wouldn't have to deal with just the women who believed in Therapy and Art, but with the Critchfields, the Thachers, and the Keiths, who lived for meddling.

Alexandra told me she'd already been to a new western city. She wanted to know if she should let herself be forced back to one of them? She looked at me directly when she asked this question, raising one brow. I was glad to see that small gesture and even the look in her eyes when she asked: the fact of the matter is that she hadn't lost her spunk. But it was clear, too, that she had every reason to be scared.

I thought that Harlow and Alexandra would come to terms, that they'd sit down behind closed doors and settle it like reasonable people. But that was a privilege they'd thrown away over the years, or that Harlow had thrown away. If Alexandra was stubborn, or willful, she'd had a damn good teacher.

Alexandra stayed at Harlow's house. In the morning after they'd agreed about trying to catch the fish, she got up early, and had breakfast. While she ate she read the local paper, and she saw in the sports section a large advertisement for the town's annual Trout Derby. In the advertisement for it there was a line drawing of an old trout, its mouth ugly, a hooked knob on the lower jaw making the head of the creature look menacing and unfriendly.

Alexandra went to town and bought some flies. In the hardware store she stood before a case that was divided into small sections, like an old printer's drawer. The flies were light and fluffy, and there were many sizes and colors. Alexandra looked at the feathers twisted around the hooks, and felt the presence of the birds themselves, the mallards and wood ducks, peacocks and geese, and the animals, the muskrats, rabbits, moose, deer, and mink, the fur of which had been rolled into the bodies of the flies.

Then she drove back to her father's house and went fishing. She walked through the field and woods, carrying her things. It was still early, and she thought her father and Xannie had gone shopping in town. She went into the woods, feeling the freshness off them, and their odd, ominous brooding, too.

There was something off about them. In the years when Alexandra had been growing up, young women had disappeared in town, or from places close by. It was bad for the families of the girls, since they had to wait for what they knew would be found, and, after a week or so, they were usually proved right. The girl's body would turn up in the woods someplace close to the river. The newspapers were always a little vague about what had happened to the girls, and they hinted that there must have been a coon or some other animal around to explain the wounds on the body. Once, a young woman had been found on Harlow's land, and the woods had been filled, for a few days, with policemen, forensic photographers, and, at the end, sightseers. Occasionally, over the years, someone was arrested, and there appeared in the paper a hazy picture of a piece of land, like Harlow's, next to one of a young woman as she had posed for her high school yearbook. No one had ever confessed, and no one had been tried, either.

After the young woman had been found on Harlow's land, Alexandra never allowed herself to be frightened about it, and had continued spending time in the woods, although the atmosphere was bad sometimes, and not as pleasant as it had been. Alexandra had always laughed at herself when she felt fear. Now she went through the woods, seeing the lizard-green of the aspen, the new, reddish-pink leaves, and the long stems of wild grapes, which were bright purple, almost glowing with the color and looking alien. There were swales filled with ferns, and when she stepped into them, not being able to see where her feet went, she felt a slight uneasiness, which was compounded by the place. She thought of the young woman who had been found there. Soon, she was fighting something like panic.

In the beginning she tried to laugh at herself. She wasn't a little girl anymore, but she was amazed how the woods seemed to rise above her, the shape of the partially filled crowns seeming darkish and suggestive. The trees, the shape of the land, the ridges and swales, had been comforting, but now all of it had an ugly aspect, as though Alexandra was lost and was certain of it for the first time. She laughed at herself again, but it did no good. As much as she tried to deny it, she was frightened, and the things around her looked dark, veined, swollen, handlike.

She told me she probably wasn't in the best frame of mind to begin with. She'd driven three thousand miles in an old car, not knowing if she'd be able to protect her child. She was certain, too, that she was a little ill with being pregnant, and being sick in the morning was the least of it: she cried easily and found herself trembling with anger that seemed to have no object. She stepped over the dead leaves, which were both light and dark brown, each color already a little rotted and having the quality of old bones, and as she worked her way toward the path that ran to the pool, she sighed deeply, feeling the panic trail away from the end of each breath. It didn't go away, though, and got worse as she walked. And, after a while, she was certain that there was someone else around. She thought again of the young woman who had been found close by, of the vague descriptions in the paper, and the reporter's odd insistence on trying to find a reasonable explanation for the condition of the young woman's skin. She told me that as she went she was almost certain she deserved to have something happen. Hadn't she tricked her father? And hadn't she thought of doing it right from the beginning when she stood talking to the used-car salesman in San Francisco? Wasn't the entire thing monstrous? She knew how angry Harlow had been, and thought there was something wrong with that, too. So she went through the darkish, clawlike woods, being trapped by a kind of moral superstition: She would be punished because she had done something wrong. Things had a way of happening to people who were in the wrong.

She came to a stop, hearing the last year's leaves around her feet. The sky was whitish blue and cast vague shadows. She breathed deeply and argued with herself, still feeling the slight tickle of panic. But, she said, she was able to get a grip on herself. She took another deep breath, shook her head, and almost laughed at herself. That's when she came to the path and found the smallish white piece of cloth.

It was a woman's nightgown. Alexandra held it up, saw the lacy neck and skirt. The thing was inexpensive, made of nylon, and it had an imitation silkiness. But as Alexandra held it up she saw that it had been burned here and there with a cigarette, and there were round holes in the material, edged with a dark, burned ring. The burns were over the front of the nightgown, through those places where, if the nightgown had been worn, the sensitive flesh would have been. There were some burns near the lower part of the skirt as well, and there had been outlined with them a crude, rough shape of a woman's pubic hair. Alexandra held the thing up, staring at it, feeling the heat of panic spread over her neck and face, and smelling the burned, synthetic material. There were some stains on the nightgown, too, and Alexandra didn't know what they were, and then she found that she was holding the thing by just two fingers of her right hand.

The woods around her and on the ridge above her had the quality of a bad dream, the suggestion of the moment just before the worst began to happen: everything looked all right, but nevertheless, for a small reason (as little as one leaf being out of place or the bark of a tree being so speckled as to suggest reptiles), there was a sense of horror just beyond the line of sight.

Alexandra was reminded of the few times she had ever been really drunk, and of the following morning, when everything had been off-color and she had been filled with some nameless fear or embarrassment.

Out of the corner of her eye she saw some movement at the top of the ridge: she wasn't certain, when she turned toward it, what it had been. Maybe nothing more than just the tip of some pine branch as it moved in the breeze. Then Alexandra felt ill. She was even afraid that she was losing the child, and that's what probably made her get a grip on herself, although by then she was in a bad way. She sat down on a stone, and waited. She heard the light twittering of some birds, the horrible hush of the leaves, the trickling of the stream that ran from the pool where she had been going. After a while she was able to stand, and then she went along the path, trailing the nightgown, not wanting to hold it, but not wanting to let it go either.

She came to the pool, going slowly, with one arm out from her side, and saw Harlow.

He was wading in the pool, casting to the top, trying to catch the fish. Alexandra sat down to watch. Harlow had waded deeply, and was holding a long bamboo rod that had come from England. It had an aged, gingerish color from the old lacquer, and the thing was wrapped with bright red silk. He handled it well, put a fly near the head of the pool, and jerked it out of the mouth of the fish when it rose to it. She heard Harlow swear.

As she sat there, watching her father, she spread the nightgown out on the ground. The smell of the thing was new, and when she touched the burned places, they were soft and seemed like they had just been made. Aside from the stains, which Alexandra saw were creamy and whitish but looking more cosmetic than anything else, the nightgown looked clean. When she looked at the tag in the neck of the thing, it was crisp, fresh and unwashed. So Alexandra sat there, looking at the thing, knowing it was a fraud, and staring at the man who had left it for her to find.

When she told me about this, she was sitting in my house, in a large, heavy chair. I had given her some beer in a crystal glass. The beer was dark, reddish, filled with good things, vitamins, molasses. She had held the glass next to her lips, and then she brought it down, hitting the table in front of her, spilling the bright, heavy beer. Her grayish eyes were set on mine, her face flushed . . . I knew she was angry enough to smash the glass. The man was cheating her, was denying her the one thing she had insisted upon, which was a fair chance of catching the damn thing. It hadn't been that much of a chance, but it had been something, the only thing that she had been able to come up with in her girlish, youthful attempt to put things right. How dare he take even that from her? And did he really think she'd sit still for it? What arrogance was that? she wanted to know. Then she took a long drink, the dark, reddish beer flowing into her, the drops of it trembling from the bottom of the crystal glass.

She said things were bad enough without the nightgown being left in the woods. Harlow knew that Alexandra had been terrified of what had happened to those young women, and why shouldn't she have been? Have you ever had someone murdered near where you live, especially if it's in some remote, unused place, and then walked by the spot and seen some peculiar imprint in the grass, some shape that suggested, and worse, proved, the existence of everything you'd never wanted to believe?

There was something else, too. By leaving the nightgown in the woods he had brought between them the horrible suspicion that women had of men. It was a man, everyone knew, who had taken those young women and left them in the woods and along the bank of the river, their bodies marked in that unusual way. Well, Alexandra told me she thought that fear should be kept out of families. When she spoke of this, she closed her eyes and said she wasn't certain that a family even existed if that fear was there. So she was hurt, too, and infuriated that he had tried to tease her, or just scare her away with that dark thing that existed between men and women.

Well, I wanted to know, what did she do?

Alexandra told me she waited a few moments more, watching her father tie a new fly to the leader. He looked competent there, like something out of a catalogue from Antoine and Von Lengerke. She waited, pushing the nightgown around with one finger. Then she stood up and walked down and picked up a stone. She threw it into the head of the pool where the fish had been working. At least, she said, he wasn't going to be able to catch the fish too soon. He'd have to wait a few hours or maybe even another day before he had a chance.

She dropped the nightgown on the bank. Harlow began to reel the line in slowly, but soon he was doing it quickly, the clicking of the thing making a shriek. Alexandra hesitated, looking at him, her face more surprised than anything else. I'm sure the man was ashamed, but he didn't know what to do. He probably growled at her, or said she should remember how tough the world can be. Or worse than tough. Something like that would be typical of him. Then Alexandra turned and walked through the woods, up to the house.

She went through the fields, feeling the weight of the sun on her shoulders and head and the quick whisk of the new grass against the cuffs of her pants. The air was fresh and clean, moist, and she breathed deeply. It didn't do much good. She was still angry by the time she got to the house, although now she was certain of one thing: She'd need help. By the time she stood in the kitchen she knew where she'd get it, too, because as she began to fill the kettle to make herself a cup of tea, she looked down on the table and saw, spread across the open pages of the newspaper, the large advertisement for the Derby, and the line drawing of that old, ugly, and cannibal brown trout.

The Derby ended in less than a week, and then there was a party for the men who had fished in it. The first prize was given out each year by a woman in costume. Alexandra remembered those pictures she had seen in the paper of men holding up enormous, fat fish. At least, she said, there, in the middle of the fishermen, she'd be able to get some help. What she wouldn't have given for a small, practical thing, a bit of advice that would allow her to go down through the woods and to the pool, and reel that ugly fish out of the water. And she didn't want to go to the party and sit there, waiting for a chance to introduce herself to the winner. She had enough sense to know that the man might be awkward and shy, and not be willing to tell her his name or give her his address in front of a roomful of scowling, failed fishermen, let alone tell her the tricks or secrets he'd used to win. The man might be stubborn. Or embarrassed and not

wanting to be noticed in public at all. What if he were frightened of strange women coming up to him and asking him
strange questions, like what was it he used for bait. Well, Alexandra said, there was only one way to do it. She'd have to be the
one, dressed in the costume, who put the award, the metal
plaque that was screwed to a piece of polished walnut, into the
hands of the man who won. At least, she said, that ought to
break the ice.

The costume made the woman who wore it look like a fish.
Usually, it hung in the closet of a shop in town, Maude's Sewing and Alterations. Each year, the award was presented by a
woman who was hired for the job, and who lived in Boston or
Albany, Pittsfield or Manchester, N.H. The Critchfields, the
Thachers, the Keiths, and the women in town who organized
the benefits for the museums and looked after children needing
"assistance" would never have permitted someone from town to
do it. In a way, I suppose, Alexandra was a little envious of the
women who put the thing on, not so much for what happened
when they wore it, but for the freedom to do so. Every young
woman in town had, at one time or another, seen the thing
hanging in Maude's closet, and had taken it out, held it up, and
looked into the full-length mirror on the wall. Some had tried it
on and worn the mask that went with it, already feeling a kind
of flirtatiousness and spunk, just in the touch of the thing . . .
but mostly, as far as their actions were concerned, the young
women in this town were supposed to keep their heels low,
their hair in a bun, and their eyes averted. And then, some
woman from out of town, hired for the purpose, came to wear
the thing. It was as though the young women were being con-
strained from it and that the town was afraid of something, and
what was it, if not the peculiar moment when the young
women pulled the costume on and decided, with the mask, it
might not be bad after all to do something other than keeping
their heels low, their hair in a bun, and their eyes averted?

When Alexandra had been a little younger, she had been fascinated by Mardi Gras, or the Carnival in Rio, and since I had
been to both, she'd ask me what really happened there. Behind
the mask, so to speak. I'm not sure I was entirely truthful about
this, but I think she got the idea. She had always wanted to go

and she had brought me pictures, from *Vogue*, of the costumes she'd like to wear. Well, there was that, and something else, too. She had been angry earlier at the pool. The pressure from her father, the tricks, the unnecessary fear, seemed to be extensions of the constraint she'd lived with for years. You can imagine what her life had been with a father who thought first, when noticing his daughter was a young woman, of finding a "conservator." Anyway, Alexandra was sick of the constraint, the maddeningly vague but nonetheless definite tug of what was permitted, whether it came from her father or the people in town who seemed to live their lives waiting for someone to make that first false step.

Alexandra stood for a moment, looking at the newspaper spread on the kitchen table, and then she went out to her car, and drove to town and stopped there in front of the Derby's sponsor, Grome's Sporting Goods. The store was in the middle block of Main Street, on the first floor of one of those brick, nineteenth-century buildings. The front of the shop had two large and old windows, the glass of which was so rippled and pitted it seemed to have water flowing over it.

Charles Grome was forty-five years old. When he was younger he'd done a fair amount of hunting, but one day he'd been shot in the face. I was there when they brought him in, his cheek, nose, and side of his forehead filled with bird shot. At the hospital they cleaned his face, and it was strange to see, since it looked as though he'd been bitten by twenty mosquitoes, each leaving a small, round bump with a hole in it. Well, he didn't go hunting so much anymore, and he sat behind the counter of the sporting goods store, a tallish, thin man, with the side of his face marked blue-gray where there were still some shot beneath the skin. He was a humble, friendly man, although more nervous around loud noises than he had been as a young man: he still jumped when anyone slammed a door, and, of course, there were people in town who lived to slam a door when he was close by.

Charley Grome was reading the brochures left by a sporting goods salesman when Alexandra came into the store.

"Hello, Charley," said Alexandra.

"Well, Alexandra," he said. He pushed the brochure to one

side of the counter. "How have you been? I heard you were out west someplace. Denver. San Francisco. Someplace like that."

"There's no place like home," said Alexandra. "I just came back."

"Well, that's true," said Charley, "there is no place like home. The other day I got down as far as Greenfield, Massachusetts, and you know what? I got homesick. Can you believe . . . ?"

A young man came in the back door and then slammed it. Charley ran a hand along the side of his face, his fingers moving over the blue-gray bumps.

"Look, Charley," said Alexandra. "I want to give out the awards at the Derby party."

"Why would you want to do that?" said Charley. "We usually get someone from out of town . . ."

"I know," said Alexandra. "I'd like to do it, though."

"Listen," said Charley, "we got some old buzzards in this town that can make your life pretty rough."

"They don't have to know," said Alexandra. "There's a mask, isn't there?"

"Yes, there's a mask," said Charley, "but if they find out, those old buzzards will think—"

"I know what they think," said Alexandra. "What do you say?"

"Well," said Charley, "we only pay twenty-five dollars. I could give that to charity, if you don't want to have it yourself . . ."

"I better have it," said Alexandra.

Charley looked at her and blinked.

"I guess it won't do me any good to ask you why you want to wear the costume, will it?" said Charley.

"No," said Alexandra. "If you pressed me, I'd just make up some junk you wouldn't want to hear."

"I've been hearing junk all my life," said Charley. He walked over to the cash register and pushed the no-sale button. The drawer came out and he took from it a ten, two fives, and five ones. He pushed them across the counter. "Here."

"Thanks," said Alexandra.

"Oh, don't mention it. If we get caught, I'll probably have to go out of business. Those old buzzards will let me have it, too. So be careful," he said.

Maude's Sewing and Alterations was in an alley, about five doors up from the sporting goods store. The door to the shop was the only one in the long brick wall. There was a window next to the door, and in it there were a dressmaker's dummy (with heavy-gauge wire at the top), some silk and lace, and a bouquet of flowers. Inside the shop there were racks of thread, the spools in them arranged to look like a rainbow, and there were two long tables, each padded and covered with cotton ticking. There was also a brownish counter with a meter that looked like a clock. Alexandra opened the door, and came in, hearing the clap of the bell above her head and feeling, too, the atmosphere that came from the women who had worried through fittings there and smelling the crisp, clean odor in the room that came from new material.

At the back there was a large cotton-covered and padded press, an ironing board, and a sewing machine on a table that had been made from a door. Maude was sitting before it. She was sixty years old, had gray hair and a small, pulled-together face that had always suggested intelligence and now suggested, in old age, something more like piercing understanding and cunning.

When Maude heard the door open and the slap of the bell, she raised both brows, and her expression seemed almost foolish with wonder, but then the features changed, and the expression of cunning was there again, although Maude said, "Alexandra! My God, there were people here who thought you were gone for good. But I told them you'd be back. Who can escape this place? Well, welcome home. . . ."

"Thanks," said Alexandra.

"Where were you?" said Maude.

"California," said Alexandra.

"Well, well," said Maude, looking sharply into Alexandra's face, "I guess it must be pretty out there."

"I guess so," said Alexandra.

Maude looked at Alexandra's face a moment longer and then turned to the water glass that sat on the table in front of her. She poured some bourbon into it from a half-pint bottle she had

in a drawer. She had a water pitcher, too, and she poured some
water into the glass.

"It's amazing how rusty the water is in this town," she said,
holding up the glass. "The whole town's gone to rust."

"You can keep a secret, can't you, Maude?" said Alexandra.

"Honey, that's all a dressmaker does," said Maude. "Why,
there are women here who are as fat as hogs, but when I'm
done, you'd think they were just plump. . . ."

Maude nodded to herself.

"Can you fix the trout costume so it will fit me?" said Alexandra.

"Now, why should I do that?" said Maude.

"I'm going to have to wear it," said Alexandra.

"Why?" said Maude.

"I have a reason," said Alexandra.

"Well, honey, you better have a good one," said Maude. Then
Maude got up and went to the closet where the thing was hung.
She brought it out and spread it on an ironing board.

"I do," said Alexandra.

"All right, all right," said Maude. "I didn't say you were
crazy. I said you better have a good reason. I've still got your
measurements." Maude opened a large loose-leaf binder, covered with black. "You remember those dresses I used to make
for you to go to dances with your father in Washington?"

Maude closed her eyes and swayed back and forth a little,
humming what sounded like a Strauss waltz.

"Maybe you better measure again," said Alexandra, and then
Maude took out her yellow tape. And when she was done, Alexandra went out the door, already hearing the pop, pop, pop as
Maude took a tool, a thing that looked like a small can-opener,
and pulled the stitches out of the trout.

Then she got into her car and drove out to see me. I was
standing in the front yard, glad to be outside in the springtime:
I swear, each winter, that I will not sleep inside, or will not be
inside until after dark all summer long: but I become jaded with
the weather, and soon I don't even notice the extra hour, and
then two and more, of daylight. It is some human flaw, some
inability to acknowledge good fortune. But when Alexandra

came down the road, I was outside, with my smelly old dog, turning over the garden. Soon, I'd have the thing planted.

I gave her a late lunch. She ate the cheese, drank milk, and asked if this year I'd plant some Othellos. She said she liked the brightness of them, the shocking blooms that came when you least expected them.

I still had hopes they'd come to some terms, some understanding, but . . . well, it was just hope, having more to do with me than them. And neither one of them knew how dangerous it was, how absolutely essential it was that they give up. If they'd really known, if they'd really had sense, or if Harlow had, the whole thing could have been avoided . . . it was criminal. The man should have known better. They went on torturing one another. There's no better word for it.

Even though they were tearing at one another, they were still polite, and in the evenings they passed the silver bowls of food back and forth when they sat down together at the same table. Xannie spent his days cooking the things that each of them liked to eat the best. They smiled, ate, and sat together in the evenings, reading books, writing letters. How domestic they appeared.

It was into this that Harlow brought the liar.

Mad Katherine

That afternoon, after walking down the road from my house, and being sleepy from the lunch and the morning at the pool, Alexandra got into bed and dreamed of Mad Katherine. Alexandra saw Mad Katherine sitting in an abandoned orchard. There was one small, cleared space, and around it there were the trees, growing wild, the limbs and trunks spiked, the crowns large and full. Between the trees there were vines, the thorns on them long and sharp, each looking as though made of shiny metal, silver or platinum, although the tips were black with something, blood or soot, as though a match had been held to the tip. Mad Katherine touched the scars on her face, the whitish lines. She was thinking of how she had been scarred, of each fight and the heat of the wounds. Alexandra stood, naked in the thorns, and watched: around Mad Katherine there were wolves. They were tall at the shoulder, their sides quivering, their coats shiny with the meat they had eaten. They watched Mad Katherine, their lids half open, their eyes set on her. All were hungry. Mad Katherine didn't move as a wolf ate her deer-skin bag, the golden hooks in it spilling from the animal's mouth. The wolves came closer, their low growling making the thorns tremble: Alexandra touched one with her finger. Mad

Katherine leaned forward, keeping her eyes on a wolf, and
whispered: the wolves sat and turned their noses upward. Mad
Katherine howled, too, making a long, high note. The wolves
turned and ran, and then Mad Katherine looked at Alexandra.
"I like my scars," she said, "it shows I have seen the worst and
am not afraid." The knotted, whitish lines on Mad Katherine's
face gave her a grinning, foolish expression, but her eyes were
moth-colored, hard. Alexandra shivered, felt the tickle of the
thorns, and didn't move. She didn't want to be seen and looked
away, since she could feel Mad Katherine's understanding of
Alexandra's own worst fears. She woke to her stifled, half-
formed choke and drowning sound. She sat up and shook her
head, still feeling the dream and thinking, What kind of slave
are you, then, if someone knows what you fear the most?

The Man Who Knew Cabot Lodge

 Now, when I sit here in winter, hearing the old dog outside, howling because the wind has gotten to his joints, I think about the liar, and I want to be careful about what I say, since just being reminded of the man makes me want to be precise. In many ways, he seemed like the other young men who had worked for Harlow in Washington. That's where he came from. Bryce McCann had been a legislative assistant to Harlow and was invaluable, too, since he always seemed to have a little dirt, just the right knowledge that helped Harlow along. I can't think of anyone who hated the truth more than Bryce. He hated the limitations of it, as though every fact were a maître d' asking if he had a reservation. Well, Bryce wasn't going to be without a reservation. He lived for those vague moments when people have both fear and desire and are willing to accept anything less than precision. It was amazing what he could do with just the shred of truth, just one small, tiny piece of it.

And soon he was in my life, too, sitting opposite me in my room or on the screened-in porch. He was uninvited, but he'd come in anyway, clapping me on the back and sitting down. Like all gifted liars, he confessed. He was always confessing to something, some minor, or maybe a little more than minor, trespass. He gave me tips on the stock market, good ones, too. I expected to lose money, but never did, and, of course, I was disappointed when I didn't. He came to find out how much I knew and worked about it in a strange, roundabout way: everything was atmosphere and gesture. Sometimes he'd give me a little bit of the truth and he'd watch me snap at it like a turtle. He could be charming when he wanted. That's critical, I think. Since there were times when you'd be around him and you'd almost but not quite forget that he was lying . . . What sitting ducks we were for him, with our old ideas of decency and our ordinary human frailties.

At thirty, Bryce was tall, and his blond hair was thinning. His eyes were a pale, hazy-day blue, and his eyelashes were long and almost white. He had gone to Boston University and once, when there, he had attended a dinner party for Cabot Lodge. At the dinner, Cabot Lodge has asked him for some salt. Bryce told other people he had become friendly with the man and that Bryce had discussed "certain things" with him. As the years went by, Bryce added that he had advised Cabot Lodge on one thing and another, and by the time it became clear that Bryce had nothing to do with the man at all, he had met so many other people on the basis of the connection, it didn't matter anymore. When Lodge retired, Bryce said he was sorry, especially since he (Bryce) had done so much to help the man.

Bryce had played basketball and resigned from the team in a point-shaving scandal. It was unclear as to who had organized the team to shave points, although after Bryce had been given immunity (at the first rumor of scandal) and accused others, saying it "was the only honorable thing to do," the other members of the team had threatened to kill him.

An odd thing happened when the Boston police first came to talk to Bryce about it. They stopped him just as he came out of a restaurant on a cold day in January. The men asked if they could walk along with him. They wanted some answers. And as they went through the cold, their feet making heavy, chilled bumps on the sidewalk, Bryce saw that no lie in the world would help him. The men began to ask some pointed questions. Bryce stopped and faced them, and for a moment he began to speak, but then gave it up. They were walking along the river in the bright, cold sunshine. That's when Bryce did an odd thing: He turned and ran. Ran as hard as he could, his long coat flying out behind him. He didn't go far, not more than twenty yards. By the time the police realized what he was doing, he'd already turned back, ready to come to some arrangement with them. Well, I guess he was panicky when lies wouldn't do him any good. I often think of him at that moment, as the panic just showed on his face and as he crouched and began to move, the wind blowing his hair and the sunlight coming off the river, the hard flash of it making him momentarily blind as he began to run.

It wasn't a big scandal, but I remember it well. There were rumors that some men from Nassau Street in Boston were looking for Bryce. Of course, Bryce left town, but after a few years in Washington he was able to do something to make it safe for him to walk the streets of Boston again. I don't know what it was. A tip, I suppose, like the ones he gave me for the stock market.

Bryce visited Harlow every month or so the winter Alexandra was in California. And now, after Alexandra had been home three days, he came again. She had been taking a nap, and when she woke, she heard voices downstairs. Bryce had been in and out of the house when she had been growing up, and even when she had been fourteen and fifteen she had turned and seen him watching her when he'd been for a visit or was dropping something off for Harlow. Then he'd shrug, or at least act hurried, and walk out of the room. Now, after her nap, Alexandra sat on the side of her bed and recognized his voice. She went into the bath, splashed cold water on her face, and combed her hair. Then she went downstairs.

Bryce sat on a love seat opposite Harlow. He was dressed in dark grayish and pleated trousers, brown shoes, and a sport jacket. His shirt was open at the neck, and he held his teacup on a saucer on the cushion next to him. When Alexandra came into the room, he rose with a little trouble, although he was in perfect health. He took her hand and kissed it and then sat down again.

"How nice to see you again," said Bryce.

Alexandra sat down and Xannie gave her some tea. She was a

little drowsy and she was glad to have it, and while she sipped it, feeling the bite of it against her lips, Harlow and Bryce talked. Harlow had been out of office since January, and Bryce now worked for the Department of Interior, in an emergency assistance program. It wasn't a hard job, or a good one, Bryce said. Ranchers, in the West, came to him with financial problems. He had good connections with the mining companies and arranged for the sale of mineral rights. It wasn't always clear when the land would be strip-mined, although there were times when it was done on short notice. Bryce was only too happy to help people in the West, glad to meet the salt of the earth. That's what he called them.

"They've learned to trust me," Bryce said.

Bryce stayed while Alexandra had her tea. She ate the salmon sandwiches on pumpernickel bread and every now and then looked Bryce full in the face. He smiled then, pulling his cheeks up.

"I do impressions, too," said Bryce, "would you like to see one?"

Bryce did an imitation of Marlon Brando in the backseat scene from *On the Waterfront,* and Harlow and Alexandra laughed. It *was* a good imitation.

Alexandra finished her tea and then went for a walk. Bryce spent the night, and in the morning, when she had gathered her fishing things, she turned and saw that Bryce was standing behind her. He was dressed in a white suit and wore an ascot at his neck. He wore white shoes, too, with soles that were pink rubber.

"Going fishing?" he said. "Like Dame Juliana? Ah. To spend an hour with 'an angle.' "

"Not quite like that," said Alexandra.

"Mind if I come along?" said Bryce.

They stood opposite one another, and Alexandra looked into his blue eyes. He smiled but didn't say anything. The air was cool and it blew against her back.

"Let's just go for a walk," said Alexandra, and she put her fishing things away.

They went down the road, going slowly. Bryce carried his hands behind his back and swung his feet out from side to side.

When they saw a bird, he identified it and gave the genus and species in Latin. Half the time he was wrong, but the other half he was right, and Alexandra found herself straining, trying to remember the natural history she knew.

"Well," he said, "I'm glad we've had this occasion to get reacquainted."

Alexandra took a deep breath and said, "Yes. Of course."

Bryce looked at her and raised an eyebrow.

"I mean, it's especially important given the honor your father has bestowed upon me," he said.

"What honor?" said Alexandra, stopping and facing him.

"Oh," said Bryce, "that's far too personal. I could never say."

"Too personal about you or my father?" said Alexandra.

"About Harlow, of course," said Bryce.

"So personal about my father, you can't tell me?" said Alexandra.

"There's no reason to be upset," said Bryce, smiling and putting his hand under Alexandra's elbow. She left it there and they continued walking back to the house.

After a while Bryce put his bag into his car. It was a red Austin-Healey with chrome, spoked wheels. The top was down, and Bryce got into the car and waved good-bye and then went down the road. Harlow and Alexandra stood in front of the house, listening to the fading drone of the engine.

"You know why I trust him?" said Harlow.

"Why?" said Alexandra.

"He does what I tell him to," said Harlow.

In the morning, Alexandra got up early and walked through the woods and saw the river, which was bluish-gray, moving, and having a definite tug. As she walked down to it the sky became light enough for the atmosphere of dreams and some other world to lift from the landscape. She scooped a handful of water from the river and tasted it, recognizing stone and brush, silt from the mountains.

At the pool, she rolled up her jeans and waded until she could reach the stones that were as big around as an egg. She picked up three or four of them, and stood on the bank and threw the stones, each one bright with water and showing mica in the pale light. They landed in the water with a *kerrthunk kerrthunk*.

There had been some nymphs at the head of the pool, their skins splitting down the middle, and there had been a dark shadow underneath them, but now it sank and became a vague shape at the bottom, although it didn't seem as indifferent as the things that hid it, the large stones, the deep holes, the greenish slime. When the pool's surface rocked with small diamond shapes, Alexandra turned. Harlow stood behind her, and stared at the pool and nodded, almost agreeing that she'd cut the odds down on her side, too. Then he turned and carried his things, walking slowly to the river.

Desire

There's something else I want to say about the town. There are times when I think the Critchfields (although not old N.B., "the Raver"), the Keiths, the Thachers, and even the Boyds and the Beamonds have gone crazy. And, of course, the other people in town take their lead from them. Everyone wants to be proper. The town doesn't understand the word. It used to mean not embarrassing other people, but now the weight of the word, the feigned knowledge of correctness, is used to keep as many people "in line" as possible. And no one knows for what reason or to what end. It is almost as though it is some horrible game, in which a raised eyebrow or a surprised expression, a simple statement of the obvious, has tremendous power, and maybe, after all, it is the power people are interested in, and manners be hanged. The Critchfields and the others believe they are better than the rest of the world, and it drives them mad that the world doesn't acknowledge it, doesn't petition them to step in and take charge. They're left with the damage they can do here.

What they hate is desire. Let's say there's a young man who works as a mechanic, and he wants to go to the Ford Motor Company school to learn something about new cars. Somehow

he lets everyone find out about it. Well, soon people are coming
into the gas station and raising an eyebrow when he puts gasoline into their cars. And perhaps he even has ordered a book
from the company, and sits in the office of the gas station, reading it. Then the people come into the station, almost forming a
line down the block. They ask him to check the oil, to change
the tires (which don't need changing), to fill their window
washers with fluid, and if the young man ever says things are all
right, there's no need to worry, they look at him and say, in a
tone of perfect vagueness, "Oh, of course, you're the one who's
ambitious." And, of course, it was never ambition, not the claw-
ing, vicious thing the word implies. It was only interest. In the
end the young man will burn the book, because he cares about
the people in town, and to prove he isn't evil, he will sit in front
of the gas station for forty years, blinking as the cars go by. The
people in town will say to themselves, "Look at young Tom,
down at the station. My God, but isn't he dull." Their hands are
always clean.

There was a young man named Willie Shaw who grew up
here. His parents were farmers, and they lived outside of town.
When Willie was born, they seemed to be pretty far away. But
the town grew, and finally they lost their land. I don't know
how, but they were able to hang on to the farmhouse and an
acre or so around it. Willie's parents started a junkyard, and
soon the acre was filled with old cars.

Willie grew up like the rest of the young men here. I'd see
him from time to time, and be amazed he had grown so much.
He was tallish, even as a young man of fifteen or sixteen, and he
had thick, almost blue-black hair and blue eyes. He went hunting on his Uncle Whalen's land, trapped foxes and beavers,
spent some time fishing. He was a good fisherman, although he
went with worms. And he was smart, too. He knew enough
never to save the money for a fly rod and flies, knew that was
something for "other people." He perfected his bait fishing.
And he even came to me to ask questions. It was done in a
roundabout way, I suppose. He came up the road in the middle
of winter, after two bad storms, and asked if he could shovel the
sun room roof. I was glad to have him do it, and paid him well,

and then we got to talking about fish. He asked some sharp questions, his face always smiling and innocent.

There were times, too, when he went fishing along the Sugar Wolf River. He went one day in June. The spring had been hot, and the water was already low, but Willie spent time slowly drifting a big worm through the deep, cool holes of the river. The day was clear and hot at eleven in the morning. Willie had walked miles along the bank, and had planned on turning around and fishing each hole on his way downstream, but by the time he had come to the end of his walk, the sky was already pale and the stones burned his hands when he touched one. The heat makes the fishing bad, so he turned around, carrying his spinning rod and the can of bait he'd dug in the back of the junkyard.

This June, Alexandra was fifteen, a year younger than Willie, and on the morning he had gone to fish the river and found it so hot, Alexandra had been digging in my garden, cultivating the dark soil, keeping the weeds from growing between the rows. She had gotten up early, when the day was still crisp, but soon it was hot. She finished in my garden, and then walked down the road, the dust in it, which was as soft as face powder, streaming away from her feet. The late morning had a dry, itchy quality. The road itself was almost white with dust, glaring in the heat, and from the dark stones of the walls that were exposed to the sun there rose minute but still definite waves of heat, like the ones that come from a wood stove: beyond them there was the undulant, steady movement of trees and drying grass.

Alexandra walked through the woods and toward the river. The river was silvery, colored by the bluish-white sky. The stones at the side of it were bleached and hot. They were warm to the touch, but Alexandra sat on them, and when she looked upstream there was that same slight quavering of the air above the stones and it made the river itself seem hot and silky. She sat there, tired and facing the rest of the hot, empty day, and others like it until the fall.

She was thirsty, and she thought of things she'd like to eat, cold pieces of watermelon, the slight pulp of it crushing in her mouth, or of grapes, light green and beaded with moisture, lem-

onade so cold as to make the bridge of her nose ache. I had taken
her to a fair where they served shredded ice in a cup with syrup
on it, "snow cones," that's what they were called, and Alexandra had enjoyed them. She sat in the heat, imagining the cold,
damp paper and the taste of the syrup. I had told her that for
Roman banquets, runners had been sent from the mountains,
carrying snow, so that the guests could have a cold dessert, and
she sat there, imagining that she was a runner who went
through the Italian countryside, the long roads and olive trees,
carrying snow in the heat: some of it melted and ran down her
forearm, the bright drops tickling her skin and then hanging,
for a moment, from her elbow.

She took off her shoes and put her feet into the river.

As she sat there she saw out of the corner of her eye, in that
same quivering heat from the stones, that someone was walking
on the bank, and going quickly, too. She sat with her head held
up by one hand, the heel of the palm against her cheek. She
looked over her shoulder to see who it was, and then Willie
stopped and said, "I wasn't spying on you. I was just up above.
You weren't here when I went up. I'm sorry."

"That's okay," she said.

"I didn't expect to see anybody on the river," he said. "It's
lonely up here."

"I've seen you in town," said Alexandra.

"I've seen you, too," he said. "I didn't mean to bother you."

"It's all right," she said.

He nodded, and looked away, his head down, his hair hanging over his sunburned face.

"The river's nice and cool," she said.

"Why, sure it is," he said, and then began to walk along,
going over the white stones. Alexandra sat, her fist against her
cheek, staring across the river and hearing the footsteps fade.
She tried to think again of running, of carrying snow . . . but
she stopped, and turned her head in the direction where Willie
had gone. He seemed to have vanished and all she saw was the
rising, steady movement of the hot air over the stones at the side
of the river. There was the sense of the sky above her, which
seemed immense and unconcerned. She sat with her feet flat on
the bottom of the pool where she had put them. After a few

minutes there was a small *plick* in the water, just ahead of her, and then another, as a pebble was thrown into the pool.

"Hey," said Willie.

He was downstream, about twenty feet away.

"Do you think we can have a soda sometime?" he said.

Both of them started laughing, and Alexandra said, Yes, sure. There was a place he mentioned in town, an ice-cream store. Then he turned and smiled and went down the river, disappearing into his own reflection in the silvery, mercury-like air just above the stones. Alexandra sat and watched him go, her fist against her cheek. Then she stepped out of the water and let the sun dry her feet. Maybe it was just a schoolgirl crush, but I'm sure she was glad to have it. The summers were long here, with just her father, her mother, Xannie, and me to talk to.

She waited for him to call, but, of course, he never did. I know good and well what happened. He began to walk along the hot stones of the river, and someplace, probably about halfway to town, or when he saw the first cars on the road, he stopped smiling and having that light feeling in his chest and face, the one you can only have when you are fifteen or sixteen and have just run across a young woman who has agreed to meet you. Of course, he'd realize that he'd been selfish, that he'd only been thinking of himself, or of just the fun they might have. Then he'd realize the trouble he'd make for her, or for the two of them together. He'd seen enough already of those raised eyebrows in town, knew how the talk began. I'm sure, for himself, he would have chanced it (not knowing, of course, that Alexandra would have chanced it, too), but he wasn't going to expose her to those lifted brows, to that voice (or voices) that said, "Oh, you're the one who takes herself so seriously." He didn't show up, and Alexandra sat in the ice-cream parlor on alternate nights for a few weeks, and then stopped going. She spent more time in my sun room, and there were times when she looked at me, and was about to ask a question, but then took down a book and began to read. I know, too, that on that same afternoon, when Willie walked down the stream and realized how selfish he might have been, he stood at the side of the river, getting ready to throw the can of bait and spinning rod as far as he possibly could. He didn't, though. Everyone here takes his licks quietly. He walked home and put his things away and just said the weather had been too hot.

He went ahead with his fishing and got pretty good at it. I'd hear things about him from time to time, that he'd caught a big fish. It took two men to drag the thing into a boat. I heard, too, that his parents died and that he had the junkyard out there beyond the town, the old farm building still surrounded by the piles of smashed and old automobiles. Mostly, though, I'd lost track of the young man.

Celebration

  Alexandra and Harlow came to a truce of sorts, at least for a few days. Harlow had to go to Washington to see his lawyer. He said it was just ordinary business. They talked about it early in the morning after Alexandra had gotten up and dressed, although she was still feeling bad and was eating chipped ice from a glass as she sat in the kitchen. Alexandra was too ill to think about Harlow seeing a lawyer. It was hard enough to sit at the table and to wonder about getting to the pool, where she'd throw stones into the water. So she was glad to hear he was going. She told Harlow she'd need five days more, and then she'd either have caught the fish or she wouldn't have. Harlow looked at her and said, "All right." It was Tuesday morning, and he said he'd be back on Saturday afternoon. So they sat in the kitchen for a while and then Harlow went upstairs and packed his bag.

Alexandra felt a little better when he came downstairs. His bag was made of leather and had brass fittings and a large leather handle, too, which was dark from the years Harlow had used the bag. Alexandra remembered him coming in the door or going out of it, carrying the bag, his face always set in the same smile of greeting or farewell. Now, he stood next to her. She sat at the table, drinking ice water and eating saltine crackers.

"I'll be back Saturday," he said.

"Be careful," she said.

"You too," he said. He sat down at the table. "What are you planning to do while I'm gone?"

Alexandra shrugged, although there was in her face the faintest suggestion of a secret: Harlow had seen it whenever she had been in trouble over the years, and he now looked into her eyes and said, "Well, what is it?"

Alexandra shrugged again.

"I'm going to get some help," she said.

"Where?" he said.

"At Grome's party," she said.

"You mean where they have a hooker up from Boston or from Albany, dressed up like a goddamned fish . . . ?" said Harlow.

"No, no," said Alexandra, shaking her head, "not from Albany or Boston. From right here."

"What do you mean?" said Harlow.

"I'm going to wear the thing myself," said Alexandra.

He waited for a moment, looking at the face of his daughter: her eyes were on his, and her expression was so similar to his own as to be almost mirror-like. After a while he sighed and said, "Would it do any good if I said I didn't want you to go?"

Alexandra dropped her eyes, and then shook her head.

"All right," said Harlow.

He sat at the table a little longer. All of the ice in Alexandra's glass was gone, and she began to get up for some more, but Harlow stopped her, putting his hand on her arm, and said, "I'll get it." Then he took a tray from the freezer and poured the last chips into a glass and put it on the table next to Alexandra's hand. She thanked him, and then he picked up his bag and went out the door. Alexandra heard him start the engine of his Jeep and then the gentle putter of it as Harlow went down the road in the early morning light.

After a while, when the day warmed up, she went to town and picked up the costume and hung the thing, which was covered with plastic, in her closet, the scales and tinsel, the bright spots on it, catching the light for a moment before Alexandra closed the door.

Alexandra waited for Saturday. She told me she didn't expect any trouble and was looking forward, in some secret way, to wearing the thing. Like Mardi Gras, I guess. After all, the costume had been the thing that reminded the young women in town that they were being kept in seclusion, groomed there for some "right" man. The thing must have haunted the dreams of the spirited women as it hung in the closet of the sewing and alterations, the scales glowing when the door was opened and let the light in.

I don't think she knew how dangerous the struggle was. Certainly she didn't know how bad it would be for Harlow. I didn't, and I was his friend, and it's sure that if I had known, I would have told her. But even as I was appalled at what they did to one another, or at Harlow's stubbornness, I was pleased by her, too. Or more than pleased. Maybe I was proud. And if it was pride, it was of a strange kind, something like the kind you'd have in watching a child grow up. You notice all the things he learns for himself, tying knots, cooking food, driving a car, understanding the dangers of the world, and then, just when the child is almost grown and seems to have good sense, he becomes a ski jumper. And then you find yourself in a crowd of thousands, watching as the child comes down the jump. Is it pride you feel when the skis just clear the lip of the thing, as the child spreads his arms and lifts into the air?

On the night of the party for the Derby, Alexandra took the costume and drove to the barn, outside of town, where the party was held. The barn was high, three stories anyway, and there was a loft at one end. The construction was peg and beam, and there were long timbers, each cut from one tree, that ran the seventy-five feet of the barn. The beams looked like masts, and the entire place had a nautical quality, as though it had been built by a naval architect. The farmhouse that had been next to it burned the year before, and the foundation hadn't been cleaned up, or bulldozed and buried, and it stood across the road, the timbers looking like a sailing ship that has run aground and has been left to the wind and rot. The barn, though, where the party was, had been looked after and been untouched by the fire. It had been used as an auction hall, a place where estates were sold quickly and where all concerned hoped for fast probate.

For the party the place was divided in half by a large piece of canvas that at one time had been a sail and was now used as a screen. Alexandra was on one side, and Charley Grome was on the other. As she wiggled into the costume, feeling the roughness and the heaviness of it in the cool air of the barn, Charley put out some bottles on the fifteen or so tables on the other side of the screen. Each one was filled with a clear liquor. The bottles had originally come from a discount liquor store in New Hampshire, but somehow the same bottles appeared year after year, the labels of them becoming chipped and worn away, although each new year they were filled again to the top. There were people who said that in his spare time, now that he didn't hunt so much, Charley had set up a still in some swale or out of the way place in the Black Mountains, and that it was from his small, carefully maintained still, the thing lovingly patched and even polished, that each year's supply of liquor came, the cost of it duly charged against the expenses of the party. And it was true that each spring, Charley packed his four-wheel-drive Scout with a sleeping bag and camping things and some fishing tackle, the rods, reels, lines, hooks, lures, net and other things still in their shrink-wrapped plastic, right off of the shelf from the store. When Charley came back, a week later, obviously bitten by mosquitoes and blackflies, he looked exhausted and pale, as though he's been drinking something, and his hands shook and he was sweating when he put back on the shelf, still in the shrink wrapping, those same spinning rods, reel, nets, hooks, and lures that he had originally loaded into the Scout.

After Charley had put out the bottles and some mismatched glasses, he asked through the screen if he could come in, and when Alexandra said it was all right, Charley came around the corner and said, "Here. This is it," and gave her the plaque for the winner. "Isn't it a beauty?"

Alexandra held the thing in her hands, surprised at the weight.

"Yes," said Alexandra, "it's not like something out of a Cracker Jack box, if that's what you mean."

"That's what I mean," said Charley. "Duke MacCalley up in Beamond Mills had a closetful, but he's dead now." Charley blinked for a moment. "Now we got this kid coming along. And I'm glad that MacCalley isn't here, because the kid's fish was bigger than any the Duke even told lies about getting away from him. See you later." Then Charley went back to the side of the screen to set up a movie projector. When he was done, Alexandra heard the clink of the neck of one of the refilled bottles against a glass and then a sigh.

The barn was dark and musty, and Alexandra felt the unlighted space over her head. There was some light next to the canvas wall, and Alexandra stood in it, holding the plaque, feeling comforted by the solidness of the thing. She ran her finger over the metal, and held it up to the light, the surface of it soft and glowing, scratched with engraving that gave the name of the winner as *Willie Shaw*. She waited there, running her finger back and forth over his name, tapping it with her finger as she thought of the young man who had come across her sitting with her feet in the shallow pool of the river behind her father's house. Then she went to the side of the building where a mirror was leaning against the wall. First she put on the mask, tied it behind her neck, and then let down her hair, which had been piled on top of her head. She took a brush from her bag, and then she leaned her head one way and then the other as she worked, hearing the steady *lick, lick, lick* as the bristles went through her hair, and while she worked she thought of the time she'd waited for him to call, and now tried to laugh at herself for having been so girlish as to be concerned. But somehow she couldn't laugh, and the memory of the time was one of things from the middle of growing up that wouldn't go away. She sat down on a chair without a back, smelling the dusty odor of the barn, which had more the atmosphere of cellars and old furniture than it did of hay, manure, and the warm pressure of the breath of cows.

After a while the men began to arrive. They came in through the door on the other side of the screen, and they took their places at a table. There was a movie projector at the rear of their side of the room, and they arranged themselves so that the projector was behind them. They faced the blank, pale screen and poured themselves the liquor in mismatched glasses. They drank and said nothing, aside from asking the time, or when the movie was going to begin. Mostly, though, they were quiet. They didn't seem to enjoy the liquor so much as to want change, almost any being preferable to the monotony they carried with them. They were farmers and woodcutters, loggers and men who worked in gas stations. They were telephone repairmen, carpenters, masons, plumbers, and almost all of them had families. Mostly, when they went fishing it was alone, stealing an hour from work or on a Saturday morning. They carried spinning rods in their cars or trucks and dug worms in the backyards of their houses. Almost all of them wore green or blue heavy trousers and shirts, and caps, although they shaved closely and kept their hair cut short, too. Some of them, loggers mostly, were hard of hearing.

The men continued to drink. Once Alexandra heard an unpleasant laugh, which was in reaction to nothing: it seemed to exist by itself, having nothing to do with any comment or story or joke, coming only from a definite, interior memory. No one said anything about the laugh, although there were some arguments now. A man said the best way to have venison was to put the whole deer through a grinder and to serve it as meatballs made with Hamburger Helper. A friend of his said it was better to grind the thing and mix it with oatmeal and pork. Both of them said their wives didn't like it any way, since they complained about the deer hair that got into the Hamburger Helper.

Charley turned on the projector and the men watched a movie about salmon. They were shown jumping into the falls, once and then again, the water coming down, in a large whitish splash, the salmon looking like streaks of trembling quicksilver against it. Alexandra watched from the back of the screen. And while the flashes of light fell over her, she stared, not really watching the movie. She didn't want to face what the town did to its young men: It was hard on them, and they aged so quickly that in some cases a few months did the work of years. There were young men, not twenty, who had grown fat, were tattooed, and whose teeth were already stumpy and dark, and when they looked at you, their expressions were blank, and if there had been some promising, delicate moment (as when Willie had found Alexandra sitting in the river and then had asked for a date), that moment disappeared in an angry, uncompromising blink. There were things Alexandra didn't want to give up, like the memory of the time when she had waited for the phone to ring while thinking of the young man with the pale skin and dark hair. She could still recall the black phone and the bright smear of light over the receiver. The memory of it had become a kind of hope. Of course, she hadn't seen Willie in years.

The movie ended and Grome gave a little speech. Then Alexandra picked up the plaque and walked into the room. It was brighter there and the light showed off the costume. It looked like a small, low-cut, one-piece bathing suit with a long wire tail at the back. The costume was made from a shiny material that was covered with dark spots, each one of which was surrounded with a silver circle, and over the spots, over all of the material, there was something like Christmas tinsel, and this was supposed to suggest the scales of the fish. In the small of the back there was a fin, made of brownish silk, and it was held up by wires that had been sewn into it. At the end of the tail, which was also held up by wires so it swung easily from side to side as Alexandra walked, there was a fan made of the same brownish silk and held up with wires too. High on the sides there were gill fins, hinged at Alexandra's ribs, and they waved slowly back and forth, each one stiff with wire, as though the trout were finning gently in a pool. The costume was tight between the legs and thin there, so that it revealed the narrow crease between her thigh and the flat between her legs. It was tight around her breasts and exposed her collarbones, the small ball of her shoulder, and her underarm and side. The scantiness of the costume was so severe as to suggest some wild, dreamlike urge. The mask was large, covered with glitter, the eyes marked with silver. It was heavy, and Alexandra felt the weight of it as she went through the room, carrying the plaque.

The room was lighted by a few bare and yellowish bulbs, and the men, in their dark green and blue clothes, sat around the tables, bent forward, each holding a glass of the clear white liquor that Charley Grome made in some hidden swale in the

Black Mountains. They watched as Alexandra came through
the room, her shoulders square, her long legs slowly swinging
out, her mask set on the back of the room where Willie Shaw sat
at a table with a small, hand-lettered sign that said FIRST PLACE
WINNER. And, as Alexandra went, the men clapped and said,
"Trout. Trout. Trout."

The clapping took on a harsh, repeated quality and the room
seemed filled with a hilarity that was balanced, just poised away
from anger. But even so, as Alexandra went through the men
she was relieved, and she almost stopped and breathed deeply,
more glad than she could ever say that those girlish (and perhaps more than girlish memories) hadn't quite yet disappeared.
Shaw hadn't changed, or certainly if he had, it was for the better. He was taller, still dark, and his skin was sunburned. He
shaved closely and his cheeks seemed smooth and a little pinkish. He wore a light blue shirt with a small patch on it that said
SHAW'S WRECKING and a pair of matching trousers. His brow was
a little furrowed as he watched her walk toward him, and his
eyes had, in the yellowish light of the room, the same reticent
intelligence as when he had come, years before, to shovel the
snow off the roof of my house.

The men went on chanting, but Alexandra hardly heard the
words. Soon she stood in front of him, and was able to see the
long fingers of his hands, the cords in his neck that ran to the
top of his chest, the lines of his face. He smiled at her, not
flirtatiously so much as to encourage her to come a little closer
and to hand the plaque over so that she could be done with it
and go home. For a moment, Alexandra didn't know what to do,
and she stood there, shoulders square, the light coming off the
sequins of the costume, her bare skin feeling the smoky heat of
the room. Then she stepped closer, and as she did, Shaw sat up.
So it was easy for her to bend down, the sequins flashing a little
as she did, and to put her face close to his, and, while the men
called out, "Trout, trout, trout," she lifted the mask from the
top, just a little, or enough for Shaw to see her face, and then
she said, her voice hushed, "I guess I've come to have that soda."

Before Alexandra had a chance to say anything else, some
men pulled their chairs up to the table, and then, of course, she
was afraid to speak. She'd talked to almost every man in the

room, at one time or another. It's a small town, and she was certain that at least one would know her voice. So she was silent, standing in the yellowish light, the tinsel of the costume wavering as she breathed, suggesting the slow, languid movement of water.

She told me it wasn't having to be silent that was the worst. It was the look on Willie's face. He stopped smiling when she let him see, for that moment, behind the mask, and when he heard her voice, when she had been able to speak, there was an expression of disbelief. Then he looked away, down at the table in front of his hands. That's what frightened her. When he looked down, when he dropped his eyes, it was done with shame. Alexandra stood there, not being able to speak, still holding the plaque, and thinking that the entire thing had been a mistake.

Of course, he'd been afraid of running into her again. Perhaps he wanted to have the memory, too, of having found a young woman who was enjoying herself in the river and who hadn't been difficult or ashamed. I'm sure it was a small, precious thing for him, especially so, since after that he had come to one of those moments in growing up that change you forever. Alexandra felt the slow, warm heat of a blush as it rose along her neck, into her face and forehead, and ears.

She still held the plaque, and when Shaw looked up, she cleared her throat, and then handed the thing over, feeling the weight of it disappear as he took it. He put it on the table, and continued to stare at her, his eyes set on the holes in the mask as the rest of the men in the room chanted, "Trout, trout, trout." Alexandra sat down in a chair, opposite him. It was a folding chair and there was space between the seat and the back for the tail of the costume. And as they sat there, the table between them, not to mention those years between this evening and the time when they had first met, Shaw leaned a little closer, his face still a little pale, his eyes passing once over the blush on her neck, and said, "It's hard to talk, isn't it?"

Alexandra nodded.

"Well, let's go someplace where we can talk," said Shaw. "Maybe we'll have that soda. I'd always planned on buying you a chocolate one, you know, in a big, curved glass that sat in a kind of silver holder. You'd have a long spoon."

They both stood up, and began to walk away from the table, and as they stepped away from the men there Alexandra said quietly, "I always liked chocolate."

The room was filled with the men's short, harsh laughter. It was all she could do, she told me, to keep from putting back her head and laughing with them until the tears streamed out of her eyes. But instead, she went through the men, toward the screen where her clothes were. The room didn't seem so stuffy and dim, and as she went, the men chanted, "Trout, trout, trout. What about us?" Alexandra went behind the screen and picked up a tube of lipstick, and then went back into the room. She pulled a chair next to the screen, and since she was still afraid to speak, she climbed on it, and then wrote with shaking hands, and feeling the greasy stick against the texture of the canvas, "See you next year. The fish." The men clapped and shouted. Alexandra was glad to get outside, where she stood with Shaw and said that she needed help, that she had to catch a fish.

Shaw laughed. They stood in the parking lot for a moment. Alexandra took off the mask, glad to have the weight of it off her face.

"Why, you've come to the right place," said Shaw. "I've got it down to a science. You come over to my house, and I'll make you the best bait there is. Period. There isn't a fish in the world who wouldn't go through hell to have just a small taste of it."

He laughed.

"Okay?" he said.

"Fine," she said, "I'll follow you. Where's your car?"

The windshield of the Ford had fogged a little, and through it the taillights of Shaw's car looked like the head of some bright, furry bloom. The costume tugged at her waist and hips. The tail, on the seat next to her, was turned up, and it made a small crinkling noise as she drove.

Shaw stopped in front of a billboard. On the front of it there were two cars crashing together, their front ends collapsing like an accordion, and out of the crash there were flames, above which there was a sign that said SHAW'S WRECKING. The back of the sign was held up by struts and latticework that looked like the supports of a roller coaster. There was a fence, topped by barbed wire, and the strands of it looked like lines for musical notation. Beyond the wire there was a small farmhouse, with clapboard siding, shutters, and with a barn attached. Beyond it, under light standards, there were some wrecked cars.

Alexandra and Shaw walked through the yard, and onto the porch of the house. Shaw opened the door for her. In the living room there was a sofa and two wing chairs and there were bookshelves floor to ceiling. A large desk was covered with open books and had a reading lamp with a green shade. There was a kitchen opposite the desk. It had an old basin with long, slender legs. There was a gas stove and a refrigerator. The refrigerator was new, at least six feet high, and it had two tall doors. The cupboards in the kitchen were made from packing crates and had chicken wire doors. The counters were made of rough-cut lumber, and everything, the planks of the cabinets and the counter, too, had been painted white.

When they stood in the living room, Shaw said, "I heard you were out west for a while. How was it?"

"It was okay," said Alexandra.

Her eyes moved away from him and to the desk covered with open books. The green light shade was cool and soothing to the eyes. There was a pad of white paper under it, covered with a small, neat handwriting. There was a pencil sharpener, too, filled with fanned and curled shavings.

"Don't mind the mess of books. I've been studying law at night," said Shaw. "Word's already gotten around."

"Has it?" said Alexandra.

"It's hard to keep a secret," said Shaw. "You sit down. I'll make the bait."

He brought her a chair. It was caned at the back and had a place for the tail of the costume to stick out, and she sat comfortably, her legs crossed, as Shaw went into the kitchen. From a shelf he took a styrofoam cup that was filled with peat and worms, and he took some of the worms and put them in a stainless steel bowl. There were boxes on the shelf over the counter, the kind that Chinese food comes in, and from each one he took some brownish and small insects, nymphs from mayflies and caddis flies and stoneflies. There were some freshwater scuds and shrimp, each one of which Shaw had collected with a net on a broomstick, not knowing when he had caught them what they were, but he was convinced that the trout had been eating them. He took an ear of corn from the freezer, cut off two kernels, and then he took a small plastic bag from the freezer, too. Inside there were the glands of fish. They were gray and shiny, something like mother-of-pearl, or like the color of clouds when they are thin and the moon is behind them. He put the glands in with the nymphs and then put in some ants and hoppers and put everything into a blender and turned it on. The high, whirring screech filled the kitchen and then Shaw added some water to the gray-brown mixture and turned the machine on again. After a minute the paste became a little thinner. On the shelf, next to the Chinese-food boxes, there was a row of rubber worms. Each one was segmented and had a collar or band in the middle and they were green, as bright as an August grasshopper. The light in the kitchen was strong and reflected by the white walls, but even in the clear, definite light it was obvious that the worms were glowing. Shaw took a syringe from the shelf, and with it he pulled up some of the liquid and then pushed the needle into the glowing worm, time and again, in long lines down each side of its belly, each time leaving a little of the scented lure under the skin. He took a large new hook, the color of a paper clip, and worked it under the collar. Then he cleaned everything up and washed his hands.

"Here," and dropped the bright, glowing bait into her hand. "That's the best I can do. Fish it deep."

Alexandra felt the almost greasy segments and the plastic give and squirm of the thing. It had the texture of a scar, and when Alexandra cupped her hand around it she saw the dim glow against her fingers, and as she sat, feeling her hair against her bare shoulders, she thought, The thing doesn't have a chance. Not one. How could it?

"Thanks," she said.

"Anytime," he said. "Be sure to fish it deep."

Then he pulled up a chair and they sat opposite one another. Alexandra looked around the room, saw the law books, the pencils and curled shavings, the shiny wire over the shelves, and finally, when she felt the silence of the room, she turned back to Shaw. She began to raise a hand, to reach out for the edge of his face. But she did nothing, and sat there as straight as she could, the glowing thing sitting against the skin of her legs. What could she do, she said to me, tell him she was already pregnant with another man's child and ask him if he'd like to complicate things further?

"Would you like a drink?" he said.

"Please," she said.

He went into the kitchen and poured some bourbon into a glass, and then brought it out and handed it to her. Their fingers touched.

"Do you have a couple of ice cubes?" she said, holding up her glass, and Shaw went to the freezer and took a plastic bag from it. The bag was filled with cubes and as he carried it spots of frost formed around the tips of his fingers where they touched the clear plastic. He stood before her, saw her eyes set on his. He opened the top of the bag and held it out for her, and as she reached forward, as she put her fingers into the open top and against the bluish rings of ice, the sack collapsed. The cubes fell with a bright, almost cheerful sound into her lap. They made a pile there, clicking like marbles when she moved against them. Shaw stood for a moment, seeing the slick, clear pile, and the look of strain on Alexandra's face as she sat with the cold and surprising weight in her lap. A few cubes fell between her legs, and the ice was as bright as the tinsel that covered the material out of which the costume was made.

"Let me get something," said Shaw.

Alexandra opened her mouth, began to speak, but then shook her head, feeling the constraint of the costume and the hard, cold surprise of the ice.

Shaw went into the kitchen and picked up a clean, folded bag, and then knelt before her. The ice cubes spread over her thighs. He began to pick them up one at a time, but there were too many of them. He put both hands into her lap and scooped up the cubes. The ice burned his fingers and against the back of his hands he felt the trembling in her legs. He scooped more of the cubes into the bag, brushed some of them from her lap onto the gray rug of the floor, where they sat, the ice seeming bright and strange. The weight of the few cubes that remained was less, but the cold was more definite, and when there was only a

handful left, Alexandra stood up. Some of the cubes had slipped
from her lap onto her knees and legs, and piled up between
them. When she stood she felt the ice as it fell away from her
knees and thighs, hitting her calves and ankles as it dropped.

As Shaw knelt, he took two clean cubes from the sack that he
spilled and slipped them into Alexandra's glass, which she held
with two hands. Shaw took the sacks to the kitchen, and the ice
made a hard, loud ringing in the kitchen sink.

"I'm sorry," he said.

"It's all right," she said.

He put his head back and swallowed. His eyes were closed.

"I'm sorry," he said again, looking at her, "but I think you
better leave."

"I know," she said, "I know."

Then they both stood opposite one another, Alexandra feeling the shoddy theatricality of the costume, and Shaw avoiding
her eyes and her face. She still felt the burning of the ice, the
ache of it along her thighs. She had dropped the bait, and Shaw
picked it up and put it into her hand. Then they went to the
door.

She thanked him.

"That's all right," he said, "use a heavy leader. Twenty-
pound test."

"All right," she said, "I'll remember."

And then, already damning herself while she spoke, she said
to him that she'd like to come back sometime. Maybe they could
try again. She told me he was polite about it, more polite than
she deserved. But, she wanted to know, was it so bad that she
wasn't able to give up hope? It's all she had. She thought he was
hoping, too, and that's what she found hard. Where did that
hope come from? she wanted to know. It was hard to give it up.
That was the problem. She said it was hard to live without it.

Alexandra stopped on a back road and changed into her
clothes, and then she drove to town and left the costume hanging on a hook on Maude's door. She turned out of town and
went to her father's house. Harlow had come back from Washington, but he had been tired and was already asleep. The light
was on in Xannie's room, but there were times when he slept
with it on.

Alexandra went up the stairs quietly, hearing them creak, the sound itself seeming old and echoing through almost all the years she could remember. Upstairs, she took off her clothes and lay down, pulling the cool sheet, which smelled of the outdoors, over her and feeling the slippery touch of the comforter. She lay on her back, staring at the ceiling, but not moving, aside from once running her finger around her lips. After a while her door opened and Harlow stood, with the light behind him, and said, "Alexandra? Are you all right?" And she said, "Yes, I'm fine. Good night, Dad. Daddy."

When the door closed again and the room was dark, she turned on her side and stared at the bait, the plastic worm as it sat on the windowsill, where it would get the first light of morning, although even now it was glowing, filling the air around it with an enlarged, fuzzy version of itself. As she looked at the glowing thing she remembered the scent of it, which she found peculiar, but not unpleasant. It reminded her of the Pacific Northwest, of long sloping beaches at low tide, the gray, mirror-like sand, and of the stands of spruce that grew above the dunes, and of the mountains, which couldn't be seen, but whose presence was nevertheless there, icily ridged, canyons filled with blue shadows, the peaks themselves bearded with mist.

A Bad Business

There are parts of this story that bother me more than others, and this is one of them. I'd like to stop, like to get out a catalogue and order caviar or plan to build a lobster pound, a small one in the kitchen, where the lobsters would sit, their claws against the glass, their shells having a green and orange color. Or I'd like to go out and touch my old dog, just to see if he's moving. But . . . Harlow knew he was dying. That's why he went to Washington. And he had been coming by my house for months and staring out the window, his face drawn, or looking angry, and I thought it was that his daughter was gone, but there was something else in his voice as he struggled, as he tried to describe the terror in things when they are about to disappear, or that moment when most of what human beings do seems false and of no consequence. He was an inarticulate man. But he was scared, that's for certain. He looked out my window. He stood for some time and then said, his breath making a round spot in front of his face, "Well, it's a bad business . . ."

What can I say? He was my friend, and I cared for him. He was charming, beguiling, and he was such a jackass. Haven't you a friend someplace you'd like to grab and shake and say,

Can't you see the mistake you've made, that life is slipping through your fingers?

Well, it was a bad business. And now, of course, Alexandra was more determined than ever. So, in the first light of morning, when the shapes were emerging from the dark, Alexandra walked toward the river, carrying the fly rod, reel, plastic worm, a large landing net, and a spool of twenty-pound test monofilament. The worm was in the pocket of her white cotton blouse and she felt it bouncing against her. The worm had the same green glow as the tubes that are twisted or broken to give light in an emergency.

It was the first really hot day of the year, and even in the morning, at the hour when things were usually moist and cool, there was already a sense of heat. The air hung around Alexandra's face. The river seemed silvery and heavy and it reflected the smoky quality of the sky.

Alexandra came to the pool, and strung up her rod, fitting each ferrule into its seat, making sure that each joint was firm. Then she screwed the reel down tight and worked the line through the eyes and tied the leader onto the end of the line. The leader was clear, but it was so thick Alexandra couldn't believe the fish would come near it. She tied the end of the leader onto the hook in the bait and then, from the head of the pool, where the small falls fell into it, she let the worm straight down into the water and watched the green glow until the thing was too deep to see anymore. She worked it across the bottom. There was a small tug, but it was just the bait pulling a little in the current, where the water seemed to boil up.

The pool was hazy and quiet, still and soothing. Alexandra wondered how she appeared to the fish, and she imagined her face and hair, her clothes and shape reflected on a satin sheet, one hung from a clothesline and moving easily in the air of some spring afternoon. Above her there were some chickadees, flitting from branch to branch. A hawk floated on the air and there was the slight creaking from the pines. The falls fell into the pool, the shape of them streaked, the water rilled, crosshatched. The fish took the bait.

It went straight down into the depths of the pool. Alexandra tugged a little, lifting the rod. The fish was heavy and it sat on

the bottom, resisting her, and as she tugged on the rod it felt as
though she had snagged the hook on a log. The fish was finding
out how strong she was. The bamboo of the rod made a slow,
long creak, and the sound was alien and even a little romantic,
or nautical, and suggested the sound of a mast in a wind. The
fish hung in the depths, and was invisible there, although in the
milky water there seemed to be a slow, side-to-side movement of
some dark thing.

They waited. Alexandra had plenty of time to think. The
pool seemed exactly the same. The birds still sat overhead, flitting their tails. Alexandra took one finger and touched the line,
plucked it like a banjo and imagined the vibration going
through the water and into the fish's mouth. She tugged a little
harder and the fish came up.

The line felt less tight, and Alexandra stared into the water.
The calmness of it was a little dreamy, and Alexandra found
herself thinking of other things: Wasn't there a stage when a
fetus had gills? Down below, there was a greenish luminescence, and then the fish showed itself. When it came to the
surface it was turning end over end, like some large paddle, and
in the sunlight, in the few clear glimpses Alexandra could get,
the fish was long, heavy in the belly, spotted and silvery, and
the movement of it, in the bewilderment of white water, came
as a spawning-like quiver. It jumped and hung in the sunshine,
just in front of Alexandra, the worm hanging from the side of
its mouth.

It turned neatly and fell back into the pool. The fish made one
run and then another, and Alexandra sat, tugging on the rod
and hearing it creak. The fish made the surface of the pool
quake, and the reflection of the sky and trees, the curve of the
landscape, trembled and disappeared in the splashy wake. Soon,
the fish seemed to be tired.

Alexandra climbed down from the ledge and stepped into the
pool. The fish was a few feet away, finning, opening and closing
its gills. Alexandra stepped into the water and it filled her tennis shoes and climbed up her legs. She stared at the fish, and
saw its large eyes, the centers of which were filled with some
dark hole. When she put the net into the water, its black stocking weave settled into the pool. The fish rested. Alexandra

turned her back and threw the net on the bank since the mouth of it was too small.

The fish was still, and the thing watched her. Its mouth was open, and Alexandra thought she could put her fist into it. The insides of it were ridged, and the gills were the reddish color of vines in the spring. Alexandra stepped deeper into the water and walked along the edge of the hole, her feet going over the mossy stones, which were large, greenish, and half hidden in the shadows. The water rose to the middle of her chest, and the air was filled with her steady panting as she tried to breathe. She became a little buoyant, and bounced on one foot. The fish broke away then, and Alexandra hit the rod hard, pulled back on it, and the bamboo broke, making a long, squeaking snap.

The fish fell away, tumbled backward over itself, and went toward the end of the pool, marking the surface with a widening V. Alexandra wound the line around her hand. The fish stopped and swung from side to side. The green worm was still hanging from its mouth, although now it was torn and the end of it was frayed. Alexandra went on panting, and then took a deep breath. The fish rolled over on its side.

She pulled the line in, hand over hand, stepping back a little. She put her fingers into its gills and touched the burred red and polypy texture. The fish flinched. The jerking of it, the electric, cold spasm of the thing ran up her arm: she felt the jerking in her shoulder. Soon the fish stopped, and Alexandra was left with only the soft working of the gills against her fingers.

The fish began to quiver: it looked as if it were a flag, rippling in a strong wind. It kept its eyes on Alexandra and she stared back. Then she stepped over one of those large, dark stones that were at the edge of the depths of the pool. Her tennis shoes slid along the mossy surface and she tried to jump, or to struggle toward the bank. As she fell, she went facedown, and hit her elbow on one of the stones, and as she opened her eyes, seeing the undulant and satiny water overhead, she felt the ringing buzz from her elbow run into her hand. Above her, and marred by the surface of the water, there were the pale green of the trees around the pool, the smoky sky, and, edged by prismatic light, the shape of the fish.

Alexandra sat up. The scales of the fish sparkled like sunshine

coming off the edges of crushed ice. It began to swim again.
Alexandra kneeled on the stones and slapped at the surface of
the water where the fly line drifted away. The sound of her
hand hitting the water came as a mild, repeated smack, like that
of one person clapping in an empty theater. Alexandra hit the
fly line with her open hand, took up a loop, and gave it a jerk, as
though restraining a vicious dog that was barking at a child.
The fish stood up in the water, almost on its tail, quivering in
the sunlight, and then fell forward, away from Alexandra, and
she was left with only the leader, loose now and coiling a little
bit toward her.

Alexandra sat down on the stones of the bottom of the pool.
She put her elbows on her knees and leaned her head forward,
and then the surface of the water slapped her face hard enough
to make her head snap back. She stared toward the tail of the
pool, hearing only the steady sound of the falls and the tinkling
drip as the water ran from her face. The fish disappeared along
the edge of the pool, and the surface was too troubled for Alexandra to see anything, not even the dark stones and shapes
where the fish could have gone. She backed out of the pool and
sat on dry ground, her head between her knees as the water ran
out of her clothes.

After a while she began to shiver. She ran one hand over the
elbow she had banged against a stone, still feeling the cold, vibrant ring down into her hands, and then she picked up the
broken rod and walked down to the river, where she could
stand in the warm sunlight. She sat there, too, feeling the
warmth on her back as she rested her head on her knees, but the
warmth didn't get beyond the wet clothes and she continued to
shiver. She didn't want to be sick, so she picked up a cool pebble
from the edge of the river and put it in her mouth, like a sliver
of ice, and as she pushed her tongue against it she tasted the
landscape through which the river ran. Alexandra kept looking
at the round white stones next to her, as though she couldn't
believe the fish wasn't there, stretched out next to her. She kept
shaking her head, stopping only when she felt she was going to
be sick. Then she stopped and waited for the cold, slow coiling
and uncoiling in her stomach to go away.

Then she felt a little better. She took the stone out of her mouth and went through the woods, carrying the broken fly rod. The tip trailed behind her. Her clothes gripped her legs as she climbed the hill and the shirt was cold when the breeze blew. The aspen was lizard-green and Alexandra didn't look at it, keeping her eyes ahead, where the fields in front of her father's house began. She went through the gate in the wall, dragging the broken fly rod.

The small orchard at the side of the house was in bloom, and since it was such a warm day, wicker chairs had been put out in the sun, under the trees and in the fallen blossoms, which lay like each tree's shadow on the ground. The chairs were green, and Xannie had planned on giving Harlow and Alexandra lunch there. As Alexandra came across the field, looking at the white tablecloth Xannie had spread on the wicker table between the chairs, she felt the cold pain in her arm. Her white jeans and blouse were still wet and almost transparent as she went through the orchard, kicking up the petals.

One of the chairs was in the sun, and Alexandra sat in it, smelling the apple blossoms. She put her head back and swallowed and thought, He should have given me two baits. The apple blossoms in the trees and on the ground, the tablecloth, and Alexandra's blouse and pants were the same color, and she sat in the green chair looking into the field.

Xannie came out of the house. He was wearing his mail-order clothes, his corduroy pants, Black Watch tartan shirt, a rag sweater, and black-and-white saddle shoes. He stood before Alexandra, his dark eyes set on hers, one of his hands held in another.

"I'm sorry," he said.

Alexandra looked up and smiled, but when she saw the rising grimace on his face, she frowned and said, "It's all right, Xannie. It'll be okay."

"No, it won't," he said, "I don't think it will."

"Why?" said Alexandra.

"Harlow's gone," said Xannie.

Alexandra looked down, away from Xannie's face, which was marked by deep lines, each feature drawn and severe. There was a light, barely hissing breeze, and Alexandra sat in it, hearing the distant field where the stalks of grass moved against one

another. She sat in the chair with her hands in her lap and
blinked.

"Where did he go?" she said.

"It's not like that," said Xannie.

"Did he leave a note?" said Alexandra.

"No," said Xannie. "He's gone. He's upstairs."

He knelt in front of her and took her hand. He cried freely,
wetting the corners of his eyes, and Alexandra felt the warm
moisture as he put her hand against his face.

"I'm sorry, I'm sorry," he said. "What are we going to do
now? Have you saved any money? Did he give you any?"

"What?" said Alexandra.

"He's upstairs," said Xannie. "He's gone. Didn't I tell you to
be careful with what you told him? Didn't I?"

Xannie began to cry, and Alexandra walked and then ran
through the white, cool petals, leaving Xannie against the chair.
She went into the house and smelled the odor of wax and plaster and climbed the stairs, taking them three at a time, feeling
her wet clothes clinging to her. She found Harlow in his room,
on the bed, the blankets and sheets and pajama top, too, pulled
away from his chest. His eyes were closed and Alexandra stood
at the side of the bed, pushing her legs against it, before she
knelt on the floor and put her face against his, feeling the coldness of her wet hair and of Harlow's skin, too. She leaned her
head on the sheets, turned it to one side, but she put a hand,
with its fingers spread, over the sickly and already fallen features of Harlow's face. She picked up Harlow's hand and
touched it against her lips, but then she stopped that, too.

The room was silent, although outside there was the slight
sound and pressure of the breeze. After a while there was the
sound of a siren on the road and soon it came close and then
stopped. Alexandra sat back, away from the bed, as the doctor
and two other men came into the room. The men wore work
clothes and were volunteers from the local rescue, and one of
them was tall and heavy and had on one side of his face a large
birthmark, as bright as pomegranate.

"I'm sorry," he said.

She had never seen the doctor before, although he was young
and could have been new in town, fresh from medical school.

The men brought a stretcher covered with starched sheets, and after they were gone, the doctor said, "How did you get wet?"

"I fell in the river," she said.

Alexandra stared at the mark that had been left on the pillow and the shape of the sheets that had been thrown back. She pushed the back of a hand to her nose and mouth and cried openly.

Xannie came into the room and gave the doctor a look of unrelieved hatred. His face was a little puffy.

"Go away, go away," said Xannie. "What can you do? You've done nothing. Go away."

"I'm sorry," said the young doctor.

"No, you aren't," said Xannie. "Go away."

The doctor looked at Alexandra and said, "I'll leave some . . . drugs. You might want to take one every few hours . . ." He opened his bag, and in the compartment built into the top he reached for a plastic bottle, but he stopped when Alexandra said, "No. Don't. I'm pregnant. I can't take them."

"Oh, well. Congratulations," he said, and then blushed and packed up his bag and walked out the door, leaving Xannie and Alexandra in the room. Alexandra sat down in a chair opposite Harlow's bed and Xannie stood there until the sound of the automobiles outside went away, the sandy, bumpy sound of the tires on the dirt road disappearing into the blooming orchards and the woods where the trees were coming into leaf. Xannie said, "I'll make something to eat," and then he left Alexandra alone, still sitting in the chair. She stared at the bed, the white wall next to it, and through the window, where, in the distance, she saw the cold flash of the river. After a while, Xannie called her downstairs and they went into the orchard, where they ate salmon sandwiches on pumpernickel bread and drank Swan beer and told old stories about Harlow. Xannie started with the one about the races at Ipoh.

"The dirty son of a bitch," said Alexandra, looking into the field. "I loved him so much."

So that's what it got them. I like to think it could have been avoided. Harlow, I suppose, would have gone along no matter what, even if he knew how it would end. Maybe it's an illusion I

keep, that it could have been avoided. It's one I cling to, since I
don't want to think they were that damned by themselves. Well,
I began to miss him on the spot, since he was the one *I* wanted
to turn to. He would have looked at me with those understanding eyes, the ones that had gotten him into so much trouble.
Maybe *that* was the illusion, that he understood at all. I wonder
if we didn't seem like strangers to him, even his daughter. What
in God's name did the man have to hide? There are nights when
I wake, hearing the dog howl, or the snow blow against the
house, and I know, before I've even realized what I was thinking about, what the problem had been. The man was just
scared, more scared than anyone I had ever met. Anyway, Alexandra asked if I'd say a few words at the funeral. I agreed, and
sat for a long time, wishing that I weren't decent at all, that I
had the backbone to stand before the people who had known
him and say, I have a story to tell you, and let it all come tumbling out. I got through it, though, and told an anecdote about
his gambling for comic relief. We all laughed.

Good Bait

   Maude made the black dress for Alexandra quickly and on credit, and said, "I'm sure you'll be able to pay for it soon enough, if a tenth of what they say is true." Alexandra wore the dress on the day of the funeral and sat in the living room of her father's house, where she talked first to a young man, only a year or two older than her, from the wire service. He had a hangover and asked almost nothing about Harlow. The editor of the local paper was better, crisper, more friendly. A lawyer called from Washington to say that he would come to see her, a few days after the funeral. He asked, too, if she knew Bryce, and when she said she did, the lawyer said he thought that was for the best.

When Bryce arrived, on the day of the funeral, he was wearing a black jacket with wide lapels and big pockets, a pair of black pants, and a black tie. The tie was wide. That year everyone was wearing wide ties, and I was amazed that he had the time to buy the damn thing. I was in Harlow's living room when he came in, and he smiled and then embraced Alexandra and said, "I had no idea the honor would come so soon. And such a great human tragedy." He wore the tie pulled away from his neck, but the tie was new and the shirt was fresh. He sat

down as though he were tired, but his eyes were clear. I should
have known right then. But I was thinking of other things, and
didn't really notice that he said "honor." Well, I found out what
he meant, and soon, and, of course, he'd see it that way. There
are times now when I wake at night, and think of him, picking
out that wide black tie. He probably took the plane to New
York to do it, in anticipation of its being needed. I'd guess he
went to Paul Stuart's. Maybe they keep a stack of them, hidden
away someplace.

He sat down opposite Alexandra and took her hand. He
frowned when she pulled it away. He said, "I understand. I
understand. Grief is such a terrible thing. But you are taking it
well. Supremely well. I'm sure you have things to do, so I'll see
you later." Then he stood and bowed at the waist. Alexandra
didn't notice, or care. I was glad no one else was in the room.
"You must understand," he said when he was at the door, "I've
come here to help."

He smiled before he went, and I can still see it, have woken in
the middle of calm, warm nights, and seen it then, since there
are times when I think it explains what happened perfectly. Of
course, it was false. The man was a liar. But it was something
else, too, something I'd never seen before. There was a kind of
emotional greed in it, as though there wasn't enough feeling in
the world to make him trust people, or to do without trapping
them. No ceremony was hollow for him. They were probably
as close to living as he ever got. He stood at the door for a
moment so we could get a good look at the tie.

Alexandra was surprised at the number of people who came
from Washington, New York, and Boston, old friends from
school, old friends from Congress, secretaries, political aides,
advisors, people from the State Department and the diplomatic
corps, all of whom had a sharp sense of ceremony. They were
strangely reserved, though, and quiet, and after Harlow had
been taken to the old graveyard, where the stones were more
like tablets than anything else, the writing on which was almost
unreadable, more like black, smoky shapes no longer suggesting
language or names, and after the black coffin had been put into
the ground, few of the guests came to the house, although there
were enough not to be embarrassing.

After they were gone, and Xannie and the caterers were cleaning up, Alexandra took Harlow's Jeep and drove back to the cemetery, and she stood there in the bright spring afternoon, where she looked at those old headstones and the vague inscriptions that seemed more appropriate to her father than the sharp new inscription on the small stone over his grave, since, as she stood before it, she was confronted with the mystery of him again, and she shivered, aware of her lack of understanding so severely as to still feel it as the drifting, thin-stranded tug of a spiderweb.

Alexandra began to leave, but she stopped and closed her eyes and found that all she could think about was the fish jerking at the end of the line. She saw the jumping convulsion, the spasm above the pool, and the splash that made the trees, land, and sky disappear. The vibrant tug still made her fingers ache and she felt in her elbow the same cold ringing as when she had fallen and hit the stone, although now the ringing not only ran into her arm, but seemed to go into the soil at her feet.

In the evening, after Xannie had been asleep for an hour, Alexandra walked through the house, looking at Harlow's things, his shotguns and fly rods, the photographs of fishing trips to Alaska, Argentina and Yugoslavia, Spain and Iceland, and of Harlow with Lyndon Johnson, under which Johnson had written, "To Harlow Pearson, the only northerner I ever met who could carve a whole hog. Your friend, Lyndon Baines Johnson."

Alexandra sat down at the desk. There were checkbooks, and bills, a book of telephone numbers. There was a large wooden filing cabinet, which she looked into and was surprised to find a large folder, filled with page after page of financial holdings. There was a code that referred to the other drawers, the contents of which dealt with records of the holdings. The pages were only an index, and Alexandra was shocked at the number of shares, of the bonds, the sheer bulk of the thing: she was amazed that her father had been so rich.

When she told me, I was surprised, too. Maybe the man hadn't been such a dummy after all. He never mentioned the money. There was no need why he should have. And I should have known he was doing fairly well, since there were times when I mentioned the beating I was taking, and he'd say, with his eyebrows raised and his blue eyes clearly showing wonder, "Why, you didn't sell short?" It was enough to make me keep my losses to myself.

Alexandra sat at the desk again and opened the bottom drawer. Inside there were letters, which had been carefully opened and stored in their envelopes, and then bound together and put into neat, although not new manila envelopes. The letters were to Harlow and written by women other than Alexandra's mother. Alexandra read them all, every one, every word, lingering over phrases: ". . . I cannot stand the prospect of no longer feeling your scent around me, or on me . . ." "It's not that I love you so much as I just don't think of myself as being separate any longer . . . when you touch me I can feel it run straight to my . . ." Alexandra turned the pages, slowly looking at the handwriting of the mysterious women, and smelling the fragrance of the paper, which was still scented after years of sitting in the manila envelope. ". . . do you remember," said one, "that afternoon at the garden party . . . with the sound of the musicians, the breeze, the taste of champagne . . . how could we have taken the chance . . . ?"

Alexandra still wore the black dress, and after a while she put on a sweater and went into the orchard, where she sat, listening to the quiet noises of early morning and having the sense of the dew as it settled over the white blossoms of the apple trees and into the grass beneath them. She sat with her legs straight out before her, ankles together. The white blossoms began to glow with the dawn, and Alexandra went back into the house and read the letters again. When she was done, she gathered them together, folded each one, making the old creases sharper by running a nail over them before putting the letters back into the envelopes. For a moment, when she was putting them away, she wanted to tear the letters into the smallest confetti, and imagined herself throwing it from the window, spreading the white and pinkish bits and destroying evidence of the past.

She told me that the entire house seemed unreal. Or just so different as to seem unreal. She was a little giddy and there were times when she was angry. But there was some maddening thing around her, something that was suggested in the way the house seemed to have changed. For a while she was simply addled, or abstracted, and she'd spend ten or fifteen minutes looking out the window and thinking absolutely nothing, or going over memories so inconsequential as to seem childlike. But when she came out of those moments, that maddening thing surrounded her again, especially as she noticed something specific, a lamp, a chair, a rug, a book of stamps on Harlow's desk. She wandered around the house, touching one thing and another with the tip of her finger, being gentle even with the walls, the shelves, light switches, the corners of the house, as though by touching them she was carefully assuring herself that these things still existed. It was the thing she couldn't touch that infuriated her: the thing that had made everything change. She went carefully down the hall, feeling that maddening, untouchable presence until she was about to scream, and as she went she became angrier. Finally she stopped in the doorway of her room.

There she unzipped the black dress and let it fall in a heap. She stepped out of it and pulled a pair of blue jeans over her black stockings and underthings. She put a dark shirt over the black brassiere, and then put on the tennis shoes she had worn when driving across the country. Downstairs, she found a brown paper bag, and after she tore a piece from it she wrote on it, "Back when it's done," and left the note for Xannie.

Alexandra took the keys to Harlow's Jeep and went outside, but before she got behind the wheel she put the windshield down flat, combat style, and then sat on the dark, smooth seats and started the engine. She went to town, going fast, or as fast as the wind would let her, seeing the dirt road, which was wet with dew, reflect the bluish color of the morning sky.

There were no lights on at Shaw's house. Alexandra stepped down from the Jeep and slipped between the cool poles of the gate in the hurricane fence. The smashed cars were clearly visible at the back of the house, and their broken lights and bent grills gave each one a grinning, cracked expression, and where the cars were piled on top of one another they looked like totems, winking, insanely cheerful. She stood on the porch and knocked, feeling in the boards beneath her feet a gentle give as he came to the door on the other side of the wall. He stood just behind it, shielding himself with the edge of it.

When he saw it was her, he opened the door and let her in. He was wearing only a pair of jeans, but then he pulled on a white shirt, fresh from the laundry, and as he did so, as his fingers worked the buttons, and as he went into the bathroom and washed his face, combed his hair, and rubbed his skin, Alexandra stood and talked in a flat, breathy voice. She said Harlow was dead, that she had been fishing when he died, and that she'd had a bet with him. Here she stopped and put back her head. She closed her eyes and swallowed. Shaw put down the towel and stared at her. She wanted to finish the bet. It was the least she could do: it was the only thing that made sense to her, and as she stood in Shaw's house, watching him brush and wash, she realized she didn't want to catch the fish, and that she hadn't come there for another bait. She wanted to kill the thing.

It came out as a stutter. After all, she had spent hours walking around her father's house, trying to make herself believe it hadn't turned to dust and blown away. And, at the time, she had no way of knowing it hadn't. She didn't even know, she told me, if Harlow had owned the house outright. She hated standing opposite Shaw, looking so brittle and feeling her face tight as a mask. He didn't tell her to calm down, didn't ask for any reason at all. She probably would have despised him if he had.

He finished washing his face, and, looking over the towel, he said, "Where's the fish?"

"In a pool in a tributary," she said, "not far from the river."

"Are there any houses around?" he said.

"No," she said.

He went back into the bedroom and came out with a small bag, one that he had used when he had been in high school and had traveled to schools where he had played baseball, carrying in it underclothes, socks, cap, and candy, bars of Bit-O-Honey. It was blue and the plastic handle was cracked and showing some white stuffing underneath. He put it at the base of a wooden cabinet, which was made of old light wood and which was closed with a brass hasp and a combination lock. Shaw worked the combination and Alexandra stood by the door, her eyes set on his fingers. She watched the shape of his ear, his shoulders defined in his shirt, the shape of his legs and hips. Her coloring was pale around her eyes, nose, and mouth and she breathed quickly, making her nostrils flare.

"You sure there's no house close by?" he said.

"Certain," said Alexandra. "The pool is on Harlow's land . . . was Harlow's land."

"Okay," he said. "All right."

In the cabinet there were two double-barrel shotguns, a rifle with a large telescopic sight, and, on a shelf at the top, boxes of ammunition. There was a roll of coated wire at the top, too. Shaw's back moved as he put things into his bag.

"Are you going to shoot it?" said Alexandra. "How can you see it?"

"I'm not going to shoot it," said Shaw, reaching for the wire at the top of the gun case. He put that into the bag and then zipped it shut. He took a jacket from a hook on the wall.

Alexandra drove the Jeep. It was day now, although there was still the gray-blue and wet cast to things. The streets were empty, and the traffic signals made Alexandra and Shaw wait for nothing and no one. Alexandra gripped the wheel with both hands.

She parked at the entrance of a logging road that was a mile from her father's house. It wasn't seven o'clock in the morning and the sky was high and blue, with only large white puffs that trailed mist. They went through the woods, which were a little damp, and as they went, Alexandra picking the way and Shaw carrying his high school bag, they heard the soft hushing give of the dead leaves. They went down to the river and along it until they came to the mouth of the tributary in which the pool was.

When they came to the pool, Shaw stared into the water. The surface was calm, smooth as tin, and down below, with the light from the cloudy sky, he saw the round and large mossy stones, the shadows, the depths that were black-green and impenetrable.

"I've seen the fish there, under the falls," said Alexandra.

He opened the bag and took from it a stick of dynamite, a small box of caps, and the roll of wire. The dynamite was a grayish-red, covered with wax, and had some print on it. He took a detonator from the bag, too, and it was small, made of hard plastic, and had two caps that snapped back and revealed terminals. It had a plunger. It didn't go up and down, but sideways, like the handle on a bathroom faucet. He had a pair of pliers with a point, and he made a hole in the dynamite. Alexandra watched his hands, and then went and sat above the pool, and stared into the water, trying to see into it. There were a few insects on the surface, but only small fish picked at them and made rings.

Shaw played out two strands of wire, attached them to a blasting cap, and pushed it into the dynamite. He stripped off the plastic from the wires, exposing the bright, almost cheerful-looking copper. There were two terminals on the detonator, each threaded and made of brass. Shaw attached the wires, putting them through the holes in the terminals and tightening the brass nuts over them. He climbed up to the ledge where Alexandra sat, and then put the detonator in her lap while he threw the stick into the pool. It made a splash shaped like the pages in an open book. The wires went into the pool, too, and they looked out of place, like electrodes attached to someone's head. The detonator was compact, not much larger than a cheap model-train transformer.

"Do you turn this?" said Alexandra, her fingers touching the black plunger.

"Yes," said Shaw.

Alexandra stood and turned it. Shaw rolled back, away from the ledge and into the brownish humus that was beyond the rock, calling as he went, "Get down. Get down."

Alexandra stood with the box as the green water made two separate movements. The first was a quick flinching that seemed to move with long and thin tendrils through the water, and the second, which came so quickly after the first as to seem to be part of it, was a boiling, a bubbling that started at the bottom of the pool and pushed up in one rising and white geyser. The noise came as a muffled thump, and then as the loudest thing Alexandra had ever heard, a kind of opening of the air that left her skin feeling numb. The geyser was as thick and as solid, for an instant, as the biggest and oldest maple, and it was ridged and as suggestive of power as the trunk of that same old tree. As it rose, as the top of it became floppy and then broke into drops, there was revealed the bottom of the pool: the water had been forced away from it, either into the air or toward the tail, and the round stones were now bright green and glistening in the early morning sunlight. In the center of the crater, or at least the bottom of the empty pool, there quivered for a moment a few strands of whitish smoke that smelled of cordite or gunpowder. Then the top of the column of water broke into the finest mist, which lingered among the new leaves of the crowns of the trees. The water fell back into the pool, leaving only a rainbow, which drifted away from the ridge. But the water didn't fall directly into the pool. It rose straight up and then away from its center, like a spout, and when the water came down it fell in a widening circle. Alexandra stood on the ledge and was hit by the curling, now ice-colored and slick water. It came with a hard, sudden smack, making her feel not its moisture but its weight, and she tried to stand up to it as though she were at the beach and a wave were breaking over her.

It wasn't just the sudden weight of the water that hit her, but what was in it, too, since the explosion had lifted not only pebbles and even stones from the bottom, not to mention mud that in the air had been blown to wet dust, but fish as well, and as Alexandra stood under the tall curve of water, she felt the brook and brown trout as they splashed against her. She felt the hard slap of them against her face and shoulders and breast, not even realizing what they were until she saw them bouncing away from her and landing on the stone at her feet, where they were left stranded by the receding water and where they bounced again and twisted, head over tail, and fell back into the now shallow pool. There were no stones in the water that fell over Alexandra, but there were pebbles and these stung, not so much in the moment, in the heaviness of the water, but later, when the water had passed and the wave of the explosion was rolling back where it had come from.

The pool turned the color of silty water and the waves rolled back and forth, from tail to head, but before the pool stopped quivering, before the separate waves had stopped, the fish began to rise, belly-up.

"Let's get out of here," said Shaw.

He began winding in the wire, not taking it from the terminals but just wrapping it around the detonator. Alexandra climbed down from the ledge. Shaw shoved the wire and the plastic box into his bag and stood in his wet and muddy clothes. Alexandra stepped into the brown water of the pool, and began looking, pushing one fish out of the way and then another before she found the large whitish and silver belly. The fish's eyes were set on hers, or on her head or just the sky beyond. Alexandra put her hand into the gill opening and dragged the fish out of the water, and then carried it with her as they went quickly through the woods, which seemed to ache with the echo of the explosion. They went straight uphill and to the car, Alexandra carrying the fish and feeling the weight of its tug backward, toward the pool out of which it had come, and as she went she gave it a hard, definite jerk, as though to stop the fish's existence, since even its weight made her skin crawl. She carried it to the back of the Jeep and stretched it out there and slammed the door, before getting behind the wheel and putting her head back and closing her eyes, feeling the last of the water trickle along her legs and sides, and the effect of the breeze, which was gentle to her face and made her arms seem cool.

Shaw got in on the passenger's side. Both of them were breathing hard and shivering. Shaw put his head back and blew air softly between his lips. Alexandra looked over and saw his profile, beaded with water and his hair falling over his forehead, one drop hanging from a damp strand.

Alexandra drove back to town, passing after a while the isolated and abandoned farmhouses, the fields and orchards having gone to blackberries and red raspberries and wild grapes and the pine already moving in from the edge of the woods. The buildings didn't seem calm, so much as desolate, and the grayness of the weathered houses and barns, which had long since lost their paint, even the last clinging chips of it, looked more like the color of stone walls.

She drove through the town, which was filled with sleepy people who went slowly along the sidewalks, each remembering the warmth of a just abandoned bed. The streets were still damp, and the Jeep's tires made a swishing noise. On the other side of town Alexandra stopped in front of the sign that showed cars crashing together.

"Well, okay," said Shaw, after he stepped out of the Jeep. "It was sure one big ugly fish."

Alexandra had one hand on the wheel and she gripped it hard.

"What do you want?" said Shaw.

She told me she didn't answer, at least not right away. The question hung in the air as she sat there, the Jeep's window down flat, combat style. She didn't want to be selfish. And what would happen, what trouble would the two of them get into, if one moment led to the next? What if they couldn't stop, and how would she have compromised him then? She didn't want to seduce him into the mess she was already in. She told me, though, she did want something, and it was just a little time, in which things would stop and she could draw her breath freely. Was that so wrong? she wanted to know. And didn't he have needs too? Of course he did, I said. She said she didn't want to be selfish, but then, in that moment, in which she was angry at herself, she said, not able to look at him and while she gripped the steering wheel hard, "I want to come in. Is that okay?" It was out before she was able to do a thing, and then she turned in his direction. There are times when I think of that movement, her hair swinging out, her face white and her eyes not quite challenging but certainly frank, honest. And to me she said, recalling it, trying to tell me everything as clearly as she could, "I didn't want to bitch him up. That's the last thing I wanted to do."

"Sure, it's okay," he said.

Alexandra turned off the engine and got out on her side. They went through the yard, from which Alexandra saw the crushed cars and the cracked glass, and the bright sky beyond. She stood inside the house door, her posture correct, but even as she said, "Maybe I shouldn't, maybe you don't . . . want," she was already opening the silk blouse and finding to her surprise the black undergarments of mourning. She took off her jeans, too, and then, as she put her fingers under the sheer stockings, she found that they were damp and tugged against her. She slipped her fingers under the nylon next to her calf and then

pushed it down to her ankle, thinking, There's still time to walk
. . . through the yard . . . but she shook her head and re-
moved the damp things. She had to lift one foot and then the
other to remove the black stockings that sagged around each
ankle, and then she stood before him, holding the dark,
strangely heavy nylons, which were wet from the pool. She
helped him with his wet clothes and they stood before one another, barely touching and feeling at the places where they did
smooth skin and their hard and mutual trembling, and while
she felt the shiver, the coldness of his skin, she said, "Let's lie
down . . . we'll be warm in a little bit."

In the afternoon, they sat by the open oven in the kitchen. It
was on, and her things were inside, drying. Every now and then
she turned them over, and she was glad to stand next to it herself, feeling the cooking warmth as it pushed against her back or
stomach. He sat on a chair just before her and smoked a cigarette. She pulled a chair next to his and sat down, and both of
them were quiet and languid before the heat, feeling the moving warmth of it against their skin, and as they sat there, and
even as Alexandra said slowly, "Come here, why don't you
come here . . ." she knew she was just buying time, but even
so, as they walked through the living room, as they held hands
and gently touched fingers, she forgot about the drive she'd
make, back along the river to her father's house, and even about
the clothes in the oven, which she remembered and came running to save when she smelled the first odor of scorching silk.

When she was dressed and standing by the door in the living
room, when she had her hand on the knob and felt the coolness
of it, she was hoping they wouldn't argue. She spoke to me
about it when she was big with the child. She looked at me, her
skin milky and filled with life. Shaw and Alexandra did argue,
though. She thought they did so rather than saying they had no
hope, rather than her just turning and walking politely out the
door. That would have been more than both of them were equal
to. And, by God, she said, maybe more than they should have
been equal to. We weren't, she said, that experienced. And she
didn't even know how they began. Perhaps, in all innocence,
and in all forgetfulness, just as though they had first met and
there were no other problems in the world, Alexandra had sug-

gested they see each other again. Then she saw the look on his
face. Of course, she said to me, he was angry. He had every
right to be. She told me it was as though they'd agreed: no
future and that was it. In a moment of relief, or calmness, she'd
broken the agreement. Perhaps she wanted to break it, maybe
she thought the entire thing was too hideous. Perhaps she
couldn't stand another minute of it. And she was angry, too. So
they stood there, both of them trembling, each waiting for the
other to say the least thing. And, of course, they did. Alexandra
found herself standing before this man, wishing that things
were somehow other than they were. It was at that moment, she
said, that she knew she loved him. Did I understand how much
worse that made things? she wanted to know. I said I didn't
think it made things easier. And when I said that she laughed
out loud, holding the large belly with both hands.

"Ah, ah," she said, "the muscles along the side hurt when that
happens."

Then she looked at me, still holding herself, seemingly angry
again as she had been that afternoon, trying to decide where it
had all begun, with her mother's unhappiness, with her father's
secrets, with his stubbornness or her own innocent curiosity.
By then, though, Shaw was speaking, raising his voice. Oh, he
said all kinds of things. What do you say in an argument, when
you're trapped and trying to make sense of the teeth that have
gotten through the flesh and into the bone? She remembered his
voice as he said that he'd have to take money from her and that
he'd need her advice not to appear like a hick. Or such a hick.
By then he was screaming and Alexandra screamed back, lying
for all she was worth, and being ashamed with each word. And
then, in the middle of the noise, they stopped, each looking at
the other, Shaw's voice falling to an ordinary, quiet inflection,
in which he said, "Don't you know what I'd give to spend a
little time with you?"

That was bad. Because she almost told him about the child
right then. When we talked about it, I could see her lips moving, almost forming the words, opening into the first letter and
then being pursed, ridged, full. She waited for the impulse to
pass. Shaw watched her closely. And you know why I didn't tell
him? she said. Can you guess? I had a good idea, but I waited

until she looked at me again and said, I was afraid he'd think the worst, the absolute worst, that I was "damaged goods." So we sat there, her glass of milk almost empty, the pale, smoky sky beyond her. The prospect of being "damaged goods" was so ugly, so horrible, she said nothing to Shaw at all. Even months later, when she sat before me, she couldn't keep her head up when she explained what might have happened: that he would have supposed she had turned to him, a man who was an outsider, a junkman who was studying law at night, because her value had been so diminished by the child. She put down the glass of milk and said, "I loved him too much to let that happen. Are you satisfied? Now that I'm finally using the word?"

At the time, when they still stood opposite one another, Alexandra thought Shaw even hated the things he had used to try to escape. He picked up one of the law books from his desk and said, "You know what this goddamned thing is? A book of torts. *Torts!*" He threw the book, with its bright, gaudy mail-order printing on the binding, and it sailed across the room, opening and closing like a bird that's just been shot. It hit the wall and slid down, the gold on the pages flickering as they closed.

Well, that was the end. I asked her if she left then, and she nodded. There was nothing else to do, she said. She went through the door and Shaw walked across the room and sat down in front of the open door of the stove where her things had been, and after a while he looked up and pushed away the chair where she had been sitting. Alexandra got into the Jeep, passing the large, silvery, and now faintly bug-eyed fish, and then started the engine and turned around slowly, waiting for him to come out of the house or to look through the window or to make some sign, but there was nothing, and then she began to drive through town and toward the isolated and cool house that had belonged to her father.

Meson, Charles, and Crump

 Alexandra had expected to find the house the way she'd left it, with the Ford parked alone in front of the orchard, but when she arrived there were two other cars. One was a long, dark Mercedes, which was driven by a chauffeur. He sat in his blue coat and hat, and stared at the woods. The other was a small red sports car, an Austin-Healey, and it was parked behind Alexandra's Ford. She stopped the Jeep in front of the dark, long Mercedes, and sat there for a moment, looking at the house. There was smoke coming from one of the chimneys, and as Alexandra sat there, gathering her dark underthings, which were on the seat, Bryce came to the door and then approached the car.

"Hello, Alexandra," he said, looking into the Jeep, his face long and serious and hurt a little. His eyes, though, were bright, hard. "We've been more worried than we can say. I'm glad you made it safely."

"I had some things to take care of," she said, already angry with herself for explaining, for saying a word.

Bryce was wearing a pinstriped suit. The stripes were very wide, and the lapels were wide, too. He wore a dark blue tie, but the knot had been opened at the neck and the shirt was unbuttoned. He nodded, closing his eyes, as though the light hurt his eyes, saying, "Yes, yes. I'm sure. There's no need to explain. At least not now. Charles Meson is here."

"Meson?" said Alexandra, getting out of the Jeep and carrying the underthings.

"Of Meson, Charles, and Crump, the prestigious Washington law firm. Harlow's lawyer," said Bryce. "He wants to see you."

When Bryce said "prestigious," it sounded as though he had a piece of watermelon in his mouth. It was the kind of word that meant a lot to him.

"Let's not keep him waiting," said Bryce.

He took Alexandra by the arm and brought her into the living room, not giving her a chance to go upstairs. The fire was set and the lawyer sat before it, drinking a cup of tea.

Charles Meson was fifty-five, almost bald, heavy. His clothes were dark, perfectly made, and his skin was pink, his hands manicured, the nails ending in a perfect, clear crescent moon. He held on his lap a manila folder, and when Alexandra came into the room he put it aside, which Alexandra realized was his greeting.

"Alexandra," he said. "Pleased."

She sat in a wing chair opposite him. Xannie was in the room as well, and he came forward to stand next to her chair.

"I am only the medium," said Meson, "I have opinions only on mechanics, on methods. Substance is of no consequence. Understood? Good. You must understand that Harlow was a wealthy man, and, with a few minor exceptions"—Meson looked at Xannie and then back at Alexandra—"you are his sole beneficiary, under the terms of a trust, which will be administered by Bryce McCann."

Bryce stood opposite her and bowed, clicking his heels lightly together.

"Index," said Meson, "is here. Stocks. Bonds. C.D.'s. Deeds. I'll leave this for later. But there are one or two legal oddities . . ."

Meson looked up from his papers, and stared at Alexandra.

"Remember," he said, "I only have opinions about execution, not substance. How. Not why. All right. There are two late provisions, entered last week. The first is, you shall enjoy the income from the estate and the right to convey the principal at your death, on the condition that you maintain a *regular morality*. Those are the terms. Regular morality. Mr. McCann is to be arbiter, and his fiduciary duty is to instruct the trust's legal officer on hearing of moral irregularities. Those are the terms."

Alexandra looked at the windows beyond Meson, at the sharp lines of the sashes, at the white walls and the severe furniture. She could smell in the room's plaster the dry, arctic odor that seemed to linger from the winters through which the house had endured. She looked at Meson's round head with the curls of blondish hair that were only at the edges of his enormous bald spot. He blinked at her and waited, his hands folded over the manila folder.

"Questions?" he said.

"Are there any recourses?" said Alexandra, "speaking only of matters of methods?"

Meson tucked his head down for a moment, making his chins defined and almost taut. He blinked at her and said, "Delaying tactic, litigation, yes. But, in point of fact, in point of result, no."

"I see," said Alexandra.

"Good," said Meson. "Pleased."

"I have your sincere best interests at heart," said Bryce, "Alexandra, I'm sure you understand that. . . ."

"Later," said Meson. "Substance. Not methods. There is one exception which was also entered last week. You are given the income of the trust and this house and all other properties, the trust to be managed by you or your consignee, provided, by this afternoon, you are able to produce from a stream off the West River, one trout, over three feet long. The pool is here described."

Alexandra sat in the wing chair and looked at Meson. His eyes were surrounded by sacks and deep creases, and although the weight of his face, the size of the bags around his eyes, should have suggested humor or goodwill, they did not. He blinked. Alexandra waited, looking at his face, and then at Bryce, who sat and stared. She then rose and walked through the room. She went through the apple orchard, through the petals, smelling their odor, the promise of apples, which in the scent of the petals suggested cider. She went through the gate in the stone wall and to the back of the Jeep, where the thing lay, its one visible eye bulging and clear as glass, set on nothing at all, its scales silver and bright in the sunshine that fell through the window of the Jeep, its fins rayed and silky and suggestive of horror. Alexandra carried it back to the house, feeling in her arm, elbow, and hand the hard ringing ache. She brought the fish into the room and stood before Meson with it.

"Fish," said Meson, touching the scales of the thing and satisfying himself it was real and cool from the river. "Well done."

Bryce stood up as though he'd been kicked. Alexandra told me he put his hands together, just at the tips, the fingers trembling. He said, "Ah, the work of Dame Juliana. Tell me, how did you catch it?"

"Method not specified," said Meson.

Xannie took the fish and smiled at it, lifted it until the eyes of the thing were almost opposite his own, even though he had to strain and to use both hands to do so, and then, with his face opposite the head of the fish, he gave it jerk after angry jerk, which made the scales sparkle in the artificial light and in the red glow from the fire.

"I'll put it in the smoker," said Xannie, and carried it out of the room.

When he was gone, Meson said, "Spoken to him previously. Twenty-five thousand for him. Job done. Pleased to have served. Wishes. Regrets as always," and then he walked through the room, shuffling toward the door, his bulk being carefully carried over the space between his ankles. He sniffed the air, and went down the slight grade of the orchard, his feet splayed out and moving faster, since when his speed increased, the size of his steps didn't. The door of the long blue car was already open, and Meson got into it, but just before the door was closed, Meson gestured quickly and said to the chauffeur, "Blossom. Blossom." The driver walked to the orchard, took a blossom from the first tree, and handed it to Meson, who put it in the lapel of his coat, and then the door was closed and soon the car drifted slowly down the road.

The Detective

 It looked as though she had gotten away. There was plenty of money. More money than she could ever know what to do with. There was the house, and Xannie wanted to stay and help. . . . But there's something in all this I've been avoiding. It's the thing that made her vulnerable . . . and it probably came from her being decent, or at least from her desire to face things squarely, head-on. It is the thing that let the liar do his worst. And I still want to avoid it. I can tell you it's better for me to look the other way and to remember the time I climbed the Andes or shot the rapids in a kayak, the water turbulent and screaming, tugging at the shell and the amazing slickness as the boat took a drop and fell into a run, where the river folded smoothly over itself and fell between two rocks. Or I'd like to think about a time in Rio, when I had fallen in love and thought it was possible to die from it.

One thing is certain: I hate lies. I hate them because they steal the world from you. And what fools they make of us all: one day the lie is revealed, and the world appears again, although in a different form . . . you're left with saying, My God, I really believed those things, didn't I? What an easy mark, what a poor boob I was. You sigh. You shake your head. But the truth is, you've started getting old.

And there's something else, too: Bryce didn't know a goddamned thing. He made a lucky guess, that's all. Years later, when he talked about it to me, he said it was a "tidy piece of inductive reasoning."

After Meson left, Bryce sat in the living room with Alexandra. He said, "Of course, everything is for the best this way . . . don't you think? I couldn't be happier for you. How the hell, by the way, did you catch that fish?"

When he spoke, his hands were together, the tips of his fingers shaking against one another. Bryce pushed them together so the shaking stopped, but he kept his eyes on Alexandra. He didn't blink, and went slowly over the features of her face. Alexandra sat on a love seat opposite him, her head back, thinking about going upstairs and running a long, hot bath . . . she imagined the silvery water in the tub, the itch of it against her skin, the slight mist rising into the air, the reassurance of the heat against her. There were still some teacups on the table between her and Bryce.

"A friend helped me," Alexandra said. She spoke slowly, not really looking at him.

"Who?" said Bryce.

"A young man from town," said Alexandra. She sat up then and looked at the dirty teacups, the jumble of them on the table.

She wanted to go upstairs, but she felt ill again, a little dizzy and nauseated. After a while Xannie came into the room and cleared the tea things away, and as he went, carrying the tray, Alexandra said in a quiet voice, "Xannie, could you do me a favor?"

"Yes, sure," said Xannie.

"Could you give me a glass of ice water?"

"Sure," said Xannie, "do you want some chips of ice too? How about a saltine cracker?"

Alexandra nodded.

"Are you feeling ill?" said Bryce.

"A little," said Alexandra.

"Of course," said Bryce, "I can understand."

He looked closely at her though.

"I wonder why Harlow wrote such a thing into his will," said Bryce. "The business about a regular morality. That was . . . well, he was a wonderful man, but don't you think that was a little harsh?"

Alexandra shrugged. Xannie brought the water and crackers into the room. Bryce watched her sip the water and eat the crackers, a small snapping bite of them at a time.

"I guess he was concerned about your having a . . . private life, you know, that you'd see men . . . intimately. But this is the modern age, isn't it?" said Bryce.

"Not around here," said Alexandra. "Excuse me. I'm going upstairs now . . . thanks for coming, but . . ."

She had already begun to stand. That's when Bryce said, "Wait a moment . . ." The house was quiet: it had the peaceful atmosphere that comes when many people have been in a room and have departed, leaving not only silence, but a kind of peace or fatigue, which suggested nothing more would happen for a while. There was the lingering hiss in the fire, the sound of running water, of some small tick as though the house settled under the pressure of another funeral, another year passed. Bryce sat there, looking at her face, her hands as she turned toward the stairs. He looked at the ice, the water, the crackers, at the shape of her, the color of her skin, which was pale, but healthy too: she looked lovely and alive.

Alexandra still faced the stairs: it was almost as though a man in a public library had been saying something rude to her, and she was trying to get away. That's how far Bryce had really drifted in the twenty minutes since Meson had left: she scarcely gave him credit for existing, or existing beyond anything aside from a nuisance. Of course, Harlow had liked the man. She imagined she would have to be polite to him, but nothing more. Harlow had had a use for him, but it had been legal, or ceremonial: she was sure that nothing private, nothing intimate had passed between them, nothing that showed Harlow's affectionate approval of the man.

Bryce said, "I know about the child."

Alexandra turned toward him, moving so quickly that her hair swung out and then fell across her face. Her skin looked as if she'd been slapped. Bryce kept his eyes on her.

"Ah," he said.

"How did you find out?" said Alexandra.

Bryce looked at her, his own eyes wide, his lips parted. There was the sound from the clock on the mantel, the steady ticking and the pendulum rocking inside. Somewhere in the house water was still running, and the cold whine of it seemed just at the edge of the room.

"Harlow told me," he said.

"When?" said Alexandra.

"When I came to visit," said Bryce.

Alexandra stared at him, her color still high. Then she gave up the idea of the long, hot bath, and sat back into a chair opposite Bryce, keeping her eyes on his features, the shape of his ugly brow and nose, the set of his lips. Bryce sat back, too, and sighed.

Outside the window some birds landed on the stone wall, each dipping a tail before flying away again. Alexandra stared at them, seeing the quick movement, the light touch and disappearance of them.

"I'm not sure how to begin," said Bryce.

"How to begin what?" said Alexandra.

"Well, to help you," said Bryce. "You do need help."

"Yes," said Alexandra, "there's no doubt about that."

"I want to be generous," said Bryce, "Harlow would have wanted me to help. That was the point of his . . . well, asking me to look after his affairs. Don't you think?"

She looked out the window. The birds were still coming and going, gray and dark, their feathers seeming dusty and without any shine.

"And I'd like to point out that under the circumstances husbands don't just come out of the woodwork. And if you have the child alone, it will be the child who pays the price. The town looks like it could be pretty unfriendly."

Alexandra laughed a little, although she still looked out the window.

"You could say that," she said. Then she stopped smiling. The laughter hadn't been pleasant.

"You know," said Bryce, "I've watched you since you were

just a kid with long legs. . . . I feel like a member of the family already."

"Already?" said Alexandra.

"Yes," said Bryce. "Don't you think we should get married? I think we could get along."

They sat silently for a while. Alexandra looked at the features of his face, the shape of his lips, the strange blond ugliness of the man. He smiled at her. Alexandra looked away and said, "I don't know. . . ."

Bryce nodded and looked at the floor between his feet. Then he went out the door, not looking over his shoulder. He got into the red Austin-Healey and drove down the road, and as he went he steered with one hand so he could hold his forehead. Alexandra watched from the window.

She spent a few days alone. She took long walks along the river and along the road. She had her lunch in the orchard and went to look for mushrooms, but found few she really knew, and was afraid of eating the others. In the evenings she sat in the living room before the fire and listened to the separate ticks of the clock. Xannie went to bed early, and she did, too, mostly lying awake and staring at the ceiling over her head. A week passed.

One morning she drove through town, passing the dark stains on the milltown buildings, the long, Fu Manchu–mustache shapes that began at the sides of every brick windowsill. Even in the springtime the town still had the atmosphere of wood and coal smoke and soot and the suggestion, just behind the stained brick and blistered windows, of the mechanical and spiritual quality of the nineteenth century. Alexandra sat at a stoplight and saw the hills beyond town, which were gentle, eroded by millions of winters and springs. She drove farther, hearing the putter of Harlow's Jeep, and then stopped in the dusty shoulder of the road next to the yard with the piles of automobiles surrounded by the hurricane fence with barbed wire at the top. There were FOR SALE signs on the fence, and the supports of the sign that had said SHAW'S had been cut through with a chain saw. Alexandra got out of the car and stood next to the new stumps that had white wood where the cuts had been made. She ran her fingers over the splintered, jagged tops of them and then looked down the road, smelling the dust from its shoulder. The FOR SALE signs were about seventy-five feet apart, and Alexandra walked through the dust, hearing her shoes squeak in it. She stood before a sign and looked up. There was some writing on it, too, in a large, sprawling hand, made with a Magic Marker, and it said, "Gone to Oregon." The wind blew through the deserted yard and the fence, too, over Alexandra's hands as she stood with her fingers pushed through the wire diamonds of it. As she stood there, feeling the wire against her hands, she was glad he'd gotten away.

Then she went home and sat in the empty house, hearing the ticking of the clock on the mantel. She felt the damp spring air around her, the lushness of the grass, the lateness of the setting sun. Xannie had gone to town, and there was no other sound, aside from the clock and her own breathing.

In the morning she sent Bryce a telegram, which said, "All right. What terms?"

In the evening she had his reply, which was "I manage three quarters."

"Of what?" she sent back.

"The income."

Alexandra sat with the yellow slip of paper in her hand with the words pasted onto it and felt the silence of the house around her.

"All right," she said, sending her reply that night. "One half."

In the morning she opened the small yellow envelope that came while she was drinking tea, and read, "You're a woman after my own heart."

It was in the winter when Alexandra and I talked about this. She was big then, and when she came to visit, she turned to her side and showed me her hump. What did I think? she said. There was no one around to say, Well, of course you look pretty. I muddled through, stuttered a little . . . it wasn't easy for either one of us. We looked through the infants' catalogues filled with clothes, furniture and toys . . . I had had a child and gave practical advice. There was a mimeographed list of things she should eat, and I had taped it to my icebox. I made her lunch, picking from the cheese, meat, and vegetable groups. She ate slowly, cutting the food into small bites. I filled out the forms from the catalogues. There were times when she sat, her eyes set on the field or the distance beyond. She seemed, for a moment, to be remembering something: she'd jerk her head and flinch, turn to the side exactly as if she'd been stung, then she'd stare through the window of the sunroom, seeing the snow, the smoky wastes of it drifting there, the stone walls showing just a little, the dark stones seeming indifferent and dead in the snow. She closed her eyes, swallowed and then went back to looking at a catalogue, the list of things she was supposed to eat, the pamphlets (the everlasting pamphlets . . . as though life came into being through them). There were times when I stood and looked out the window, unable to take it for a minute, a second more. Once, when I stood with my back to her, looking at the snow, the brilliant bits, each surrounded by a spectral flash, I said (already hating the words as they came out of my mouth), "What is it?" She must have stared at my back as she said, her expression pale and incredulous, "Don't you know? I thought you understood. I was the one who killed Harlow. It's hard to take . . . sometimes. At least he approved of Bryce. That's something, isn't it?"

Soon she got up and went out the door, her figure large under the coat. She went along the stone walls, her feet turned a little to the sides, since she was big enough to go with a splay-footed gait. She carefully avoided those places in the road where she could fall, and there was a slight bounce in the hump she carried. After a while, when her figure disappeared along the walls, I heard the snow blowing along the clapboards and the light tick of it against the window.

BOOK II

My Own Heart

Mad Katherine

So they were married, and after the baby came, a girl who was named Anne, Alexandra dreamed again of Mad Katherine. The river was frozen and Mad Katherine stood on the ice. It must have been twenty below and the sky was the color of tarnished silver. There was no wind and the mist rose from Mad Katherine as she spoke. It's cold. It's cold, she said, but now that we both know some things, I'll show you where I'm hurt. She opened the coat that was made of bear skin and showed the cold silver scars on her chest, and when Mad Katherine touched them, they made a clear, sharp, and beautiful sound. Here is where my daughter was and here the town and here the men, she said, metal is what's left. Isn't the sound beautiful . . . ? It carried on the arctic air. Alexandra touched her own flat stomach and ran a finger over her one scar, the cesarean section out of which Anne had come. Don't you want to come with me? said Mad Katherine. No, no, not now. I need my daughter. And the men. Some man. We'll see, we'll see, said Mad Katherine, trailing skins and bright fishhooks on lines, all of them splayed like strings on a harp.

A Good Quiet Hotel

Bryce and Alexandra were married a week after they sent each other the last telegrams, and it was done quietly at a justice of the peace across the river. It was a moist, cool day in late May and the sky was filled with puffs of clouds that were gray underneath. Bryce wore evening clothes even though they were married at eleven o'clock in the morning. His shirt was too big at the neck and his jacket and pants were baggy and hung as though they were a size too large, which they were, since Bryce had bought them that way: he was gaining weight and thought no one would notice if he wore clothes that didn't fit. He wore a mink bow tie, a large one, and they drove across the river in his red Austin-Healey with the top down and the cold, moist air blowing around them. Alexandra wore a white skirt with a silk blouse and a blue jacket, and in the car she had a scarf tied over her hair. When they were done, Bryce took a bottle of champagne from the ice bucket behind the seat and opened it in the middle of the bridge. He popped the cork over the side of the car and the bridge, too, and he watched the long, curved fall of it until the surface of the river was marked by a ring. He sprayed the windshield with a floppy stream while he watched the cork, and then he drank, letting the champagne

run down his chin and over the mink tie. He offered the bottle
to Alexandra. A car went by and honked as she took a sip and
passed the bottle back.

A truck passed them, blowing its air horn, and Bryce turned
up the bottle.

"We'd better get going," said Alexandra.

"In a minute," he said, turning toward her and offering the
bottle. "As man of the hour, I won't tolerate a long face. I'll
make a toast, don't you think . . . ?"

"Bryce," she said.

"Of course, of course," he said, "I'm just delirious with happiness. But let's not kid ourselves. We are to be congratulated that
we know a marriage is based on a firm understanding of money.
How mature you are. How grand."

He put his hand on her knee, and when he saw her face, he
took his hand away.

"What would you have done without me?" he said.

"There would have been a scandal," she said, "the child
would . . . have paid for it . . ."

"That's right," said Bryce, looking at her, "that's absolutely
correct. Do you think I will have to remind you of that?"

Alexandra shook her head, and Bryce sat with the drops of
champagne quivering from his chin. He took another long
drink and put the car into gear as another truck passed.

"It's just as well," he said, "that we get things clearly established."

They went back to Harlow's house, which was now Alexandra's and which was where she had decided to live: no matter
what the terrors of the town might be, they seemed preferable
to other places. It was home, and Alexandra didn't want to see
any more strangers. She understood the place, knew what was
expected, and that was a comfort. She knew the schools, and as
they drove through the bright green fields, she thought of what
it would be like to teach the child to fish in those same places
where she had learned from Harlow. When Bryce and Alexandra arrived, Xannie had lunch ready for them, and he served it
on a white linen cloth on a table under the apple trees. They ate
cold smoked pheasant, endive salad, and a chocolate souffle.

They sat quietly and at the end, Bryce leaned back, put his foot on another chair, and undid his mink bow tie.

"I know the solemnity of the occasion, if not the magnitude of it, has impressed you. I'm not so bad. I know you are still grieving, so we won't have any celebration. I'll go back to Washington, and I'll move up here slowly," he said, and after he was finished with lunch he bent at the waist, kissed her hand, and then got into his car and drove down the road, leaving Alexandra sitting under the apple trees.

Bryce did move slowly from Washington, and even when he had given up his apartment there, he only spent a night or two a week in Alexandra's house. He had bought a small building in Boston on Beacon Hill and said that he needed a civilized place to attend to "business." When he had come with the first load of his things, tennis rackets, skis, books, and an aquarium, Alexandra had made arrangements at the bank to have his share of her income paid to him directly.

"You are a woman of your word," he said, looking at her, his face frowning a little, his eyes looking at hers. "I'm flattered, of course. You'll learn, too, that I'm not just interested in money."

A few months later, Alexandra received a call from a motel manager about a young woman Bryce had left there. Alexandra was already beginning to be heavy in the stomach. She got into Harlow's Jeep, which was now her car, and drove the thirty-five miles to the motel, which was just off the highway. The motel was a long row of rooms, one next to the other, each covered with a modern pitched roof that had asphalt shingles. The parking lot was empty, and Alexandra went into the one open door, where she found the girl sitting on an unmade bed. She was seventeen, had long dark hair and a dark complexion, and she sat in her underwear and a shirt that was buttoned through the wrong holes. Alexandra paid the bill at the motel and drove the girl to the bus station and bought her a ticket home (to Manchester, New Hampshire). She gave the girl a hundred dollars, and as the girl stood at the entrance to the bus, carrying her backpack, she said, "The man wasn't a liar. He just said black was white."

When Alexandra mentioned the call to Bryce, not wanting an explanation, but telling him about it if only because she saw no reason to lie to him about his own actions, he said, "You know, she was one of these girls at the side of the road in blue jeans who obviously needed a meal and a place to stay. Can you believe that she was hitchhiking? Who knows what kind of person would have picked her up? But what gets me is that people call me about her, as though my generosity is boundless or that I had adopted the poor creature."

Bryce was in Boston when Alexandra went into labor. It was January and it was cold and snowing. When the contractions began to come regularly, she called Xannie and they took the bags they had packed weeks before and got into Harlow's Jeep. Xannie's was a round duffel bag from L.L. Bean and Alexandra's was an old leather one of Harlow's. They went down to the car slowly, Xannie behind her, both of them feeling the light, cold bites of the snow, although neither said a word about it. Alexandra told me the roads hadn't been plowed, but the Jeep had four-wheel drive. The contractions weren't that close together. Fourteen minutes. As she went through the drifts across the road and the piles of new snow, she wasn't thinking about the weather. She was terrified of being torn open, and that somehow the ordinary, trusting world would desert her. It was strange to feel deserted, she said.

It began to snow harder. It was a light, dry snow, and it piled up: the edges of everything, the fences, barns, signs, cars, brush, and woods became soft and indistinct. It was impossible to tell where the road ended and the shoulder or ditch began. Alexandra drove slowly, feeling disoriented and dizzy, and soon the Jeep was beyond the shoulder. It turned to one side and slipped into a drift.

Xannie got out and began to push the snow away from the tires. There was a snow shovel in the back of the Jeep, and Alexandra got out and worked too, feeling the snow around her legs, under the maternity dress. For a moment both of them stopped, Xannie looking up, his eyes wide, Alexandra holding the shovel. When she told me about this, she kept her eyes on mine, and she said that what passed between the two of them as they stood in the snow was a kind of terror, since in that moment they knew that if they couldn't get the Jeep back on the road, they'd have the child in the back of it. Xannie said, as the snow moved around them, that he'd helped other women. In his village, in Malaysia, there were no doctors or hospitals. And then, said Alexandra, as she stood in the snow she felt their isolation, the distance to anyplace where there would be help. The wind blew. The snow made a sandy rush against the car. And Alexandra could feel the power of the child, of the birth, and she knew that if she had to, she'd do it alone, squatting in the snow. Somehow she was relieved, although more terrified than ever for the child. There was some wind and the snow came in straight, fuzzy lines, and in the headlights they looked like the marks a glass-cutter makes on glass. Alexandra stood, knee-deep in the stuff, holding a shovel. Her waters broke then, and she felt the warm tickle as it ran down the inside of her legs. She lifted her skirt and saw the silvery fluid run down her knee and into the top of her long socks. The contractions became more painful. Xannie dug out the winch at the front of the Jeep and wrapped the cable around a tree on the other side of the road. Soon they were both back in the cab, going toward Boston, neither saying a word about what had happened, although once, as Xannie sat with the watch, his teeth began to rattle and he started shivering, too, as though with tremors of birth.

In Massachusetts, Xannie said, "You should be having another about now," but Alexandra had already had the sense of a belt tightening around the large frontal hump she carried. They talked about names, and Xannie said he thought it should be called Harlow if it was a boy. And when Alexandra woke from the anesthetic, feeling the sores in her mouth and the stitches in the cesarean section, she asked about the child and was told it was a baby girl. She decided to call it Anne, in honor of Alexandra's mother.

On the few days a week that Bryce was in Alexandra's house, he helped with Anne. He didn't walk the floors when she was sick with fever and crying and vomiting, but when she was older, he read Shakespeare to her, acting out the parts before the fireplace, walking back and forth with the book open. He went to the school shows and took photographs, taught her to play Chinese checkers, and chess, went to the hospital when she broke a leg (and drew a large picture of Bugs Bunny on her cast), brought her jeans, tennis (and then running) shoes from Boston, made sure there were pretty dresses, and coached her for her College Boards.

When Bryce came from Boston, he was full of gossip and stories, and he mimicked the roles in the latest movies he had seen. He especially liked to do imitations of Barbra Streisand (the songs, too), and when Alexandra and Anne saw in the paper or a magazine that there was a new Barbra Streisand movie, they waited for Bryce and then laughed until each of them felt the muscles in her stomach burn. Bryce bought a dog, a poodle, that he left in Alexandra's house. The dog had a "lion cut," and whenever the dog saw Bryce, it bit him. Bryce called such behavior "the hallmark of the breed" and then had the dog put "to sleep." The UPS truck was always coming up the road, and when Anne or Alexandra unwrapped a present, they found parasols with wide lace at the edges, new electronic games from Japan, a boom-box (a two-foot by three-foot radio that was to be carried in the street), an inflatable rubber boat, and an ant colony. Bryce was good at managing his financial affairs, if only because he kept his connections in Washington and once made (as he said) a "bundle" on the advance information of which particular drug company was going to be licensed by the FDA to test a cure for cancer. He *could* give good advice, especially as to what people needed or wanted, and was entertaining. Alexandra found there were times when she looked forward to his visits.

One evening when Anne was six, Bryce was home. It was fall, and Bryce never missed the leaves when they were at their brightest. Anne played on the floor in front of the fireplace and Bryce watched her closely. The firelight was reflected in the child's eyes and on her blondish, almost ashy hair, and Bryce sat with his face set in a long, faintly jowled expression. After Anne went upstairs (not being allowed to leave the room until she gave Bryce a kiss), he said, "It would be terrible, wouldn't it, if Anne ever found out I'm not her father. You know, she'd never trust you about anything, or anything about you. Who knows what lies she'd suspect you of having told, or what stories she'd believe about you? Of course, you can count on me to say nothing. I know you'd never give me reason to say anything, would you? For instance, you'd never think of divorcing me, would you?"

"If I did," said Alexandra, "it wouldn't change your receiving half of the money. You wouldn't have that taken away."

"No," said Bryce, "that's not what I asked."

They sat opposite one another, Bryce's bluish eyes set on hers, his brow wrinkled and raised, his lips set in a straight line. The coals collapsed in the fire.

"No," said Alexandra, "especially not if you'd consider that a reason to tell Anne."

"Me?" said Bryce, still looking at her, although pouting, turning down his lips and looking at her from under his brows. "I don't understand how you could say such a thing to me. Sometimes I think you don't understand me. I think it would be a tragedy, an absolute tragedy if word should somehow leak out."

"I'll give you no cause," said Alexandra.

"There's no need to speak this way," said Bryce, "no need to be so intense. I was speaking in a merely abstract sense."

When Alexandra told me this, I sat opposite her, hearing that flat, faintly breathy voice, speaking as though the words meant nothing at all. The difficulty was that Bryce wouldn't woo her, wouldn't make any attempt to win her over. There wasn't any need for brutality. She was grateful, in a way, that Bryce was available and that he hadn't done anything worse than threatening her. That's what Bryce was condemned to. He knew that if "word leaked out," he'd be packing his bags. So he was trapped, too, and there were times when Alexandra felt sorry for him. She said he never really thought he could ask for what he wanted. He was forever trying to get things without asking. He never wanted to be seen as having a desire or a need. Wouldn't someone just use it against him? Well, that was a pretty hell. No, he wouldn't woo her, and what do you do if you can't use the threats you have? Why, you come up with new ones. Even I could see that early on. So Alexandra came to visit and we talked, and then a week or two would go by, and I'd find myself waking, early in the morning, when the light was blue, and then I'd sit at the side of my bed, wondering what he'd do, what trap he'd set.

Of course, he came sniffing around here, inviting himself in to see me, trying to find out if I knew he was blackmailing her. So, I'd sit opposite him, not giving away a thing. That was always my terror: that I'd say something. And if I ever did, I'd only betray Alexandra and give him more reason to hurt her. So he sat in my house, drinking my liquor, and we had our friendly, neighborly chats about the weather, about men's fashions, politics, movies . . . the usual civilized blab.

It was at this time, when Anne was six, that Alexandra took a trip to New York. She was twenty-six years old, and she was thin and tall and her hair was streaked by the sun. Her clothes came from Paris, and when she walked into a room there was about her tallish good looks an aura of severe restraint: these occasions, when the men and women in a room turned toward her and then looked away because they were touched or intimidated, took place in Boston, where Alexandra went when she was invited to weddings and christenings. Mostly, she lived alone in Harlow's house, saw old friends, took care of Anne, paid the bills, and looked after her financial affairs. When the boxes came with the smallish underthings and the clothes from Paris, Alexandra waited until Bryce had spent his day or two in the house and returned to Boston. Then she went upstairs, and after Xannie was asleep and Anne was in bed and sleeping too, Alexandra ran a hot bath. She did this in the wintertime especially, since there was so little to do in the evenings. She ran the water until it was hot and put bath salts in it and then undressed and got into the tub, feeling the sting and itch of the water, the heat of it, which, after a while, made her feel as though her skin had disappeared. She sat in the water, feeling the salty curl of perspiration on her upper lip and forehead, the tickle of it along her neck, and imagining the dry, cold arctic night outside, the stars there against the dark, the trees creaking in the cold. She added more hot water, felt the creeping warmth around her legs: there were mirrors in the bathroom, and she put her head back, seeing the mist rise and obscure the image of herself as she put her calves and ankles out of the hot water and pushed her head against the rim of the tub. Then she toweled herself and put on a robe and went down the hall, feeling the cold slap of the air there, and then went into her room, where she unwrapped the packages and opened the boxes and spread the things on the bed. She held them up and spread the skirts against her knees, picking up one thing and then another, touching the cloth, draping it across her legs. She dropped the towel and stood before the mirror, then pulled on the brownish and lace-edged underthings, feeling the new, slick band over her shoulders. She sat before her mirror, put red, wettish-looking lipstick on, brushed out her hair, and put on the clinging clothes in their muted colors: gray the color of the underside of clouds, yellows, burgundies, browns like cinnamon.

She had shoes sent to her as well, and after putting on stockings, she tried them, too, the muscles in the calf of her leg defined as she slipped her feet into shoes that didn't weigh more than a few ounces. Then she walked back and forth in front of the mirror, before cleaning up the room, hanging up the things she had tried on, and then, still dressed, going downstairs, where she sat before the windows in the living room and looked outside into the orchard white with frost or later, deep in snow. She had a glass or two of good brandy and smoked a long cigarette, turning her head to one side when she exhaled. She wrote letters she never mailed.

She went upstairs, stopped in Anne's room, and sat on her bed. She put her hand on the child, touched her through the comforter, and for a moment it seemed Alexandra had been out for the evening to a party where she had drunk champagne, and smoked and stood talking to men in evening clothes, and that now, tired and satisfied, she had come home, climbed the stairs, feeling their height, and checked on her daughter. It was cool in the child's room, and Alexandra sat, feeling the girl's deep sleep, the flesh that was collapsed and numb with resting. She waited, not wanting to go back into the hall, where it would be clear she had been no place and had not said a word that evening.

Alexandra didn't dress in the new clothes that often, and in the morning she woke and looked out the window, hearing Anne already coming down the hall to slide under the covers with her. And on these occasions, Anne said, "You smell funny, Mom. Mom. What's that smell?"

Alexandra looked out at the gray trees or the snowy landscape and said, "That's what perfume smells like."

She sat with the child under her arm and with her head against the pillow she had propped up so she could see outside (in the winters doing this so that she and the child could watch the dawn, the reddish light that seemed as though it were mist). Alexandra remembered the texture of the clothes and the words of the letters she had written the night before, and although she felt the coldness of the rooms more keenly after a night of dressing up, it seemed to her that it wasn't so bad after all, if only because she wasn't withdrawing from the world so much as trying to stay alive enough for it not to leave her completely behind.

After these evenings, Alexandra cleaned the house, polished the woodwork and the furniture, scrubbed the bathroom, polished silver, and brought, from town, cut flowers to put into vases, and all the time she did these things, the cleaning and polishing, she stopped and looked out the window and felt cold and awkward.

She told me about the evenings she spent, and she spoke about them in that same uninflected voice. There wasn't much she kept from me. If nothing else, I have always been a good listener. She told me that on those days when she stopped and looked out the window, she remembered the evening before, the illusive promise there was in *getting ready* for something. She could suspend judgment, it seemed, was able to tell herself there was some relief, some way of letting the pressure flow out of her, and that it was coming up shortly. She only had to wait. She didn't smile when she said this . . . her face was angry and white. But she was willing to live that way, to go on endlessly anticipating something that she'd never let happen, if she thought the child was protected. And, she told me, she'd done a pretty good job of that. Anne was growing up beautifully. Hadn't I seen the child with my own eyes? Just looking at her gave Alexandra a sense of correctness, of certainty. So she continued with those evenings, in which, more than she could ever admit, she was endlessly making herself a promise and endlessly breaking it. She thought she'd be able to go on forever, that her resilience was infinite, that she'd be able to make do with the odd imitation of life and that it would never drive her crazy. Where the child was concerned, where continuing, day by day, was concerned, she thought there was no limit to the extent she could live with anticipation. She couldn't see how dangerous this was, not even when the signs were on her, when, after one of these evenings she'd stop in the middle of the next day and put her head down on a table, feeling the cool, waxy surface, her hair splayed out on the polished wood.

One evening, when Alexandra was dressed up and sitting downstairs, Bryce drove up to the house. He had forgotten some papers and had come back to get them. Alexandra ripped up the letter she was writing, but she still sat by the fire and drank her brandy when Bryce came into the room.

"Are you going out?" said Bryce, standing in his coat with the outdoor air curling around him. It blew across the new silk clothes that Alexandra wore.

"No," said Alexandra. "Some new clothes came and I thought I'd try them on."

"They look nice," said Bryce.

He sat down opposite her, still wearing his overcoat with the fur collar that started at his belt. He wrinkled his brow and stared at her.

"We have no reason to lie," he said. "Are you going out?"

"No," said Alexandra.

"I, of course, would never hold it against you if you did," said Bryce. "You could never think such a thing, could you?"

"I wasn't going anywhere," said Alexandra. "I told you I'd give you no cause to tell Anne anything or to be displeased."

Bryce stared at her and sighed, and then he wrinkled his brow and put his head back.

"You know," he said, "I think you should get away. I really do. It will be good for you. I'm big enough to admit you might not want *my* company." He stopped for a moment and raised a brow. "So I think you should go by yourself. New York. You could go out to dinner. Aren't there still friends of Harlow's there? Or your own?"

"No," said Alexandra, "I know almost no one there."

"Good," said Bryce, "it will be an adventure, then."

They didn't say anything more about it, at least not that night. Bryce looked at her, and sat in his coat. After a while he got up and took it off, but even as he opened the closet in the hall to hang it up, he turned and looked over his shoulder, his face and thin blond hair set against the white walls. Alexandra sat in the living room, before the fireplace. Bryce watched her, and stayed up late, something he didn't usually do. She didn't use the telephone and no one called. No one arrived at the house, and when Alexandra went to bed, Bryce sat up for a while, sitting with his elbows on his knees, the tips of his fingers pushed together, his lips pursed and his brow wrinkled. When Alexandra hesitated on the stair that squeaked, it made a low moan.

Bryce came to see me, smiled, and asked if I'd noticed anything different about Alexandra. Did I think she was hiding anything? Did I think she was capable of betraying him?

Anyway, the day after he had found Alexandra dressed, Bryce insisted that she take a trip. It would give her time to think. He said he thought it would do some good and take a little of the pressure off. So, three weeks later, Alexandra went to New York.

She was able to leave Anne with Xannie, and then, in the morning before driving to the train station, she took a long, hot bath, although when she stretched out her legs and put her arms behind her head she had trouble taking those long, even breaths she had enjoyed in the middle of winter. Now the water seemed hot and the salty tickle of perspiration made her want to turn or to rinse her face, and she felt a slight quiver of a muscle in her thigh. The house was quiet, and the only noise was that of the water in the tub, which made a plash as she turned and slowly washed. Then she dressed and got her things into a new leather bag, and carried it to the car for the long trip to the train station.

She wore a light gray skirt and jacket, a white blouse, and she walked up and down the platform slowly with her coat unbuttoned and blowing open like wings. There were people who turned and looked at her, but only from the side, and when she wasn't able to see them. It was a cloudy, coolish day, and the leaves were blowing along the platform. When the train came, Alexandra found herself standing close to the tracks. She felt the air on her cheeks and the dampness of the steam that leaked from the train, and smelled its swampy odor, too. She got onto the train and took a seat next to the window.

The train ran along the river. It was wide and still, silky gray from the sky. The hillside on the far shore was covered, as the train went farther south, with trees that were still bright, having almost Mediterranean colors, soft pastels, oranges, pinks, marked regularly by the browns and blacks of the telephone poles that went by in a not quite solid flash. Alexandra had a book, but it sat on the empty seat next to her while she watched the far shore and the water. She put her fingers to the dirty glass of the train, and then took her hands away. She looked at her whitish fingerprints there against the land and the water as she waited for the train to pull through the dark space of Grand Central station. She got out there, carrying her one smallish suitcase, and went along the cement platform, going slowly, feeling the air hum with the engines, and lingering in the expectant sound. She had waited until most of the passengers got off the train, and then walked along the platform almost by herself, going slowly and putting one foot down in front of the other.

While she went, smelling the air that seemed to be filled with ozone and particles of metal, she saw the long, narrowing platform ahead of her and the stairs that rose into the noise and light of the station. She held her bag in one hand, and swung it back and forth a little. She still breathed irregularly, although she was able to keep her face set in a cool and even expression. While she went she was glad there were no other people on the platform, although when she was about halfway to the stairs, she heard a noise, the sound of a step behind her.

For a few moments she continued, walking a straight line and feeling herself under her clothes in the dark and smoky space, but as she went it seemed to her that the steps behind her were coming in time to her own. She breathed deeply, not being afraid, but more expectant, or concerned not about being robbed as something else: some brief, half-formed idea of an encounter, however awkward or inconsequential. She continued, and as she went the footsteps came more definitely in the pattern of her own, and it seemed to her that the cadence was more one of following or of stalking than the unconcerned gait of someone who was trying to get to the stairs. She walked a few steps more, then stopped and turned. There was a man behind her, in his late thirties, dressed in a leather jacket and gray pants and a turtleneck sweater. He was looking at some papers in one hand and carrying a leather bag. He looked up when she turned. He smiled and then went on, walking quickly into the yellowish light of the station. Alexandra blushed, and felt the heat in her cheeks. She climbed the stairs and came into the open noise and light.

Alexandra stayed at a hotel on Fifth Avenue, just up from the south side of the park. It was a good hotel with light, airy movement downstairs and the hush of coming and going of people around the desk. When Alexandra arrived, it was late in the afternoon, and when she was left in her room, she sat on the double bed and looked out the window at the park and the buildings on the other side. The room seemed quiet, so much so as to press against her, and then she took a bath, again unable to sit in it, and dressed, finding that as she used a brush or comb or as she tried to hang her clothes, she dropped things. In the moment, aside from the sense of being someplace strange, she couldn't have said why she was having difficulty.

The hotel had a bar downstairs. Its windows were tinted glass and the ceilings seemed low. It was a black bar and black tables, and it was usually crowded, but when Alexandra went into it, there were still some tables by the window, and she took one. She had a brandy, and carefully raised the glass to her lips. It was such a place she had thought of in those evenings in New England, and now that she was here, there seemed to be something wrong, as though she were having a dream in which she was supposed to say something but didn't know what it was. She smoked a cigarette, and drank brandy, and it seemed to her that across the room, sitting with a woman who was dressed in black and whose hair was red, there was the man who had walked behind her in the station, although she dismissed this, and had another brandy, blushing at her thoughts in that subdued and excited room. For a moment as she sat there, dressed so carefully and seeming so handsome and yet not fitting at all, she felt her hands moving along the table and the almost physical sense of panic on her face, but she sat, looking coolly at the dark mirrors beyond the bar, pretending the man she waited for was not only a little boring but unable to get anyplace on time, too. She had another brandy, and the waiter brought it and took away the ashtray where she left the long ends of cigarettes. Finally, when she realized she was too lonely to eat in public, she went to her room and ate there. She had a bottle of champagne and looked out the window, and then went to bed early.

She walked as much as she could the next day. It was a high, clear day with the winds New York has in the fall. Alexandra went through the park, the museums, Sotheby's, where she held a vase that was a thousand years old, and as she touched the thing she felt the desire to take it and smash it on the floor. She didn't, though. She put it down carefully, hearing the bottom of the thing make a small click against the wood of the stand where it usually sat. Then she went on with her walk. She stopped in a bar in the Village in the afternoon, and had a drink, but no one spoke to her, and she took a cab to the hotel.

She went to the theater and while she stood among the people in the lobby and as she smelled the perfume, the smoke of cigarettes, and heard the quick conversations and laughter, she thought of the winter nights when she looked out the window. For a moment she was terrified, since there came over her skin the almost tactile certainty that if she disappeared, no one in the room would notice. She stood and smoked a cigarette, holding it carefully, touching the end with her thumb. The cars outside went by in the purplish light and the people behind her continued to speak, to laugh, and she waited, rocking one foot back and forth, rolling it slightly back on its heel. She heard, as she waited with the cigarette, someone say, "Really, I have much more than I can use . . ." The tone was one of being overwhelmed, or bored, and Alexandra listened, but she kept her face toward the street and the purplish light there.

In the morning she took an early train, and then drove from the station. Anne was at home, waiting for her, and Bryce was there, too. Anne ran out, through the leaves in front of the house, and Alexandra bent down. Anne's busy pressure, her moving hands, touched Alexandra as the child said, "What did you do? Mom. Mom, what did you do?"

"I had a wonderful time," said Alexandra.

"What did you do?" said Anne.

"Oh," said Alexandra, "I saw some things . . ."

"What things, Mom?" said Anne.

"I saw a vase that was a thousand years old," said Alexandra.

"A thousand years?" said Anne.

Bryce stepped down from the doorway and stood in the leaves. A breeze blew around him, made the long strands of blond hair move gently.

"I'm glad you had a good time," said Bryce. "Of course, I never thought you'd have less."

Alexandra picked up her bag and went into the house, and when she'd put it down, she picked up Anne and said, "My God, I missed you."

Bryce watched her, and then went into his study, where he had his papers spread on a desk.

In two weeks, though, Alexandra returned to the city. In the days that passed while she was home, she dwelt on the silence in the room at the hotel, the possibility it suggested, and while she sat at night, after Anne had gone to sleep and Xannie was in his room, she thought of the trembling of her fingers when she held the vase, or of the shaking quality there had been in her legs as she went along the hard pavement of the city. She lingered over the memory of the vibration of the train as it came into the high, indifferent station, and she remembered the hotel bar, the people there and the possibilities they implied, and her own keen edge as she had pretended she wasn't watching them. So, Alexandra had said to Bryce she was going back, and he had nodded and smiled, saying, "You see, it does do some good, doesn't it?"

On the way back to the city, Alexandra sat by the window of the train, and watched the smooth, stretched surface of the river, and the reflection of the trees, which were now without leaves and had a gray, clawed quality against the sky. She had a book with her and this time she forced her eyes to move across the lines, although she didn't see more than every third or fourth word. Her hands felt stiff as she held the book and her thighs and calves ached with the sitting in the seat, and when the train came to Grand Central, she sat, looking out into the gloom, the darkish, dusty space lighted here and there by a dim bulb, but she didn't move, didn't give her legs relief until everyone, it seemed, had walked off the train. Then she went sedately, or seemingly so, down the platform, feeling the hardness of the concrete. The air above her had a grayish cast against the dark ceiling and the station itself seemed distant, golden, filled with people. There seemed, too, that someone was with her, or almost, and Alexandra heard again the harsh, regular cadence of the footsteps, but this time, even though she found herself thinking of . . . someplace, a corner in the darkness, in the throbbing vibration of the engines of the trains, where she could half stand, where she would . . . be able . . . to reach out freely, where it would all happen so quickly in the smoky air. She shook her head and blushed so hard that there were tears in her eyes, and as she came to the stairs to the station, the man who was behind her passed, and when she glanced quickly at him, she saw that he was wearing a pair of pleated gray pants and a well-made European leather jacket. She didn't see him that well, but she thought it was the same man who had been on the train with her the previous visit. She came into the station and felt the flutter of people around her. For a moment she stopped and put a hand to her forehead and then her lips, but she stopped that, and picked up her bag again and walked through the almost roaring quality of the station.

At the hotel she sat in her room with her bag at her feet, and then, when the silence of the room seemed to touch her skin and made her try to squirm away from it, she went downstairs and into the bar, already feeling, as she walked across the room, that same panic and disorder from knowing she could disappear and leave not so much as a raised brow.

She sat down and ordered a brandy, and, at the table next to her, there was the man who had been on the train, who had been behind her both times when she walked toward the lighted station, and, later, when she was stretched out with her head on a pillow and her eyes closed, she still heard the resonance or echo or a kind of lingering hum of his voice as he sat in the bar and returned her hurried glance and smiled and said, "Well . . . ?" Alexandra heard the sound of the taxis in the street as she lay, curled next to him in her room, smelling the cut flowers and hearing his regular breathing, and then the powdery, dry sense of the skin on her own back as she put a hand on his chest and . . . pulled him . . . hearing, in the hall as she did so, the long, gentle but unstoppable roll of the wheeled room-service table, which was covered with a heavy linen cloth and had a large silver food cover where the lights and ceiling of the hall moved in fish-eye distortion. Alexandra heard, too, the black shoes of the man who hurried with the cart, the steady pat of them as he went down the hall, the ice tinkling in the water glasses and the silver jarring against the china plates.

They had food from room service, and Alexandra waited in the bathroom while it was rolled in. They ate smoked trout and champagne and Alexandra sat with just the heavy napkin in her lap, feeling the starched tickle of it and hearing, below, the honk of the taxicabs.

The silence still seemed to linger in the room, even though he was there. They didn't spend that much time sitting opposite one another, talking, although Alexandra liked the feeling of the napkin and the tickle of champagne. He said he was a photographer, and Alexandra nodded, only saying about herself that she lived in New England. The man asked about the cesarean scar, touched it . . . with his tongue as they sat back on the sheets.

They didn't leave the hotel for the three days of her visit, and Alexandra was only alone on those occasions when the man walked down to his room to get something, a toothbrush or a new, crisp shirt, and when he was gone Alexandra realized that she wasn't aware of any feeling aside from the warmth and buzzing sense of isolation that came from living, for a short time, without restraint. She bathed, and they ate lunch together and drank brandy, and then there were times when she found that she was able . . . to hear the sounds of the street and the hotel again. There were times, too, when the stillness and the intensity dissolved into laughter. They teased one another. There was a time in the midst of the teasing and laughter (which verged on the hysterical) when the photographer went to his room and brought back a camera. It was a Polaroid and he said Polaroid had asked him to do some advertisements, that they had given him thousands of exposures. Alexandra took the

camera and began taking pictures of him . . . some, or all,
coming out ridiculously, so much so that she began to laugh
when the figure emerged from the dark emulsion, although,
when she stopped laughing, and when he napped, Alexandra
looked over the side of the bed to where the photographs were
scattered on the floor, and there she saw through the mild,
warm light of the gauzy curtains the lines of his chest, the shape
of his arms, the bright, slick skin, the man's grinning, embarrassed, bewildered expression. Alexandra stared at the lines of
him on the photographs and kept her foot against his hip. She
put her hands behind her head, arched her back and saw the
smooth white ceiling and listened to his breathing, knowing
that soon he would . . . wake, and they would begin. There
were times when Alexandra's laughter became tears and laughter again without even her knowledge that the change had come
and gone, and when her stomach ached with the work of it, the
man took the camera and began to take pictures of her, and she
posed for him, turning, rearranging herself on the sheets. She
heard the click and whine of the camera, and then reached for
the bottle of champagne in the cooler, took from it an ice cube
and pushed her lips and tongue . . . against it. The photographer drank champagne, too, and stood before her, still laughing.
He had a tripod for the camera and a timer. They posed together and more than posed, hearing, in the distance the slip
and whine of the camera. Alexandra took her scanty things . . .
dressed in them, undressed. Alexandra thought of the room as
hidden, somehow slipped between the others in the hotel, and
not even having so much as a number. They drank more champagne, and continued, Alexandra feeling, once, over her wrists
and ankles tight knots and hearing the camera click and whine,
and then demanding the thing herself so that she could arrange
herself with the man in ways . . . that suited.

They drank more and went to sleep, waking on the morning
of the day that Alexandra was going to return, and as she
opened her eyes to that same gauzy light and heard the breathing of the man next to her, she looked over the side of the bed at
the pictures there . . . her dress pulled up, bunched around
her hips, legs long and taut . . . her head back, long neck exposed as she knelt . . . the dimples on her back, the smooth

skin there as she looked over her shoulder, her tongue almost touching the green champagne bottle . . . In others there were the two of them when they were no longer concerned about the camera or playing any games.

She sat up and felt the weight of her hangover. When the man awoke, he ordered a bottle of champagne, which he drank. Alexandra drank black coffee, then took a long bath, washing her arms and legs, going over them and her back, her neck, looking for any mark, and, to her surprise, finding none. When she had dressed in the skirt and jacket that were gray as the undersides of clouds, and when she stood in the room smelling fresh and clean and with her clothes neatly arranged, she saw that the man had gone. There were still some photographs on the floor. Alexandra cleaned them up, put them in the trash, feeling the quaking shame of the alcohol, but nevertheless taking one or two and putting them in her bag, shaking her head, putting her hand to her face and blushing. The man came back before she left, and they exchanged addresses. He smiled, kissed her, and then she took her bag and went downstairs.

On the train, she stared out the window, keeping her face without expression, although the day was cool and the river looked cold, and Alexandra wanted to lean her head against the glass, or to put her hand against it. The feeling of the train, the vibration of it and the swaying as it went around a turn in the river, made her put her head back, feeling the alcohol, but remembering the room, too, the silence of it as distinctly as those nights after a day's sailing, when she had been in bed and unable to sleep because of the sense of the pounding of the boat's hull. She felt ill and when she opened her eyes she stared at the river, hoping it would make her feel a little more steady and that the pressure in her head and the sense of weight in her chest would go away. There was, beneath her scrubbed and carefully dressed appearance, the desire to laugh, or to at least giggle, and mixed with it so perfectly as to be indistinguishable, there was a desire to cry, too, the two forming a high, strangely exultant state. Through it all, she found herself saying, Thank God. Thank God. And even then, she said to herself that she'd only see the man one more time, only one, and just as a curiosity. . . . Then the train went around another long, gentle curve, which made Alexandra close her eyes and feel the presence of the room again.

When the train was almost to her station and Alexandra was staring across the river at the hillsides, which were humped and looked like three or four buffalos, one standing just next to another, it didn't seem as though she could disappear so easily or that if she did, no one would notice. She put her hand to her face and blushed again, amazed, really about how she had spent the time, but underneath it being strangely proud, and drawn to it, if only because of the violation of the thing, the intensity and the danger. She told herself it probably wouldn't happen again.

She drove through the mountains and opened the window, glad for the air with the hint of rain and snow, too. She drove slowly, wondering if she had been changed, but as the car went down into the valley, she was surprised to decide that she hadn't been, if only because the man hadn't mattered: the intensity and the danger had, and they came from something that had nothing to do with him.

She stopped in front of the house, and found Anne waiting. She ran to the car, demanding a present and being glad for the soap, the shoe-polishing rag, and other things that Alexandra had brought from the hotel. They went inside, and Alexandra sat with the busy, squirmy presence of her daughter while they watched the fire in the fireplace, and Anne said, "What did you do, Mom? What did you do?"

"I missed you," said Alexandra. "What else could I have done?"

"What about the old vase?" said Anne.

"No," said Alexandra, "I didn't see the old vase."

"What would happen if you'd broke the vase?" said Anne.

"They'd make me pay for it," said Alexandra, her hand touching Anne's head.

She was shocked by what had happened, and she came to see me. It was a late fall day, filled with the softest light imaginable. The leaves had blown away, but in the afternoon the light lingered, and everything, the tree in front of my house, the stone walls, the fields, had a lingering afterglow. Alexandra came down the road, and I saw her walking through the after-

noon light. Then she came in and sat down. She asked for a cup
of tea, and I gave her one. She told me she hadn't really liked
the man, that she was amazed by the entire thing. I raised an
eyebrow, since I was surprised. Hadn't she spent those evenings
waiting, pretending something was about to happen? Well, still,
she was surprised, and maybe a little afraid it would get out of
hand. She was worried what would happen if Bryce found out.
I was, too, for that matter. What innocents we were. And at the
time I was in my fifties, and let me tell you, I'd seen a little of
the world. Before we changed the subject, before we went on
about my cooking, my dog, the work I still did, she took from
her pocket one of those Polaroid pictures. She held her hand
over most of it, but she let me see her face. The expression there
was what fascinated me, since the face was one of a pretty
woman who had been living in hell and for one minute found
herself in the upper world, on a road in front of my house, say,
where she could take a long, deep breath of the fall air. Then
she threw the picture into the fire. I got up and made myself a
brandy and then we had our usual talk, chitchat really, about
my dog and why he wasn't any good on grouse. Well, I had my
theories. Soon, she got up to leave, and I watched her going
along the road, her figure becoming smaller as she hugged herself into her jacket and bent a little into the wind, and even
from where I stood, it looked as though she breathed deeply and
enjoyed the feeling of it against her face.

Bryce visited the next weekend. After he had gone for a walk
on Friday afternoon, he sat in Alexandra's living room. Anne
was upstairs and Xannie was outside. Anne had been playing on
the floor, and her toys, plastic bricks, paper and crayons, were
lying there. Bryce drank a glass of Swan beer, and said, "Anne
is so lovely."

"Yes," said Alexandra, "and growing up, too. So fast."

"Of course, I'd like to protect her," said Bryce.

"What does she need to be protected from?" said Alexandra.
"It's safe here. Her school is good. She's healthy."

"Oh, I wasn't thinking of measles, or anything so mundane as
that," said Bryce. "You manage these things so well, I never
have to worry."

"Well?" said Alexandra.

Alexandra sat in a wing chair, her shoulders curved a little as
she leaned back, her wrists and fingers hanging over the chair's
arms. She was wearing a blouse with an open neck, and her
collarbones were defined in her slouch, her relaxed sitting before the fire. She looked toward Bryce, who was sitting back on
the love seat. He had furrowed his brow, too, and it appeared as
though he were uncomfortable, or that he was about to bring
up a subject he had no taste for. Alexandra sat for a moment,
watching him, and then her hands stopped being languid. She
pulled them into her lap, sat up with her shoulders square, her
back straight, and her longish neck rising from the blouse she
wore. Some strands of her hair had fallen around the side of her
face, and as she looked at Bryce she pushed them behind her
ear, touching her face with her fingers as she did so.

"You know the last thing I want is to alarm you," said Bryce.
"I really want your life to run smoothly and comfortably, and
for you not to do anything to hurt Anne. She needs a stable life,
don't you think?"

"Yes," said Alexandra.

"I knew you'd think that way," said Bryce, "but you are im-
pulsive. Who knows? You might, in some moment of impulse,
decide to get a divorce. I'm sure it might pass your mind, and
you'd not have . . . well, the time to know what a really horrible mistake that would be. I'm speaking for Anne's sake, of
course. But, as I'm sure you'll admit, it would be horrible,
wouldn't it?"

"We've talked about this before," said Alexandra.

"Yes, I know," said Bryce, "I'm never able to realize that
things don't change. Have you seen these?"

Bryce was wearing a sport coat made from Irish tweed and it
was gray and light blue, heavy, filled with lanolin. The pockets
were large, big enough to put a book into. He looked away from
Alexandra, toward the chest in front of him, and with that air of
duty and responsibility and being in a position that was forced
upon him, Bryce reached into the pocket of the coat and took
from it a pile of Polaroid photographs. They were held together
with a rubber band, and Bryce picked at it for a moment and
then pulled hard and broke it. The photographs spilled from his
hands onto the chest, and as they sat there before the fire, and

with Bryce looking at Alexandra from under his brows, she saw
the small squares, and the things that were on them. She
reached forward with one finger, touching one and then another, pushing them for the briefest moment, her finger trembling as she did so, until the pictures were square, one next to
another. She saw her own face looking toward the camera, her
lips stretched over her teeth, her eyes looking down the middle
of the lens . . . While she looked at Bryce, her finger wandered
from one of the photographs to another, touching them, but she
didn't look down at them anymore and kept her eyes on his.
After a while, Bryce looked away, and then, in the room, there
was only the light, almost inaudible sound of the pictures as
Alexandra touched them. Bryce took a sip of his beer.

"Well," said Alexandra. It came out almost as a sigh.

"Of course," said Bryce, "the other night when I came back
and saw you dressed up, I knew you were thinking . . . of
causing trouble. You'd hurt the child, I could tell. You'd force
me to do things that . . . I don't want to do. I won't let you
force me to expose you."

Alexandra still sat with her hands over the photographs, her
eyes set on Bryce.

"Well," she said again. It came out slowly and almost lan-
guidly. She sat back, and her arms went to the side of the chair
again.

"How did you get them?" she said.

"I don't think that's the point," said Bryce, "is it?"

"I think so," said Alexandra.

She crossed her legs and let her wrists relax again and pressed
her head against the back of the chair. Some strands of her hair
slipped forward and fell across her face, but she didn't move
them and looked through them at Bryce.

"No, no," said Bryce, "don't you see, the point is that I had to
protect you so that I'd never have to let Anne . . . take a look
at these. What would she think? And who knows what'd she'd
believe. . . ."

"How did you get them?" said Alexandra.

Bryce shrugged.

"Of course, the man came to me," said Bryce.

"Did you know him before I met him?" said Alexandra.

"It might have been possible," said Bryce, "you meet all kinds in Washington. Or perhaps New York, but—"

"How much did you pay him?" said Alexandra.

"How can you accuse me?" said Bryce, "you don't see any photographs of me in these poses, do you?"

"That's not what I asked," said Alexandra. She still sat with the hair falling across her face and her hands over the arms of the chair. She spoke slowly and it seemed as though the words passed over her lips softly. She was almost whispering.

"I don't know how you can be so insistent," said Bryce.

Alexandra looked at the photographs for a moment, and as she stared, as she moved a finger across her lips and cheeks, Bryce said, "All right. I paid him. I gave him enough so that he was pleased."

"Before or after he took the pictures?" said Alexandra.

Bryce looked at her and frowned.

"Well, well," he said, "I'm surprised I caught you at all. Don't you see, we're really more alike than you've ever thought."

"So it was before," said Alexandra.

"You forced me to," said Bryce.

Bryce began to pick up the photographs.

"I'll give you no reason to show them to anyone," said Alexandra.

"Of course," said Bryce, "I knew you'd understand. I'll put them someplace safe and then we'll forget the whole thing. Won't we?"

After this she walked down the road to my house. She came with a steady, careful gait, almost as though she were counting her steps or measuring the distance. Both of us knew Alexandra wouldn't take another chance. It was Bryce's style to try and catch her again. So Alexandra was condemned to those long, quiet evenings, to the lonely teasing, those hours that promised so much and gave so little. Or maybe it would be worse: she might not even want to be caught at that, and to see the look in Bryce's eyes when he found her trying to keep herself alive.

In all this there was a piece of unfinished business. Alexandra went home after talking to me, and in the morning she was up and gone before daylight. She had knocked at Xannie's door and asked him to make sure that Anne got her breakfast and that she got to school all right. Then Alexandra went to her car (the old Jeep that had been Harlow's, and which was then kept running only because of the efforts of Harlow's mechanic in town) and drove to the train station, where she stood on the platform in the cold morning, wearing a pair of blue jeans, a sweater and a raincoat, the front panels of it this time not blowing in the breeze but now buttoned tightly and held against her with a sash. Alexandra didn't see the train coming in from the north, although she felt it in her legs and hips as she stared due south, toward the city. She climbed the steps and took her seat, this time not looking out the window at the river or the hills reflected there. Her eyes were set on the back of the head of the woman just in front of her and she felt the endless, repetitive sound of the train as it went over the rails (hearing, too, Harlow's voice as he had said, years before, "You know what they say? Cut your head off. Cut your head off. Cut your head off"). She fingered in her pocket the slip of paper that had the man's address on it. He said that he stayed in hotels when he had been working hard and couldn't stand being in his own place. And as she felt the clicking of the train beneath her, she didn't think of what she would say or do so much as she dwelled on that moment when she had heard the quiet, hushed rolling of the room service cart. She had been sitting at the side of the bed, her elbows on her bare knees, her head in her sweaty fingers, hearing her voice say, "My God, my God. I've forgotten what it's like to . . . touch someone else." Then the cart came down the hall, rattling a little and moving softly over the carpet. And even though she told herself the only reason she wanted to see the man's face was to be certain that Bryce wasn't lying about where he got the photographs and even though she was already certain that the man had sold them, she nevertheless felt the warmth and itch, which this time, to her surprise and fear, were even stronger than before, when the man had turned to her in the hotel bar and said, "Well . . . ?" There was something about the man, in his vain ability to be wicked, that made her close her eyes, swallow, and make a soft, barely identifiable sound.

She didn't linger on the platform either, but was almost the first one off the train (not having any luggage to worry about),

and then went through the gloom and dust and into the golden
light of the station, and then through it and into a taxi, giving
the driver the address. It was a downtown address, north of
Wall Street and south of the Village. The pounding of the taxi
seemed distant, and she sat, feeling the tightness of her raincoat,
already imagining the man's face at the door, the small lines
around his mouth and dark eyes, his hair combed straight back,
and as she thought of it, she still wasn't sure what she was going
to do, but she hoped he'd show surprise or maybe fear. And
even as she kept her eyes on the cars in front of the taxi, she
knew that if the man was unfazed, if he was just cold, she'd take
a look and turn away. But if the man hesitated, if for one moment (because it would never be more than that) he seemed
surprised or shocked or better yet *intrigued* (which would bind
them together), she'd go through the door and start unbuckling
her belt and taking off her coat, while saying or just looking but
certainly getting across that he was supposed to come . . . next
to her. And even then, when she imagined this, she still wasn't
certain she wouldn't kill him anyway.

"Let me out here," she said.

The taxi stopped at the cross street, and she got out, feeling
the strength of the wind and seeing the pigeons as they turned
overhead, seeming torn and shredlike as they passed against the
little bit of sky above the street. There were cars parked there,
although the street itself seemed to be deserted. There were
bricks for pavement and they were irregular, moving up and
down with the slight contour of the earth. The fire escapes on
the buildings seemed weblike and clinging, and the buildings
themselves had ornamental spikes along the roofs, which only
enhanced the claustrophobia of the street. Alexandra walked
slowly, holding the slip of paper and hearing the soft, distant
pop of the pigeons' wings. The sidewalk was broken here and
there by stoops, ironwork, and thick round and clear tiles that
gave light to the cellars. The doors that led to them were covered with a small, raised pattern, like a fleur-de-lis, and when
Alexandra stepped on them, they boomed in the lonely, empty
street.

The building she wanted was in the middle of the block. Alexandra looked at the slip of paper and then at the building and

back again. There were no windows in it, or at least no glass
and the space for them had been covered with large pieces of
aluminum or tin, and the new shiny and airplane-colored pieces
of metal were the only things about the building that showed
any human, or any recent human, touch. There was a door, but
it was filled with the same new metal. There was a FOR SALE sign
on the building, but it was rusted and half torn and the space in
front of the stoop was covered with cardboard, packing crates,
and broken glass. Alexandra stood, hearing the pigeons' wings.
She dropped the slip of paper and stood there for a moment,
feeling the breeze push against her and smelling the ocean on it,
thinking of the man's face, and of the ache in her stomach that
had come from uncontrollable laughter. Now she heard the
slight tick as the slip of paper turned over in the gutter and
blew away, and then she turned and walked back to the corner,
feeling that lingering desire and rage and the pressure of the
street's emptiness, too.

She took the train, seeing the river again and breathing a
little more slowly and easily, and then she got into her car and
drove over the Black Mountains and home. Bryce was in Boston
and the house was warm and friendly when she got there. Anne
was reading by the fire, stretched out before a book that was
open, like wings, on the floor.

"Hi, Mom. Where have you been?" said Anne.

Alexandra sat down by the fire and watched the light of it in
her daughter's hair.

And, of course, Bryce came to see me. He came down the
road, walking or driving that long, new red car of his, and he'd
get out of it, a smile on his face, and then he'd knock on my
door and say he'd come for a "neighborly chat." He spent a few
hours trying to see if Alexandra had said a word. I didn't give
her away. He wanted to know if he had ever told me about a
man he'd met in Washington, an interesting fellow, you could
say, good-looking, a model who was out of work . . . . he was
depraved, really, and did I want to hear about the things the
man had done? Of course, I sat there, snapping like a turtle.
Bryce watched me closely then. It was a long winter.

Well, they settled down to it. You might even call it a truce.
Bryce watched Alexandra and saw nothing aside from the fact

that she was careful. He enjoyed coming and going to Boston, and he even told me once he thought of himself as a squire. *Squire.* He was at the height of his power over her, and he enjoyed it. I'm not sure what he did to her, but I'm sure Alexandra amused him on those times he was away from the city. He even asked me if I thought it would be a good idea for him to take up trout fishing. Maybe it was the only good thing I could do, since I said it would be a bad idea. It was her one escape from him, and at least she still had that, teaching Anne to fish in the same streams where she had learned from Harlow. Outwardly, Alexandra and Bryce were normal enough, if a little peculiar. Bryce spent most of his time away. Alexandra brought up Anne. Xannie helped. Maybe it wasn't that bad, given what people do to one another. Bryce was a little giddy with his success and he thought nothing would be denied him. Things went along smoothly, and then, of course, Anne turned seventeen.

Ross Critchfield

The town didn't accept Bryce. Of course, this bothered him, but there wasn't much he could do. He didn't have the money to buy the bank, although I'm sure it occurred to him it would be worth a try. But even that wouldn't have done any good. The Thachers, the Critchfields, the Keiths have nothing to do with money, more's the pity. Well, none of them except N. B. ("the Raver") Critchfield, since he still owns the bank. The people in town couldn't understand the marriage. They thought Bryce was a bounder, and they let him know it. Oh, they took his contributions to the museum and for the new wing at the hospital, for the emergency relief, and they spoke to him (when they had to), but Bryce knew it wasn't much use. He even let it slip, once, that he'd tried to "get something" on them. I think he paid a private detective, but, my God, they're all so dull. It was hopeless.

But Bryce thought they'd come around. He gave more money than he should have to the Garden Society, the Annual Dinner Dance, the Charity Drive of New England, and finally he volunteered to work in a prison. He came to me in his smiling, mock-serious, confessional way and told me about it. He asked, in that way of his, that I keep it in the strictest of confidence, although his tone suggested it was a secret I could share. I have only seen Ross Critchfield laugh once, and that was when I told him. It wasn't much of a laugh, to be sure, a kind of cough, as though the man had swallowed a feather.

The prison sat on a hill above a river. There was a large wall, like the Great Wall of China, that went around it, and there were turrets, too, where the guards stood. There was a parking lot, and beyond it there was the entrance. It had small glass windows, old wooden doors like a high school's, and milk glass fixtures. The first night Bryce was there, inmates were painting the entrance. One held the pan of paint, one held the roller, and one looked after the drop cloth. Each one guarded his job.

Bryce was amazed by the prison, especially the getting in and out. He went through a metal detector, then five or six barred gates, and finally he got into a bus. The bus went about fifty yards and stopped before a gate that seemed almost medieval: it was made of small, narrow bars, each one topped by a spike, and the lower part of it was covered with heavy screen. The thing went up and down, as though in front of a castle, and Bryce watched the gate as it was raised, and from the bus he saw the high brick wall, the turrets, the rolls of barbed wire on which there were sharpened pieces of metal. There was the stench of skunks, too, since they had been caught within the walls when the prison was built, and no one bothered to trap them. But Bryce liked the place. He told me, although not in so many words, that it made him feel better to be able to come and go and leave the prisoners behind. It was like, Bryce said, belonging to a club.

Bryce taught reading and writing to murderers. The classroom was in a converted cellblock, and it had some blond wood desks and an American flag on the wall. Bryce didn't have much luck with the students. They sat and stared and put in time so that they'd look a little better for the parole board. There was, however, one student Bryce liked. He was a short, palish man with gray hair and a flat face. He was probably thirty. His nose was short, snubbish and his mouth was small. His skin seemed pale and gray, too, because of the scars on it from acne. He did his work seriously, diligently, and he was always waiting behind the door when Bryce arrived. The man's name was Sonny, and when it came time for his parole, Bryce got him a job at a dog pound in central Massachusetts. Sonny's job was cleaning up after dogs had been killed.

Bryce continued to teach at the prison after Sonny left, although he only did so for a month more. There was a new man in his class, one who filled Sonny's place. He was heavy, tallish, and wore shoes made from alligator. He was a murderer, too, and resigned to doing a long time in the prison. His name was Sam. He always watched Bryce closely, and one night, when the other inmates left the classroom, he said, "Didn't you play ball for B.U.?"

"Yes," said Bryce.

He began to gather up his papers.

Sam said he had worked for a bookmaker in Boston and what did Bryce think about that?

"I did nothing wrong," said Bryce.

Sam laughed and then stared at Bryce again. After a while, he said, "Sure. But you know something. The boys at Jake Hearth's weren't happy about you. You're lucky you're still walking around." Then Sam went out the door and down the hall.

Bryce told me this while he sat in my sun room, leaning forward, out of his chair. The sun hit him in the face, made his eyes bright with a reflection of it, blinded him for a moment, but he didn't mind that. He went on with his story, but by the end he had raised his voice, and he was almost shouting, his head thrown back a little, those bright spots still in his eyes, his face colored a red-gold from the blush and the color of the sun. He got carried away and told the truth. It didn't happen very often.

Bryce didn't know what to do about Sam. It wasn't so much that Bryce was afraid his students would find out. It would have been embarrassing, but, in the moment, he didn't care about that. On the night Sam spoke to him, Bryce went downstairs, away from the classroom, and stood outside, where he waited for the van and looked across the yard at the medieval gates and the walls topped with razor wire, the thin blades of which were glowing in the moonlight. It was all Bryce could do to keep himself from turning around and running back into the building to look for Sam.

Bryce imagined himself climbing the cement stairs, opening the steel door at the top of them and then going down the hall, still carrying his books, his sport jacket flying open as he went from one cell to another until he found the one he was looking for. Bryce imagined Sam sitting on a bunk, smoking a cigarette and slowly turning the pages of a magazine. There would probably be a caged bulb overhead, the shadow of the cage falling in longish rectangles over the walls and bunk. Bryce wanted to lean over Sam and explain himself.

The first time Bryce had been paid for shaving points, he'd been given his money in a bar in Harvard Square. It had been winter, and the bar was crowded, filled with young men in winter coats, and there was an atmosphere of beer and steamed sausages and sauerkraut. Bryce took the money and walked back to Boston, and as he went he understood some of the dirt of the world. He thought that was worth something, that understanding. And when he was in the middle of the Harvard Square Bridge, he stopped and thought about a woman he had seen there in the springtime.

She had been dressed in a shortish, pleated white skirt and a loose-fitting sweater made from cotton. The sweater was a little baggy, had a large neck, and clung to her small figure. She had thin, definite shoulder bones, a long neck, and shortish, neatly clipped blond hair. There were sculls going by, under the bridge, and she leaned against the stone wall, standing on one foot, having drawn one ankle up until it leaned against her knee. The sculls emerged from under the bridge . . . she waved and then stopped, put one knuckle to her lips.

The money in Bryce's pocket made him feel a little less cut off from her. He stood there, flipping the corners of the bills. And on the night Sam had spoken to him, Bryce had wanted to go up the stairs and find the cell where Sam sat in that weak, yellowish light, and say, his voice filling the cellblock, the vibration of it in every brick and piece of steel, "Can't you see? Can't you see? You could have her! You had to understand the dirt of the world. You had to be shrewd. No fool was going to have the promise of her. What wasn't she worth!"

Bryce wanted to say that there was in her stance, in her movement and expression, the certainty that she was utterly decent and still knowledgeable about the world. Why hadn't she been injured by it! Nothing would shock her. She was equal to the world and spirited enough to have in her eyes a smiling understanding of men.

It was all Bryce could do to keep from turning away from the barbed wire, climbing those stairs and saying these things. But he didn't, probably because he was afraid of the smirk on Sam's face and the look in his eyes as he said, after listening to Bryce, "Go on. Get the fuck out of here." Bryce told me that after he had been given his money, he spent the evening looking over whores until he found one who reminded him of the woman he had seen on the bridge and he paid for her with that heavy, earth-scented money.

Then he said an amazing thing. Didn't Alexandra suggest the same thing as the woman he had seen, and hadn't she suggested it even more so when she was seventeen, eighteen, nineteen years old? What did I think?

What could I say? I stared at him for a while. Then Bryce said he hadn't gone back to the prison. He resigned his job and told Alexandra he'd done enough good for a while. I listened while Bryce said that Sonny had stayed in touch with him. Bryce received, every year, a Christmas card with glitter on it. And Sonny sent a shirt each year, too, wrapped in plastic and having a long, broad collar. Bryce never said he threw them out.

Perhaps I should have described Ross Critchfield. He is tall, has no chin, or a chin that recedes into fleshy rings. He has a long nose, thinning hair combed straight back, and he sits with his legs crossed at the knee. His clothes are tweeds and his pants are almost always worn until they are shiny. Anyway, it all came down to his dry, feathery laugh.

A Day at the Races

 As I've said, Bryce and Alexandra made a kind of peace, or truce. Or, to be honest, Alexandra lived with his bullying. I guess that's the best thing to call it. There were months, or even a year, when Alexandra came to visit and we only talked about pleasant things. There were times when I heard her laughter in my house, and when I could imagine she still was the young woman I had known years before, and that she was telling me one of those horrible jokes she brought home from school. Or that she was grown up, had married an ordinary man, and that we were still friends, having a comfortable visit. We had caviar on black toast, served with chopped boiled egg and minced onion. We split a bottle of champagne. Alexandra sat with the golden light of late summer coming through the window behind her. The dust made the air seemed lined, and I saw her fingers in it, opening from a fist, spiraling out, making a shape like the spokes of a nautilus shell.

I should have been able to see it coming. Those summer afternoons when Alexandra had sat talking in her normal and pleasant voice, when we had a snack and enjoyed ourselves, when things seemed so beautifully ordinary, well, they had taken their toll. I'd grown sloppy in my thinking.

At seventeen, Anne was tall and thin, with square shoulders and long legs. She rode beautifully and was an excellent fly-caster. She had fine features, a smooth nose and high cheek-bones, and she had her mother's ashy eyes and blond hair. Over her there was the quality of youth, which was so severe as to seem like makeup or lighting or something physical that was felt by everyone in a room when she walked into it. When she was surprised or shocked, she blushed so hard as to bring tears to her eyes and she liked to tell long, funny stories, and she laughed easily. She liked men and was able to be naturally frank around them and beguiling, too, although beneath the smile there was a stark intensity toward them, which more than once had surprised Anne. Alexandra had taught her to fish and had given her one of Harlow's cane rods, after it had been refinished and wound with silk that was as bright and shiny as the skin of a Delicious apple. And by the time Anne was sixteen, her cast-ing was as good as Harlow's had been, and Anne and Alexandra went to fish together not only the Sugar Wolf, the Battenkill, and Otter Creek, but the Ausable and the headwaters of the Delaware in New York. They had gone one summer to Iceland to fish for salmon, and to the far West for steelheads and cut-throats. Once, when they were together on a clear, dry day in Vermont in June, Anne saw a fish rising in a pool on Otter Creek, and said, "That's a big fish there. I bet I can catch him. You want to bet?"

"All right," said Alexandra, "what do you want to bet?"

In the summer after Anne had turned seventeen, she had a job. She was good at mathematics, and had been encouraged by Xannie in the beginning because he had needed help with the speed charts. Later she studied trigonometry, mathematical analysis, probability, and calculus, and they were used in the room behind the kitchen, where Xannie sat beneath the framed photographs of horses at the finish. Anne had finished school in the spring, and was going to Berkeley in the fall to study mathe-matics. Her trigonometry was excellent, and she had been hired by a surveyor.

She got up early and dressed in blue jeans, a work shirt, and boots. She wore her hair up and put a bandanna around it, and then put on her Day-Glo vest, packed her black lunch box, and then waited for her ride in the orchard, sitting on a stone wall there, and filling with lead the mechanical pencils she kept in a plastic pouch in a pocket of her shirt.

There were evenings when she brought home the young men she worked with. They were tall with longish hair, and they wore the same Day-Glo vests and blue jeans, and they sat in the kitchen with their sunburned hands and faces and drank the cold beer that Xannie put on the table. Their hands were stained black with the pine resin that came from the softwoods they cut away when they were marking a property line, and the kitchen had the odor of their tired, sweaty bodies and the slight scent of sticky resin. One night, when Anne was left alone for a moment with one of the men, she bent her sunburned face close to him and whispered, while her fingers moved to the back of her head and let down her hair in one sun-streaked fall. Bryce stood in the doorway and then abruptly turned away. Later, Alexandra told me, she saw him sitting in the living room, drinking from a glass without ice in it and watching the lights of the young man's truck as it went down the road with the two of them inside.

In August, Alexandra, Bryce, Anne, and Xannie went to Saratoga. It was a hot day, near the end of the season, and Xannie filled a basket with fruit and cheese and small chicken sandwiches. He got up early, before five, and went to town for the racing form and then sat in his room, doing the speed charts with his calculator. Bryce wore a white silk shirt, a blue silk ascot, and a summer-weight oatmeal jacket. He wore brown shoes, too, and he had spent some time in the kitchen polishing them, holding them up to see the reflection of his face there. Anne wore a white skirt and jacket and a pale salmon blouse, and Alexandra wore a dress with small blue flowers on it.

They went in Alexandra's car, which, while no longer Harlow's almost military or safari-like Jeep, was nevertheless still a Jeep, although it was white, a station wagon, and had power steering. When they were walking up to it, Xannie with the basket and dressed in his mail-order corduroys, pullover jersey, and saddle shoes, Bryce opened the door and said, "Xannie in back with Alexandra. Anne's going to do me the honor of riding in front. With me. Big Daddy."

They drove through the Black Mountains, seeing the haze of late August and the reddish cast of fall already on the trees. And as they went into the valley where Saratoga was, they felt the heat rise.

"Do you think I'm still attractive?" said Bryce to Anne.

"To young women who are interested in older men," said Anne, looking at him and smiling.

"Are you attracted to older men?" said Bryce.

"Not recently," said Anne, and then she picked up a magazine from the front seat and began to fan herself, with short, quick movements.

"You mean there's still hope?" said Bryce, touching his ascot and looking over at Anne, raising his brows and smiling.

"Mother," said Anne, "if I were you I'd divorce him."

"Maybe I will," said Alexandra.

"There's not much chance of that, is there?" said Bryce.

Xannie sat in the backseat, next to Alexandra. He wore large aviator dark glasses, and he sat with his racing form already folded so that he would be able to slip it through the slats of the benches at Saratoga, so as to reserve a seat. He sat, with one hand on the basket, and Alexandra could see through the dark lenses that his eyes were set on the back of Bryce's head, and that they were unblinking, constant in their stare.

"Would anyone like a sandwich?" he said.

Then it was hotter yet, and even though it was early, the valley around Saratoga was reddish with dust. They went through the small towns on the way, passed the fields with corn so high it looked like giant bamboo. The race track itself was surrounded with large, makeshift parking lots, and Bryce parked in one and they got out. Xannie walked with Alexandra, and Bryce and Anne went ahead.

By the eighth race, Xannie had won eight hundred dollars. He sat on the side of the stands closest to the small park where the horses were saddled. His program lay in his lap, neatly folded, since he had already decided about the next race. Alexandra sat next to him. People strolled in front of her, but she didn't notice the women, dressed in silks and high-heeled shoes and broad hats, who had tense, fluttery smiles for the men in well-fitting clothes, and who stood coldly in line at the two-dollar windows. There was the smell of washed and groomed horses, the odor of perfume and alcohol, and the atmosphere, too, of the squirmy excitement of the crowd. The stands themselves were nineteenth century, not high, and the supports and roof were a little weblike and spidery, hinting of darkness. Alexandra had her dark glasses on, too, and as she sat next to Xannie she looked toward a terrace where Bryce sat with Anne.

They sat at a small table, which was covered with a white linen cloth. Below them the horses, mounted by jockeys in silks so bright as to seem like wet flowers, went around to the starting gate. The earth of the track was brown, loamy as finely ground coffee. Anne and Bryce drank champagne. When she finished her glass, Bryce picked up the bottle and offered more, smiling at her and shaking his head when she once put her hand over her glass. He lifted it away, not quite putting it to his lips, but holding it for a minute and then putting it on the linen tablecloth. There was the slightest breeze, and Anne's hair moved in it. The people around them were drinking and talking, and there was the air of perfume, the rustling of racing forms, the movement of eyes and fingers, the sophisticated, expensive, and subdued laughter of people who were enjoying the sun of an August afternoon at the races. Bryce frowned and puckered his chin, looked at Anne from under his brows, and then smiled after she spoke. He sipped his champagne, and looked over the glass at her, and then Anne stood up and began walking through the crowd, her hips moving gently among the people who sat watching the horses.

When Anne stood in front of Xannie and Alexandra, both of them saw her smooth and slightly sunburned skin, through which it was clear she was blushing. Her eyes watered and then she laughed, although not easily, after looking at the jockeys who sat on horses walking with a tired, sleepy, almost doglike gait.

"I hope you're driving home," she said to Alexandra.

"Why?" said Alexandra.

"Dad's had too much champagne," and then Anne blushed again. "Xannie, who do you like in the ninth?"

Xannie still held the racing form between his fingers. There were the numbers he had written for each entry in his upright, narrow script, and he turned the paper so that Anne could see the name of one horse with a scratchy, large ring around it.

"Indian King," said Xannie.

The breeze blew Anne's hair, but she kept her eyes on Xannie.

"There's almost no record of his races. He comes from South America."

"That's right," said Xannie, "that's why."

"I thought you'd gone scientific," said Anne.

"Some things aren't scientific," said Xannie.

"Why?" said Anne, now raising an eyebrow.

"Owners love to win at Saratoga," said Xannie, "and if they're willing to ship a horse from South America, it means they've been hiding something. I'd bet a million on a horse shipped from Antarctica for Saratoga. If the price was right." Xannie sat in the light breeze and in the gentle sound of rustling paper, the luffing of silk skirts and tails of summer jackets, the hollow, ringing bounce of an empty waxed cup that blew along the rail. "Indian King's owner is on the racing board. Do you think that will help in a close race?"

Xannie and Anne walked through the crowd to the windows, leaving Alexandra in the dusty sunlight. It was hot and she felt her clothes clinging to her. She stood and walked away from her seat, going along the rail and into the park behind the stands, where the horses were waiting with their grooms and owners and trainers. She stopped there, and looked at a Cuban trainer. He was in his sixties and fat, bald with the last of his hair combed over the back of his head. His eyes moved with the quick, darting search for an assassin, and he wore plainly on his face his memories of Batista. The owner of the Cuban's horse was tall and thin and he smiled when he spoke to the trainer, but the Cuban didn't respond and kept his eyes moving over the crowds.

Alexandra went back toward her seat, and when she stood by the rail, watching as the horses approached the gate on the far side of the track, she turned toward the tables in the sunshine and saw Bryce. He was still sitting down and the seat opposite him was empty. There was another bottle of champagne in a stainless steel cooler, beaded with moisture in the heat. Bryce had his lips turned down, his chin puckered, and a sharp expression in his eyes, but as they moved across the crowd they came to Alexandra. Her face was whitish around her mouth and eyes, and she stood with her shoulders square, feeling the heat that rose from the asphalt around her. Bryce smiled, showing his large white teeth, pulled up the corners of his lips, and waved, raising his arm over his head and wagging it from side to side with his palm open.

Alexandra told me that she didn't turn away from him. Not immediately. She said that she waited in the sunlight, in the busy movement and slight breeze of the afternoon, hearing the clink of glasses, the quiet voices and in the distance the squeak of leather and the clink of a bit. There was the peculiar sense, on her face, that she was becoming numb. She thought she'd kept her end of the bargain and that she'd done it well. What had she denied the man? Well, there he sat, in the sunlight, smiling at her and waving . . . and thinking, too, what to do next with Anne, how to approach the girl without seeming unnatural. Perhaps they could find themselves alone together and a little drunk. These things happened, didn't they? It would be good for Anne, an experienced man like himself. It would be so *French*. He smiled and waved at Alexandra. He thought he was being sophisticated. Well, that's what made him evil: he was more capable of delusion than any man I have ever met.

Alexandra went to the windows, and there she emptied her handbag on the metal counter. She picked through the compact and lipstick, and found her wallet. She took the money from it and the folded bills from the bottom of the bag and then pushed them across the counter, not counting. Her tickets came out of the metal slots, the paper new, thin and clean, and being pushed up with a mechanical suddenness.

The race was a photo finish. It looked to be a dead heat, but the horse from South America was given the race. It paid eighteen twenty, and when Xannie and Alexandra stood in line with their winning tickets, Xannie said, "Maybe it will blow over. Maybe it's nothing."

They left before the last race. It was late afternoon, but still hot, and the air was even more reddish and dusty than before, if only because of the cars that had turned up the dust in the unpaved, makeshift parking lot. The cars that left early went faster than the later ones, since the drivers had lost everything and hadn't been able to stay as long as they would have liked. Alexandra, Bryce, Anne, and Xannie walked through the red-brown air and the heat and came to the white station wagon. Alexandra and Xannie were on one side and Bryce and Anne were on the other.

Anne had taken off her jacket. As she stood between the cars and next to Bryce, her youthful figure, her small breasts and round hips, were defined as the breeze pressed against the cotton blouse and skirt she wore. She had a small line of perspiration on her upper lip and she waited while Bryce searched in his pocket for the keys to the car. When he found them, he reached over Anne. He put one arm around her, and stayed there, fumbling with the keys, pressing against her hip and arm and side, moving slowly in the heat of the afternoon. Alexandra and Xannie looked over the roof of the car. After a moment, Xannie looked away, and then Bryce opened the door and said, "That wasn't so bad, was it?"

"Can you drive?" said Xannie to Alexandra.

"Yes," said Alexandra, "but Bryce isn't so far gone. Bryce is perfectly all right, aren't you Bryce?"

Bryce raised his eyebrows and smiled, and said, "Of course. What a charming afternoon we've all had, we'll have to do it again soon."

Anne looked at Bryce and then slid across the seat and sat next to the door, and then they drove through the dusty air, going eastward, and seeing before them the mountains that were almost invisible in the dust that rose from the dry valley.

James Purdey

 There's something else I've got to tell, as much as I'd like to avoid it. There was a young woman who's name was Aster. I find it hard to believe that anyone would have given that name to a child, but there it is. She was Anne's age and was a boarding student at the school where Anne went during the day. Aster was tall and dark, thin, with the bluest eyes I have ever seen. The color was dark and soft, like the sky in the late evening when everything is black against it. She was pretty, and a little sullen, not unfriendly, but given to arguing about small things, like whether James Dean was a better actor than Marlon Brando. She thought James Dean was better. Aster's mother had been a Rockette (at Radio City Music Hall), but was now retired and living in New York. Aster's mother had been married to a man from South America, but the marriage had come to nothing, and the man had gone back to Brazil. Her father seemed a little cavalier, we all thought, about leaving, especially when he had done so while the child was young, but the fact of the matter was, for however more it makes him understandable, Aster was adopted. Her parents had kept it from her. There were times when Aster went to visit her mother, and the woman was sometimes away, so that Aster had the run of the apartment to herself. She was lonely, and soon she was going to places where she could dance (and where, because she was pretty, she was allowed in . . . these places weren't too particular . . . there were many young girls at them, some younger than Aster, who was sixteen). She had about her a slight . . . oh, I'd like to find another word, but there it is, a *sultriness*. You could feel it when you came into a room and found her curled up on a sofa, reading a book, and slowly rubbing one foot across another. She seemed to have a good time in the places where she went to dance, and was gone for days. Of course, she took drugs, cocaine being something she enjoyed, and there were times when she was a little wild . . . there was even some trouble one night, when she went driving with a young man she had met. He had a new car, and he let her drive. A policeman tried to pull her over on Park Avenue, and when she began to slow down, the young man told her that she shouldn't stop, since the car was stolen . . . there was a chase (the young man screaming, as they went, This is like the old days in Puerto Rico!) and Aster got as far as White Plains before she ran off the road. It was a little bit of a scandal, and I remember being in Alexandra's house, while Aster sat at the table, a large plate in her hands, showing how she had driven when the police had chased her. She made a very good imitation of a siren, and she took a carrot from the icebox and made a kind of speedometer with it, and she sat, holding the plate, and every now and then she'd move the carrot and say, "Then I was driving *this* fast. The cops were excited. I don't know who was enjoying it more, me or them." We all laughed nervously, and then she said, "Of course, I was lucky. They could have killed me."

There was an evening in New York when she brought some of her friends home to her mother's apartment, and there they drank champagne and took cocaine, and Aster mentioned her mother had been a Rockette. The young people wouldn't believe her. One of them said, "No one is really a Rockette."

"Oh," said Aster, "but there you're wrong."

"Prove it," said the young man.

"What will convince you?" she said.

"A uniform. One of those little suits they wear."

Aster and the others went into her mother's room and looked

through the drawers, in the closets, and on the shelves, opening
boxes, drawers, prying into things. They were young and full
of life, and I don't think they meant any harm. But they found
nothing, and when Aster pried open a box on the top of a shelf,
hoping for a photograph, or some carefully hidden thing, she
found the papers for her adoption.

She didn't read them then. She got rid of her friends, and
then she read them. For a while she did nothing at all. Not a
thing. She sobered up and came back to school (where she was
already in trouble), and then she came to Alexandra's house,
and in the kitchen, at the yellow table before the window, she
started crying. She went on for hours. She wanted something to
drink, and Alexandra resisted. Perhaps it was a mistake, not
offering that drink. As the girl sat there, staring at Alexandra,
and then at Anne, she seemed to change before their eyes: Alexandra had never seen anyone more angry. The girl ended by
insulting them both: it was amazing that she knew such words,
or combinations of them. Then she walked back to the school,
refusing the offer of a ride, or of anything. Soon she had left
school for good, and was living in the city: every now and then
we'd hear something, that she had no use for the people she had
known before, that she was interested in finding her mother,
that she was working as a "waitress" someplace "downtown."
Of course we were concerned, and Alexandra went to find
her . . . she asked people who knew of her, but found nothing,
and at last she was reduced to walking those streets around
Times Square, up and down Eighth Avenue, going into bars,
finally showing a picture to women on the street. It wasn't the
first time they had seen a well-dressed, polite, and handsome
woman showing a photograph around, and of course they despised her: one woman asked her if she wanted something with
a man and a woman, or just a woman alone. Perhaps the whore
could find a girl Alexandra liked. I always thought it was melo-
dramatic that Alexandra was beset by her own fears and nightmares about the possibilities of things. Of course, I said nothing. Anne was a little frightened by it all, and spoke about Aster
with a false nonchalance. But we were left more unsure of
things than before. Then, of course, one day, when Alexandra
drove into the city and went in through a tunnel, she saw Aster,

dressed in platform shoes, a short skirt, and a scanty, spangled pullover top, walking to the cars where men sat at the wheel, waiting to pay the toll. Alexandra tried to talk to her, but Aster pretended she heard nothing.

Alexandra came to me when she got back. I have never seen her look so bad, so terrified. She mentioned Aster's name and then sat, looking at me, her lips beginning to move, to describe what she had seen . . . we sat together for a while. Finally, after lighting a fire, after giving her a drink, I made dinner, and in the middle of it, as we sat opposite each other, she put her silver down, hitting the plate so hard I thought it had been shattered, and said, "Look how easily it happened. . . ." She took a sip of wine and looked across the rim of the clear, perfect glass, her terror now making her hand absolutely steady. "Bryce is capable . . . if I gave him reason enough . . . of giving Anne the same shock. The *same*. Or worse, since the man is a liar . . . what tales do you think he'd tell about me?"

For a few days after Saratoga, Alexandra thought nothing was going to happen. Bryce had only been teasing. It was what he loved to do . . . he'd hint, make overtures, get everyone to thinking the absolute worst, and then he'd smile and slap you on the back and say, "My God, what a dirty mind you have." But she watched him closely. Anne was leaving for Berkeley in ten days.

Alexandra was wrong about being teased. Bryce took Xannie aside and asked if he had ever seen anything "incriminating" in Anne's room. Anything at all, really. Who knows what kids are up to, especially young, pretty, and smart ones like Anne, who had gone to a progressive high school? Had Xannie seen some pot, or white powder? Did she keep a diary? Were there any letters from friends? Xannie told Alexandra that Bryce had been insistent and that he had taken money from his pocket, a stack of new, crisp one-hundred-dollar bills. Bryce also brought out a small paper package, about the size of a single razor blade, and he held it up, and asked if Xannie had found *this*. Xannie looked him in the face and said, no, he hadn't found any cocaine in her room and that he didn't want any money, either. Bryce smiled when Xannie spoke, but I'm sure he was thinking, One day I'll get rid of the chink too.

Well, Bryce continued to snoop around. I guess he spoke to the parents of Anne's friends at school, or the friends themselves. I don't know what it was exactly. But Anne was a spirited girl, full of life and curious about things. She was itching to get to Berkeley, and she was at the age when almost any excess seemed glamorous and exotic. He found something though. I don't imagine it was very bad, considering what passes for normal these days. Alexandra knew he had found it, since he went around the house with his head hung a little as though he were thinking of some old memory that hurt him.

When there was little more than a week left, Alexandra, Anne, and Bryce had dinner together. When Anne and Alexandra had sat down, Bryce came into the room carrying a bucket in which there were two bottles of champagne, their necks crossed and with a white linen towel over them. In his other hand he had a drink of ice and vodka, and he finished it, rattling the ice, and put it down on the sideboard beyond the table. He looked at Anne and smiled, and then at Alexandra.

"I thought we'd have a little celebration," said Bryce, opening the first bottle, twisting the cork from the neck with his hand and leaving it on the table beside his plate. He took champagne glasses from the sideboard and filled them, leaving one at each place.

In the beginning, the dinner seemed pleasant enough. Xannie had made a rack of lamb and small, round potatoes with dill. There was an endive salad, a dessert. Bryce poured wine, talked, but kept his eyes on Anne. Alexandra supposed he was drunk, or at least incautious. Anne said she'd come back in the springtime, and that she and Alexandra would fish the Ottauquechee River, or maybe on Anne's Christmas vacation they'd splurge and go to Patagonia to fish for sea-run browns. Bryce asked if Anne would come on a trip with him. He'd seen some pictures of resorts in the Poconos, where the rooms were decorated in an unusual way and where there were tubs shaped like hearts. Of course, they were garish, but then Bryce didn't think Anne's education would be complete without a trip to a place like that.

"Of course you're kidding," said Anne.

"No," said Bryce, "I've never been more serious."

"And you want me to come along?" said Anne.

"Absolutely," said Bryce, "we'll have a wonderful time. Consider it an experiment."

"I don't know," said Anne.

They were all silent, hearing the hiss of the fire. Bryce filled his glass.

"Why don't we talk about something else?" said Bryce.

"I think that's a good idea," said Alexandra.

"Why don't we talk about secrets," said Bryce. "Don't we all have some?"

He looked at Anne.

"Don't we?" he said.

"I guess so," said Anne.

"Bryce," said Alexandra, "I want this to stop."

"What do you know about secrets?" said Anne.

"I've done a little checking on you," said Bryce, "no one else seems to care."

Anne blushed, and sipped the champagne.

Alexandra sat with her shoulders square, one hand in her lap, her eyes set on Bryce.

"Anne," she said, "I want you to go into the other room or upstairs."

"May I take some champagne?" she said.

"Of course," said Bryce, filling the glass, "of course."

Anne went through the door and upstairs, and they heard her slow tread on the stairs. Xannie came into the room and cleared the plates, took the one from Alexandra on which the food had been moved more than eaten.

"Leave Anne alone," she said, "I have never threatened you, but I tell you to leave her alone. I won't have it. . . ."

He moved his head back the smallest amount, as though he'd been shocked or insulted, and with it there came a small *sniff*. For a while they said nothing: there was almost no need for words. Bryce had thought about things, the sniff included. That was the worst, said Alexandra. She was supposed to watch. And nothing more. Or she could sit, restraining herself. Maybe Bryce wanted to see her trembling fingers while she sat, pretending to ignore him.

"Leave her alone," said Alexandra.

"And what will you do?" said Bryce.

He jerked his head back and sniffed.

Alexandra finished her glass of champagne, and then left the table and went into the kitchen. When she put the glass down it broke, and she carefully picked up the pieces. Xannie was still at the table there, and when he looked up at her, his face was long, as though the muscles were paralyzed. Then he gathered up the old racing forms he'd been reading and went into his room, where he closed the door, leaving Alexandra alone and hearing the whine in the old pipes of the house as Anne ran a bath for herself upstairs.

When Bryce left the dining room, Alexandra went through it, and stood by the fire, seeing her enlarged and shifting shadow on the wall opposite her, the harsh glint on the glasses and silver and on the green bottle of champagne. Then she went upstairs and into Harlow's study and when she had closed the door, she pushed her back against it, glad of the wood's hard pressure.

The study had white plaster walls, a chaise made of walnut with leather pads, a gun case, and a case for fly rods, a desk and a chair and a worktable. There were bookshelves around the windows, floor to ceiling, and on one wall there was an Audubon print of canvasback ducks. Alexandra sat down at the table and opened the drawers and took out white feathers and thread, and some hooks, too. She tied five small white flies, Harlow's favorite, a kind they had fished in June together on the Sugar Wolf River. When she finished, she put them in a small aluminum box, and then, taking a plastic trash bag from the bottom drawer, she gathered the wings of ducks and geese, the tails of peacock, the hair of moose, the fur of muskrat, beaver, and seal, the hare's masks, the saddles of chickens, and put them inside. She heard the bathroom door open.

Alexandra opened the door of the study, but not much. She could see through the inch or so the door was open. Anne was in the hall. There was a mirror there and Anne stood before it, wrapped in a towel. She touched her forehead, her cheek, and then started toward her room. Bryce was standing on the stairs beneath her, his hands on the round bars that held up the bannister. When Anne saw him, she was surprised and she dropped the towel, and for a moment the two of them stared at one another. Anne stood straight up and there were pale marks on her skin from her bathing suit, which had come from South America and was small and severe. Then she looked away from him and reached for the towel, her stomach contracting into its tight, youthful segments.

"You know," said Bryce, "you can always trust me. There might be some small favor I might ask, but I'd never tell what I know about you. Not to your mother."

"I don't think you know anything," said Anne a little drowsily.

"You'd be surprised, my sweet," said Bryce, "you'd be surprised. Would you want even to risk your mother's being hurt . . . would you?"

"What is it you want?" said Anne.

Bryce put his fingers on the floor, stretched them toward her foot.

"Oh, don't worry," said Bryce, "we'll have plenty of time to talk about that. Why don't we get together in a few days? Some cozy, quiet place. You can think of something by then."

Anne looked at him for a moment, and then turned, hitching the towel together tighter under her arms. She walked to her room, moving in her languid, drowsy gait. "I think we've both had too much champagne," said Anne, as she turned into her room.

Alexandra hesitated at the threshold of Harlow's study, and then went back in and sat down. She must have sat there for twenty minutes. Then she stood and worked the combination on the gun case and let the dark wooden door swing open. There were ten guns or so altogether, a Schonauer deer rifle, a long goose-gun, double-barrel pheasant and duck guns, a twenty-gauge grouse gun with a long stock, and another that was Alexandra's, a twenty-eight-gauge James Purdey that Harlow had given her when she was fourteen. They had gone grouse-hunting together sometimes in the fall. There were boxes of ammunition on a shelf.

Alexandra sat in a chair opposite the row of rifles and shotguns. She looked up, away from the open cabinet, and saw the maps, the leather rod cases, and Harlow's silver hairbrushes, which were still on top of a high bureau in a corner.

Alexandra reached onto the top shelf of the gun case for a box of shotgun shells. She took Harlow's twenty-gauge with the long stock, broke the breech and put two shells into it, then snapped it shut. She stood behind the door, certain that Bryce was already down the hall, lying in bed, his face and head clearly shown in the greasy, greenish light of the digital clock. The shotgun felt heavy in her hands, although on her palms and fingers and thumbs she had the odd sensation of being close to her father. She reached for the door handle, but then stopped, and felt some nagging, distant pull, but it lasted for less than a minute and Alexandra opened the door.

She went down the hall quietly and stood at the entrance to Bryce's room. He was lying on the bed, with the light out, although his profile was clearly visible, smooth forehead, pointed nose, thin lips, turned-up chin. Alexandra walked over the floor, feeling the soft give of the gray carpet. Bryce usually slept deeply, and he didn't stir as Alexandra put the barrels of the shotgun next to his head. She stared at him for a moment and then saw the slight, almost infinitely small flicker as one of the numbers in the digital clocks changed. The room seemed warm and cozy, and as Alexandra stood there, seeing the greenish light reflected along the barrels of the shotgun, she pushed off the safety, hearing the small, metallic *cling*.

Bryce breathed deeply, and the slight, airy whistle of his breath came and went. There was no noise from the house around her. The trigger didn't require that much pull, and Alexandra felt the flattened part of it against her finger. She sighted down the barrels and saw the flash again of the digital clock. She was amazed at how silent, how still Bryce was, and how fallen or inexpressive his face was. There was an almost inaudible squeak, which at first Alexandra thought was Bryce's whistly breathing, but then she realized it was a new generation of rats, calling in the walls, lost there. When she heard the sound, she didn't look away from the barrels and she felt the slight stickiness of her palm against the side of the shotgun.

So she was waiting, feeling the curved pressure of the trigger under her finger, when Anne came into the room. She stood in the doorway, dressed in a T-shirt and pink briefs, her hair in a silver and blond aura over her head, lighted from the hall, her figure defined as a shadow against the white cotton of the T-shirt. She stood for a moment, waiting for her eyes to become adjusted to the darkish room, and then she stepped forward, saying nothing, but putting her hand on Alexandra's shoulder, and whispering, "My God, my God . . ."

Bryce opened his eyes. Alexandra stood with the pressure of Anne's hand against her arm. She saw the long, greenish smear from the clock on the barrel. Bryce blinked, but he didn't move. After a moment he furrowed his brow.

"I've been thinking," he said.

"About what?" said Alexandra.

"That Anne can go to Berkeley anytime. Isn't that right Anne?" he said.

"Yes," said Anne.

"Your living arrangements have already been made, haven't they?" said Bryce.

"Yes," said Anne.

"Then you should start packing," said Bryce, "tonight. Right now."

Anne's slight irregular breathing filled the room and there was about her a faint, sleepy and bedlike odor, childlike and almost sweet, like ginger. She put a hand to her hair and pushed it away from her face and shifted her weight from one foot to another.

"I mean right now," said Bryce.

"Mom?" said Anne.

"Go on," said Alexandra.

Anne turned and went out of the room, the frail material of the briefs and T-shirt giving as she went. Her feet made a light padding sound in the hall. Alexandra held the shotgun lightly, and there was in the barrel the rise and fall of her pulse, which made a tap tap tap against the side of Bryce's head.

"All right?" he said.

Alexandra put the safety on, and the small, metallic *cling* pierced the room, and lingered, too, as though she had been alone and clicked shut the lid of an old gold watch. Bryce closed his eyes.

"All right," said Alexandra, and turned out of the room. She went into Harlow's study, where she unloaded the shotgun, put the ammunition into a box, and slammed the gun into the cabinet and locked it. She sat down, too, and put her head in her hands, feeling the light, watery trembling in her legs and arms.

Anne was already packing, and when Alexandra came into the room, Anne looked up, but she didn't stop. She said, "What were you going to . . . do in there?"

"Nothing," said Alexandra.

Anne picked up a hair dryer, some sweaters, a nightgown, and put them into the open bag on the bed.

"I was just making a point," said Alexandra.

"Please don't do it again," said Anne. "Please."

Anne was shaking a little.

"I promise," said Alexandra.

"For sure," said Anne.

"Yes," said Alexandra.

"Please," said Anne.

Alexandra sat down on the bed.

"I promise," said Alexandra.

Anne shook her head, closed her eyes.

"It'll be all right," said Alexandra.

"Will it?" said Anne.

"I promise it will be all right," she said.

Anne folded a sweater and put it into the bag.

"Maybe it will be better when I'm in California," Anne said. She kept her face down when she said it, and then she crossed the room and pulled Alexandra's head against her. They stayed that way for a moment, and then Anne went back to packing. Alexandra helped, piling things neatly next to the open suitcase. There were times when she went down the hall to get something of her own and left it on the bed, or on a pile of other things. Anne closed her bags and the latches made short, hard sounds in the room. They sat together until the sky began to turn gray, and just before they got up, Anne said, "I love you." Alexandra closed her eyes and nodded, and then they took Anne's things downstairs.

At the table they drank coffee and ate a piece of toast. Alexandra made Anne wait for a moment and then came downstairs with an envelope, which she pushed across the table, saying, "You'll need some cash. This came from Saratoga."

Anne felt the weight of it, but didn't look inside, and put it into the pocket of her parka, which she had hung on the chair next to her at the yellow table.

When they stood and were about to leave, Xannie's door opened and he came out wearing his tartan robe and a pair of black slippers that were made to look like cats: their faces were turned up at him as his feet slipped into their bellies. In the morning his skin looked old and a little grayish and his beard on the chin looked salty.

"Anne," she said, "Anne . . . you take care of yourself. You hear me?"

Anne stood at the door, holding her typewriter, and behind her there were the white-and-black birches, the greenish aspen.

"Don't worry," said Anne.

"I'll worry," said Xannie.

"I'll remember what you told me," said Anne. " 'Speed on the rail.' "

The bus stop was in a parking lot of a restaurant near the highway. There were no other cars in it, and there were still some lights on in the restaurant. Anne and Alexandra waited in the car, seeing the pale first light of morning. They planned to get together by springtime, at the latest.

The bus pulled into the parking lot and groaned over the entrance to it. The door opened, and Anne got out of the car. She pushed her head against Alexandra's and then said, looking into her face, "I'm sorry you and Dad had an . . . argument." Anne turned up just the corners of her lips into a tender half smile.

"We'll get to South America yet," she said.

Alexandra nodded.

"Everything will be all right," said Alexandra.

Anne looked into the window of the car and smiled again and said, "Okay," and then walked to the bus. It went to Boston, where she'd get the plane. The driver shut the luggage bay and the door, and Alexandra waited while the bus groaned out of the parking lot.

Then she came to my house. It was early, and even with my

old man's half-slumbering rest, I was still in bed. When I came downstairs, I found her waiting, already in my study. It was obvious she hadn't slept. She was pale, and there were strands of her hair falling over her face. I came down in my plaid bathrobe, which smells of the dog and my solitary life, and then I stood, feeling the damp, cool summer morning. It is one of my favorite parts of the day. But I stood there, holding a coffee cup in my hand, and asked, right out, in a way I usually didn't, "What now? What has he done . . . ?"

She said nothing for a while. She sighed and shook her head. Then she asked if she had gone crazy. Did I think it was possible? Certainly I thought it was possible, so I said nothing, and sat down, sighing a little and feeling my old bones settle into my old chair. And did I know, she asked, how much she had wanted Bryce and the rest of hell to go away in one bang and flash of light? I nodded. Then I asked if she needed the sheriff, or a lawyer, or both, and she put her head back and laughed. I laughed, too, as though that would help, and then we both sat, hearing the quiet hush of the summer morning and feeling the reassuring moisture of it. It was a long time before she started speaking again. The only sound, while I waited, was from my empty coffee cup, which was shaking in the saucer, rattling there. Neither one of us had noticed. I put it on the table.

When she had finished talking, we went into the sun room, where there were some late butterflies on the screens, their wings dark, night-sky blue with black, lacy markings. When Alexandra sat down, they moved slowly, just beyond her head. . . . We were silent. Alexandra looked at me, her head up, skin a little pale, one brow half raised. No jury in the world would have convicted her, not one. She could have had that moment, that flash and bang, the hideous smell of smoke. No, the jury would have let her go, especially after I had told my tale. We sat there, feeling the heat of the sun and seeing the tender movement of the insects' wings. Then why? Why didn't she pull the trigger and be done with it? Well, Bryce had done enough to her without that last thing. She wasn't a murderer, and wouldn't be made into one.

But Bryce was in danger. There was something brittle in her expression. And why shouldn't it have been? She was thirty-seven years old and had every reason to be impatient. How much life was she supposed to let slip through her fingers before she came to the point where she didn't give a damn and pushed the liar on his long slide into hell.

And he knew it, too. He came to see me and asked if Alexandra had ever been spiteful. Had she ever taken revenge? Just in the abstract, he said. I stared at him and said nothing. I'm sure he thought of me as just another old shoe of a man, another silly ass who was only concerned with leaving the world no worse off for having been here. But he was scared.

What should I have done? Told Alexandra he was frightened of her losing her grip? What encouragement would that have been to her? And who was I to give the whole thing a shove one way or another? It was a delicate position for me . . . Alexandra and Bryce were balanced, poised opposite one another, and who knows how long they would have lasted like that if nothing had happened.

Then Alexandra and I talked pleasantly. The day had warmed up, and we went outside to drink coffee there. She went through my bulbs, handling the small, onion-like things, feeling the silky skin give way between her fingers. There were some small strawberries I had planted and we talked about those. Then we sat in the sun. There were insects in the air and one of them bit her, and when I got up and began to go for some ammonia to take the sting out, she said, "No. I like the itch of it."

Mad Katherine

Alexandra dreamed of Mad Katherine. It was springtime, and Mad Katherine was stealing eggs from birds' nests, small, blue robin's eggs, the spotted ones of bigger birds, the buff-colored grouse eggs. She ate them like jelly beans, putting the warm shells into her mouth. She caught a turtle, cracked the shell, stripped the meat from each leg. There were only a few pieces of jerked venison left, which hung like dark shoelaces from the frame where Mad Katherine dried meat. She sat in the afternoons, warming herself, opening the skins she wore to the clear, hot sunshine of late May. Alexandra watched from a distance, only seeing Mad Katherine through the bright, lime-colored leaves. Alexandra felt the heat of the day on her back, as though her shirt weighed fifty pounds, and the golden pressure of it pushed her closer, toward the place where Mad Katherine sat, sewing deer hide with an antler needle and thread made from the deer's tough sinew. Then they sat together, and Alexandra watched Mad Katherine as her fingers held the needle, and the smooth skin of the deer. "I hate the spring, too," said Mad Katherine, "the gaudy hope of it. I need no hope. I'd rather have the ice of winter. The water rises now. There are big trees in the water. The fishing is hard." Mad Katherine sunned her scars, the slick, long lines of them bright as mother-of-pearl. Alexandra touched the scars, felt the coldness of them. "They never warm up," said Mad Katherine. "Never." "What do you miss from town?" said Alexandra. "A glass of beer, a piece of cheese, a dance," said Mad Katherine. "A laughing man. My daughter. I hate spring." Alexandra sat, watching Mad Katherine sew, and in the evening, when Mad Katherine had finished making a sack, she took it to the river. The white stones along the bank had been in the sun all day, and they were hot. Mad Katherine filled the sack with them, and then took it to her bed, where she kept the sun-warmed stones against her scars, along her stomach and legs. "It helps," said Mad Katherine, "It helps sometimes in the worst days of spring."

Willie Shaw

I usually get away in winter. It didn't matter, really, where I went, and I didn't care so long as I didn't have to shovel the drifts of snow away from the house: there have been times when the snow covered the middle of the windows and I had to make a tunnel to get to the mudroom door. It's odd, but the memory of the light in that tunnel, blue as a shadow in the snow, means a lot to me. But, instead of the tunnel, instead of the ice and snow, I usually went to Georgia to hunt quail, or to some lonely, dull beach where there was gambling at night. Sometimes I found myself farther south, in Mexico, at Guadalajara, digging through the thieves' market there, trying to find some small, important thing. But not this winter, not when Alexandra and Bryce were so perfectly balanced. I didn't think it would last, and I didn't want to be standing at the base of some sandy pyramid when I detected in the lines of some perfectly polite note from Alexandra that things had come unraveled.

There's something else I want to say here, too. Over the years Alexandra and I had a chance to talk about many things, but the one subject she kept coming back to, almost as though by accident, or as if she weren't aware of it, was what it was like to care about someone for a long time over a great distance. We talked about this at the suggestion of many things, a movie, a story, a bit of gossip. Alexandra said she hated listening to music, and then she laughed at herself because of it, but there was a brittle glance in her eyes, some desperate self-mockery. Of course, she thought about Willie Shaw, and was ashamed to find herself imagining a chance other than the one she had. She laughed at herself for having any hopes at all: but the fact of the matter is people came back to this town all the time, and not only the Thachers and the Critchfields, but just ordinary people, too, who found, for one reason or another, that the terrors here were preferable to the terrors elsewhere. Every now and then, she'd say, "Harold Taylor came back," and I'd say, "Yes, that's right, he pitched a no-hitter his second year in high school." But mostly Alexandra prided herself on being realistic about things. She had a private, interior life. It had nothing to do with the world, not anymore, or so she told herself.

The winter started early, and I found myself thinking, at night, as I tried to go to sleep, of dark jungles, pierced here and there by long rays of light, through which the parrots moved, bright as circus posters. The flutter of their wings and their shrieking voices woke me up, and then I'd sit, hearing the shutters banging in the wind. I'd try again, concentrating on the flat, gray mirrors of the upper reaches of the Orinoco, where the fog piled up and where all the leaves over the water dripped, making small rings. But, by the end of the second big storm, after I'd found that the wind had blown long tendrils of snow across the floor in the mudroom, I looked out the window and saw Alexandra working her way through a drift. I opened the door, and when she came into the kitchen with her coat smoking from the cold, she turned to me and said, "He's back."

She went into the living room and sat down, at the edge of a stool there. Her fingers were spread out, flat against her hair, pushing against the weight of it as she bent toward the fire.

We rarely talked about Shaw, at least not in so many words. I wasn't such an ass to say, when she seemed a little abstracted or when she frowned at some difficult memory, "Well, do you miss him? How would it have been otherwise, you know, if you'd had a chance?" I valued her trust and I wouldn't have had it

long with idiocy like that. But she did think about him, about
the promise of that time . . . if things had been a little different. And, no matter what, years before, she had behaved well to
Shaw and had not failed in any way. How many chances do you
get, when, without any warning, whoever or whatever you are
is thoroughly tested, and either you were up to it or you
weren't? The memory meant a lot to her: it was when she had
been at her best.

Anyway, she sat there, before the fire, face up, her eyes showing a little of what she must have felt. We both were aware of
something in the room, the sense of life coiling and uncoiling,
rearranging itself for its own purposes and leaving us with the
slight, slimy touch, the gentle push toward disaster.

She told me she'd seen Willie in town. It was a cold day and
even at noon it wasn't above zero. Alexandra had parked behind
Grome's Sporting Goods and walked through the store to get to
the main street. Grome was behind the counter, his hair now
white, his face thinner and more deeply lined, but the shot in
his cheeks and forehead looking all the more definite, as though
his skull had small bumps on it. Grome liked people to use the
store to go from the parking lot to the street. He'd read an
article in *The Wall Street Journal* about impulse buying, and he
liked to say you could never tell when someone would reach out
for a baseball bat, a glove, a bow, a basketball net, a pair of
skates, a gaff, a canoe paddle. People bought odd things in the
middle of winter.

Grome keeps the place hot, too, as oppressive as the jungles I
thought of when I tried to go to sleep. Many stores and houses
are that way, especially those in which there are wood stoves,
and when you come in, out of the cold, the heat has an effect.
There is a moment, especially if you've come in from weather
that's below zero, when you feel sleepy or disoriented, and
there is the sensation of the floor slowly rising and falling, as
though you were standing on the deck of some large ship in a
swell. Everyone here lives with it, and many times I've walked
into a store or house, and stood blinking, waiting for the sense
of sickness to go away.

It was a cold day, and Alexandra came into the store and was
disoriented by the heat. It felt as though she had taken a short

nap in some hot room, and woken, feeling a little dizzy and not knowing exactly where she was. She continued walking, though, through the store, feeling the rise and fall of the boards beneath her feet, the odd, slight movement of the things around her, the tennis shoes, golf clubs, fish hooks, compasses, and flashlights. When she came to the front of the store, the effect of the heat hadn't gone away, and she waited, her head down a little, her hand on the brass knob of the front door.

Someone leaned over the counter and spoke to Grome. Perhaps the man was looking through the glass top at something inside. Alexandra heard his voice and then she pushed down harder on the brass knob, while she swore, under her breath, at every overheated room she had ever been in. She stood, blinking, looking into the street, watching the slow glide of the cars in the snow. The voice went on and she shook her head, trying to make the haunting sound of it go away. There had been times when the memory of Willie's voice had come back, and the suddenness of it had surprised her and made her feel that she had little or no control over her thoughts: it had come back to her when she had spent those days in that good, quiet hotel. Now, in the heat of the store, she used the usual things to push it away. What was on her shopping list? Had she turned off the stove? There was ice on the steps . . . should she get some salt? The voice went on, even though the floor stopped its slow rise and fall and the basketballs, shotguns, running shoes, sweat pants, targets, and cans of black powder no longer were bewildering and seemed to be sitting in exactly the right places.

She saw Willie from the side. His hair was longish, dark, just touching the collar of his shirt, and there were a few lines of gray in it, too. His skin was tanned, youthful, and there were a few small lines around his eyes. His lips, nose, and forehead were sharp and clean. She still held the brass doorknob, now feeling that movement in the floor, since it had started again. She thought she was ill. The voice continued, the same one she had heard at night, or in those nightmares of regret and self-recrimination, when she was unable to explain the world to herself or anyone else. She waited for a moment more, her head down, still feeling the heat. For a moment there were no cars in the street, and no one on the sidewalk either, so the store was quiet, and as she felt the cold brass in her hand, she heard the voice say, as clearly as she had ever heard it, "And a box of twelve-gauge, too."

Alexandra stepped through the door, where it was ten or fifteen below. Outside, she was disoriented again, the cold rushing up to her, and she was left, leaning against the bricks of the old mill building and hearing the steady thud as people went by in their heavy, insulated boots.

She went into a market in the middle of the block, and in it on beds of ice there were vegetables. Alexandra stood with her hands trembling in her pockets and looked at the bright, damp heads of Boston lettuce, the tender carrots and heads of broccoli, which were as green as money and sparkling with ice. When Alexandra reached for the things she needed, her fingers were stiff and light, awkward, and when she looked around she saw that Shaw had passed the front of the building, his breath leaving a windblown strand in the air. She put her hand to her forehead and then realized there were people in the store, and she went carefully to the cash register and paid, splattering ink when she wrote the check.

Then she went outside, glad for the cold, anonymous quality of the street. At least she'd be able to walk along, like everyone else who came to town, the lot of them knowing better than to be outside on such a day, but doing it anyway. Up ahead, she saw Shaw turn into the bakery.

Alexandra walked down the street, seeing her reflection in the shoe store, the pharmacist's with the neon mortar and pestle in the window, the bookstore, the department store with the biggest window in town, so large, in fact, it trembled in the wind and made the people who were reflected there stretch and contract and disappear. Alexandra carried her bag and even thought she'd passed the bakery when in fact she was already climbing the steps.

Inside, out of the cold, there was that sense of fuzziness, but there was the odor of raspberry and blueberry tarts and apple pies, the scent of cinnamon and raisins. Shaw was sitting with his back to the window, and all she saw was a heavy cotton shirt, a bluish one that had been washed until it was pale and soft. Alexandra went through the room, carrying her bag of groceries and feeling the panels of her coat fly away from her. She wore a white turtleneck sweater and a pair of jeans. She went through the small shop, passing the tables that were close together and the people who sat at them, and she probably even told herself she wasn't really going to do a thing. Then she sat down opposite him, put the bag of groceries on one side and said, keeping her pale face on his, "Hi. Do you remember me?"

Then, Alexandra said, it seemed so ordinary. They just sat there, having a cup of tea. A cup of tea! she said. Just like old friends. Shaw told her he'd been to the Pacific Northwest, had been married and divorced, and that he worked in the woods, these days marking trees for loggers. There were people who came and went in the coffee shop. There was the clink of spoons against saucers, the sound of the cold chest being opened and closed, a telephone ringing, the sound of an oven door gently thudding against the frame as someone closed it after looking inside. There were things he'd missed, Shaw said. And his uncle and aunt, who lived outside of town, were old and needed some help. Shaw told her there were some orchards he remembered that still had morels, and he asked if she'd like to come with him in the spring. Alexandra nodded. He told her that he'd missed the landscape: he was old enough to be reassured by the things around which he'd grown up. Did Alexandra know, he said, in passing, and just to be conversational, that he'd missed seeing grouse? The females, when they were sitting on a nest, covered their backs with leaves so that when they flushed, when they flew away because they were frightened, the leaves fell over the eggs and hid them. It was pleasant enough, said Alexandra.

And in the middle of it, as though everything between them had been spoke of, she found herself saying, "How am I going to stay away from you? I'm married." And Shaw said, "I'll help you." He smiled and she shook her head and said, "No, no, that's the last thing I want. . . ." Well, then they went back to drinking the tea, and after they finished they both got up and went outside, into the cold air, hearing those people walking by, their heavy boots making a muffled thud on the cold sidewalk.

They said good-bye to one another. They made no plans. How could they? Alexandra wanted to know. She held the bag of groceries in both hands, kept her eyes on his face as they

stood outside: she wanted to take a good look. Then they turned
and walked along the street, each pausing to look in a window
or to say hello to an old friend. It's a small town. Certainly the
two of them had seemed ordinary enough. Hadn't they? asked
Alexandra. It was nothing more than a cup of tea. And, when
she got into her car and began to drive home, she was still using
this piece of foolishness to keep herself calm. It was nothing,
she said to herself, nothing at all. Then she came out of the cold
and into my house. . . .

She said she cared for the man. And she could trust him. He
wasn't a liar. She was thirty-seven, she said, how much time had
she given already? Was it a crime to want to be touched, or to
have some small, decent thing of her own? I sat opposite her
and shook my head. It was the least I could do. And then there
were times, in that same long afternoon, when she said, The
hell with him. I'll live exactly as I have for years. I'm good at
denying . . . things. I've done it for years. I'll leave everything
as it is, I'll do nothing at all. Then both of us sat and looked out
the window, listening to the wind moan in the chimney.

"Or," she said finally, as she stood at the door, "if I do anything, I'll be damn careful."

Then she stood, with her back against the door, shaking her
head, amazed at the vulgarity of the thing: she didn't want to
have to be "careful." It seemed to be an insult, a kind of sneaki-
ness she despised. And who was she to bring these difficulties
into the man's life? He'd lived thirty-eight years, and that was
enough to have seen some trouble. Maybe he just wanted to
come home and live quietly. She tapped her head slightly
against the door, and then opened it and went into the snow.

She thought about things for a while, although she went
about her business, too. She told me that no one would have
known a thing. I wanted to say, the hell with them, to hell with
anyone who'd interfere. But we both knew there wasn't luxury
enough for that. Alexandra and Xannie cleaned the house to get
rid of the pent-up atmosphere of winter. They polished the
floors, the furniture. And as she worked, she thought perhaps
she could have some small thing . . . nothing serious, nothing
that would cause any trouble. Then she'd turn on herself with

scorn. What was it going to be, she asked herself, just a kiss? Then she found something else to do.

She went into Harlow's study and looked at the fly rods in the wooden cabinet. The finish of some of them was cracked above the grip, almost stripped by the insect repellent she and Anne had used. Others though were in good shape, still smooth and having the brownish, lacquered bamboo color that was soothing to look at. Alexandra stood before the open door of the case, and touched one of the fly rod's sections to her lips, felt the glassine texture of the thing, the sharp angles where the strips of bamboo had been glued together.

Alexandra came to see me, and we'd talk about books, about the weather, tropical diseases, man-eating tigers, the annual pumpkin-growing contest. One afternoon, I was desperate enough to suggest a game of cards. She looked beautiful.

I sent her flowers, too. She was probably disappointed when she found my card in the bottom of the box. I sent freesia and orchids, and she arranged them and took them upstairs and put them by a window, where she sat, smelling the clear, exciting odor of the freesia and seeing the ridged and shiny lips of the orchid. She raised one finger and held it against a petal, trying not to touch it, but seeing it quake with her pulse. When she came to my house for a polite, five o'clock visit, she said, quietly, almost as though she had sighed, "Well. All right . . ."

A Day in the Country

 The next afternoon, she called Willie.

"Hi," she said, holding the phone against her ear and leaning forward. She felt the slight tremble of the instrument against her lips.

"Hi," said Shaw.

"It's Alexandra," she said.

"Hello," said Shaw.

"I'd like to see you," said Alexandra. She turned and looked through the window.

"Right now isn't such a good time," said Shaw.

"Why not?" said Alexandra.

"I was going out to see my family," said Shaw.

"Oh," she said, "well, maybe some other time."

"That might be better," he said.

They sat, each holding the black receiver of a phone, Alexandra looking out the window and Shaw sitting in the kitchen of his apartment. They said nothing for a while, each hearing between them the dark buzzing of the telephone. It was as though the sound suggested something about them, their awkwardness and their isolation, too. It scared Alexandra and made her shake her head, pressing the receiver against her ear and hearing the black hum of the wires. In the moment, it seemed horribly important that Alexandra go along with Shaw, just to visit and to be ordinary with some old people wanting company. Certainly they couldn't be denied that. And what did it mean if they were, if even something that small couldn't be managed? So they sat, hearing that horrible emptiness, until Shaw said, "Would you like to come along?"

Alexandra dressed and drove to town. She met Shaw in front of his building, where he was waiting in the street. He was dressed in a blue shirt and a pair of pants, heavy boots and a green parka. They got into Shaw's truck, a blue one, the color of a hazy sky, the fenders marked with gray primer. The softly edged spots of it looked like clouds.

They went out of town and into the hills, and when Shaw stopped the truck to set the hubs for four-wheel drive, Alexandra got out, too. She was thirsty, and she picked up a clean handful of snow from the side of the road. It was dry and she felt the ache of it in her hand, and when she touched her tongue to it, the snow tasted of harsh, arctic mountains. In the cab of the truck she still felt the pricks of the snow in her mouth and the tickle of it in her nose. She touched him once when they went over a bump. She apologized. He said it was all right, but he didn't look at her.

The road before them came into a valley, a meadow or field that was flat and through which there was a small stream. Beyond the field at the top of a rise there was a house and barn. The house was two stories, and had three chimneys, and smoke was coming from two of them. The siding had been white, but was now gray, the color of firewood that has sat in a pile for two years outside. There was plastic around the foundation, and there were parked in front of it a tractor, a baler, and a harrow that were not covered with anything, not even a tarp, aside from the snow. There were two older four-wheel-drive cars, a Jeep truck, and a station wagon. The roof of the barn sagged and the doors wouldn't close: it looked as though the tractor, the baler, and harrow had been left outside in the fall because someone had been afraid that if they were left in the barn it would fall on them. There were no lights in the house, at least bright electric ones, and after a while, as they drove toward it, Alexandra saw the paler, yellowish light of a kerosene lamp.

Shaw parked behind the older Jeep, got out and took from the back a box of groceries, dry goods and cans mostly, although there was some fresh meat, too, stewing meat and chicken. Alexandra took the other box and they worked their way around the two cars that were parked ahead of them. They went single file, up the house steps, which had been kept clean and didn't have any ice on them, and then through the storm door. Shaw kept the outside door open with his back and knocked on the inside door with the hand that held one side of the box and then opened the doorknob, and they went in.

They stepped into a small foyer. Through a door on the right Alexandra saw a large room in which there was a brick fireplace. The opening of it was long and high, almost big enough to stand in, but now it was filled with a large black wood stove. It was going and the room was filled with the heat from it, which, when Alexandra stood close to it, seemed so definite as to be almost furry. In front of the stove there was a rocker with arms that were stripped with use. A kerosene lamp hung from the ceiling and the bottom of it cast a round, pale shadow on the floor.

There was a woman sitting in the rocker and her hair was gray and neatly combed, and her eyes were the pale, clouded blue of blindness: she stared toward the stove, not because of being able to see even the bright chrome on it, but because of the heat. A man stood before the stove.

He must have been in his sixties anyway, and his face was lined and heavy. The lines from his nose ran to the sides of his chin, and it made the lower part of his face look as though it had been put together in segments, like a ventriloquist's dummy. He was tall and heavy, too, going to fat and having a belly that had begun to sag, although just noticeably, over the top of his pants. He wore glasses that had black frames and there were two large moles, or growths, on one of his cheeks.

Alexandra had seen him before. Usually it was when he had come to town and was walking as he did his errands, his face set straight ahead. He acknowledged no one else on the street. He went to the grocery, the pharmacy, the hardware, and then came out, carrying his smallish brown bags in which there were food, medicine, or a handful of nails, screws, a hinge, or a mantle for a Coleman lantern. There were times when Alexandra saw him waiting in line at the theater, his arms folded across his chest, his face set toward the box office. He waited in line for *2001, Fantastic Voyage, Planet of the Apes, Invasion of the Body Snatchers,* and with him there were mostly kids, but he was oblivious to their laughter, shoving, jokes, and their sharp cries when they waved to someone in a passing car. Alexandra only knew that his name was Whalen. There were times, though, when she passed him on the street, when he turned his eyes to her and seemed, when she was close, as though he was going to speak. Then he went back to his slow, definite walking or to his quiet standing in the line with the teenagers who were waiting to see *Alien.*

Now Alexandra and Shaw stood in front of him, each of them holding a box of groceries. The woman in the chair began to rock, and the boards under the runners made a steady *kerriiik kerrriiik.*

"Why, it's Alexandra, isn't it?" said Whalen. "You're Harlow's daughter, aren't you?"

Alexandra nodded, and smiled. Whalen stared at her. Then Alexandra and Shaw put the things in the kitchen. There was a wood range there with four top burners. There were rings in them that could be taken out to expose the flames in the stove.

When they came back into the living room, Whalen said, "Yes, of course it's you."

The tall, heavy man looked at her eyes, face, her hands.

"You got your daddy's eyes," said Whalen.

Shaw came away from the table where he had left a box.

"I got everything you wanted. That corned beef from South America. Special K breakfast. There's a bag from the pharmacy . . ."

"Thanks," said Whalen, but still keeping his eyes on Alexandra.

Then he broke off and went into the kitchen, where he poured bourbon into a glass. He went back into the living room and stood before the stove, back to it, one hand in his pocket, the other holding the glass.

"This is my Aunt Katherine," said Shaw.

He knelt before the rocking chair and touched her arm, and then lifted one of her hands and put it against his face, moved it over his features so she could tell who it was. She didn't make a sound, aside from a small noise. Alexandra stood, watching the two of them, and hearing that noise, which she realized was Aunt Katherine's crying.

"She can't hear, either," said Whalen.

Shaw tapped his fingers against her forearm, and there was about Aunt Katherine the air of someone who is listening. Aunt Katherine's chair began to move again on its runners. Outside there was the sound of a dog: it scratched at the door, whined a little, and then made a small, high yip.

"I got a one-eyed dog," said Whalen, "a setter."

"What's his name?" said Alexandra.

"He doesn't need one," said Whalen, "he knows when I'm talking to him. Quiet!"

The dog was quiet.

"Did you know my father?" said Alexandra.

"Did I *know* him," said Whalen. "If that doesn't beat all . . . yes, you could say I knew him."

"Why don't we have dinner?" said Shaw, who still knelt next to the chair. "Maybe Alexandra's hungry. I am."

"Yes, let's eat," said Whalen. "Yes. I want you to sit down at my table."

Before Whalen went into the kitchen, he took a package of cigarettes from the mantel and lighted one. The cloud of smoke spread through the golden light, and then stretched out and hung, island-like, in the air. After a minute Aunt Katherine began to rock again, making a quick, urgent creaking.

In the kitchen Whalen took some cold baked potatoes and sliced them and fried them in butter until there was a light crust over them. He scrambled some eggs and cooked some sausage, too, and then he put the plates on the kitchen table. While he cooked he kept drinking the whiskey, and when he told them to sit down, he said, "I killed a hog last fall. The sausage is good."

While the three of them ate, Whalen kept his head down, although from time to time he looked up and stared at Alexandra. Shaw asked some questions, and Whalen answered with short replies, and when they were done eating, Whalen said, "When your father won his first election, it was damn close, you do know that?"

"I heard it was close," said Alexandra.

"Yeah, oh, yeah," said Whalen. "It was ten goddamned votes. That's how close it was. Do you know anything about *them?*"

Alexandra shook her head.

"Where are your manners," said Shaw, "or your hospitality? What's wrong?"

"The hell with my hospitality," said Whalen, "I've been waiting years. A lot of years . . ."

He looked at Alexandra again.

"Take it easy," said Shaw.

Whalen looked at his nephew, and then turned away, and began to stare out the window.

Shaw cleared the dishes from the table. Then he poured some soup into a bowl and he and Alexandra went into the living room, where Shaw began to feed Aunt Katherine, a spoonful at a time, gently knocking the spoon against the lip of the bowl and making a light click between each mouthful.

Aunt Katherine ate with large, exaggerated movements, her lips anticipating the presence of the spoon. She didn't eat neatly, although Shaw had brought a paper napkin, and touched it to her chin. Whalen came into the room, too, and leaned against the mantel. He tried to look out the window, or at the yellowed walls. He opened the stove and inside there was the bright, almost glistening pile of coals, wavering in the draft and in the glassine heat. He put another piece of wood in, closed the door, and tried to look out the window again. The room was filled with the gentle, regular clink of the spoon against the bowl. Whalen put his hands in his pockets, then took them out and crossed them over his chest. He sighed and turned to Alexandra and said, "All right. I want to show you something."

He went to the window and picked up a Coleman lantern from the sill, pushed a match into it, and turned up the gas. The room was filled with another harsh sound of a lantern. Then Alexandra and Whalen went through a door and down the steps

to the cellar. The stairs were wooden, worn enough to look thin
and gnawed, as though they'd been cut from a corral where
horses had worked at the fence with their teeth. Whalen held
the lantern up and they walked in the swaying circle of light,
and by it there were visible rusty hoes and rakes, broken, bluish
Ball jars, rolls of wire, glass panes, piles of magazines, and a
woman's large, dusty straw hat, the brim of it frayed from the
summers it had been worn by Aunt Katherine. And next to it,
on a high, broad shelf, there were bottles of liquor, each one
furry with gray dust and each with a card taped to the neck.
The card was a small, rectangular, ordinary calling card.
Whalen reached for one of the bottles and took it down, his
fingers becoming thick with dust, and he held the bottle under
the lamp, close to Alexandra's face. He rubbed the card so Alexandra saw in the raised, expensive printing of the thing, the
words *Harlow Pearson.*

"And why the hell do you think your daddy was sending me
liquor?" said Whalen.

"I don't know," said Alexandra.

"Because of those goddamned *votes,*" said Whalen. "I knew
the election was going to be close, and I went to your daddy
before the election, and I told him it would be. He said he
needed help, all the help he could get. And he was right. He did.
At the time I was working on the road crew, had a mess of men
to order around and do whatever the hell I liked. You know
Maple Hill Road? That long, narrow road . . . ?"

"Yes," said Alexandra, "Amy Critchfield lives up there."

"That's right," said Whalen, "and her father, Harold. There's
a whole nest of them up there. A nest of Republicans in there,
and there's only one way out. Down Maple Hill Road. You
know they were always complaining about the road being icy in
the winter. All the damn time. I couldn't keep enough sand on
it. The problem was, there were too many trees growing next to
the road. All it needed was to have some of those trees cut down
to let some light on the road and it would have been like a state
highway. So, on election day, I went up there and cut every one
of those goddamned trees down. Dropped straight across the
road. That nest of Republicans had to sit tight, since they

couldn't have gotten out with a tank. So, there you had it, twenty registered Republicans, and not one of them got out."

"But my father was a Republican," said Alexandra.

"You've got to know your Republicans," said Whalen. "Those, up there, those Critchfields, they knew Harlow. He didn't realize where he was living. They would have voted against him, just to laugh in his face."

Alexandra listened to the lantern and stared at the bottles.

"At first," said Whalen, "Harlow wouldn't believe it. I went to see him. There was a stink about the road being blocked off on election day. I lost my job. Harlow said I was a fool, but then he went home and thought about it. Maybe he saw their eyes, those up there on Maple Hill, when they congratulated him. Then he started sending me those bottles of liquor, one every year."

Whalen put the bottle back on the shelf and stared for a moment at the gray dust on his hands and said, "And when they came, I brought them right down here."

He turned and went upstairs, wiping his hand on his pants and for a moment Alexandra stood in the darkened cellar, feeling the air there, cold, dry and dusty, and the presence of those bottles on the shelf. Then she climbed the stairs.

They sat in the living room. Whalen brought a bottle from the kitchen, and he sat with it, pouring long drinks into a water glass. He stared at Alexandra while he drank, and then looked out the window. Shaw slowly fed Aunt Katherine. There was the sense of the cold outside, and in the room there was the sound of Shaw tapping the spoon against the edge of the bowl and the bump of Whalen's glass when he put it down on the table next to his chair.

"Don't you think Harlow owed me more than those bottles of liquor down there?" said Whalen.

"Yes," said Alexandra, "I'm sure he did . . . is there anything I can do?"

"No," said Whalen. "No. I didn't want anything. There isn't enough of his goddamned money in the world to pay me for that. I think he should have come up here and stood outside this house and thanked me. I didn't want his goddamned liquor or his goddamned money. That's what those goddamned weak

chins up there on Maple Hill Road would have done. I didn't
expect it of him."

Shaw turned away from Aunt Katherine. The room was filled
with the sound of the rocking chair, the *kerrrriiiik kerrrriiik*,
which now came fast.

"That's enough," said Shaw.

"No," said Whalen, "no, it isn't." He looked at Alexandra.
"And *now you* think you can come up here?"

"I'd hoped so," said Alexandra.

"Hoped," said Whalen. "God damn it. Hoped."

Alexandra looked toward Willie.

"You've had too much to drink," said Shaw.

"That's right," said Whalen, "and I'm going to have more.
Who the hell are you to tell me a word about it?"

The three of them stood up.

"I've been thinking about it years now," said Whalen.

"That's enough," said Shaw.

"And then she comes up here to get her eyes full," said
Whalen.

Aunt Katherine made a small demanding noise. Whalen
stepped closer to Alexandra. There was a clink and thud as
Shaw put the spoon in the bowl and then the bowl on the mantel. Aunt Katherine began to move the chair again, although
more quickly now, the runners of it making a steady *kerrriiiik,
kerriiiik*.

"Someone was up here a couple of years ago and wanted to
take my picture standing out there by that busted tractor," said
Whalen, "and he's lucky I didn't kill him. My kin don't even do
that."

"I don't want to take your picture," said Alexandra.

"Oh, yeah, oh, yeah," said Whalen.

"Look," said Shaw, rising from the floor, "now look here—"

"You stay out of this. Don't you dare interfere," said Whalen,
although he kept his eyes on Alexandra.

She bent forward, toward him, and said, "I'll go. Right now."

"Yeah, oh, yeah," said Whalen. "Maybe you want to take a
picture of *her?*"

He pointed over his shoulder with his thumb, toward Aunt
Katherine.

"What's wrong with you?" said Shaw.

"There's nothing wrong with me," said Whalen. He turned to Alexandra again. "We all know our places and we're going to keep them. Why don't you go back up the hill there and stay with the rest of those weak-chinned bastards . . . ?"

The three of them stood in the yellow light of the room.

"Don't bring her back," said Whalen, "I don't want to be bothered again, you hear me?"

Shaw nodded, but said nothing, although his eyes lingered over Whalen's face.

Alexandra put on her coat. She went through the foyer and opened the inside door, and as she opened the storm door, too, and stood between them, she heard Shaw's voice, in the room behind her, as he said to his uncle, "What the hell's wrong with you?" Then Alexandra closed the storm door, and as she stood in the cold she heard the voices inside, the quick noise of them, their rising edge as the two men went on talking. As she walked away from the house she saw through the window that Shaw and Whalen stood opposite one another, their mouths moving quickly. She stopped. Overhead the stars were out, and above the house there were the cold, winking flecks. In the distance, beyond the ridge, there was the soft glow of the town. Alexandra put her hands in her pockets. In the window, between Shaw and Whalen, there was the regular gray sweep of Aunt Katherine's head. Then Shaw picked up his coat, and came into the cold, and as he opened the door Alexandra heard Whalen's voice saying, ". . . Maybe I have done enough damage for a night, but I've been thinking about it for years. . . ." Then the door swung shut, and there was the sound of Shaw's boots in the snow and the memory, in the cold black air, with those flecks of silver overhead, of the rocking chair's steady *kerrriiik kerrriiik*.

They got into the truck and went downhill.

Afternoon Light

The next day Alexandra came to see me. I was in the greenhouse, carrying a leaking watering can. I like the weight of the thing, the wooden handle that's worn to the shape of my hand. The spots on it remind me of some old dog, long gone and half remembered. Alexandra stood there with me, her face looking a little reddish on the cheeks, especially so since she stood in the afternoon sun. It seemed as though she leaned into the long, reddish rays, needing to have them play over the faintly roughened skin of her cheek. She hesitated, although she wasn't embarrassed. She wanted to give me an accurate version of what happened. So she was careful, hearing the can drip, and having the slow-moving light of the afternoon wash over her face.

Shaw and Alexandra drove home from Whalen's house. It was cold in the cab, and the heater made noise, but didn't blow any heat. The air seemed to be filled with dust from ice ground as fine as powder. There were the gentle clinking sounds of tools and a chain saw on the floor, the paint cans (which Shaw used to mark trees for loggers) making a hollow *cling cling* every time the truck went over a stone or hit a pothole.

Alexandra didn't know how they began. Maybe there was a large pothole in the road. Maybe Shaw slammed into it and her arm touched his cheek. Maybe that's when they began. Alexandra probably said she was sorry, that she didn't mean to touch him and then she saw his eyes. . . . He probably began by saying his uncle was a horse's ass, and that he'd wished he had money for every time his uncle had caused trouble. Alexandra said maybe the man had a right to be angry. Shaw said it didn't matter. His uncle should have minded his manners. Shaw was raising his voice by this time. Alexandra said Whalen had been trapped and hurt. Shaw asked her what the hell she knew about that?

Then they started in earnest. She didn't even know what he said, or what she said, for that matter. Near the end, when they came to town, she even had trouble following his words. He stopped in front of the building where he lived. It was in the middle of town, on Main Street, above a shoe store. There were people on the street, men and women dressed in heavy clothes against the cold, but it was a Saturday and there were a lot of them, and as they went by, each one slowly turned toward the truck and almost, but not quite, raised a brow.

As I stood opposite her, letting the can drip, I said, "Ah. Ah. You didn't stop then?" Alexandra shook her head. I wondered who had been on the street, but Alexandra didn't know. I imagined Nancy Thacher, or Charles Keith, their faces flushed as they went, both of them giddy with something new.

No, they didn't stop. Shaw opened the door of the truck, but Alexandra didn't get out. She stared through the windshield. People crossed the street, went into the bookstore. There was a line in front of the theater. Shaw said, "No one has ever made me so angry. No one!" The words hung there, where those people went about their business, their sluggish walking and window-shopping.

But she hadn't gone crazy, and she hadn't forgotten where she was. She stepped into the street and said, in a voice that everyone there could hear, not because it was loud, but because it was clear and everyone was listening, "I'm sorry you're having trouble with your girlfriend. But I called you to buy a piece of furniture. Is it upstairs?"

Yes, he said, it was upstairs.

They didn't stop so much as agree to a slight truce, just

enough time to get across the sidewalk, through the downstairs door, and then up the staircase, where they were free to begin again, if only because Shaw lived on the third floor, at the back, and he was the only tenant in the building. They climbed the stairs. Well, she said to me, we'd got a grip on ourselves.

They stood in front of the apartment door, and Shaw's hands were stiff and awkward with the fight, the fingers trembling, and he dropped his keys. Alexandra stood still, waiting, almost as though she were counting or trying to remember some distant thing. When she stepped inside the apartment, Alexandra saw it was a loft, now painted white. Before Shaw had moved in, it had been a cabinetmaker's shop, and even though the paint was fresh, there was still the odor of fir and cedar, the tang of walnut, and the smell of pine. At the end there was a large window, through which Alexandra saw the river and the dark shape of the hill beyond. Shaw closed the door and they stood opposite one another.

Shaw wanted to know if she thought Whalen and Aunt Katherine were "quaint."

Alexandra almost hit him. She stepped closer, felt her right hand rise.

How dare you? she said.

Did you? he wanted to know.

Is that what you think of me? she said.

And worse, he said.

How much worse, she said, what could be worse than that?

That they were rustic, you know, like those pictures of poor people you see from the Depression. Rustic, how about that?

God damn you, she said.

Oh, sure, he said, I know about you.

Only a fool would think so, she said.

They stood opposite one another, each having hands clenched. They heard nothing, not the sound of the fire siren, or the rumble of a heavy truck in the street.

So, he said, we've come to that. To calling names.

You've earned them, she said.

Oh, God, he said, why don't we just admit it's a mistake?

Yes, she said, why not?

We'll just forget the whole thing, he said.

That's right.

The sooner the better, said Shaw, right now.

All right, she said.

What a mistake, said Shaw.

Go to hell, she said.

Then she closed her eyes, put her head back and swallowed. Shaw went across the room and turned back the covers on the large bed by the window. There was a blue down comforter that collapsed like a parachute as it landed on the floor. Alexandra went across the floor, toward him, already thinking, she told me, that she'd tell him of the moments, of the things she'd dreamed of, of the fantasies of him she'd had in that good, quiet hotel, and that she'd not keep back a thing, not the smallest detail. She felt the slip of her clothes as she let them fall and then the rustle of the clean sheets as she sat next to him and said, "Don't be shocked . . . please . . ." She stretched out beside him, went over his chest and arms, tasted the skin and whispered, telling him those things she'd wanted or needed to say. She stretched out on the cool sheets with him, already feeling a chill on her skin, which was something like the tickle of snow held to her nose, or the sense that the dust in the room, the fragrant fir, walnut, cedar, cherry, the dry pine (from the cabinetmaker) was in the air and was settling over her bare skin. She heard her voice, wet and muffled as she spoke with her teeth together, clenched, her face pressed against his shoulder.

The sound in the room came back, seemed to drift in, like smoke. She heard the hush of the river and the tick of the nineteenth-century building, the slight, almost inaudible settling or sagging, which came almost as an ache. Then she got up and pulled the blue comforter over them. After a while they lay in the warmth trapped by it.

"Well, all right," said Willie. "Let's be careful, though. I don't want to turn into gossip. Not after all this time."

"Yes," said Alexandra, "I know. We'll be careful."

After a while, Alexandra got up and put on her clothes. Shaw sat nude, at the table in the kitchen, drinking bourbon from a water glass. When Alexandra left, he was still sitting before it, drinking, looking at the shape of the dark hill beyond and the river, too.

When she stood opposite me in the greenhouse, she wanted to know if she'd done anything wrong, and of course I didn't think she had. But I was amazed she thought she could do otherwise, that she still thought she'd be able to escape. Maybe you have to be my age to know how little chance there is of that . . . I've bought my few square feet in a cemetery up the road, and I've stood on the plot. I know what I'm talking about. Well, she was still young. And she was frightened what Bryce might do to Willie. Some vile, monstrous thing. She'd be careful, she said. I stood, holding the watering can and looking out the window. After a while Alexandra said, "How much time do you think I've got? Before I'm found out?" I said I didn't know. Of course, she said, they'd go on as though they'd never be found out, knowing full well they would. That would be bad, she said, and as she spoke, she turned away. Then we went down the long trays of dark earth, where new leaves had pushed up, and where there were rows of Boston lettuce, the heads bright and green and such a surprise in winter.

Neckties

 In this town you can't do so much as to buy a necktie without hearing about it from everyone you meet. Your life will be divided into two periods, the one before the tie and the one after. It takes months for the color of the damn thing to be forgotten. Well, Alexandra and Willie were careful, and I guess, for a while, they passed as old friends on those few times they were seen in public. Maybe people thought he was working for her. I don't know.

And they were lucky, too, because the town hated Bryce. There wasn't a soul here who would have called Bryce a friend. And here, giving information about one's wife or husband isn't seen as injury so much as friendship. Gossip, in this town, is a kind of sacrament, reserved for insiders, passed from one old citizen to another. You could live here thirty years and never hear a damn word, if you'd been born in Chicago or New York. You'd think the town was the soul of propriety. And maybe it is. The Critchfields and the Thachers are so dull, but they have their moments. I even saw Harold Critchfield at the Ritz in Boston with a two-hundred-dollar whore. He came over to me, his face red with bourbon, and said, "You understand, old man, how it is . . ." Well, he could trust me to keep my mouth shut.

But for years, when I saw Harold Critchfield at the endless cocktail parties of fall, spring, and summer, he'd brace himself and look like a hog who sees the knife. And he traded in gossip, too, just as soon as he got his hands on something juicy . . . perhaps he thought it made him better, or more impeccable. They were such predictable jackasses. It was almost comforting.

Anyway, they hated Bryce. They hated seeing him in town or at the cocktail parties. They smiled, nodded, talked about their gardens, a bird they'd seen, a bear that had come out of the woods . . . the usual chitchat, but they all sighed with relief when Bryce moved on to someone else. Maybe it came down to this: whether the town hated Bryce more than the enjoyment they'd get from their maliciousness. It wasn't pretty. And they left me in the middle, waking at night, hearing my dog howl, or just imagining it, and feeling around me that dark, threadlike drag of the last of a nightmare. Then I sat up and rubbed my head and wondered, Which will it be?

So Bryce was stuck with bringing his suspicions to me. There was nothing definite, nothing he could put his finger on . . . but, he was a kind of genius. He came down the road, his hands behind his back, and when I saw him coming, I'd reach for a Parcheesi set. I have always hated Parcheesi or those other board games. It will be what the worst sinner in hell does for an eternity. And when Bryce came in the door, I'd be unfolding the board and rattling the dice in a cup: it didn't faze the man. He sat down with a smile on his face. Maybe he actually liked the game.

Wasn't it wonderful how well Alexandra seemed? he said. I gave him a horrible token, one that looked like an Indian temple. He was thinking of moving up from Boston for good. Perhaps he'd invest some money in New England. Skiing looked good. What did I think? He had heard that everything was for sale on a ski slope. He said that even the broken legs were for sale, that a doctor paid for the right to treat them. He wondered if any brokering went on, if a doctor bought a thousand legs at fifteen dollars apiece and sold them for twenty-five. Maybe to someone just out of medical school and desperate. I said I thought anything was possible. He watched me closely, though. . . . I looked him in the eye and talked about the weather, the river, the land, what crops looked like. The kind of thing he hated. But he knew something was up, and it made him uneasy.

Alexandra still came to visit, too. I don't want to give the idea that she was selfish or uncaring. She was the most polite woman I have ever known. I'd like to think it was more than that, but I'm old, and the last thing I am is vain. Anyway, she never made me feel as though I'd been discarded. She enjoyed coming, and she still did. There were times when I hardly noticed the difference, at least as far as the number of her visits were concerned. It's true she didn't stay quite so long, but I was glad to see her just the same. We'd sit in the sun room, and we'd have our usual talk. She laughed now, and told me of things she'd heard, or read in the paper. The world didn't seem, for the time being, such a horrible place. We didn't talk much about what she was doing . . . but I could guess, could give a perfectly accurate account, from the few words she said. Anyway, she sat in the sun, holding a glass of lemonade, or a small sandwich, which she ate with such appetite, the sun slanting around her, and making her seem surrounded by those small, bright points of dust.

More than anything else, I think, she was happy. I don't think even she realized how much she had craved the ordinary. . . . She was pleased to find she was curious about Shaw's life, about what he did in the woods. Why did he decide to take one tree rather than another? What was the difference between rock oak and white oak? He wasn't a liar, and it took a while for her to get used to it . . . she had been used to the claustrophobia of lies. Without it . . . well, she was able to enjoy an orange, a lamb chop and wild rice, mushrooms that Willie brought home from work and sautéed for her . . . they ate them with a glass of beer. Once I asked her what she'd been doing and she said, her face warm with the memory and her lips smiling, "Oh. We just went for a walk. It was so dull. . . ."

Twelve Gallons a Minute

September is a dry month. It seems as though there is always someone in September who runs out of water. I have woken in the middle of the night, hearing in the cellar the ominous sound of the pump running: it loses its prime and comes close to burning up. The water table falls. I go down to the river to bathe sometimes, taking a sandwich with me and a big towel.

In early September, Alexandra went to town to do errands. She drove the Jeep and had the windows down, feeling the dry air blow around her. She went along the back roads, thinking that no one else was on them, but as she passed Albert McManus's house she saw there were twenty-five or thirty cars parked there, and some trucks, too.

McManus is an old man, Alexandra's closest neighbor on the side away from me. He can't hear and he's almost blind, but he still cans the things in his garden and makes five hundred gallons of maple syrup every year. He says one year he'll die doing it, and that's fine. Sometimes, in a dry season, he runs out of water.

Alexandra is friendly with him, and there are times when she helps him with the syrup. So, she came down the road and saw the cars, and for a moment she thought McManus had died in the heat and the dry air. She pulled in behind the other cars and then got out on the dusty road.

In the field behind McManus's house there was a crowd of people. Men and women, young and old. There were a bunch of kids, too, solemn as at a funeral. Some of the women were wearing hats in the heat. There were fifty people anyway, most dressed in jeans and cotton shirts that had been bleached until they were pale as old flowers. The boys and girls walked closely behind the adults, and when the grown-ups stopped, the kids bumped into them. Alexandra walked through the gate in a stone wall and stood at the side of the crowd.

In the middle of the people was a man who stood with his back to Alexandra. He wore a pale blue shirt and brown trousers. The tops of the trousers were pushed into the boots he wore, and even from the back Alexandra knew, and not by anything physical, nothing like hair or a scar, that the man was Whalen. He trembled there, and then began to move, turning a little with the piece of willow he carried, which was forked and newly cut. He held it between two hands and went back and forth, over the dry field, where the last of the Indian paintbrush made the grass look dull as old money.

The men and women were silent. Their shoes and pants made a swishing hiss in the grass they walked through, and the children made signs to one another, put fingers to their mouths. McManus came out, too, with his cane and heavy glasses, and he stared, blinking in the sunlight, bareheaded with one wisp of hair blowing across his nearly bald head. Then Whalen turned and trembled, and the piece of willow began to move downward.

He was sweating in the sun, and the veins in his arms looked wormlike under the skin, as though he'd been invaded by some gray parasites. His forehead was bright, and his thick glasses were shiny in the sun, the moles on one cheek casting long, dark shadows across the man's lips and chin. He stood with his legs apart, his feet splayed, as though he were trying to stand up to the weight. Then Whalen grunted and bent over, pushing the piece of willow into the ground.

"Well?" said McManus.

"That's it," said Whalen. "You drill right there. I'll leave the stick."

The men and women stood around the piece of willow, the children looking down with the same blank, disbelieving faces as the old people. The dry wind blew the long hair of the women around their shoulders. McManus took from his overalls a large wallet, held together with a rubber band. He opened it up and took out some bills, holding each one up to his glasses, and then he put the money into Whalen's hand.

"Hey, you there," said Whalen, pointing to one of the boys who wore a man's work shirt with sleeves cut in half so that the boy's forearms and hands were free. "Go into the house and get me a cold drink of water. From the icebox."

The crowd waited around the stick, and then the boy came back, carrying a large thick water tumbler, filled with water and already misting a little. Whalen stood in the sunlight, slowly raising the thing, drinking until the water ran away from his cheeks, the bright, clear moisture trembling at his chin and falling onto his shirt.

"Right there," he said, and then he turned, and began walking through the crowd. The people made way for him, and then he was left, facing Alexandra. Whalen had the front of his blue shirt unbuttoned, and it blew away from him like wings, leaving the old, patched undershirt visible, curved around his stomach. He was taller than Alexandra, and he hesitated there, seeing her face. The wind blew through the brown grass of the field.

"Damn dry season," he said, and then pushed past her, walking through the tall grass, toward the four-wheel-drive Jeep Alexandra had seen parked in front of Whalen's house in the early winter. It started quickly, and then Whalen went down the road, leaving a long line of dust that drifted over the crowd of people and then beyond. It left them standing as though they'd emerged from a dry fog. The people stood quietly and watched him go. Alexandra got into her car and started the engine, feeling the grit in her teeth and over the skin of her face.

The next day was clear and hot, and all of us turned out in time to see Billy Harness drive up the road, hauling his drilling rig behind him. Alexandra and I sat on a stone wall with the

kids, and soon Billy had the derrick set up, and we all watched
the small butterflies moving around in the air as the bit began to
cut through the rock: it was too loud for anyone to talk. But it
was nice to sit there, in the shade of the tree, watching the gray,
pulverized rock oozing out of the ground. I had brought a sandwich, sardines on rye, one for me and one for Alexandra, but I
didn't have time to eat it, since by eleven-thirty, at forty-eight
feet, the well brought in twelve gallons a minute. McManus
could have started a Laundromat if he'd wanted. Then all of us
lined up, kids, women in their plain skirts and hats, men in
their faded jeans and dark glasses, Alexandra in her light cotton
dress, and we all had a drink of that cool, sharp water, as Billy
hooked up a hose to the new pump, and let us all have a drink.
Then we went back down the dry, dusty road.

It didn't rain, though, and there were other wells that went
dry, and Whalen was asked to find a place to drill. I don't know
how Alexandra found out about them, but she was there when
Whalen drove up in his truck, already carrying the piece of
willow he'd cut from a river bottom, and she was in the middle
of the crowd of kids that went along with him as he walked
slowly across the field, or a swale, and after the willow was
drawn down and left in the earth, Whalen began to walk toward the owner of the field, already having his hand out and
then getting his money. Then he went back to his truck, and
each time Alexandra was there, or close to it, and he'd see her
tall, thin figure, her face set in a not unfriendly, questioning
expression, and the first time he saw her, he said, "Good afternoon," but not more. The next time he saw her among the
crowd, her hair moving in the slight, dry breeze, her hand over
her eyes to shield them in the bright sunlight, he stopped and
stared, but said nothing. When he saw her again, at the edge of
another dry field, he said, "Do you need water? Is that it?" And
when she said no, he stood in the bright sunlight, one eye half
closed, the other set on her face. "Well, be careful where you sit.
Snakes move in dry weather, looking for water."

Finally, though, it rained, and those people, who'd been
thinking of driving out to Whalen's and asking him for help,
sighed instead, and went back to their old ways, letting faucets
drip and taking long cool showers. Alexandra didn't see him

again, but at the end of the month she came down the road and showed me a note, written on a piece of brown paper cut from a shopping bag and mailed in an envelope made from one, too. It said, "All right. Let's talk. Will you come out to my house on Saturday? Uncle Whalen."

Twenty Votes

I didn't see Alexandra for a week. There was an Indian summer, and then it got cool again. When the warm weather was over, I went to see Shelley Blackburn.

Shelley Blackburn has his store down along the river. He sells headstones and monuments, and I went down there, wanting to have all the details in order. I have bought the few square feet in the cemetery up the road. I'm at the age where it gives me a certain security to stand on that cold, humming piece of ground. It takes my mind off things, and makes me not so concerned about the stock market. Well, I wanted to pick out a headstone, too, to keep some relative from giving me a pink one with gaudy lettering on it. There's some nieces and nephews who'd probably jump at the chance. I went down to Shelley's and we talked about the World Series for a while and the designated hitter rule, and then we looked at the stones. He has a small warehouse and a yard, too, filled with gravel. In the summer, spring, and fall the stones are outside, and that's where I stood, looking at them. Shelley left me there, and I was standing in front of a piece of gray marble, the color of morning doves, when Alexandra walked into the yard.

She wore a gray skirt and a blouse, and a sweater. It was a late fall day, coolish. There had been a little snow a few days before, but it had melted. I was glad to see her, since there was no one else I could have trusted to be a good friend and make no fuss. We stood in front of the pieces of marble. I stepped back from one. For all the world I could have been buying a pair of shoes and looking at them in a mirror. This one's nice, I said.

I wanted her to sit down on it. If nothing else, I am practical: young people could sit on the thing and have their lunch. Alexandra sat down for a moment, but then she stood up. I asked if she thought a decoration was in order. I thought of Everett Dirksen pleading with Congress to designate the gladiola as the national flower. I like begonias better, and wanted to have them on the gray marble. Expense be hanged. But then, as I stood there, reciting Dirksen's speeches ("And what can compare with its lucent corolla, the veined majesty of the stem . . . ?"), the horror of the yard, the gravel, and the blank stones came over me like a blush, and I felt vain and old, too: she'd been waiting to talk to me, and didn't want to intrude. Well, I stopped, and asked if she'd like to go down the street to the coffee shop. It's comfortable there in the afternoon, in a large booth with the lined shadows of the venetian blinds laid across the table, the steam from a cup of coffee rising slowly into the slats of light. But we could talk more easily in the gravelly yard. Shelley Blackburn is a discreet man, and he stayed inside. I was glad to hear her voice. It made me feel as though I were still among the living.

Alexandra sighed and began, her voice drifting over the gravel and the gray marble.

On Saturday, she said, Shaw had driven her to Whalen's house. It was morning, and in the fall sunlight the house looked old and brooding. The air was filled with unmoving smoke that had risen from the chimney and then collapsed around the house. Alexandra got out of Shaw's truck, and when she looked up, Whalen was standing in front of the house.

He wore a pair of brush pants and a blue shirt, one that had been washed so many times as to be indistinguishable from the hazy blue of the sky, and when he walked against the gray woods or fields, there was the impression of a tunnel through them, in the shape of a man, that let you see through to the sky beyond. Now, though, he stood in front of the house, the smoke from the chimney falling around him.

"Why don't we take a walk?" he said. "Winter will be here soon. What do you say?"

"I'd like to," said Alexandra.

"We'll go for a long one," he said, "I've been cooped up with Aunt Katherine for a week. Don't you worry. I've got lunch." He put his hands against the two large front pockets of his shirt.

Shaw went inside to stay with Aunt Katherine. Through the window Alexandra saw the dog with one eye. It had been sitting next to Aunt Katherine's chair, leaning against it so as to be rubbed when the chair moved. Shaw lighted a cigarette. Aunt Katherine began to move her chair, but just a little, in a quick, short stroke, her hair pulled into a small bun and her shrunken, almost monkey-like face concentrating on the cigarette Shaw held just before her lips.

The dog came out of the house, emerging into the smoke and being, for a moment, hidden by it. Then the wind changed and the dog stood there, head and tail down, one eye squinted shut, the other set on Alexandra.

"Don't you worry about that mutt being blind in one eye," said Whalen. "Being that way makes his nose sharper. Most things are better hurt, if it doesn't kill them."

They walked. The air became hazy and yellowish, and Whalen, Alexandra, and the dog went through the woods, where the ground was covered with brown, pale yellow, and rose-colored leaves. They came to a wood road and went along it and came to piles of slash left by loggers, the tops of trees that lay there, each looking like an enormous piece of brush. The tops were surrounded by wild grape and Alexandra felt the vines wrap around her legs and knees as she pushed through them.

It wasn't so far into fall that all the leaves were gone, and around Alexandra and Whalen there were the pastel leaves of the maples, birch, and popple, which were soft, almost Mediterranean, more like pomegranates, lemons, and oranges, each one soothing and easy to look at. Whalen said nothing as he went, keeping his eyes on the land ahead of them, going steadily, his

legs moving in a definite, infinitely repeated pattern that reminded Alexandra of the ticking of the clock in the front room
of her house. He didn't look at her, or even acknowledge that
she was there, although if she caught her leg on a wild grape
vine, or stepped into some briars, he waited for her to come
along next to him. Sometimes they'd flush a woodcock, and then
they'd see the rise of the thing, the quick, bouncing flight of it
that seemed to have the same movement as a stone thrown
across the surface of a pond, skipping from one place to another.

"All right," said Whalen, "it's time for lunch. Here."

The pockets of his shirt were large, and out of one he brought
a sandwich wrapped in plastic. Alexandra took it, and thanked
him. Whalen looked at her, half closing one eye. They stood
next to a few apple trees, which were gray and which had scraggly crowns, without leaves, and the limbs of them were covered
with thorns. The thorns were as thick as knitting needles,
sharper, but only about two inches long, and black, almost
sooty-looking. Alexandra stood in the grass in front of the tree
and unwrapped the sandwich, which was made on slices of
thick white bread, not cut by any hand aside from Whalen's,
and between the bread there was some lettuce, a slice of onion,
and some mustard. Whalen looked at the hillside and took a
bite, and when Alexandra tasted hers, she felt the mustard as it
rose into her nose and the crunch of the lettuce and the onion.
Whalen reached an apple from the tree and threw it to her. The
apple was yellowish on one side and red on the top and had
dark spots where the birds had pecked it. It was small, too, and
Alexandra put her fingers around it before having a bite, which
was sharp, juicy, and made her not thirsty anymore. The skin of
the apple was a little dusty, and it tasted of bark and even the
slaty and gray hills before her.

"One time I was here and I shot a grouse," said Whalen. "He
flushed up over there. When I found him and picked him up, it
turned out he was only stunned. I was holding his legs when he
started flying away. He liked to dislocate my shoulder with the
jerking. For a moment I thought he might be able to lift me off
the damn ground. Then I wrung his neck."

The one-eyed dog came over to Alexandra, and she reached out and patted the dusty fur of its head.

"We got a lot of coons up here, too," said Whalen. "When I used to grow some corn, they got into it."

"What did you do about them?" said Alexandra.

"Well," said Whalen, "I'll tell you a secret. Coons don't like music, and one of the things that kept the farm going as long as it did was I'd take a portable radio I got with Green Stamps, and put it out in the middle of the fields. I turned it to a station in New Hampshire that only played Frank Sinatra. The coons hated Sinatra."

"Did you ever try Barbra Streisand?" said Alexandra.

"No," said Whalen, "I didn't want to *kill* them, I just wanted to scare them away."

Then they turned and went through the orchard, down through the pine and around the slash left by a logger, the tops of the trees fallen together and filled with vines, raspberries and blackberries. It was colder as they went downhill, and when they came out of the woods, and onto the road, it had clouded up. They went toward the house in that same tired, regular gait.

Whalen stood at the door, which he held open, the yellowish light behind.

"Come into the house," he said, and then Alexandra climbed the steps, and heard the sound from the other room where Aunt Katherine was rocking. Alexandra went past the foyer and stood before the fireplace, where the room was filled with a steady *kerrriiik, kerrriiik, kerrriiik*. And while Alexandra stood there, glad for the warmth of the room, she heard the sound of Whalen's boots on the stairs and the hiss of a lantern, too, and after a moment the cellar door opened and Whalen came out, carrying one of those dusty bottles that had Harlow's card taped to it. He took a rag from a hook near the top of the cellar steps and cleaned the bottle until it shined, showing the reddish old liquor under the glass.

"I have a favor to ask you," said Whalen.

"What do you want?" said Alexandra.

"I've got a mess of this stuff in the cellar," said Whalen.

"Yes," said Alexandra.

"There's a lot of it down there, near three gallons," said

Whalen, "and I was wondering if you'd help me drink it. It'll probably take all winter. And then, by springtime, I'll stop thinking about those goddamned twenty votes."

"I thought you'd never ask," said Alexandra.

Shaw stood next to Aunt Katherine's chair, but then he went into the kitchen and came back with three glasses. Whalen poured some of that old, pale liquor into each one.

"There!" said Whalen, looking at his nephew. "There! You see! I've got manners after all."

"I know it," said Shaw.

"Ha!" said Whalen. "Here's to a damn long winter."

The liquor was smooth and easy to swallow.

Whalen had gone grouse hunting the day before, and he sat down to draw the birds. Alexandra sat in the kitchen with him, feeling the snow melt in her hair and run down the side of her neck. As the feathers came out of the birds there was a steady, small popping sound. Whalen broiled the birds, and after a while they ate the broiled grouse with hot German potato salad and beer. When they'd finished, Alexandra took a breast and some potato salad and knelt next to Aunt Katherine. Alexandra brought a drink, too, from the dusty bottle, and the lids over Aunt Katherine's blind eyes fluttered when she tasted the liquor and when she tasted the meat, too.

When Shaw and Alexandra were leaving, Whalen came to the door and said, "There's one thing I don't want to forget. And that's the look on Ross Critchfield's face when he came down the road in that little car of his. A Morris. He got out and looked at the trees across the road, and, by God, he looked like he'd eaten a toad, webbed feet and all. And then the rest of those black birds came and stood around, but all the hard looks in the world weren't going to move one of those maple trunks. It took us working with chain saws two days to do that. And I'll tell you something else. Every election since then, Ross Critchfield votes by absentee ballot, just to be on the safe side."

Then Whalen turned and went into the house to sit there under the lantern while Aunt Katherine rocked until she was tired.

Then Indian summer came, and Alexandra and Willie drove out and looked for mushrooms on Whalen's land, large Chicken of the Woods, which they brought home. Shaw dusted them off, sliced the almost coral-like shape into long strips, sautéed them in butter, and then they ate them. Afterward, Alexandra looked out the window and saw the ridge above the Sugar Wolf River, and as she stood there, hearing the splash of water in Shaw's bath, she felt the anxious, faintly euphoric tug of the woods.

They drove to Whalen's house and after helping bank the house with hay or stacking wood, they sat in the screened-in porch next to the kitchen and felt the light of the afternoon sun. They ate pea soup with large pieces of bacon in it and drank dark beer, and Alexandra sat in the warmth of the screened porch and listened, as she drowsed, to the last buzzing of a fly near the door. Whalen said they could use a piece of ground in the spring, and Shaw and Alexandra thought, as they drank the dark beer and felt the smoky silence of the land, that they would plant potatoes, green onions, cherry tomatoes, long cucumbers. Alexandra imagined the crisp, sharp taste of a radish and wondered if she could get sage to grow, too.

Then Indian summer was over, and Alexandra found me at Shelley Blackburn's, where she stood, pressing her fingertips against the shiny and gray marble. Perhaps the coldness of it helped her. Of course there was something wrong. Or worse than wrong. She spoke of Whalen, of Indian summer, and all of it had come in that flat, breathy voice, and when she spoke, she stood, one hand trembling and reaching out to touch the surface of that cool, gray stone. Well, I waited. Across the street there was a greenish house with a front porch. There were chairs on it, and in the warm weather the people who lived there came out to watch Shelley's customers as they stood in front of the gray, white, and pinkish headstones. The people on the porch drank iced tea and lemonade and were silent as they watched. Occasionally I glanced at Alexandra, at her pale face and her fingers as they turned white at the tips, pressed there against the marble. She turned to me and raised a brow.

I wondered why I had been so stupid. Maybe it was having to pick out the marble. Maybe I'd become self-centered in that. I don't know. Of course, I knew what the problem with her was. Bryce had found them out.

"At least," she said, "he saw us in the street. No one told him. That's something."

I supposed it was, and then both of us stared at the empty porch. I could taste the lemonade in summer, sharp and sour. She told me she'd been unprepared. Of course, they stopped. They didn't really talk about it. Alexandra went to the loft and took her things away. She didn't have a small suitcase, so she put the few dresses, makeup, pants, and underthings into a bag from the grocery. She wished she'd had a suitcase, she said, so she could have walked out of the building with it, for the entire town to see. I wasn't ashamed of anything, she said. Not a thing! And then she sat on the cool marble stone.

Of course, both of us knew that now the town would begin to tell Bryce, just to watch his face, to get a good close look. And I wanted a look, too, maybe I'd be the first one in line.

She stood up and wrinkled her brow for a moment, but then she got a grip on herself and we walked away from the headstones. Shelley had been waiting just back inside, by the cash register, and when I came out, I said, "That one. The gray marble. I'll take that one right there. Put some begonias on it and some gladiolas, too."

"They're eighty dollars apiece," he said.

"Fine," I said, "I'll take a dozen."

He wrote it up and I signed for them.

"Who do you think is going to win the series?" he said.

"The Pirates," I said, "you can't stop them."

BOOK III

The Bottom of the Falls

Gangland

 I want to tell a small story here. It didn't seem to be more than a moment in Alexandra's life. Or in mine. How many bits and pieces of half-heard or half-thought-about information come your way each week or month? The kind of thing you overhear at the grocer's, the gas station, the dry cleaner's, the florist's? Well, some years before, when Anne was growing up, Alexandra used to sit in my sun room, or outside when the weather was cool and nice. We'd eat and talk, as I've said. But I don't want to give the impression that there was never anyone else around. Of course the Critchfields and Thachers, their cousins, and assorted fuddy-duddies were around. We got rid of them as quickly as we could, especially if we had something private to talk about. It was amazing how they could linger on, though, each sitting with legs crossed and holding a teacup and saucer, eyes half closed. You'd think they were asleep, the vipers, but they weren't: they were waiting to hear a little juicy bit. Well, after a while they'd get up and go, and then we'd be able to talk frankly. It was a breath of fresh air.

But there were other people, too. People from the Soil Conservation Department, engineers, and old classmates of mine from Berkeley. There were clients and ex-clients, men and women who worked for the wildlife foundations, pleasant, charming people, some of whom were obsessed by silt flowing into trout water, or the loss of wetlands for ducks. And there were just old friends, men and women I had known. One of them was Tommy Goshorn, who at one time had been an assistant police commissioner in Philadelphia.

One summer Tommy and I were sitting outside in the garden in green wicker chairs I'd put out. We were eating Liederkranz and sardines with slices of onion and large pieces of tomato with parsley and vinaigrette. Tommy and I knew a few secrets about one another, and some old stories, and we sat there enjoying the afternoon and some memories we didn't get to talk about too often. Alexandra came down the road, walking slowly, enjoying the summer day, the sound of the leaves in the wind, the movement of the insects above the field. Alexandra smiled and sat down, and I got up to get her something to drink. Of course, sooner or later with Goshorn, the subject of murder came up. He had been a homicide detective for years, and knew some stories, which he told, leaning forward, fixing his eyes on you, and then, when he wanted to make a point, he threw himself backward into a chair and laughed, although he still looked at you. I felt like confessing to almost anything when I saw that look.

Well, I asked him what it was that made for what the papers called a "gangland style" murder. They're always saying that. Or "professional" killing. Or some other phrase that suggested people who live in a gray, peculiar world, in which there are only modern, expensive, and anonymous hotels, car-rental agencies, airlines, and restaurants that struggle to suggest the presence of money . . . one never thinks of the "professional killer" as sitting around in the summer in a pleasant garden, drinking beer and talking to old friends. Or eating a sandwich, or being in love. Perhaps they never do . . . I don't know about such things.

Goshorn leaned forward, his elbows on the arms of that green wicker chair. He had a sardine on a piece of toast, and held it in one hand. The sun hit it, and the shiny skin looked as bright as polished silver. Goshorn leaned his bald head downward a little, and stared at me, and then, perhaps in an unguarded moment, or just because he was old and didn't care anymore, he said, "It always boils down to two things. A large-caliber, untraceable gun. Left there. If the killer is really well connected, the gun will have been stolen off a ship. But, it could be just a large-caliber gun that's never been written up. It doesn't have to be new." Then he threw himself back into his chair and laughed, although he continued to look at me.

It wasn't really more than summer conversation. There were insects around. The sun was bright and the leaves in the distance blew in the wind. But Alexandra sat opposite him, watching his face, although she seemed a little brittle. She smiled, though, and kept up her end of the conversation. We talked, but she kept looking at Goshorn.

When he left, Alexandra said good-bye and smiled pleasantly enough, but when he was gone, and we were alone, she started shaking. For a while she tried to deny it and we talked about politics and movies, but then she gave that up, too. And when she sat there, I realized she'd been given information that might come in handy. And she was tempted by it. Or worse than tempted. Maybe she knew she'd just put the information aside and sooner or later she'd find a use for it. What she despised was being reduced to someone who would pick up such things and think about them seriously. What self-contempt there was as she sat in the dappled sunshine, her hands shaking, as she looked at me and said, "Of course, I have one like that. Harlow had two or three, in the bottom of his case, that were never written up."

Anyway, that was some years ago. She lived with the knowledge. I mention it because it was the kind of pressure that built up. . . . Well, things went along as I've described them, at least, that is, until a week after Bryce found her out. Because, a week after that she was gone. . . .

There was no note, nothing. And Shaw was gone, too. Xannie told me she'd left. Had she packed a bag? Xannie told me she had, a medium-size one. Not large. She took no papers, nothing aside from her wallet and a checkbook. Just some clothes. I'm not certain she knew what she was doing. All I knew was that she'd gone, and that I was left to wait.

It didn't take long for Bryce to find out she'd gone, too, and he came running. He sat in my living room, his head in his hands. His blondish hair was combed back, and his skin was pale. It was one of the few times he was honest, and I listened carefully. There was a moment when I almost felt sorry for him. He was trapped, too, and he was so tired of things. He said he might have "twisted Alexandra's arm" a little, just to keep her in line . . . that's the way he spoke when he was being honest about blackmail. But he didn't want her to be "loyal" just because her "arm had been twisted." He had been lonely. And there was something else that was bothering him. He was getting old.

He never thought he'd get old, and it came as a shock that he was now forty-seven. He had been successful with women. That was the word he used. It was becoming harder and he hadn't found them as satisfying, either. What was the use of scaring them, or "twisting their arms"? Not physically, of course . . . my God, that was the last thing in the world Bryce would have done. It had grown stale. He had the sense about himself that his life would continue, having no surprises and no romance, until he was left with the certainty of his old age. He couldn't understand why Alexandra didn't love him.

I sat opposite him, being surprised the glass I held didn't shatter in my hand. If you're going to have fools around, buy glasses of good quality, the kind that are heavy and can take some squeezing. . . . The fact of the matter is that I had never heard such sentimentality. For a moment, I began to let my jaw drop in wonder, but I stopped it, and made a strange, half-yawning, uneasy face. At least, if nothing else, Bryce proved how evil sentimentality is.

He wanted me to know about a party Alexandra had. A coming-out party. That's what he called it. He spoke as though I hadn't watched her grow up, and as though I hadn't been at the party he described. When he talked about it, he leaned forward, out of his chair, staring at the dark fields beyond the window and pressing the tips of his fingers together until they became cloudy beneath the nails.

He said the party had been at a house on the beach north of Boston. It was a large house, three stories, and had an irregular shape. It was covered with shingles and had about it an air that was both nautical and Germanic. In one corner there was a circular structure that went from the first floor to the top of the house, and because of it, each floor had a small place where you could sit, among cut flowers, in a comfortable brocade chair, and look out the window at the ocean. There was a large room downstairs, and on the night of the party a band had been there. The party had been on a foggy evening.

Alexandra and a friend, Bryce said, had been uncomfortable and expectant before the party. They went for a walk on the beach, hearing the hush of the ocean in the fog, and then they returned, seeing the house at a distance, the yellow light from it streaming through the mist. The band leader played the trumpet, and as they approached they heard the muted sound of it, and the house had a romantic, glamorous quality. The party began.

The young men had worn evening clothes and starched shirt-fronts and they wore bow ties that were small and black. Their hair was neatly parted and they wore dark, broken-in shoes that were nevertheless polished and shiny. The young women were dressed in clothes of the season, longish gowns that were without straps and showed young shoulders, long necks, the tans they had gotten during the long, heavy summer before. They had had a long, late supper, where there were toasts and laughter. Later there was more dancing, more champagne, and then the young men and women took off their shoes and went outside, onto the beach, where there was fog, through which they could all smell the tang of the ocean, the seaweed and iodine scent, and as they walked along the beach, feeling the coolness of the damp sand, there was the sense of the future (which was elegant and exciting) as definitely around them as the squeak of the sand under bare toes. There was the moaning of the fog horns, the clink of some pulley on an unseen yacht, and the bewilderment, seriousness, and flip dismissal, too, of those who walked there in the fog with the future just before them.

Of course, the jackass had gotten all this from Alexandra. He spoke carefully about it, as though it were a speech in a foreign language. When he finished, he still had his hands pushed together, and then he said, with more hatred than I have ever heard, "Well, I was never invited."

But he had it all wrong! I was at Alexandra's party. In the middle of it I was called into an upstairs bathroom. Perhaps someone asked me in the bright, drunken champagne glitter of the evening to go into the room because I was an engineer, a man of science, something like a doctor. Well, someone was sick. Or a lot of young people were sick. I knocked on the door and then went in. The bathroom was large. It had two sinks, large mirrors above them, a large bathtub. There were large white tiles on the floor, white walls, heavy chrome racks for towels. The racks had heaters in them to make the towels warm. The bathroom was filled with young women who had drunk too much. One was at the toilet, her skirts bunched up as she knelt, her long legs in stockings stretched out behind her. At each sink there was a young woman, each bending over it and throwing up there. And there were two more at the bathtub, each one holding her skirt so as to keep it clean as they stood there sick and miserable. I heard the young woman who was at the toilet say to herself, or the others in the room, or to the entire party down below, "Jesus. Oh, Jesus. It's really begun, hasn't it?" And of course it had: that phantom-like thing was already tugging at the young women there, pulling them toward marriages, children, divorces, which would leave them older, more confused, and without youth. The young women had every right to be drunk, and the young men, too, who were downstairs, doing the same thing in the bushes behind the house, at least some of the young men, who knew the same thing was happening to them, and they would be left drinking a triple martini in the morning before going into the office where they had become stockbrokers. And the young women were wonders, those in the bathroom, because in ten minutes they had splashed water on their faces, put on more makeup, sucked on a Life Saver, and were down below, hearing the music and sipping, just sipping, a new, cold glass of champagne.

Well, Bryce wouldn't have understood even if I had wanted to tell him. And it's certain I didn't want to. He was convinced I felt sorry for him, and he was almost on the verge of tears. If he had shed just one . . .

He told me something else that day, and I find myself thinking about it from time to time.

"I always have been terrified," he said, "of people I can't trust."

One thing was certain. He wanted to know where Alexandra was. And he wasn't going to let her "get away with anything." I said nothing and squeezed my glass. After a while he got up and left, and then I sat, hearing the wind in the chimney while I held my dog's gray muzzle in my lap.

In the morning, I woke to that gray, deadly light of fall, and in the dim room I wondered where Alexandra was. I went about my business, answered my mail, saw my lawyer, ordered groceries, cooked my food and let it sit on the old chipped plate I used. I took a long hot bath, feeling the heat around my chest and stomach, the soothing pressure of it sink into those organs that itched with disease. I hated the silence. I wore my comfortable clothes, old boots, brown pants, and a large, blue sweater. Took a stick and poked it into old stumps, stirring up the ants.

Bryce came back the next day. He stopped in front of the house and honked the horn, and when I came out, he said, "I know where they are."

"How do you know?" I said.

He didn't smile when he told me he'd called the telephone company. They'd given him a list of the long-distance charges on Alexandra's bill. He'd gone through the numbers, marking off the ones he knew or were listed in Alexandra's book. That left one that had been called twice. It was the number of an inn up toward the Canadian border. There was nothing else to do, he said, but to go after them.

Of course, I tried to argue. I stood by the car, feeling my words blown away by the wind, becoming pale in it. I spoke as an old friend. I think I made a joke, too, advised seeing a lawyer. Perhaps he wanted to come in and have a drink. Maybe, I thought, I'd get him good and drunk.

"You don't understand," he said, "I know where they are."

In desperation, I asked what the name of the place was . . . he smiled and shook his head, then turned his car around and went away, going fast and leaving behind the eddies of air that moved the leaves from the side of the road and left them gently falling onto the gray dirt surface.

I finished the chores for winter. I stopped eating and waited by the phone, reading Watson's *Gardener's Assistant*, and tried to imagine the right combination of things to grow in a bed for cut flowers: it seemed, as I sat by the phone, that whites, reds and salmon-colored ones would be best, and I thought of Tahiti begonias, Everest phlox, Prairie Sunset lilies, cornflowers, and some ferns to mix with them. Perhaps I'd even find some place for gladiolas. Well, I thought of bringing the flowers in, in the heat of summer, the shape and odor of them looking and smelling cool and refreshing on a table set in the sun room. I waited eight nights.

The rain begins in the fall, and it will last for days, coming down solidly, and there is something about the cold, gray insistence of it that makes you long for snow. While I was waiting, the rains began. They kept me up, leaving me to lie awake and hear the sound on the roof, each drop as definite as one of the points of a chill moving over your skin. It rained for two days and in the middle of the second, the fog boiled up from the river and filled the valley. I sat in the white, opaque air, in the damp claustrophobia of it, and stared at nothing at all. The sky turned blue, and then dark, and I went to bed, still hearing the rush of the rain against the roof. I didn't really dream and didn't really sleep: I have an old man's broken, half-delirious rest, and in it I thought of a man I knew when I was young, a deer hunter, who said, "Wouldn't you know if someone came into your house? Wouldn't you? Well, the woods are a deer's house. Do you think he knows when you're there?" Then I woke, hearing the endless, numbing rain, the tick of it as it fell from the slate tiles of the roof onto the hard ground outside. I knew someone was in the house.

It was as though the air was different. Perhaps a door had opened, and the breeze blew in. I don't know. But I sat on the edge of my bed, looking for my slippers. I didn't hear any broken glass, or the sound of a lock being forced. Everyone knows I never lock a door. If someone has a business with me, he can find me anytime. I pulled on a robe and went downstairs, not seeing a light, or hearing any movement, but when I came into the sun room, I heard the sound of the rain much louder and I saw, too, that Alexandra was standing there.

She was dripping wet, and her hair was wet, too, stuck to her face. The late night had its own gray light, and it showed her eyes as mirror-like, and gray, too. In the sound of the water running from the roof, there were others, two or three of which were fast, and we stood there, hearing the quick *drip drip drip*. There was some water in her jeans, and it made a small tick, too, as it hit the stone of the floor. Whenever I think of the time, it's the sound of the dripping I remember, the insane tick of it as Alexandra reached with her fingers for a strand of wet hair, which she pushed out of her face, tucked behind an ear, and said, "Bryce is dead. That's what I came to tell you."

She didn't say anything more. I waited. We listened to the constant, harsh sound, the horrible dripping. I imagined holding her by both shoulders and shaking an answer out of her. Her lips were bluish and they trembled: perhaps she tried to speak. I kept my hands in the pockets of my bathrobe, the fingers of my large old hands made into fists. Then I said, "Maybe you need a towel?"

"Yes, thanks," she said.

I went into the bathroom and took from the cupboard there two large ones. They were neatly folded and heavy, and I brought them out to her. She took one and sat down on it in a chair and shook out the other.

"I'm sorry about the floor," she said.

"That's all right," I said, "I've been worried. . . ."

"Have you?" she said.

She put the large towel over her head, and worked at her hair with both hands, the fingers spread out as she worked. She went about it with a rough, shaking motion and said, "Ah. Ah. That's good." I sat there, hearing the steady *drip drip drip*, and all I could think about was who would come to the man's funeral. There'd be plenty of people: no one, in this town, is ever buried alone. It's a good funeral town.

We sat there, Alexandra drying her hair. And after a few moments, after she looked at me and the things in the room, almost as though to reassure herself, to guarantee where she was, she began, in that same, slow voice. I wanted to know if she had . . . killed him, if she had finally used one of those guns of Harlow's, but when I asked, or hinted, she looked at me and put her head back and laughed, and when she was done, she put her hand to her eyes, to wipe away the tears there, and said, "No, it was worse than that. . . ." Then she touched the side of her eyes again.

In the end, it turned out, it was a look, a glance that had killed him: just that. And maybe, when I read back over what I have put down here, it seems to me that that moment, that glance, is what I have been trying to avoid. Well, Alexandra had been, too, but it caught up with her just the same.

The Camel's Back

 When she had finished drying her hair, she looked up and shook it out, touching it with her hand, making the curled strands bounce around her face. Then she said that after she'd been found out, after she'd taken her things from Willie's loft, she decided that she'd go on living her life as it was before he'd come back to town. She knew how to be lonely. In a way, she almost looked forward to it, since it was cleansing and had its own devotional quality. At least, she said, she knew how to allow the ordinary details of day-to-day life to take care of her. But, when she tried to do it, she found she'd lost the touch. It was harder than she'd ever remembered. Anne was away at school, and there didn't seem to be quite so many of those day-to-day details as there had been before. I was amazed she thought she would be able to cut things off and go about her business. After all, she loved the man.

It was fall, and there were things to do for the winter, and Alexandra put up the storm windows, banked the house with hay, put antifreeze into her car, drained the outside pipes, drove small wooden wedges into the windows so they wouldn't rattle in the wind and then she caulked them, too. She started early and finished late. The jobs were done quickly, and then she and

Xannie were left in the sealed house, both of them listening to
the silence outside and feeling the oppressive quality of the last
warm afternoons of fall.

After Bryce found her out, he went to Boston for a few days.
It is typical of him that he'd be generous after he'd done some
harm. And after she'd gotten the house ready for winter, and
was sitting uneasily in it, he came back. She was looking out the
window when the new red Turbo pulled up in front of the
stone walls.

They had dinner together and went to bed early. Alexandra
got up early, too. They went shopping together and for a walk.
They didn't talk about what had happened. It was as though
they were in a strange play. She heard Bryce moving around
the house late at night, the clink of the toothbrush in his glass,
the squeak of the board in the hall as he stepped on it, the sigh
of the bed as he got into it. At night there was the slow whistle
of his breathing, as she lay awake, staring at the ceiling. In the
morning she made him breakfast. Xannie had gone for the paper already, and Bryce sat at the dining room table, turning the
papers, making a slight *lick, lick* as he went from one to the
other. Alexandra brought him a piece of toast and a soft-boiled
egg, and then she went back to the kitchen, but as she went she
stopped and turned, hearing, as she had for years, the *chit, chit,
chit* as Bryce took a spoon and tapped at the top of the egg.

The sound made her stop and stare out the window, and for a
moment she thought of nothing, until she heard the tapping
again, and while she heard it she knew what it reminded her of,
or what she thought it was like: grave robbers, digging at gold
in teeth. She turned and looked at the man, listening to him,
hearing the slight *lick* of the knife and fork, a squeak of the
chair, and the slow crinkle and sigh as he turned the pages of
the newspaper.

She went upstairs. There was a mirror in the hall, and as she
heard the noises she stopped in front of it. The mirror was old
and there were gray, bare patches around the edges that reflected nothing, but there was enough silver left in the center to
make a clear, sharp image. The glass was held in a wooden
frame and had been polished over the years until the wood was
dark, almost the color of dried blood, and shiny. Alexandra

stood in front of it and stared at herself. She saw the figure there reaching out to her, their fingers touching at the tip. The cold glass made the two figures separate with a start. Alexandra couldn't stand the touch, or the reflection of her face, either. It was a little like looking into one's own grave. She had always believed Bryce had never really gotten to her and hadn't done anything to change her: it had been her strength to believe it. And, as she reached out and touched the reflection of her hand, as she stared into her own eyes, she saw it had been delusion. She had always thought she'd get away with it, with the arrangement she'd made. It was a shock to see that she wasn't going to. The reflection of the carefully controlled woman was haunting, since she was someone Alexandra had never wanted to be.

Alexandra sat down on the bench in the hall and pushed her head against the hard plaster. She tried to sit up straight, to fold her hands neatly in her lap, to hold her neck as though she were balancing a book on the top of her head, but all she felt was a peculiar softness, and she sat there, breathing deeply. From downstairs there was a click as the door opened and Bryce went outside for his walk. The house was quiet, aside from the steady ticking of the clock downstairs. Alexandra got up, went into her room, took down a suitcase and started packing.

The suitcase wasn't large, and she was careful about what she put into it. Alexandra walked back and forth between the closet, bureau, and suitcase, moving with a sense of lightness and ease, almost as though she were drifting on some downhill grade. Although in the middle she sat down, holding a scarf and a sweater in her hand, and rested for a moment. Outside, she heard the sound of Bryce's footsteps in the road, and she imagined his legs swinging out from side to side, and his hands held together in the middle of his back. She got up to continue packing.

It didn't take long. Then she sat on the bed. She looked up at the long cracks on the ceiling, which she had spent nights staring at, wondering what rivers they suggested, the Mississippi, the Yukon, the Amazon, the Nile, the Elbe. . . . Well she sat there, looking at the long, veinlike cracks, as a car stopped in front of the house.

From the window Alexandra saw a woman standing at the gate in the stone wall. The woman was wearing a gray suit and gray stockings and she had a new tan overcoat over one arm. She looked up at the house, her eyes moving over the windows, and then, with a certain obvious determination, she began to walk toward the front door. Alexandra went downstairs to meet her. When Alexandra opened the door, she saw the woman had dark hair, but that there were some streaks of gray in it. She had pretty features. She was tall and slender, and her figure made her seem younger than she was, although there was a downward tug in her face that suggested her years, or her years and a little more.

The woman introduced herself as Debra Carey. She had been a friend of Harlow's in Washington years before. She had always wondered what Harlow's house had looked like. The inside of it, she meant, and since she'd finally come to New England, and wasn't staying very far away, she thought she'd drop in, if it wasn't too much of an imposition.

They went through the house. Alexandra looked at Debra Carey's face as they went around a room, and the features seemed both strange and familiar, and as they went Alexandra realized she'd seen the face before: there was a photograph of Debra upstairs, and there was a note that went with it, written in a crisp, neat hand: ". . . we should never have taken the chance . . . with the breeze moving the white curtains and the orchestra playing below in the garden . . ." ". . . I can't stand this separate feeling, as though there were a large transparent thing that fit over us both, and now that you're away, I feel the light dragging of the empty part that used to fit over you . . ."

Alexandra and Debra sat down in the living room. Xannie brought them each a cup of tea, and Debra sat with hers carefully balanced on her knee.

"It would be terrible, absolutely terrible if I spilled it," said Debra.

Debra had neatly folded her raincoat and left it on the cushion next to her.

"You know," said Debra, "I was a little in love with your father."

"I know," said Alexandra, "I've seen a picture of you."

"There was one of me on a balcony . . ." said Debra. "It was taken in Mexico City. We went down there together. . . . We had a good time."

Alexandra drank the tea, glad for the heat of it.

"There were times when I made your father happy. But they were just moments," said Debra.

Alexandra nodded.

"He was lonely," said Debra. She shrugged a little, then sipped her tea.

"I'm sure he was," said Alexandra.

They sat quietly in the living room. Debra looked around a little and then concentrated on holding the teacup.

"There are still some letters upstairs, and that photograph of you, too," said Alexandra. "Would you like to have them?"

"Yes," she said, looking down into her cup. "I would."

They finished the tea.

"You know," said Debra, "I was never in his house in Georgetown."

"Well," said Alexandra, "this house is still pretty much the same as when he lived here."

"And the way it was when your mother lived here?" said Debra.

"Yes," said Alexandra, "and my mother too."

"I'm sorry," said Debra, "I shouldn't have come in. I'm acting like a bitch."

They went upstairs and into the study, where Alexandra opened the bottom drawer of the filing cabinet, and then Debra knelt before it, putting her shins flat against the floor. Her fingers went through the envelopes quickly, stopping once over an envelope that wasn't hers. Her fingers went through the rest quickly, and then she came to the notes in her handwriting. She picked them out and the photograph, too, of her as a young woman in Mexico, sitting on a hotel balcony, a drink in her hand and the breeze blowing a few strands of her hair across her face, her full lips set in a smile, which suggested not only a delicious secret about herself, but about the man who took the photograph, too.

Debra put the letters into her bag, pushed the drawer shut, and then the two of them went downstairs. In the foyer, behind

the door, they stood opposite one another, and Alexandra saw
in Debra's face an expression like the one she had seen in her
own, upstairs, when she had looked in the mirror: Debra had
probably never thought she'd spend a day like this one, either.
There was a soft, kind glow from the fanlight. Debra lingered
for a moment and then thanked Alexandra and went out, her
shoes making a slow, diminishing click as her heels hit the flagstones that led to the gate in the stone wall. Then Alexandra
was left in the empty house, hearing the clock.

After a while, Bryce came back. It was Sunday, and there was
more of the paper to read. They had lunch. Bryce had to leave
early to be back in Boston to be up first thing on Monday.

"It was a pleasant visit, wasn't it?"

"Yes," said Alexandra.

"And maybe we'll get along," said Bryce. "We've had our
difficulties, like everyone else. But maybe we can put them
aside. You know I care for you."

Alexandra nodded.

Bryce gathered his papers together. He never had to pack,
since there were things for him in his apartment in Boston and
in Alexandra's house, too. He smiled when he went out the
door. He stood next to her and kissed her, not noticing that she
looked over his shoulder when she did so, her eyes set on the
window, beyond which the woods seemed to be running together in the old, distorting panes of glass. Bryce went out, and
she sat down in the hall.

Then she told Xannie she was leaving for a few days and that
he shouldn't worry. He blinked at her and took her hand, which
he shook a little formally, before he went quietly into the room
behind the kitchen. Alexandra went upstairs and called an inn
near the Canadian border. It was a beautiful place and she
called and made a reservation. Just like that! she said. When she
told me, she took a short, shushing breath, as though she still
had a chill from being wet. Just like that, she said.

She went out to her white Jeep, taking the bag with her. At
the time she even laughed at herself when she tried to lie by
saying she'd be gone for just a little while. She just needed a
little time. Then she got into her car, gently putting the bag on
the backseat. She drove along the darkened road, seeing by the

headlights the trunks of the trees, each one looking gray and enormous, like the leg of an elephant.

She went to a small town about twenty miles away, which had a square surrounded by white buildings with green shutters. On the outskirts of town there were motels. Alexandra went into one and registered and then went to a pay phone and called Shaw.

She waited in the rented room. There was paneling on the walls, pieces of pine that looked nicotine-stained, yellowish, a carpet that could be washed with a hose, a picture on the wall that had been made in a factory, and thin, gauzy curtains that were starched and new-smelling. She sat on the bed, dangling her legs over the baseboard, and looked at herself in the mirror on the wall opposite. Her face was white around the eyes and lips, her hair loose and not brushed out. She listened to the cars passing by outside, and untied the tennis shoes she wore, pulled the laces back, out of the holes, jerked them free. Shaw found her in her bare feet, sitting in front of the mirror, staring at herself.

"Come here," she said. "Please."

Shaw sat next to her, hearing the sigh of the motel bed. Then both of them stared at their reflections in the cheap mirror. Shaw had just come from the cold, and his face was reddish, almost as though sunburned. Outside there was the sound of trucks and cars as they went by on the interstate highway, which wasn't far from the motel. Alexandra sat, trying to face the images of the both of them, stared into her own eyes, not flinching, not seeming to notice the motel room, the airy despair of the place, or the expression on the face of the man next to her.

"Will you stay with me for a while?" she said.

"You know I will," he said.

She was absolutely still, only moving her eyes as she looked at the room, the furniture covered with thin veneer, the painting on the wall in primary colors, the cracks on each side of it where the Sheetrock had been badly taped, the carpet that was the color of split-pea soup. There was a heater and a slight tinny whir from it. Alexandra looked at each object, and tried to stand up to them, to brace herself and look into the mirror, but she let her head move a little more, the smallest bit imaginable, and then she said, looking up again and facing the mirror, and sighing a little, too, "I just got tired. That's all."

Then she stood up and while Shaw took off his coat, she turned down the bed and took off her clothes, doing so quickly, in a girlish manner, dropping things on the floor around her and getting between the cool, rough sheets.

"Please, lie down next to me," she said. "I haven't been able to sleep. Maybe we can sleep."

"I'll turn up the heater," said Shaw.

"Yes," she said, "I'm cold."

Shaw lay down next to her and pulled up the light blanket. She pushed her back and buttocks against him and said, "I just want to sleep."

"Okay," he said. "Fine."

They listened to the tinny whir from the heater.

The trucks and cars went by outside, but the sounds stopped being harsh and grating, and after a while, they seemed fuzzy, almost smokelike, and then they seemed to disappear as the bed got warmer and as the sound of the heater disappeared, too.

In the morning, after the night in the motel, they began driving north, along the river. There wasn't ice in it yet, and Alexandra saw some ducks there, flying over its surface, just skimming it.

"All I wanted to do," she told me, when she came into my house out of the rain, "was to keep moving. That's what seemed important." And, as she went along in the car, she thought about nothing at all. There was the reflection of the hills in the river, the sky there as shiny as silver, the land itself that passed with a sure, haunting indifference. But, she said, she always knew Bryce was coming after her. She never doubted it for a moment. There was the sense of him just beyond the sight of things, or in the gray, scraggly crowns of trees or in the exposed rock of the mountains. Sure, she said, she had known Bryce would find them. It was the man Bryce brought along who came as a surprise.

Bryce and Sonny

Sonny had been Bryce's best student in the prison, and when he got out he moved to Bridgefield, Massachusetts. The most prominent thing about the town is a cemetery and some mills that have closed. The cemetery was begun as not much more than a squarish field, but over the years it grew, and now it covers the hills that surround the original piece of land. There are monuments of large gray stones, and the names on them can be read from a hundred yards away. The grass is carefully mowed and green, and it is the one place in town that looks well kept. The mills are closed up and have their windows broken and the river that runs behind them is an unhealthy green color. It looks like crème de menthe and milk mixed together.

In the end, I went to Bridgefield. I wanted to talk to Sonny. I had talked to everyone else, had spent years listening . . . well, I wasn't going to be cheated of the whole story. I got into my old station wagon, smelling the dirt of it, the dust from the jobs I had done. It was twenty years old, had wood on the sides, and it swayed a little when I got into it. The seat fits me well, and my dog likes to sit up front with me, putting his blind old head out of it and slobbering in the wind. I wear dark glasses when I drive, and my dog can't see a thing. He moaned and whined and moved his head up and down when we passed the cemetery in Bridgefield. At the end of the cemetery there is a large sign with a blue-and-white eye and words beneath it that say CRIME WATCH.

A little beyond the cemetery there is a row of houses. Or, there is a long building with a pitched roof, and it is covered with green asphalt shingles that are the same color as the river. The building is two hundred feet long, but it has doors here and there, cut into it, so that the entire thing looks like six buildings put together under one roof. In front of the building the dirt is packed down, hard as cement, glittering with broken glass and the cardboard wrappers from six-packs of beer. There are no bottles, though, since a deposit is charged on them. One of the buildings is a boardinghouse and on the wall of it someone has written, with a can of blue spray-paint, WELCOME TO CLOUD NINE. Inside the door is another small sign, which says NO COOKING IN ROOMS.

I climbed the stairs and knocked on Sonny's door. He opened it and stared over the night chain that was new, a bright golden color. The chain quivered as Sonny held the door against it. I introduced myself.

There was a click and a rattle and then the door opened. Sonny was in his late thirties, and his grayish face was filled with small features. His cheeks were pitted, scarred from acne, and his eyes were dark brown, the color of maple leaves after they've spent a winter under the snow. His hair was dyed as dark as stove blacking, and he wore it slicked away from his forehead. He was dressed in a Hawaiian shirt, blue jeans, and a new pair of yellow boots. He had been smoking a cigarette, which he'd left in an ashtray, making a smell of burning paper and hot tin. He picked it up when I came into the room.

It was a smallish room, almost filled by a double bed, a bureau, a chair, and a table. There was a hot plate on the bureau, and above it there were a few cans of beef stew and Campbell's Manhandlers. There were two plates, a couple of glasses that had once been jelly jars, a large jar of peanut butter, and a loaf of Wonder bread.

I came in and sat down, drawing up my long knees. Sonny

told me he was only living there temporarily. He shared a bath across the hall with a woman.

"She's sleeping now," he said, "but last night I come in and she's in the bathroom. She won't open the door and she won't talk through it. So I push in and she's, you know, regurgitating on the floor. I look at her like she's just a dog, but she doesn't care. She's taken some pills and she's brought them up and she's, you know, picking them out of the stuff on the floor. I said, 'Millie, you should go to AA,' and she says, 'Sonny, that's right,' and then goes on picking up the pills and taking them. . . ."

"She should go to AA," I said.

Sonny shrugged.

"It's only temporary," he said.

He told me he remembered the morning Bryce came to see him. He hadn't seen Bryce for years, not since Sonny had left the prison. Sonny said he always sent Bryce a shirt at Christmas, and a card, too.

Sonny hadn't felt well the morning Bryce came to visit. He had gotten up and then gone into the bathroom and leaned against a wall, feeling heat on his brow and the sense of something slowly coiling and uncoiling in his stomach. He stayed in the bathroom for a while, and then went back to his room, where he drank some medicine from a bottle. The medicine was pink as bubble gum, thick, and Sonny drank it and sat and looked out the window, where he saw the blue-gray morning and the large eye of the CRIME WATCH sign. His teeth hurt, too, and he made a paste of brown sugar and aspirin, and sucked it slowly off the spoon until he felt a little better. Then he went across the hall and tapped on the door and said, "Millie, Millie, my teeth hurt," but there was no sound, and Sonny stood, feeling the cold floor against his feet and knowing he wasn't going to get a codeine from Millie. He put on his boots and then went down to the corner store, where he bought a quart of beer instead. He drank it quickly, the carbonation making his eyes tear. As he drank the beer he sat on the side of his bed, hearing the moaning sag of it. After a while he stood up and went into the bathroom, where above the sink there were two cupboards. One was his and the other was Millie's. Both had locks on them.

Sonny's was a combination, but Millie's took a key, since she couldn't remember numbers. She hadn't locked hers, and Sonny opened it and looked inside and saw the makeup and lipstick tubes, some toothbrushes (one for "guests"), a disposable douche, a box of Tampax, an eyelash curler, paper towels, and a compact. There were some medicines, too. Sonny went through the things and found, in a piece of foil that had come from a stick of gum, a half of a codeine. He took it and chewed it when he sat on the sagging bed, pleased by the bitter and salty taste of the thing. He finished the beer, and was feeling the warmth of the codeine, when Bryce knocked on the door.

"Well, Mr. McCann," said Sonny, "Mr. McCann. Come on in. I haven't seen you in years. . . ."

"Call me Bryce," said Bryce, "we're old friends. Really."

"Of course, sure," said Sonny, "Bryce. I didn't mean to be, you know, formal."

Sonny offered Bryce a seat, but he stood, looking at Sonny. It was quiet for a while, and Sonny heard the noises in the building, Millie's snoring from across the way, some voice downstairs, and the sound of a television. Bryce waited, his hands in the pockets of his coat, his brow furrowed as he stood above Sonny, looking down.

"Did you get the cards and the shirts I sent?" said Sonny. Bryce nodded.

"You were always the smart one, weren't you?" said Bryce. "You always stayed in touch because you knew I'd need your help, didn't you? Sure you did. You were the smart one, weren't you?"

Sonny blushed and felt the warmth of the beer and codeine.

"Well, I was always pretty smart . . ." he said.

"Of course you were," said Bryce, "don't deny it for a minute."

Bryce spoke in a cool, flat voice. Sonny said it was like an announcer on TV for the golf matches when someone's trying to make a long putt. Bryce stood there, looking at Sonny, and then he sat down in the chair by the bureau.

"Maybe you'd like something to drink," said Sonny.

"Yes," said Bryce and without saying anything more, he picked a twenty-dollar bill from his wallet, which Sonny took, glad to feel the clean, new money, and went out and down the street, where there was a store that sold liquor. He brought back some bourbon, Cheez-its, and a handful of beef jerky. He wished there had been more codeine to go with the bourbon. When he came back, Bryce was sitting in the same chair, staring out the window at the hard-packed and gray dirt of the yard. Bryce drank little sips from the bottle, and Sonny poured some into his cup. Sonny told Bryce about Millie, who had worked in Vermont once, at a ski lodge. She was a chambermaid and she saved the toothbrushes that had been left behind during the season, and then she tried to sell them.

Bryce sat in his chair, looking out the window, and laughed for a moment. Then he and Sonny began talking a little about Bryce's problem. That's what Bryce called it. Somehow, Sonny got the idea that Bryce's wife had run off with another man. Well, that was pretty bad. Anyone had to admit that. They talked a little more. Sonny said he might help. Bryce nodded, and then they talked about other men who had been Bryce's students and finally they were quiet, hearing the sound of the television and the footsteps in the hall as Millie went toward the bathroom. Bryce offered Sonny a thousand dollars. Sonny said he wasn't born yesterday. He wasn't going to let that kind of money slip through his fingers. He knew what Bryce wanted, but he wasn't going to kill anyone. He knew better than that. He was just going to take the money, and then maybe he'd throw a scare into the man who had gone away with Bryce's wife. It was bad, though, about the guy bothering Bryce's wife, said Sonny. Wasn't it? Bryce was going to go after them. He wanted Sonny to come along and help out. Sonny agreed. The whole thing made him angry and there was some money to be made, too. He packed a bag and Bryce watched as Sonny put the things from the almost empty drawers into it. Sonny was wearing his Hawaiian shirt, jeans, and new yellow boots, and he put a sweater over the shirt, took a jacket from his closet, and then they went down to Bryce's car, leaving the bare coat hangers in the closet, where they made a slight, repetitive *ting*.

They drove out of town. Bryce kept his eyes on the road, and they went past the mills with the broken-out windows, the greenish river and the cemetery. Sonny was feeling pretty good,

sitting in the newish Turbo, and feeling the softness of the seat.
There was the bottle of bourbon in the car, and every now and
then he'd have a little taste. Not too much, he said, because he
didn't want to get drunk and say something he shouldn't. He
hadn't collected the thousand dollars, but he was thinking about
it. They ate in Burger Kings and McDonald's.

Sonny had kept it clear, at least to himself, about what he was
and was not going to do. But, he said, Bryce was good at stirring
things up. Bryce knew Sonny had been raped in prison, and as
they went along in the comfortable car, seeing the bare trees of
fall, Bryce talked about it. At first, he just hinted a little, but
later he said, "Did somebody hold you down when they did it?"

"I don't want to talk about it," said Sonny. "Let's talk about
something else?"

"Didn't somebody sit on your back?" said Bryce.

"Yeah," said Sonny. "That's right."

"Were there more than one?" said Bryce.

Sonny shook his head, and reached for the bottle of bourbon.

"Well," said Bryce.

"There was more than one," said Sonny.

"Did they say anything?" said Bryce.

"They said some sweet stuff," said Sonny. "Honey. Baby
stuff."

They went along the highway, Sonny biting his lip a little
and blinking.

"Well, don't start blubbering about it," said Bryce.

"No," said Sonny, swallowing hard and biting his lip, "I
won't. What do you think I am?"

"Well, just don't start crying," said Bryce.

There were still some Cheez-its left and some beef jerky, and
Sonny ate a little, just to hear the crunching sound. He began to
chew the beef jerky and think about the thousand dollars. After
a while, Bryce turned off the highway and went along the service road.

"Let's take a little break," said Bryce.

"Sure," said Sonny. "Okay."

On the service road there was a miniature golf course, and it
sat in a small square piece of land, two hundred feet on a side.
There was a windmill, and a castle, and other buildings into

which a ball was hit and out of which it could come through some different openings. There wasn't any grass, although in front of each of the small buildings there was some Astroturf. There was a small office in front of the golf course, and there was a sign that said CLOSED.

"Do you like miniature golf?" said Bryce.

"Sure," said Sonny.

Bryce got out of the car, and then Sonny did, too. The air was cool, and Sonny wished he had been able to get some codeine for the trip. The windmill moved a little in the breeze. There was a neatness to the arrangement of holes, a clean painting of white lines on the concrete and crisp arrangements of Astroturf that Sonny liked to look at. There was the sense of order there, and a certain amount of control.

Bryce walked back to the house behind the office. It had two stories, and white, newly painted clapboards. There was some lawn furniture on the porch and it had been covered with plastic. The place was ready for winter. Bryce knocked on the door, and after a while a man came out. He was bald, and had short hair around his ears. He wore a T-shirt and a pair of dark pants.

"My friend wants to play a couple of rounds," said Bryce.

Sonny had come to stand on the porch, too.

"We're closed until spring," said the man. He turned and began to go back into the house, but Bryce touched him on the arm. The man looked at Bryce and then at Sonny and said, "I told you. We're closed until spring."

Bryce leaned down, close to the man, and said, "I'll make it worth your while."

"Everything's locked," said the man.

Bryce took fifty dollars from his pocket and said, "Unlock it."

The man looked at Sonny and said, "All right. Suit yourself."

There was a small shed behind the office, and the man came out to it after getting his keys. He opened it and inside there was a line of clubs, and a basketfull of balls.

"Pick your stick," said Bryce.

"Any will do," said Sonny.

"Come in here and pick your stick," said Bryce.

Sonny came in and took a club from the rack. Bryce made the

man give Sonny a small pencil and scorecard. Then they went outside, and Sonny looked at the course, which was clearly numbered. Bryce leaned against the fender of the car, watching, and Sonny went around, tapping the ball, shooting toward the windmill, the imitation hedges, and the other places, his gray face stopped over the ball and his hands holding the club with a professional grip. As he went, the panels of his coat opened and showed the bright Hawaiian shirt he wore. He went around once and then Bryce told him to go again, and Sonny went, sometimes going through the holes two and three times, bending carefully in the wind when he made his shots. Then they got back into the car.

"Is there anything else you want?" said Bryce.

"A portable radio," said Sonny. "I never had a portable radio."

They drove into the closest town and bought a small red portable radio.

That night they checked into a motel. There were two large beds in the room. The walls were a light Caribbean blue, and the beds were covered with mustard-colored spreads. The lamps were screwed down, and the television didn't work. Bryce had stopped at a liquor store and had bought a bottle of wine, Pouilly-Fuissé, for Sonny. He taught Sonny how to pronounce it and then lay back on his bed, while Sonny drank it. After a while, Bryce took from his bag a pistol, a "belly gun," Sonny said. Sonny didn't know where Bryce had got it. And Sonny sat on the side of his bed, loading and unloading the thing and listening on the radio to a Country and Western station that played "I'm giving you a chance to miss me. . . ." Bryce stretched out, under the covers of his own bed, staring at the ceiling. They could hear the cars outside, the hush of the tires on the highway.

"Having a man fool around with your wife is like being raped," said Bryce.

"Is that right?" said Sonny. "Is that right?"

He snapped the cylinder shut.

Of course, when Sonny told me about the gun, I knew where Bryce had got it. It came from the bottom of Harlow's cabinet, and was unregistered. Well, they stayed there, listening to the radio. Then they went to sleep, since Bryce said the next day would be a long one.

When Sonny told me about it he said, Bryce was good at stirring things up. Real good.

Geese

 There is something else, though, in all of this, and I want to say it here. I haven't said much about Willie . . . but then, I didn't know much, not until I had a chance to talk to him, and that was after he'd come back. One afternoon, which was gray and cold and about to snow, I found Willie standing in front of my house. He was wearing an old bird-hunting coat, one of the brown ones with a game pouch, and a pair of jeans. He had a one-eyed dog with him, and a shotgun over one arm. He said, "I'd like to come in. I'll leave the dog outside." Of course I asked him in, and he took a chair, while his dog and mine sniffed at each other and then sat down like old pals.

We talked for hours before he'd admit he'd gone away with Alexandra. He was a reticent man, and even on the basis of what he said, I had to fill in those enormous blanks he left for me. But he said that when Alexandra called him, and when he'd gone to the motel, he was thinking that once before, years ago, he had let the chance of spending time with her slip through his fingers, and he'd be damned if it was going to happen again. He was going to sleep through the night with her and wake up in the morning and find her still there, and they were going to live that way for as long as they could. They weren't going to look over their shoulders for a while. He said he was "fed up" with it all, the sneaking around, the town's odd pressure, the fear of gossip, and Alexandra's resistance, her plain refusal to leave Bryce. He knew they'd be caught, that Bryce would come after them. Well, then Alexandra . . . would leave Willie again. There wasn't a damn thing he could do about it. But he wasn't going to be cheated of what little time he had with her.

It was obvious, when he spoke, that Alexandra hadn't said a word to him about the blackmail, the pictures, the damage that Bryce had threatened over the years, or Bryce's attentions to Anne, either. Not a word. I suppose she knew the world wouldn't be such a pretty place for him after she talked about these things, or at least the time he spent with her wouldn't be so pretty anymore, and she couldn't stand that. She wanted whatever time they had to be untainted. Things were difficult enough as they were. Not only did she want to get away from Bryce, she wanted to be away from his effect, too. And there were other good reasons for being quiet. Alexandra was afraid things could get out of . . . hand. Who knows what would happen in an unguarded, angry moment between Willie and Bryce? She didn't want to find out.

After the first night in the motel, they went north. Alexandra sat on the right side of the car and Willie drove. Alexandra stared at the river. The high, fall sky was reflected there, and the geese were flying, their wings working in a busy, untiring cadence, a quick flapping that seemed insistent. The honking made the air seem ancient and comforting.

There was a time when Alexandra turned around and looked at the road behind them, staring at the concrete and the lines on it as they streamed away. She saw a red Turbo coming quickly, and then she faced the front, her head up, looking at the rise and fall of the highway. The yellow lines seemed to go under the car with an almost audible tap. Alexandra sat with her hands in her lap, her back held a little off the seat. The red Turbo came quickly, but she didn't look back. She felt the slight vibration in the Jeep, heard the rattle of something in the glove box, a slight squeak from the engine. The red Turbo passed, the driver unfamiliar and the license plate one she had never seen before. She let herself slouch against the seat, and then she turned to Shaw and said, "Why don't you pull off at the next place?"

Shaw looked in the rearview mirror.

"Let's take a chance," she said. "I don't think anyone's after us yet."

So they left the highway at one o'clock in the afternoon, and found a motel. The white Jeep was the only one in the parking lot, which was gray earth and spread in front of the long line of doors on either side of the room they'd been given. They spent a few hours there, napping sometimes, hearing the sounds from the highway. When Shaw was asleep, Alexandra dressed and moved the car, parked it behind the long building so, from the road, it looked as though no one was there.

In the morning, they began going north again.

The inn where Alexandra had made a reservation was a longish white building, two stories, with green shutters, dormers, and a slate roof. There were gray, leafless woods around it, brightened by a few pines. There was a chimney at either end, and they trailed long strands of smoke. It was cool even in the evenings of August, and it was nice to sit by the fire on a summer evening. It was early November now, and the place was about to close for the season.

Alexandra had been there before, with Anne, to fish the river beyond it, and now she gave directions to Shaw after they got off the highway and drove through the town where the inn was. It was after dark when they arrived, and they drove along the back road, feeling the dirt there becoming solid with frost.

There was a car parked just above the entrance to the inn's drive. Alexandra was sitting close to Shaw, pointing out the turn, when she saw it. She supposed it was red, but it might have been black. There was something familiar about it, but she was thinking of the inn, of the room upstairs, of being ordinary. Shaw and Alexandra spoke quietly to one another, not saying more than a few words about directions. As the Jeep went up the drive, which was a narrow dirt road lined with pines, the lights fell across a man who was walking downhill.

He was in a curve of the road and the lights swung over him quickly, but even so he was clearly visible. There was a moment when he crouched a little and was obviously thinking about hiding in the pines, but when the lights were most on him, he stood up and smiled, facing the Jeep. He was thinnish and short, and he wore a Hawaiian shirt with a jacket over it, jeans, and new yellow boots. His hair was black and shiny, combed back from his forehead. His face had smallish features. His cheeks were pocked and his skin seemed grayish. He hadn't shaved for a few days and there was a little stubble on his chin, upper lip, and below his sideburns. As the lights washed over him, his eyes were brightened by the reflection. Then he turned and went down the road toward the car parked there.

It seemed, as the man faded into the darkness, that there was something heavy in his jacket pocket, and the thing swung from side to side as the man went along. Alexandra sat next to Shaw, now staring over her shoulder, into the darkness, but seeing nothing: it had happened quickly, but she sat, touching a hand to her face. There was something in the small features, in the flattish gray expression that she saw again, floating at the side of the road. She put her hand on the seat behind Shaw and let it touch his shoulders and said, after sighing, "We'll be there in a minute."

"Did you see that man on the road?" said Shaw.

"Yes," said Alexandra.

"Who do you suppose that was?" said Shaw.

"I don't know," said Alexandra.

There were no other guests, and the white Jeep was the only car parked in front of the place. There was a woman waiting for them when they came inside. She was gray-haired, wore a print dress with a sweater over it. She asked if they'd like dinner.

"No, I don't think so," said Alexandra. "Are you hungry?"

"We'll have something in the morning," said Shaw, "thanks."

The woman told them there was a Coke machine in the closet downstairs if they got thirsty. Then Alexandra and Shaw went up to their room, which was small, with slanted ceilings and a dormer. There was a double bed with a white metal bedstead, a bureau, a large wing chair with a reading lamp. There was a bathroom with a long white tub. A fire had been set in the fireplace, and after the door was closed, Alexandra lit it, saying, "It'll be warm soon."

In the middle of the night she woke and felt cold. The com-

forters were on the floor, and she picked them up and spread
them over Willie. Then she put on a robe and sat in a chair,
looking at the last of the fire's dull glow, the coals of it having a
kind of quaver or shiny blinking as the chimney drew. Outside
there were the fuzzy tops of pines and over them the bluish-
purple stars, each one seeming sharp and clear, close.

Alexandra woke early in the morning, and she dressed and
went downstairs, carefully closing the door so Shaw could
sleep. She sat at a table that had been set in the dining room
near the window. There was coffee and toast and strawberry
preserves. The whole berries were clearly visible, each one red
and bright as a candy apple. They were large and sweet and
they still had the slight yellow markings on their sides. Alexandra heard the domestic sounds from the kitchen, and she sipped
her coffee. It was comforting and warm by the window, and she
stayed as long as she could.

Alexandra went outside. It had been cloudy before dawn, and
it had rained, but now the sun was coming out, and the air
around the pines near the house was filled with a bright mist,
that moved like dust, and defined the long rays of light that
came from the tops of the trees. The sun was warm, too, and the
ground steamed with the heat. Alexandra went uphill a little
and came out near the river. It was broad and gravelly, and in
the fall and spring the inn was filled with fishermen, but the
season was now closed. The brown trout were spawning. They
came upstream, into the gravel, and the males made a nest in it
and waited for the females, who looked over the waiting fish
and picked a place to lay their eggs.

Alexandra was glad to walk along in the misty sunshine. Every now and then she saw one of the trout holding in a pool,
gently finning there. Up above, around a curve in the river,
there was a sharp, quick noise, like someone blowing up a bag
and popping it. Alexandra walked slowly around the large
stones, her hands in the pockets of the sweater she wore. When
she came around the bend in the river, she saw two boys standing at the side of the stream.

One of them had a small-caliber, lever-action rifle. The fish
were holding in the water, and the boy with the rifle shot into
the pool. He shot once, the water splashing up, and then he

gave the rifle to his friend. Sometimes they were able to catch the fish as they floated away, but mostly they didn't. Alexandra stood back from the river, on the brown pine needles in a grove of softwoods, watching them. Then she went farther upstream.

For a while, she still heard the snap of the rifle, but she kept walking until the sound of it disappeared. Some of the rocks in the sun were dry, and she sat on one, putting back her head for a moment. There was no breeze, and no sounds, aside from the clear hush of the river. After a while the geese began flying overhead and honking as they went.

When Alexandra heard them, she sat up, and began walking back toward the inn. The geese passed overhead, and she heard the insistent shush of the river, the light snap of water falling into a pool. The sky became a little darker, or hazy, and her shadow became a gray pool at her feet. She turned away from the river and walked toward a stand of softwood above the inn.

Sonny was waiting for her there. He was still dressed in jeans, Hawaiian shirt, a jacket, and his new yellow boots. The boots were covered with mud, since he had been out watching the house in the rain.

"Hi," said Sonny. "It's a nice day for a walk, isn't it?"

His face looked even more gray in the sunlight, and the features seemed flatter. His chin, nose, eyebrows, lips, and forehead all seemed to be flat like a board, although the scars in his cheeks were deep and definite. He looked hungover and thirsty. More than anything else, the expression in his eyes suggested he didn't see Alexandra as anything more than a life-size photograph of herself, the kind of thing that is sometimes stood up in the lobbies of movie theaters. Perhaps he wanted to step over to the river and have a long cool drink.

Alexandra stopped in front of him.

"Aren't you married to Bryce McCann?" said Sonny.

One of Sonny's hands was in the pocket of his jacket. He opened his mouth, and with the fingers of his other hand he reached inside and squeezed a tooth, or the gum around it. He winced, shook his head, and took his fingers away.

"Come on," he said, "step over here."

Alexandra shook her head.

"I'm going back inside," she said.

Sonny took the gun out of his pocket. The day was so hazy now that his shadow didn't show, or it was absorbed by the gray cast to the ground. There was the sound of the trees and the distant hush of the river. Sonny pointed the pistol at the center of her chest.

"Let's go up here," he said, "someone might see us."

Talking hurt Sonny's teeth, and he winced.

Alexandra stared at the gun. It had dark, wooden grips, and there was a ring at the butt for a lanyard. It was oldish, and there were some silver marks on the barrel where the bluing had worn away: she recognized the thing as having come from Harlow's cabinet.

"Where's Bryce," she said.

"Down in the car," said Sonny.

"What's he doing down there?" said Alexandra.

"Waiting," said Sonny.

The geese started honking again. Alexandra imagined she saw their necks stretched out, the movement of their wings, the V shape of them against the clouds.

"There's somebody waiting for me," said Alexandra, "I'm walking back."

"How come you're treating Bryce the way you are?" he said. "Shacked up here . . ."

"I wouldn't talk about it like that," she said.

"What are you going to do?" he said.

He kept his eyes on hers and winced.

"I'm going back," she said.

"Listen," he said, "do you know what having a man play around with your wife is like . . . ?"

Alexandra shook her head.

"I don't know what I'm going to do with you," he said.

"What does Bryce want . . . ?" said Alexandra.

"He doesn't say," said Sonny, "he just stirs things up."

"What things?" said Alexandra.

"You know what having someone play around with your wife is like?" he said again.

They stood there in the cool, damp air, without the sunlight. The geese continued flying.

"Bryce is upset," said Sonny, "he's my good friend."

Alexandra swallowed and said, "I'm going back down the hill."

"No, you aren't," said Sonny, "you step back in here."

Sonny reached into his mouth and squeezed his tooth or gums. Alexandra turned and began walking. Sonny grimaced, put the cool barrel against his cheek, pressed it so the metal soothed the gum or tooth underneath, and stared at Alexandra. After Alexandra had taken a step or two, she didn't hear the sound of the gun going off, but there was the sure, two-toned click as the hammer was pulled back.

"I was supposed to warn your friend," said Sonny, "but I'll take my business up with you. You're the one who did it. You make me sick."

Alexandra went slowly. Her legs were heavy, a little rubbery. The trees before her were clear and bright, and Alexandra saw the sheen of light on each separate needle. When she had gone a few steps more, the house was visible, the white clapboards seemed so bright and clean, so white as to make her want to look away, even in the coiling smoky air. Alexandra had eaten almost nothing in the previous days, and she felt light-headed as she kept her eyes on those white boards, the neat squares of the house's windows, the shutters that were as green as the deepest pool in the river. When she passed the last pine, and walked onto the brownish lawn, she turned toward Sonny. He stood again with the cold barrel pressed against his cheek. He winced a little at the touch of the steel.

When she came upstairs, Shaw was sitting in a chair, fresh from the shower. He was tying a shoe. He looked up and smiled at her, but then he saw her face.

"We're going to have to go," said Alexandra.

"We just got here," said Shaw.

She shook her head and pulled out a suitcase. She pushed her things into it, her fingers catching on a shirt as she pushed it down.

"We have to go," she said, "please. Will you promise to come along. That's all I ask. Please."

Shaw looked at her for a moment and said, "What's happened?"

"Just come along," she said, "that's all I ask."

"Look," he said.

"Please," she said. She picked up his suitcase, too, and began to put things in it. "We haven't got much more time."

He looked at her for a moment, and then said, "All right."

They left some money downstairs, and then went outside, into the soft, shadowless morning. They got into the white car, and Shaw put the keys into the ignition, and as he started the engine he said, "You know I love you, don't you," and she said, yes, she knew that.

When Alexandra told me about this, after she'd come into the house and sat there, dripping rain, after she'd sat down and dried her hair, leaving the golden and silver strands curled against the skin, she said, "Don't you see? There was nothing else for me to do." I sat opposite her, hearing that steady, maddening drip, and nodded. She'd made her peace, and even though Bryce made her walk through the valley of death itself, or close to it, she went ahead, just walking, as ordinarily as you please. At the moment, it seemed as though there was nothing else to do. So I sat, watching Alexandra as she went back to drying her hair, knowing how close she'd come. What was it, how thin had it been . . . well, maybe just a toothache, or the irritation that comes from one and makes someone not want to hear a loud noise.

I got up, not able to sit still, and went into the kitchen. I didn't really think about what I was doing, aside from having an idea of feeding her. I took a piece of Stilton cheese from the icebox and some Bremner crackers, and put them before Alexandra. She had a piece on a cracker and said, "Hmm. That's good. That's delicious."

Mad Katherine

The next night, after leaving the inn, Alexandra and Shaw stayed in a motel, and Alexandra dreamed of Mad Katherine, who sat in the trees not far from the river. Her coonskin coat was open to her stomach and showed her white breasts and the scars on the center of her chest. It was cold, and Mad Katherine's breath rose as she waited in her tree, on the branch porch she had made there. She had a deerskin bag with her, in which there were the things she needed to hunt in the snow, a white cape she spread over her arms and legs. She had a hood, too, which she wore, so that she appeared to be invisible, the same color as the snow or her own white breath. Alexandra stood not far away, holding a fox skin over her shoulders, and feeling the cold air against her naked legs and stomach. "The trick is being still," said Mad Katherine. "You must not move. Must not shiver. Your breathing must be slow. Make no sound, so nothing, absolutely nothing knows you're there. Then you drop. It's better than stalking, when all you do is scare what you want." Mad Katherine looked toward the frozen river, and saying, with her teeth chattering with the cold, making a sound like an instrument made of bone, "It's not the killing that's hard. It's the waiting."

Fall Rains

I have always hated the fall rains: they remind me of those months in August and September when I stood outside, with my dog beside me, looking at the sky and seeing not so much as a cloud. The flowers wither. The grass turns brown, and my dog whines when it smells the water I bring outside to him. The well runs dry. I stop doing the dishes and bathing and sit up at night, looking at the hot, dry darkness, and thinking what good a little rain would do me. It is then, in the fluttery dryness of these nights, I think of those women I have loved and how much we had been trapped, and I wonder, too, where they are on those comfortless nights when it's hard to breathe, and if they roll over in the heat and curse my name. Well, some of them probably do. Then the rains come, cold and useless, futile, since everything has stopped growing and it won't even be stored as snow.

Alexandra and I sat, hearing the useless patter. She finished drying her hair, and it began to fluff out a little. She ate another piece of cheese, and thought for a while, sometimes looking at one of her hands, which she held out before her, back up, her fingers stretched out. Her expression was the one of a woman who has seen something that left her wide-eyed, and then, in the instant before looking away, her face shows disbelief, as she asks, My God, does this happen? Or worse, My God, so this does happen after all.

Because then Alexandra came to the moment Bryce was killed.

After she and Shaw had left the inn, they traveled west, through New York. Alexandra noticed the small difference in the rooms they stayed in, the colors of the carpets or the plastic wallpaper, the texture of the sheets, the number of bulbs in the bathroom, the angle the sunlight came into the room in the morning, the direction from which the sound of the highway came, the brand of the television that sat on a stand with wheels, Zenith, Motorola, Quasar. They went through New York State, toward Buffalo. It took three days . . . Alexandra wanted to be around people, and they stayed late at the Holiday Inn they stopped at the second night: it was Saturday, and after dinner they went to the bar, where there was a Country and Western band, the men in it wearing western shirts with scalloped backs and sequins. There was a woman who sang, and she wore a one-piece, sequined dress that shimmered and flashed in a rose-colored light. Her hair was long and probably bleached, and the dress was low-cut. The woman looked as though she had been in an automobile accident and that she had had plastic surgery: it wasn't a good job, and left her face with a slight, haunting asymmetry. Alexandra was careful when they went back to their room, watching the shadows of the parking lot, the movement of windblown paper, alert to the slight, scratching noise of it.

They even thought they were getting away . . . but of course they weren't. Bryce and Sonny followed, at a distance. Sonny told me Bryce was "quietlike," brooding, as they sat in the parking lots beyond the rooms where Alexandra and Shaw spent their nights. But Bryce was stirring things up, and he made Sonny tell him the story of every Christmas Sonny could remember. Sonny didn't want to, but it seemed to make Bryce feel a little better. Once, after Shaw and Alexandra had come out of a room, Bryce and Sonny went into it, and Bryce sat on the side of the one double bed that was unmade, staring at the mustard-colored wall with the Picasso print on it. He laced his

fingers together and sighed. Sonny sat on a chair and turned on
the television, a Motorola, and changed the channels, while
Bryce sat there. After a while, Bryce pulled back the covers and
stared at the sheets. Then he went into the bathroom and
looked in the medicine chest, on the shelf beneath it, and finally
he went through the wastebasket, taking out the tissue and
Kleenex, touching it. He washed his hands and came back into
the room, and when Sonny had turned off the television, Bryce
said, "Goddamn her. I don't think she's using a diaphragm."
Sonny picked up the Gideon Bible from the drawer, and then
they went out, where Sonny put the Bible into the backseat of
the Turbo. They started west, toward Buffalo, and Bryce said,
"Tell me about the Christmases you had. What about the ones
in prison? Were you raped near Christmas?"

In Buffalo, Alexandra decided to turn back, and in the morning, after sleeping late, she got back into the Jeep with Shaw
and they began going the way they had come, passing the same
landscape, which was changing quickly, the leaves mulling fast
now. Alexandra was glad to see the rocky hardness emerging
from the yellow leaves: it was cool and reassuring. They drove
and watched the road slide by. In the early evening, when everything white was glowing, and when the Jeep had climbed a
long, gentle grade, from the top of which the land could be
seen, the ridges of it pushed against each other in the distance,
Shaw pulled to the side of the road, at a rest stop, so they could
get out of the car and look at the hills before them. They stood,
feeling the wind. The place was deserted: around them there
was only the empty parking lot of the rest stop, the hills in
the distance, the highway behind them, which was divided by
the median. The floor of the woods was yellow with leaves, the
light from the last part of the day lingering there, making the
woods seem filled with their own soft illumination.

Bryce and Sonny had been waiting when Alexandra and
Shaw had come from their room in the morning, and when
Bryce followed them to the highway, where the white car got
on the side going east, back the way it had come, Sonny said,
"Look. They're turning around. Why are they doing that?"

"I don't know," said Bryce.

"I'll bet they're tired of each other. Yeah, that's it. The good times are over."

Sonny was thinking about how he'd collect the thousand dollars: he thought it might be the easiest money he'd ever made.

Bryce stared at the white car in the distance, and slowed down. "Maybe you're right. Maybe she's come to her senses after all. She wants to come home," he said.

Bryce had lost the white car, since he'd slowed down. He followed at a distance for most of the day, sometimes getting closer, others falling back, his face puzzled. In the afternoon he fell even farther behind than usual as he sat for a moment at the side of the road. After a while, when the Turbo was shuddering with the passing of large trucks, Bryce said, "I think you're right. They're probably arguing right now." Bryce bit his lip. Sonny grunted. Then Bryce pulled back onto the road, going fast now, his eyes set on the distance. He didn't see the white car in the rest stop until he had passed it.

He stopped for a moment in the fast lane and shifted into reverse, but both Sonny and Bryce looked at the cars coming toward them, and then Sonny said, "Go on. We can turn around. There's an exit up ahead. I saw the sign."

Bryce got off the highway, went under it, and then got back onto it. After a while he parked opposite the rest stop, on the shoulder of the highway. Between him and Alexandra there were the highway and the median in the center of it. Bryce stepped out of the car, and stared: in the rest stop on the other side of the highway Alexandra and Shaw stood, looking at the hills which were humped against one another, the ridges of them darkish in the failing light. Sonny got out of the car and leaned against the fender, one hand against his cheek. His teeth were still killing him, and he felt a little ill, too, as though he had blood poisoning.

Alexandra stared into the distance, hearing the highway behind her, the maddening hush of it. She was fascinated by the shape of the hills, the endless certainty of them, and then she turned away and saw Bryce standing on the shoulder of the other side of the highway.

He was wearing a pair of dark pants and a grayish jacket. He wore a white shirt, open at the neck, and he had on a scarf, too,

an ascot, and as he stood there, his clothes luffed in the wind.
Bryce began to walk through the traffic, picking his way carefully. Some of the cars and trucks had their lights on, the mirrors of which looked like they were made from gold foil.

Bryce came to the median. The grass in it was longish, brown
and yellow, and looked dormant, already waiting for spring.
Bryce walked through it, his hands behind his back, his head
down. He seemed tired. Alexandra crossed her side of the highway, and began to walk through that tall, dead grass, her shoes
swinging through it. She had on a sweater, and she crossed her
arms in the cool air. They met there, in the middle, and stood
opposite one another, Bryce slouching a little, Alexandra standing before him, tall, her hair blowing in the wind of the highway. They stood there, looking at one another. There was the
sound of the trucks shifting down and climbing the grade. Alexandra's face was cool and matter-of-fact, and Bryce seemed, for
a moment, fascinated by it. He even raised a hand and began to
touch her cheeks or lips, forehead or chin, but then he stopped
and stood with his hand outstretched, the fingers of it shaking.
There was a momentary stillness in the traffic. Bryce stopped
slouching and his hand still floated in the air, his fingers slightly
curved, although they no longer had the aspect of reaching out
to touch her cheek and lips so much as already beginning to
ward her off. He seemed pale as he hesitated in the brownish
grass. Alexandra stood before him, hugging herself. He dropped
his hand and then turned and ran through the grass of the median, his coat flying out behind him, his arms and legs moving,
his head down. There was a frenzy in his movement, a kind of
wide-eyed panic, as though there were behind him some slimy,
quickly moving creature from a nightmare.

When Alexandra spoke to me with the rain ticking behind
her, she held the towel she'd used to dry her hair. And when she
glanced up, she let me see the same expression Bryce had seen,
and then she looked down at the wet shapes her shoes had made
on the stone floor. So it came to that, I thought as I sat there
looking at her and hearing the rain and her voice, breathy and
almost inaudible as she said, "He'd seen I'd kill him, the first
chance I got. That's why he ran."

Alexandra hadn't thought about what she'd do, not specifically. That would take care of itself, and one night Bryce would feel the tickle along his neck as he slept, and when he awoke he'd see the edge of the razor Alexandra had used along the vein. He'd see then, when he awoke, the same look as when they had met in the middle of the median on the brown and yellow grass with the sound of the trucks shifting down.

Bryce covered the ground quickly, his jacket flying out as he climbed the slight grade of the median. It was getting darker and the jacket looked like some cape or wing. The tops of the trees beyond the highway were like black lace, the thin branches of the crowns perfectly visible against the pale gray sky. Bryce came to the top of the median and his shoes, with their thin, expensive soles, made a lonely sound against the concrete. He'd run like that before, in Boston, when he'd been asked about shaving points, and now he may even have been confused for a moment. Were there, just behind him, the police who had asked if he had been paid by a bookie? He wasn't thinking really, although perhaps he remembered the cool air of Boston, the dirty ice that had been on the river, the grubbiness of the things that were frozen in it at the shore. The long, deep sound of an air horn must have jarred him. At least he knew he wasn't going along the river, although the sense of being unable to breathe, of the harsh, acidic landscape, the indifference of it, or the plain hostility of it seemed the same, as did the numbness on his face, which was so definite as to feel chemical, as though it came from a local anesthetic. Nothing in the world seemed as important as finding out whether or not Alexandra was coming after him, and he glanced over his shoulder, seeing that she continued to walk up the bank, one arm out, her hair moving lazily in the wind. Bryce went along, his legs trembling, shaking down into the joints, which were loose and watery. He felt the wind again, saw the lacy tops of the trees, the platinum twilight above them. There was the greasy air of the highway and the vibration from the moving cars and trucks.

He went twenty-five yards and stopped. He stood still, his eyes set on the horizon, on the space above the furry, animate shapes of the trees, the sky above them looking gray and as soft as a piece of expensive silk. In the sky there was a caressing quality, a slight tactile sense of smooth, delicate, and soft skin.

When he turned to face her he still stood on the concrete of the highway.

From the distance there wasn't much he could see, but he couldn't forget the look on her face. He still saw the raised brow, and the details of the eyes, the pale lines radiating across the iris, the gray pebblelike color of it. There was about her eyes the quality of water running in a stream: cool, indifferent, but nevertheless certain and more real than anything Bryce had ever seen. He would have found it impossible to say where in her expression the change showed the most, in the faintly tired set of her mouth, the relaxation or smoothness of her forehead (aside from the slight lifting of one brow), or in the skin at the side of her eyes: in all there was a certainty and a lack of wanting to hide anything.

For a moment he must have begun to be angry. Didn't he have plenty on her? He stared at the pastellike sky and there he saw through its luminescence the photographs he had of Alexandra: he remembered, or clearly saw a vision of her, a few years younger than now, her arms straight behind her as she sat up, her breasts showing the white shape of her swimsuit, her head thrown back, her eyes closed, or he remembered another in which she stood, her skirt bunched at her waist, the long thin straps of the garter showing, tugging at the top of a stocking: the freedom of it, the brazenness of it was so apparent as to still be shocking. Bryce remembered the images of her and was amazed she could have done such a thing . . . my God, how could she have behaved this way and so injured him? Of course, he'd find a way to use what he had on her . . . it was best to be shrewd. He'd begin by confessing to something. Even something important. It had worked before and he saw no reason why it wouldn't again. And as soon as he was safe, as soon as he had got rid of that look, why, then he'd get down to cases. As he thought of the photographs, as he became angrier, he began to walk toward her, now feeling the cold northern wind and seeing the tops of the trees, blacker now as they began to move in the wind, each feathery bit of them having a dark, claustrophobic insistence.

One of the lights of a truck winked. In a second it came back on, and in the sound of the brakes and in the sharp stopping of the truck, Bryce moved, one arm snapping across his chest, and then he was left lying on one of the thick yellow lines of the highway. There was a lowing, a mourning of horns, and the shriek of more brakes as the cars and trucks stopped behind the first truck. The air was filled with blue-gray smoke from the burning tires, and it drifted slowly in front of the golden headlights. Bryce shook his head and waved an arm back and forth.

Sonny stood at the side of the road, his flat, hungover face turned toward Bryce. Cars were still coming to a stop, and some tried to go around on the shoulder. Bryce moved his arm from side to side, as though beckoning, and then Sonny stepped into the traffic, into the shrieks and honking horns, crossing the lanes on a direct, slicing angle that left him unharmed and standing next to Bryce, the pistol, which was still in Sonny's pocket, swinging back and forth as he stood and stared. People climbed down from the trucks and out of cars, their legs making long, scissors-like shadows that fell over Sonny. He said, as he looked at Bryce, "Oh, Jesus, oh, Jesus, what are we gonna do?"

The place had been deserted a few minutes before, but now there seemed to be people everywhere, and as they came down the road, with the headlights behind them, Sonny stepped back, into the shadows, and stood there, the thing in his pocket still swinging a little. Now eight or so men stood around Bryce, their figures blackish against the lights of the trucks. One driver put a blanket over Bryce's chest.

Alexandra came up from the median and stood behind the men. Sonny stood a few feet behind her, his hand on top of his pocket. "Oh, goddamn, goddamn," he said. From up above, more people began to walk, making the lights wink.

One side of Bryce's face was untouched, and he lay in the harsh light from the truck. It made the skin on the untouched side of his face seem pale, and his blue eyes were bright. Every now and then he blinked, and one hand, which was bleeding, picked at the blanket that lay over him.

The man whose truck had hit Bryce put another blanket under Bryce's head. Then he stood up and said, "He ran out in front of me. He didn't even look. . . ."

"I saw him," said another man, a truck driver who wore green pants and a green shirt.

"Did you?" said the first driver.

"Yeah," said the other driver. "He was in the median. What the hell was he doing out there?"

"He just ran out and stopped," said the first driver, "that's all I know."

"He doesn't look so good," said the other driver.

"No," said the first, "did you really see him?"

"Yeah," said the other, "he ran out."

"What's your name?" said the first driver. He took a pencil from his pocket and someone gave him a business card to write on. The other driver frowned, and looked toward his truck.

"I was a pretty long way back," he said.

"But you saw," said the first.

"Yeah," he said, "I guess I did."

The men stood around Bryce in a half circle, all of them facing the headlights, their heads bowed as they looked at the man in the blankets on the ground, and as they stood they appeared tall, their dark work clothes looking stained and well worn. Their bent heads, long faces, the dark greens and blues of their clothes, their silence and the lack of motion, gave them an air of antiquity, and a military quality, too, as though they were the survivors of a battle, hung with blankets and standing next to a campfire at night. In the distance there were the flashing blue lights of the state police and the sounds of sirens.

Alexandra stood next to the men, and when Bryce saw her, he said, "Please. Oh, my God, please keep her away from me. . . ." He tried to point with the hand that had been picking at the blanket.

The driver of the truck turned his worried, taut face to Alexandra. Inside the circle of men it seemed brighter than day: it was like standing next to a beacon at a movie premiere. All of the faces were bright, each looking almost powdered because of it.

"Who are you?" said the driver.

"I'm his wife," said Alexandra.

"Well, he's hysterical now," said the driver.

Alexandra nodded.

"Maybe you should keep back," said the driver.

"All right," said Alexandra. "Maybe that's best."

"He's in shock," said the driver.

She stepped back, into the shadows, although Bryce kept staring at the darkness into which she had gone. The ambulance came along the road, its light flashing, the long, V-shaped beacons swinging through the evening air. There were so many cars stopped now that the ambulance had to drive on the shoulder of the road. It was a large van, with a driver and an attendant, and the word *ambulance* was printed backward across the front of it. When its lights swung over the concrete, they showed one of Bryce's shoes, which looked as though it had fallen out of a car and had the forlorn air of something discarded. Soon the ambulance stopped and the driver and the attendant got out and put Bryce onto a stretcher, their hands lifting him and covering him with quick, simple movements. There was a doctor inside the van, and he asked Bryce if he knew what his blood type was. Bryce shook his head. The doctor was young and pink, not much more than a student.

"Why were you out in the middle of the road?" he said.

"Why?" said Bryce. He turned toward the wall, where there were gray smudges from other people who had leaned against it. "Because I wanted to be loved."

Alexandra stood at the back of the ambulance. The doctor began to look into the deep wounds on Bryce's head, working quickly, trying to stop the bleeding. Sonny came up, too, and as he stood next to Alexandra, he said to the doctor, "Hey, have you got any codeine?"

"Can't you see I'm busy," said the doctor, without looking up.

An attendant closed the door, got into the front, and the ambulance crossed the median, going sloppily over the ground there, climbing the bank on the far side, its lights flashing and the siren wailing. Alexandra stood and watched it go away, the red light on the top spinning like the rotor of some enormous helicopter.

The ambulance light was very strong, and it took a while before it disappeared. Alexandra and Sonny stood back from the men who watched the thing go, and while they waited in the darkness Alexandra's face and Sonny's looked as though they were standing under some neon sign, a red one (for a hotel, say) that flashed on and off. Sonny came a little closer to her, his hand over the pocket where he had the pistol.

"I never have any luck. . . ." said Sonny. "Bryce was going to give me a thousand, but I didn't get it. . . ."

Alexandra only looked at him.

"Listen," he said, "you got to take this."

He touched his pocket. "I'm on parole. I'll go back if they find it on me."

Sonny reached into his pocket, and Alexandra saw that his hand was around the butt and that his thumb was probably on the hammer. The lights of the state police were sparkling down the road, and Sonny's eyes were filled with it. He stepped closer.

"Bryce has something on me," said Sonny. "I'm not going to start blubbering. He didn't want me to start blubbering."

Sonny closed his eyes for a moment.

"He was harping," said Sonny. "All the time. Well, I should have killed him. But he was going to give me a thousand."

Sonny shrugged.

"You understand?" said Sonny.

Alexandra looked across the road, over her shoulder, where Shaw was standing, alternately visible and disappearing with the flashing lights from the police cars.

"Yes," said Alexandra.

"Ah," said Sonny, "how can you understand?"

"You'd be surprised," said Alexandra.

"Is that right?" said Sonny. "Well, what am I going to do?"

"Give it to me," said Alexandra.

"What?" said Sonny.

"The pistol," said Alexandra, "in your pocket."

She put out her hand. The people around them looked toward the sparkling lights, and for a moment it seemed as though Sonny and Alexandra were alone, as though in one flash of the police cars' light everyone else, the drivers of the trucks and cars, the people on the shoulder of the road, had disappeared. Sonny took the thing out of his pocket, the barrel pointed at her, his finger curled through the trigger guard. He swung it up, in the flashing light, the metal glistening in the dark, the bore passing across Alexandra's chest. "I won't start blubbering," he said, keeping his eyes on hers. For a moment the pistol hesitated as he looked at her, and then with a shrug, he said, "Here. Careful. It's loaded," and put the sweaty, cool thing into her hand.

Then Sonny turned and walked back across the white concrete of the road and went to Bryce's car, where he reached into the backseat and picked up a bag. He put a Gideon Bible into it, and then reached into the front seat and took from the dashboard a small red portable radio. The light from the sky was almost gone now and Sonny appeared to have almost no color, or not much more than purple, which left him looking like a dark shape that went along the road, holding the small radio to its head. He walked with a repetitive, slightly limping gait, the bag he carried going up and down, one shoulder rising and falling, the radio held with a kind of fierce ownership. The slight dip and limp suggested, as he was absorbed by the darkness, an infinite patience.

I don't know exactly what happened in the ambulance, aside from the fact that Bryce died there. Perhaps the doctor asked the driver to go faster, or said that he was having trouble. Perhaps he pounded on Bryce's chest and gave him a shot of Adrenalin . . . I don't know what kind of equipment was in the van. Anyway, Bryce was left with his head against the grayish, shadow-like mark on the wall, feeling the unsteady swaying of the ambulance and hearing the failing siren.

Well, Alexandra and I sat opposite one another, hearing the rain. She held the towel in two hands. It was getting a little lighter, and I saw that when she had come into the house she had brought something with her and that she had put it on the floor. And now, as she looked at me, she reached to the floor, where she had left a brown paper bag, the kind that comes from the grocery store. It was wet from the rain, crumpled together, the brown paper dark because of the dampness. Alexandra's hands lifted the thing up, carefully holding it at the bottom, so that the small, heavy thing inside wouldn't rip through.

"Here," she said, "I thought you could get rid of this for me."

I put my hand inside and felt the cool, damp surface of a pistol, and the small diamonds of the grip. It was heavy in my hand and made my old fingers seem frail. When I broke the cylinder and shook the cartridges out, they made a dull, repetitive thud, thud, thud in the bottom of the wet sack. I put the pistol carefully inside, and we both sat there, hearing the gentle click of the thing and the moist rustling of the brown paper as I squeezed it shut. She'd put the pistol in her sweater when Sonny had given it to her and hidden it in her car before she talked to the police. She said things had been difficult enough without having to explain that away, too.

There were other things to be done. She followed the police to their barracks. She sat, drinking coffee from a styrofoam cup. They talked to her for a few hours. Bryce had run into the road. Other drivers had seen him. That's what it came down to, and then Alexandra went out the door, into the night, hearing the bump of the styrofoam cup she had thrown into the trash can in the corner of the new, institutional room. Then she made arrangements for Bryce to be sent home.

Shaw and Alexandra spent the night in a motel. It was close to the road, and as they sat on the large bed, each leaning against a pillow, they heard the quick popping as the trucks on the highway began climbing a long grade. In the morning, they slept for a few hours. Then Alexandra got into Bryce's car and Shaw got into the Jeep and both of them began the long drive home to town.

It was raining when Alexandra stopped in front of her house. She went inside and stood in the kitchen. She had put the pistol on the counter, and she stared at the dark bore and the metal shine of the thing . . . she didn't say, but there must have been an impulse, a horrible moment when, with a jerk of self-hatred, she touched the checkered grip, the grooved cylinder, the ring in the butt, the textured thumbpiece on the hammer, the stubby, thick vane on the front of the barrel. Perhaps she picked it up, and stood in the kitchen, feeling the steady weight of it as she put the large bore just behind her ear, or against the temple and looked out the window into the black and blue light of the fall rains. . . . I don't know. But soon, after that, I found her in my sun room, dripping water on the floor, carrying the pistol in a brown and wet paper sack.

And after we'd talked, after she'd told me about Bryce, about

the time she'd spent away, and after she'd dried her hair and
had gone home, wearing one of my jackets, I took the pistol into
the woods. I climbed over the deadfalls, and the undergrowth
was wet. Soon my clothes were damp, although it was good to
be outside and to feel the height of the sky. After a while I came
to an abandoned farmstead, which was just stone walls and
briars now, the barn lying in a gray heap, the cellar filled up
with vines. I looked until I found the well, where I dropped the
pistol. The bullets went in, too, each one making a small, sweet
kerrthunk. Then I started home, already wondering which of the
Critchfields, the Thachers, and the Keiths would come to the
funeral. And by the time I got home, I was certain that not one
of them would miss it for the world.

The Bath

 When I came back, I was cold, and I went upstairs and ran the tub, making it hot, and seeing the steam rise into the air. I am a tall man. I have a long, porcelain tub. It is narrow and has feet like a lion's. I dropped my clothes and avoided the mirror, not wanting to see my old skin, which fits me like a gray, baggy suit. I am thin and my knees seem enormous, the size of grapefruits. I got into the tub and felt the water coming up to my neck, and I sat, breathing slowly and feeling the motion of the water as the air went in and out. My blind dog sat out in the hall, thumping the hard floor as he scratched at something.

There is one thing left to tell. Of course, there was a moment when Alexandra knew she'd kill Bryce. She didn't know when the change took place. I don't think anyone ever does. But she did say that when she had been in Buffalo, Willie had taken her north into Canada for a few hours. They went along the river, passing the tall, sticklike figures of the power lines, and came to Niagara Falls.

The place was almost deserted. There was only an off-season tour bus, filled with Japanese newlyweds, who stood, in twos, before the edge of the falls, and took their own pictures with a camera left on a tripod and having a timer that allowed the groom to run from behind it and stand next to the faintly smiling bride.

It is possible to take an elevator and go down behind the falls, and to walk out of a tunnel there and to stand just behind the water. Alexandra and Shaw went down in the elevator, and before they walked through the tunnel, they rented black slickers with hoods, black rubber boots, and then they walked along the cement hall, the walls of which had been made of poured concrete and still had the texture of the wood forms. There were small yellow lights overhead, each one held in a wire cage. They came out to the back of the falls.

The vibration there and the noise were horrible. The water came down, not more than five feet away, the wall of it gray, and textured like a curtain made of glass beads. Alexandra stood on stone that was trembling. There was a hard mist in the air, and as Alexandra reached out, as she tried to stand closer to the water, she heard the quick slap of drops as they hit the rubberized and black hood she wore. The two of them stood there, before the water, alone, appearing nun- and monklike. The light was pale and luminescent. Alexandra probably opened her mouth to speak, or to scream, but it was useless. She was left with the taste of the river and the hard, unrelenting pounding of it, and the everlasting fall of those glasslike beads. It was the trembling, the shaking of the falls that haunted her: the noise and the pounding, the unstoppable quality of them, the strength of them seemed otherworldly or at least so large or hard as to dismiss any human thing.

They couldn't stand there long. Alexandra and Shaw went along the trembling hall. They returned the slickers and took the elevator to the surface. The Japanese were still there, the cameras making a kind of insistent, light clattering. Alexandra was tired, and she went with Shaw into a coffee shop, where they sat down at the counter. She was cold and she held the cup in both hands, feeling the warmth of it in her fingers.

The room behind her was a gift shop. There were floor-to-ceiling windows on the side that faced the river, and on shelves and counters there were displayed cups and plates, clocks, mugs, ceramic calendars, plaques, ashtrays, and glasses, and all of them had a picture of the falls. It was done in bright reds, blues, and gold. Alexandra walked into the room. In differing sizes the same picture spread around her, on the walls, shelves, and counters, and it seemed, for a moment, that she was looking at the room through an insect's compound eye. Then she turned, trying to get away from the endlessly repeated thing, the gaudy image, and there before her, through the glass, was the river.

It was fifteen feet thick, dark green, and it slid over the edge and streamed away. From below the mist boiled up as though the water was hot. It seemed to Alexandra that everything in the store was shaking from the falls, and she reached out a finger and put it against a large, heavy plaque that sat on a counter.

Shaw came up to her. When she looked at him, she slowly raised a brow.

"Do you want to go home now?" he said.

"Yes," she said, "I'm ready to talk to Bryce."

Well, it wasn't long before she met him in the middle of the highway. . . .

I sat in the tub, thinking about the falls, the greenish water tumbling over, the streaks in it, the unstoppable noise and shaking of the stone. The water in the tub was still, rising and falling with my breath. It was clear and soft to the touch, caressing, seemingly as far away as possible from that beaded wall at the bottom of the falls. But even so, I wanted to get out of the tub, and then I stood, hearing the water gurgle in the drain. I toweled my skin until it burned.

Timber

The Critchfields, the Thachers, the Keiths, the Campbells, and even the Hawleys turned out for the funeral, and they showed up in black suits and dresses, the cloth of which was shiny with use, almost greenish on the seats, knees, and elbows, like the coloring of a fly. They came in, pale in the face, one at a time, all of them sober, aside from N.B. ("the Raver") Critchfield, who always said a funeral was only worth going to if you hated the man who died or if you were drunk, or both.

I was there, too, dressed in my dark suit and dark tie. I wore black shoes. They had a nice shine. They are the clothes that I wore to bury my wife and friends, and at least they aren't shiny with use. The men and women outside the church told me I was looking well, and this, I know, is a bad sign.

Shaw was there also, dressed in a dark blue suit. There was a crowd in front of the town's Episcopal church, waiting for the thing to begin. Shaw stood away from the rest, smoking a cigarette, his eyes set on the hills outside of town where his uncle and aunt lived. It was a damp, drizzly day: Bryce would have approved of the weather. It would have been worse, I think, if Shaw hadn't come. The Thachers, Critchfields, and Keiths would have taken his absence as an admission of some wrongdoing. They believe in correctness of form, in attending funerals no matter what. . . . They knew Shaw and Alexandra had spent evenings and afternoons in his loft. Well, maybe they liked him the better for it after all, that he'd dare to be there for all to see. It wasn't spiteful, but maybe Ross Critchfield thought it was, and maybe that's why he stepped out of the mass of people in his shiny, fly-green suit and said to Shaw, holding out his hand, "Ross Critchfield."

Willie turned from the mountains and looked at the tall, pale man before him, at the pinched features and thinning hair combed so closely to the scalp as to seem painted on. Ross Critchfield's accent is so severe, so warped from its Groton beginnings, as to sound like a speech impediment. He did not look friendly. But then Willie was never a stupid man.

"Willie Shaw," he said.

They shook hands, Willie feeling on his palm and fingers the cool, long, and delicately fleshed bones of Ross Critchfield. I have never seen Ross Critchfield linger so long and to be so interested in the eyes of another man as he was then, standing in front of the Episcopal church. He gave Willie's hand three quick jerks and hesitated and then dropped it. Usually when he has shaken someone's hand he reaches for his handkerchief, but now he stood and went without it. Usually he wipes his hands with a handkerchief that is the size of a dinner napkin, and, for all I know, may well be. It is the kind of economy the man approved of, turning the Egyptian linen of his great aunt's trousseau into handkerchiefs. I imagine that every time he used one he thought, Mildred (the great aunt's name), Mildred, do you remember the summer in the Adirondacks when you had a chance at that Morgan boy, the one with the squint? Muffed it, didn't you?

"Pity about McCann, isn't it?" said Critchfield.

"Yes," said Shaw.

"A young man, too," said Critchfield, still keeping his eye on Shaw, "wasn't fifty, was he?"

"No," said Shaw.

"Well," said Critchfield, "it's not for us to wonder. Is it?"

"No," said Shaw.

Critchfield bobbed his head once, in short, economical approval. The rest of them, the tight, dark circle, began to turn their heads: even they are capable of awe, and the sight of Ross Critchfield talking to Shaw made them open their eyes. They waited, thinking that Ross would return and enter their circle with his short, dry laugh, but that didn't happen. He continued talking to Shaw, or they stood opposite one another in the cool breeze and drizzle and every now and then Ross said, "Dry fall," or "Saw a grosbeak, remarkable bird," and Shaw nodded or said that he had seen a "cedar waxwing." Critchfield said, "Waxwing. I'll be damned."

But they lingered even beyond that, and the dark, greenish, and shiny group turned their small eyes on Shaw and Critchfield. After a while the two men shook hands again. I don't hear as well as I used to, but I am certain there was a murmur of surprise when this happened. Then Critchfield went back to the dark circle, walking slowly and dragging his leg a little, and told them he'd arranged to have his timber cut. Mr. Shaw had agreed to oversee it.

Althrace Thacher is ninety-five. She is short, and on this day was wearing a longish black skirt, and a matching jacket. Her face is small, the wrinkles in it so symmetrical and fine as to look like decorative tattooing. She has short, absolutely white hair, and when Ross Critchfield spoke to her, she reached into her pocket and squeezed the battery of her hearing aid. She walks with a cane, and she wears one out every year: she doesn't approve of canes having rubber tips. Hers is made of walnut, and she keeps the tip bare so she can rap it sharply on the floor to get someone's attention or just to express an opinion.

She now came out of the group, moving a little crablike around her stick, and went across the sidewalk to where Shaw was standing. She turned up her white face, looking into Shaw's eyes. He didn't flinch or look away. I'm sure he could hear her sharp, shallow breathing. Then she rapped her cane on the stone sidewalk. It made a sound like a policeman hitting something hard with a nightstick.

"I have timber," she said, "needs to be cut, too. Well?"

She squeezed her hearing-aid battery again.

"Don't trust loggers," she said.

"You shouldn't," said Shaw.

"Ha!" she said.

She rapped her cane on the sidewalk again.

"So, we're in business," she said.

"If you'd like," said Shaw.

"Of course I'd like," she said. "Call me. I'm in the book."

Then she turned and went back across the sidewalk, still going in that side-to-side, crablike gait, and when she returned to the circle of her friends and relatives, she stood next to Ross Critchfield. They were obviously to one side, separate, and pleased with themselves. Althrace rapped her cane on the walk, jerked her head back as though something had stung her. Ross took the handkerchief from his pocket and blew his nose, and then they blinked at one another, not so much as a smile changing their features. Althrace looked toward the church, and said, "That Shaw is a decent fellow. Can see it plain as your face."

The rest of them didn't wait long. Soon they were easing across the sidewalk, coming in their shiny dresses and suits, their wrinkled shoes (some of which had a piece of cardboard in the sole to cover a hole), all of them appearing faintly luminous with the flylike cast of their clothes. Shaw looked up once when he saw them approach, and I'm sure that he was never closer to turning and running: his eyes widened a little, although he was man enough to keep his jaw from dropping. Well, he had his chance to get away. Maybe it was then I realized how much he actually loved Alexandra.

They drifted over, in ones and twos, offered their dry, thin hands. Shaw shook every one. They all owned land and none knew the first damn thing about it. They flinched and nodded and one of them almost smiled. It was a hundred times more than Bryce had been able to do in nineteen years. I found myself oddly cheerful, given the occasion, and was glad when N.B. took me aside and offered his silver, engraved flask that was worn almost smooth in the middle with use. It was still warm from his hand when I took it and walked to the side of the building, out of the way, and tilted it up. These days I can only have a short one, although I wanted to have more. It was strong, good, and warming. I liked standing in the alley, feeling the people beyond me, just around the corner on the street. Then I went back and gave the flask to N.B., who weaved on the sidewalk and said, in his deep, harsh voice, "Never liked that Bryce. Was a damn bounder. Had pictures of clouds and sunsets on his checks."

The Raver stood on the sidewalk, glaring at the people around him, daring any to return his gaze. He grunted again, and waited. There was a murmur and nervous snuffling, a blowing of noses, a black huddling, and a strained staring into the distance.

"Checks should be green, with a slight, discreet texture," said N.B., "blue is not altogether bad. Yellow is passable. People have forgotten that checks represent *money.*"

The rest of the mourners were quiet, although they moved from side to side. Some of the women touched their dark hats, and others noticed a few cars that went by. But at the back of the group there was the sound of a sharp rapping, like a policeman's nightstick, as Althrace struck the sidewalk in agreement.

"Yes," said N.B., now turning his eyes on Shaw, "come down to the bank for a sample check!"

Then the crowd of people were absolutely still, their protuberant eyes showing, in some of the more weak-livered, the slight cast of fear, which seemed to have a color like the bellies of fish. Some of them were less timid, and their eyes showed a certain keen pleasure in N.B.'s having gone too far. There was the hard, single rap of disapproval from Althrace, the sound ringing clear and cold in the air in front of the grayish church.

Shaw had been staring at the hills, but then he slowly turned his head in N.B.'s direction. His face was pale, and I'm sure there was a trembling in his hands, neck, and shoulders, and he stood there, the breeze slightly moving his dark hair. Of course he looked angry . . . I have never seen him so definitely so. There were no cars passing in the street, and we were all silent. N.B. stood up a little straighter. After a moment, Shaw jerked his head back, that same small amount (as though stung by something), the gesture itself showing disapproval and control. N.B. stared, blinked, and said, "Well done. Well done," and then turned and went into the church, where he sat in the back row, and was soon asleep, blubbering into his neck.

Althrace's cane rapped twice. I stood there, gaping at Shaw a little, and I knew then, as all the rest of them certainly did, that he was a harder nut than anyone had given him credit for, and I wasn't so worried about him. Not anymore. The smarter of the Keiths, Critchfields, and Thachers looked a little uneasy as Shaw stood on the sidewalk, now turned away from them again, staring at the place where Whalen and Aunt Katherine still lived. Of course, Shaw had grown up here, and knew the rigamarole as well as anyone. I was glad N.B. had given me the drink.

Alexandra, Anne, and Xannie arrived in a long, dark car. They were dressed in dark clothes, Alexandra and Anne in skirts and jackets and black stockings, too. They stepped out of the dark car, onto the sidewalk, and hesitated for a moment before going in. Alexandra nodded to the group of people there, her face serious, but not grief-stricken: everyone understood. Anne seemed a little worse, but she wasn't crying. Xannie came out of the back of the car, too, dressed in a black suit with a black tie. His face was palish, and he went along, next to Alexandra.

There was no hypocrisy in it, at least not for Alexandra. She had been married to the man. He was dead, and she wanted to bury him properly. That was all: she believed it was the right thing to do. They stepped inside, and then the rest of us turned. The black-dressed people began to flow, as though pushed by some gentle wind, into the church.

Bryce had known a fair number of people in Boston, men and women who had been stockbrokers, real estate agents, and managers of the buildings he had bought. Who knows what women he had known there? None of them came. There were many notes, with the excuses not particularly imaginative. There were many flowers, so many, in fact, it looked as though Bryce had ordered them himself. But as we began to move toward the church a car stopped in front of it.

It was orange with large tires at the back. It was about ten years old, but looked as though someone had once tried to race it, or thought of doing so. There was a roll bar in the back, and an air scoop on the hood, but the fenders were rusted to a fine, trembling and brownish lace. The muffler was loud. The windows were dark and rolled up, but after the car stopped a woman got out of the driver's side. She was thirty, heavyish, and her face was round, puffy and flushed. Her hair was pulled into a bun and she looked as though she was having trouble staying awake. She wore a purple dress and a gray coat, and she stood in the street for a moment, blinking at the mourners, before she went around to the curb and opened the door for Sonny to get out.

Amy Critchfield doesn't see very well, and she stood at the curb, her eyes looking like the imitation ones used by a taxidermist when he mounts a deer head. Amy's have the same lack of focus. Even she, though, was able to see the new large and white cast on Sonny's leg.

"I had an accident," said Sonny. "I was hitchhiking."

Amy Critchfield stepped back, holding the brooch she had pinned to the neck of her dress. Her mouth opened and closed a few times and then she turned her eyes away.

"Of course," she said, "I see."

Then she made her way toward the dark shape of the church door.

The driver of the car had to get a wheelchair, which had been folded up and put into the backseat. Then Sonny worked his way into it, the white cast on his leg supported by a platform on the wheelchair. He wore a pair of dark green pants, a blackish jacket that had on its elbows the same shine as the clothes of the other mourners. He wore a white shirt with a clip-on bow tie, the kind Bryce despised. Sonny's hair was brushed back, and when he had been rolled into the church, he sat, his head glistening in the pale, clear light, his flat, scarred features turning toward the people as they came in. Millie, the woman who had driven Sonny from his boardinghouse, sat next to him and began to doze. During the service, Sonny touched her with his elbow and said, "Pssst. Hey," and she opened her small leather purse and took from it a codeine, which Sonny put into his mouth, and then sat there, his expression softening as he chewed the thing slowly and listened to the service. Sonny sang the hymn very loud and with real feeling.

The casket sat in front of the church. It was large, black, and had silver handles. It also had a large silver monogram on it, the letters being at least three feet long. The thing was closed, and the ceremony was short, and soon the members of the congregation began drifting out.

Sonny was still sitting in the aisle when Alexandra came out, and for a moment they stood opposite one another, Sonny glancing at her and then looking away. Millie was sleeping on his shoulder. He reached over and pushed her up, but her chin fell sharply against her chest. Sonny blushed. Alexandra still hesitated, and then finally she nodded to him.

"Is there going to be a party afterward?" said Sonny.

"No," said Alexandra, "we hadn't planned anything."

"That's too bad," said Sonny, "Bryce would have loved a party."

There were two black cars parked in front of the church. The gaudy box was in one, and Alexandra, Anne, and Xannie were in the other. No other cars went toward the cemetery, and as I got into my station wagon and began to start the engine, Shaw opened the door and said, "Do you mind if I ride along?"

"Not at all," I said.

He sat in front, with me. The back of the station wagon was filled with things I'd left there, picks, shovels, a microscope, and there was the everlasting dust from the dirt I'd tracked in. Shaw stared at the black cars ahead of us. I asked him if we should put the lights on, and he said yes, since he thought we were part of it. I turned them on, and then we brought up the rear, the station wagon swaying on its old springs, the tools bouncing in the back, as we established a procession of one car.

It had rained, and the small road that led into the hills was black and shiny. The hills were a fuzzy gray of leafless trees. The cars ahead of us passed a small river, and then turned onto a dirt road that ran along it. The river was the color of tea, a deep reddish brown, and it formed pools behind boulders. After a while we came to a small cemetery.

There was a small fence around it, made of chains, but they had rusted, and a couple of lengths lay on the ground. There was grass between the headstones, but it wasn't anything more than timothy and crabgrass that had been mowed. The mowing was done by a boy who had hair so blond as to seem white. In the summer he drove his father's pickup truck (illegally, since the boy didn't have a license) to the graveyard, rolled the machine off the bed on a piece of plywood, and then pushed the mower around the stones. There were many brothers in the family, and the job of mowing the grass in the cemetery was handed from one to the other, like a worn-out coat.

The black station wagon had stopped there, and the other long car had pulled up in front of it. The grave had been dug with a backhoe, and it was now parked at the top of the cemetery, just behind a few spruce that grew there. The driver of the backhoe was tall, had thin hair he kept cut short, and it was fuzzy as it stood up from his head. He leaned against the yellow machine as Alexandra, Anne, Shaw, Xannie, the two drivers of the black car, and I got out and began to carry the gaudy black box from the back of the car to the grave. Alexandra and I looked at each other as we went, both keeping our eyes on the other, and neither of us flinched when we felt the slight roll and shifting of the weight inside. Shaw kept his eyes on the hills above us, and one of the drivers said, "Easy, easy, easy," as we went along, trying to be careful where we put our feet and hearing our mutual and slightly harsh breathing. Then we put the thing down on the straps over the hole. The silver monogram seemed very bright, and then the man with the fuzzy head and the large nose walked from the backhoe and let the thing slide slowly into the ground.

Then we turned and went home. The sky moved quickly, the clouds there going so fast as to make me dizzy. Shaw rode back with Alexandra and Anne, and I went down the road myself, bringing up the rear, and seeing, in my mirror, that the yellow backhoe had come from behind the trees and darted toward the hole.

Light Cahills

I didn't see Alexandra for a few weeks after we'd gone to the cemetery. She was just down the road, but she kept to herself for a while. I saw her walking on the road and she waved. I thought she had gained a little weight, and that seemed like a good thing. If I was sad, it was, much to my shame, that my job was done: she didn't need someone to confide in, or at least she had someone else. And in all honesty, that was for the best. We'd be just friends now, and we'd sit in the garden, eating the light things I made, and we'd be able to talk freely about nothing in particular. Maybe there'd be some fungus, or insects in the Judy Langdons. She'd tell me not to use poison. I go out and spray anyway. I knew that soon the weather would be warm and she'd sit opposite me, her face a little tanned, her streaked hair in a pile on her head, the insects, like bits of gold filament, rising and falling behind her. I looked forward to those days. Now, though, the ground was freezing, turning white: in the morning you saw the white marks on the ground where the early shadows had been.

One afternoon I was standing outside, dressed in the coat I used to wear to hunt when I was young and my bones didn't ache so much. It is a red-and-black plaid, lined with a cashmere blanket, and was like magic against the cold. My pointed elbows have worn through the sleeves now. I was gathering up the tools I'd left here and there and taking them to the shed. I went back and forth, tottering over the dirt in the garden, dragging a hoe. Alexandra walked along with me, picking up the things I dropped. Then I invited her in.

She kept her eyes on mine as we sat in the study. I made the fire up. I made some small cucumber sandwiches. Cut off the crusts. Put out some small pickles, too. She didn't eat. But all along, she kept looking at me. For a moment I thought I was turning blue. I looked in the mirror. My color was fine, so I sat down and listened to her as she talked about what she'd seen in a magazine, some local gossip, her plans for a greenhouse. We never came to things quickly. She kept looking up, though, and I could feel her coming closer to it, the chitchat falling away and the words coming more slowly over her lips.

She told me she was pregnant. What did I think? And in spite of myself, knowing I shouldn't ask, I did anyway, and even though I was ashamed to hear my words, I was glad to get the answer. The child wasn't Bryce's. It wouldn't have mattered, I suppose, but still, I was . . . relieved. I sighed. She asked if she could have a glass with crushed ice. I went into the kitchen, put some cubes in a towel and began to hit them with a hammer, feeling the ice shatter beneath it. What did I think? My God, I was an old man, facing the grave, and what could I say about some new creature pushing into the world? And, as I hit the ice and was glad to feel it give in the cloth, I felt around the house, or around me, the sense of life rearranging itself for its own purposes and not giving a damn about any of us. I was ashamed, too, that I had been smug enough to think that things ended.

"Don't hit it so hard," said Alexandra.

"Sorry," I said, and then brought the powdered ice into the room and sat down. Alexandra put the bright, glassy chips into her mouth, let some of them linger for a moment on her lips. She looked as though the ice was good, cold and bracing.

She had already told Shaw. They had been alone, at her house, and afterward they sat together on the brick steps by the front door, both of them with their forearms on their knees and both staring into the distance. They sat that way for a while, and Alexandra knew that they were going to have the child.

"I guess we'll have to get married," said Shaw.

"Yes," said Alexandra, "I suppose so."

"Where will we live?" he said.

"Here," she said, "where else?"

He opened his mouth as though to speak, but then stopped, and said, "All right."

He said, though, that he wanted to keep his job. He didn't want to be all dressed up with no place to go. She said she'd never asked him to, and then both of them sat, feeling the house at their backs and seeing the river in the distance.

They were married at Whalen's house by a minister who was an old friend of mine. I suppose you could say I gave the bride away, and was bridesmaid, usher, and family. Whalen stood up for Shaw. The preacher is older than me and he rocked back and forth on his heels. Alexandra looked into his eyes and said her vows softly. Shaw said his, and then the preacher had a drink and went away. Aunt Katherine's chair rocked back and forth throughout. Whalen stood straight, breathing hard, glaring for a while. We all were happy to have it over, and we stood quietly in the kitchen, hearing the *kerrik, kerrik, kerrik* of Aunt Katherine's chair.

"How's your well?" said Whalen.

"It runs dry in September," I said.

"I'll find you a new one in June," he said, "on me."

"I'd appreciate it," I said.

We drank a lot and talked. I had a camera and took some pictures. Whalen demanded that I give the small black box to Alexandra, and then we all went outside. He was careful about where he stood, and when he was satisfied, he made Alexandra take a picture of him standing in front of the broken-down tractor in front of his house.

In the late spring, Anne came home from school. Alexandra asked if I'd like to fish with them, and I was glad to come along, carrying my old waders over my arm. Soon, we all stood out on the river, Alexandra in hip waders, her belly large and round. Anne was farther out, and Shaw was upstream a little. Xannie sat on the bank with a brown bag of peas and a stainless steel bowl. He shelled the peas into the bowl, and as we stood out in the water we heard the steady, metallic *pick, pick, pick* of the peas as they fell into the bowl. Shaw's casting was long, graceful: the line moved over the water. I suppose that's the way they fish the western rivers. Anne's was not so long, and a little more delicate. Alexandra's was shortish and gentle, and around her gold and silver head and her white shirt there were the rising mayflies, small white ones. Cahills. Not more than a sixteen hook. They rose into the air, and we stood there, casting to the heads of pools or into pocket water. There were a few rising fish, which surprised me. Anne hooked one and I watched it play for a while. Alexandra's face seemed dark now, with the sun, and she wore dark glasses. After a while, she hooked a trout, too. All in all, the fishing was pretty good, considering how acidic the water has become.

Mad Katherine

When Alexandra was pregnant, she had one last dream of Mad Katherine. It was late fall and the fog came up from the river. Mad Katherine sat on the bank, her gray hair filled with small drops from the fog. She ate dried berries, which were the color of rose leaves. Around her on the ground there were the knives, fishhooks, axes, the skins of bear, the long leather tongs from deerskin, the claws of bears, each made into a needle. She also had a hard leather cup and in it there were the vertebrae of deer: she rattled the bones. "I am blind now," said Mad Katherine, showing her milky eyes to Alexandra. "That's why I love the fog. It makes no difference then." Mad Katherine's hands went over her things, discarding fishhooks, needles, knives, the things she used. Instead, she picked up the berries, smoked fish, and meat, and the paddle of the canoe. "Where are you going?" said Alexandra. "Away from here," said Mad Katherine. "I'm finished here. I've heard this river leads to oceans. There are whales, salmon, and sharks in oceans. That's where I'll go. You can feel the whales heave over in the sea, their backs bending in the waves. The sharks bite hard." Mad Katherine smiled. "Good-bye, my dear," Mad Katherine said, "when you see water, think of me."

West Dover – Westminister West
1983 – 1985